Praise for the Work of Larry Niven

"As eclectic a volume as Niven has ever issued. Niven started writing during the original era of "the sense of wonder;" now he is readably, vigorously advancing into a new one."
—*Booklist* on *Scatterbrain*

"One of our finest. . . . Jams ideas for several novels into each one he creates."
—*The Sun Times*

"The premier hard SF writer of the day."   —*Baltimore Sun*

"Great storytelling is still alive in science fiction because of Larry Niven."
—Orson Scott Card

"For three and a half decades, nobody's done it better than Larry Niven . . ."
—Steven Barnes

"Niven is an undisputed master in the field."
—David Gerrold

"*Ringworld's Children* provides another fascinating and intriguing look at Ringworld, its implications, and its history, all while telling a fast moving page-turner."
—L. E. Modesitt, Jr.

"*Ringworld's Children* is the most exciting Ringworld novel since the first, which makes it one of Larry Niven's best ever."
—Spider Robinson

"If there isn't really a Ringworld out there somewhere, we ought to build one someday. Until then, we have Larry Niven's. A rich and fantastic story."   —Fred Saberhagen

"Outstanding! . . . The best ever by the best in the field."
—*Tom Clancy* on *Beowulf's Children*

"One of the best teams in science fiction . . . a tale of space conquest that makes *Aliens* look like a Disney nature film."
—*The Washington Times* on *Beowulf's Children*

P9-AZV-671

TOR BOOKS BY LARRY NIVEN

N-Space
Playgrounds of the Mind
Destiny's Road
Rainbow Mars
Scatterbrain

WITH STEVEN BARNES

Achilles' Choice
The Descent of Anansi
Saturn's Race

WITH JERRY POURNELLE AND STEVEN BARNES

The Legacy of Heorot
Beowulf's Children

SCATTERBRAIN

Larry Niven

TOR®

A TOM DOHERTY ASSOCIATES BOOK
NEW YORK

This is a work of fiction. All the characters and events portrayed in this book are fictitious or are used fictitiously.

SCATTERBRAIN

Copyright © 2003 by Larry Niven

A Tor Book
Published by Tom Doherty Associates, LLC
175 Fifth Avenue
New York, NY 10010

www.tor.com

Tor® is a registered trademark of Tom Doherty Associates, LLC.

ISBN 0-765-34047-X
EAN 978-0765-34047-4

First edition: January 2003
First mass market edition: July 2004

Printed in the United States of America

0 9 8 7 6 5 4 3 2 1

This book is for all of my collaborators. Thank you for your endless generosity. My life would have been quite different without you.

CONTENTS

INTRODUCTION
WHERE DO I GET MY CRAZY IDEAS?

Yes, I finally figured it out!

It's the same reason I can't remember your name, or face, or where we met.

My brain has a lousy retrieval system. Data does surface, but there's no reason to think it'll be the data I went looking for.

I got 99.9 percent on the California high-school system's math aptitude test in 1956. What made college so difficult was my daydreaming in math and physics and chemistry class. Something would spark an idea—the second law of thermodynamics, say—and off I'd go, following the implication that the most efficient heat engines will be built on Pluto. I broke more glassware in chem lab than anyone else.

I dozed and daydreamed through psychology, too, but that got me an A. What they teach in psychology class is fiction without internal consistency. Dreaming helps codify such stuff. Where was I? The point is, my brain will chase a datum through pathways no sane mind would ever consider and come out matching data that never belonged together in the same book, or library, or mind.

So. Early in my career, thirty-odd years ago, I noticed that time travel is fantasy. There appeared to be no way to make time travel consistent with the laws we think govern the universe. But the best stories are told as games of internal logic, as if time travel were science fiction.

So I dreamed up the Institute for Temporal Research, though the title came from elsewhere. I wrote these stories as a Green pessimist. Thus: By A.D. 3100 most of the life-forms we know are extinct. The United Nations rules the world, and the Secretary General is an inbred idiot who likes animals. The ITR keeps sending its agents back in time for animals out of a book for children.

I only sold one story to *Playboy* magazine in my life, and it was the one in which agent Hanville Svetz has to kill the great sea serpent to retrieve Moby Dick.

The joke played out after five stories, so I quit.

Then a funny thing happened. Carl Sagan got the mathematician Kip Thorne to build him a plausible time machine. *Now* time travel is science fiction.

And a notion was playing around in my head.

Any student of mythology *might* consider that Yggdrasil the Norse world-tree, and "Jack and the Beanstalk," and "Jacob's Ladder" are all stories that belong in the same box. Every one of them is a tower to Heaven. Several human cultures have believed that the world has an axis, a center point. Yggdrasil runs through it.

Many physics teachers and most science fiction writers will understand the concept of an orbital tower—a tether with its center of mass in a twenty-four-hour "Clarke" orbit, and one end anchored on the equator. Sometimes it's called a Beanstalk. Such a thing would have to be stronger than any material we know how to use. We can postulate stronger materials, and the likeliest are based on carbon: monofilament crystals or fullerine tubules.

Plants are good at manipulating carbon. Thus, any madman might dream that an orbital tower could be a real plant.

The easiest place to build (or to grow and cultivate) an orbital tower isn't Earth, it's Mars, with its low gravity and high spin.

Mars had a canal network before the probes arrived.

Are you buying this? And if all of that were to come together in one mind, true madness might pick up a few oddities on the way:

Time travel was pure fantasy until Kip Thorne got involved. Then the mathematicians started competing for the *cheapest* possible time machine. They use wormholes and exotic matter, and they all look more like a highway than an automobile. You can't travel to any time where you haven't already built the highway.

Now it's science fiction. But earlier than that . . . a horse from medieval times, picked up by a time machine, has a horn in its forehead. Ranchers removed it to tame the beast.

And Mars was populated, and covered with canals, until the recent past. Hell, we've got maps of Mars dating from a century ago, and it's *all* canals. They must have been there until just before the probes arrived.

We called it *Rainbow Mars* instead of *Svetz and the Beanstalk*. Tor Books published it in March 1999.

I seem to have a bumper sticker mind.

The surface of the Earth is the last place you would want to fight a war.

This may sound simplistic, but during the Cold War there were loud voices proclaiming that the last place we want to fight a war is space! Most of us *live* on the surface of the Earth! The only exceptions are aboard Freedom space station.

Think of it as evolution in action.

In *Oath of Fealty* Jerry and I used this as a running theme, mutating from a chance remark to a suicide's manifesto to a graffito to a bumper sticker . . . but it's a useful concept in real life. The Jonestown massacre really bothered my brother; "Think of it as evolution in action" was what I told him. It helped.

I hike with Jerry Pournelle and his dog on the hill behind his house in Studio City. We solve the world's problems up there. Jerry is sure that the exercise sends blood to our brains and makes us temporarily smarter. It beats drinking, which is what we used to do.

We come down the hill with bullets.

When I was on a panel at Houston, I heard one of the

panelists describing bullets. NASA loves bullets. A bullet is the short, punchy statement you put on a screen while you're making a speech, in the hope that someone will remember *something* ten minutes after you've stopped talking.

And on that panel, I said, "The dinosaurs didn't have a space program!" and the whole audience went, "Ooo!" I heard Story Musgrave quoting me that night.

So Jerry and I talk about space colonization, and why we don't have a Moonbase, and presently I'm saying, "If we can put a man on the Moon, *why can't we put a man on the Moon?*"

Or we're talking about President Bill Clinton. I listen to radio talk shows while I drive. I learn that Clinton has been exposed as a sexual bandit and an habitual thief, he's selling political favors to China, and his popularity is up above 70 percent. None of the talk show hosts or the call-ins can figure it out. And on the hill I hear Jerry talking the same way.

But it's obvious!

The Soviet Union has fallen. Some of what brought them down happened at my house, with Jerry officiating, but that's another story. George Bush Sr. could have snatched some of the credit for the Soviet collapse, but he tried to prop them up instead.

Seven years later, the celebration was hitting its full swing. *Clinton had taken on the mantle of the Corn King.* Anything he does with any passing woman helps to fertilize the fields. Anything the Corn King wants is his. Talking about theft is missing the point. He was even getting tribute from foreign powers!

Somebody should have told him what happens to the Corn King if the crops fail.

But the stock market didn't plunge until Clinton was about to leave office.

So one day Jerry and I were talking about evolution. Some human genes improve the odds of survival, but some genes are junk. They only ride along with the survival traits. It seems that evolution never allows a creature to do an editing job on its own genes.

WATCH THIS SPACE. We're right at the edge of being able to do that.

Meanwhile Jerry and I were talking about death, and senility, and why these traits haven't been bred out of the human race.

When you think of human evolution, you want to picture tribes of about a hundred hunter-gatherers. Less than that, the tribe's not too successful. Evolution may be about to lose them. More than a hundred, they break up so they can find enough to eat. So it's a hundred people including a few wise old men in their forties.

Wise old women, too, for all we know, but they mostly didn't talk to the men. This notion of men talking to women is fairly recent. I've got no information on the wise old women. Ask Ursula LeGuin.

If the old men weren't there, everyone would have to learn everything the hard way, over and over. But too many old men would be eating up the resources, and that's why we haven't evolved away from death. So far so good.

Alzheimer's hits about one out of five. We used to say *he's gone senile*, but that was when we thought everyone was at risk. Turns out it's a genetic thing. One in five.

Now, if one old man out of five loses his mind, the tribe can still survive. Jerry's argument for the survival of Alzheimer's disease is that natural selection doesn't care.

But wait.

Old men aren't always right. Clarke's law applies here. Times change, and we geezers can't always follow. There are times when we—sorry, when *you* shouldn't listen to the geezers. We should at least be required to justify our hoary old copybook maxims.

And the elders will damn well have to, if one out of every five is a drooling idiot who can't remember whether his grandson is his brother for more than ten minutes at a time.

And that's Niven's theory for why Alzheimer's has survived.

* * *

I want to tell you a writer's story.

In 1980 or so, I went to Steven Barnes's to work on our second novel. Steve's a black man from South-Central Los Angeles. He was a Heinlein fan at age ten. He owned a house with a picket fence in Grenada Hills, north of me.

I got there. He showed me *Dream Park*, Ace Books, just out. This is the book that generated a subculture, the international Fantasy Gaming Society, that runs live role-playing games up mountains and across deserts and down rivers. Mark Matthew-Simmons borrowed the name from our book, with permission.

My name on Dream Park was bigger than Steven's.

This is an insult to us both. In publishing tradition it implies that he did the work, and I put my name on it to sell more copies. I've actually had such an offer, once. Dammit, if my name is on it, I did my 80 percent! And so did my collaborator!

So I said, "This isn't my fault!" Hell, *he* knew that.

Steve said, "But what do I tell my friends and neighbors?"

"Tell 'em it's because I'm white."

Heh-heh. But of course I told that story to Jerry Pournelle . . .

1990. Four paperbacks arrived from England on a Thursday afternoon. *N-Space*, *Lucifer's Hammer*, *Oath of Fealty*, and *The Mote in God's Eye*. My name showed on *N-Space* in wonderful embossed curved letters in reflective silver. The other three looked very similar . . . because Jerry's name in each case was much smaller, in flat white.

I took them to the Los Angeles Science Fantasy Society that night. Jerry caught me. He said, "If you show those around, I'll kill you."

Ralph Vicinanza, our agent for foreign monies, got copies too. He wrote the company, Macdonald Futura Publications

Ltd., and demanded they withdraw the books. Their answer was, "There's nothing in the contracts that says we've got to make the names of both authors the same size."

"We'll see about that!" Ralph began looking through the contracts.

In the meantime I learned a little of the background.

Macdonald was a British billionaire who bought up everything in sight, including Futura. Then he disappeared off a yacht. It was discovered that he was a billion pounds in debt. Notice that there's still no good reason to think he's found a watery grave. He could have found a plantation in Brazil.

So Futura Publications ended in receivership, and the business administration graduate who found himself in charge of keeping the company going may never have met a live author. Certainly he couldn't guess how Jerry Pournelle might respond to having his name made barely noticeable on three book covers.

By 1990 Steven and Jerry and I were all at work on *The Legacy of Heorot*. Jerry had expanded his office into a cavernous space, so we all worked there.

I really wanted to see Steve's face when he saw those covers. I got to Jerry's house in time that morning, but I'd hurt my knee: a torn meniscus. I inched my way up the stairs and I got there too slow. They were laughing like maniacs, and then Jerry told me Steve had—nope. There really are things I can't tell you.

I had no idea Steve had that power. I asked him to show me his robe, but he wouldn't.

Meanwhile, Ralph Vicinanza was still looking through contracts. What he discovered was that the term limit had run out on *A Mote in God's Eye*. They didn't have the right to reprint it at all.

What made that *really* interesting was that Jerry and I had just finished *The Moat Around Murcheson's Eye*, published in the States as *The Gripping Hand*. If we could sell those two books as a package, they'd be worth a lot more money.

And we did that.

There came a letter from Macdonald, saying (in essence): "I was in America when these events took place. I'm now in charge at Macdonald. We're really sorry." I have no idea where the man in charge of making these covers disappeared to.

And there came a stack of books, very similar to the ones that had been pulped except that the authors' names, embossed in curvy silver letters, were of the exact same size. They got that by making the letters in Jerry's name narrower.

Intelligence tells you what your rights are, but not whether to exercise them.

There was nothing to tell a business administration graduate that the entire publishing industry is based on *trust*. We see contracts *this* thick. We argue fiercely about the clauses. But—

When he was negotiating for *Lord Valentine's Castle*, Robert Silverberg got Pocket Books to write in a clause calling for $60,000 to be spent on publicity. Innovative idea! Might have worked. Came the time, that clause just got forgotten. Oops. Did Bob Silverberg sue? He did not. Writers would rather be writing than in court.

When Jerry and I wrote a sequel to *Dante's Inferno*, Pocket Books had no faith in it. They put it in a royalties pool with *Mote*. Instead of sending us royalty money for *A Mote in God's Eye*, they were applying it to the advance money for *Inferno*.

Now, that's not uncommon, but there *is* an implication that the damn book will be published! But Pocket Books had a shakeup, and *Inferno* sat forgotten for two years. By publication date they had paid *no* advance.

Book contracts are based on mutual trust. The publisher can ignore any clause, knowing that the writer hasn't time, money, or inclination to bring him to court. The writer is guessing when he says he can finish a novel at all, let alone tell you when.

There are authors who will sign a contract for peanuts, spend the advance, and *then* decide they've been cheated. The whole industry comes to know who they are.

The publisher bets on the author's guess, and his honor.

Only wisdom can tell a bean counter not to declare war on people whose weaponry he doesn't understand.

A writer's best friend is his editor.

Don't buy that? Try this: a writer's most valuable unpaid servant is his editor.

I'm raising the subject because many good writers don't understand it, and those included Robert Heinlein, who missed very little.

The reasons seem to be historical.

The generation of writers ahead of me came out of an era of censorship . . . which may have lasted tens of thousands of years. Allowing people to speak their piece is a new thing for governments *and* religions. So the most conspicuous thing an editor could do, during the pulp era, was to tell a writer what he couldn't publish.

Robert Heinlein was the first science fiction writer to become too powerful to be censored, at least in this country. In England, Arthur Clarke may have had the power to demand that an editor do it his way, though he rarely used it. Thing was, Robert Heinlein *should not* have used that power. His early stories were lean and dense with ideas. He was the most copied writer since Dante. But his later novels sprawl all over the place. They needed an editor!

Alfred Bester needed Horace Gold. *The Demolished Man* and *The Stars My Destination* date from the Horace Gold era. *Golem 100* was written without Gold.

I can describe what one or another editor has done for me.

Frederik Pohl bought my first four stories. He published "World of Ptavvs," the novelet (named by Judy-Lynn

Benjamin), in *Worlds of Tomorrow,* but he also ran it down the street to Betty Ballantine, who bought it as a novel to be expanded. He once intended to commission articles on the oddest entities in the astrophysical zoo and pair them with my stories set in those same places. The scheme fell through, but he had me thinking in terms of the odd pockets of creation: a habit I've kept.

Judy-Lynn Benjamin was a power source at Galaxy when Galaxy was worthy. She became Judy-Lynn Del Rey. She was editor at Ballantine, then chief editor at Del Rey Books, named for Lester Del Rey, her husband. Our relationship was long and fruitful, and I miss her. I still have in my custody one of her pets, a stuffed bull.

Robert Gleason has an uncanny perception for which books will be successful. He bought *A Mote in God's Eye* and *Inferno* from me and Jerry Pournelle. While at Playboy Books he told Jerry: "Write a novel about an alien invasion of Earth in present time." Jerry told me. I laughed. I said, "I hope you broke it to him gently that it's been done." By the time we got done talking, it had become both *Footfall* and *Lucifer's Hammer.*

He told me and Steve Barnes how to write *Dream Park*; but that wasn't the novel we intended to write. That's not to say he was wrong. He worked on *The Burning City* too, though it didn't end up at Tor.

Owen Lock was the best damn proofreader in the business. He was absolutely meticulous, but he had no sense of the rhythm of words at all. He proofed for me even after he became chief editor of Del Rey Books.

John Ordover makes me feel old. He was in place at Simon & Schuster when Jerry and I sold them *The Burning City*. He had interesting, useful suggestions—negotiating with bees, for instance. He was ready to edit this book, and its sequel, because he read *The Magic Goes Away* as a kid.

Thank you all.

DESTINY'S ROAD
EXCERPTED FROM THE NOVEL

The heart of this story was the road.

Like this: Two landing ships founded the colony on Norn, renamed Destiny. Sometime later, one left the colony. Riding on its fusion drive and a ground-effect skirt, a few meters off the ground, the ship left a trail of melted rock behind it, first in a spiral, then off into the unknown.

Hundreds of years later, a boy sets off down the road from Spiral Town to find out what happened to the ship. We follow the boy.

Irresistible, isn't it? I can't guess how many years that sat in my head before I did something about it.

But I had never told a man's life story from childhood to middle age. Most of Robert Heinlein's early novels fit that description, but I wasn't sure I could do it. I flinched.

I turned the novel in to Tor four years late.

When Michael Whelan wrote his wonderful cover painting, he did it from my outline; but he thought the book was near finished. The plant he painted in foreground became the "fool cage" in the book.

Michael, and Tom, and Bob, thank you for your patience. The book came out precisely as I had hoped.

A.D. 2722 SPIRAL TOWN

Junior at fourteen had grown tall enough to reach the highest cupboard. She stretched up on tiptoe, found the speckles shaker by feel, and brought it down. Then she saw what was happening to the bacon. She shouted, "Jemjem-jemmy!"

Jemmy's eleven-year-old mind was all in the world beyond the window.

Junior snatched up a pot holder and moved the pan off the burner. The bacon wasn't burned, not yet, not quite.

"Sorry," Jemmy said without turning. "Junior, there's a caravan coming."

"You never saw a caravan." Junior looked through the long window, northeastward. "Dust. *Maybe* it's the caravan. Here, turn this."

Jemmy finished cooking the bacon. Junior shook salt and speckles on the eggs, sparingly, and returned the shaker to the cupboard. Brenda, who should have been stirring the eggs, and Thonny and Greegry and Ronny were all crowded along the long window—the Bloocher family's major treasure, one sheet of glass, a meter tall, three meters from side to side—to watch what was, after all, only a dust plume.

They ate bread and scrambled hens' eggs and orange juice. Brenda, who was ten, fed Jane, who was four months old. Mom and Dad had been up for hours doing farmwork. Mom was eating poached platyfish eggs. Platyfish were Destiny life; their bodies didn't make fat. Mom was trying to lose weight.

Jemmy wolfed his breakfast, for all the good that did. The rest of the children were finished too. The younger kids squirmed like their chairs were on fire; but you couldn't ask Mom and Dad to hurry. They weren't exactly dawdling, but the kids' urgency amused them.

The long window was behind Jemmy. If he turned his back on the rest of the family, Dad would snap at him.

Junior emptied her coffee mug with no sign of haste, very adult, and set it down. "Mom, can you handle Jane and Ronny?"

Seven-year-old Ronny gaped in shock. Before he could scream, Mom said, "I'll take care of the baby, dear, but you take Ronny with you. He has to do his schoolwork."

Ronny relaxed, though his eyes remained wary. Junior stood. Her voice became a drill sergeant's. "We set?"

Brenda, Thonny, Greegry, Ronny, and Jemmy surged toward the door. There was a pileup in the lock while they sorted out their coats and caps, and then they cycled through in two clusters, out of the house, streaming toward the Road. Junior followed. The younger three were half-running, but Junior with her long legs kept up with them. She wasn't trying to catch Jemmy, who at eleven had no dignity to protect.

The sun wasn't above the mountains yet, but Quicksilver was, a bright spark dim in daylight.

The line of elms was as old as Bloocher House. They were twenty-five meters from the front of the house, the last barrier between Bloocher Farm and the Road. To Jemmy they seemed to partition earth and sky. He ran between two elms and was first to reach the Road.

To the right the Road curved gradually toward Spiral Town. Left, northwest, it ran straight into the unknown. That way lay Warkan Farm, where four mid-teens stood in pairs to watch the dust plume come near.

The Warkan children had been schooled at Bloocher House, as had their parents before them. Then, when Jemmy was six, the Bloocher household computer died. For the next week or two Dad was silent and dangerous. Jemmy came to understand that a major social disaster had taken place.

For five years now, Jemmy and his siblings and all of the Warkan children had trooped three houses around the Road's curve to use the Hann computer.

The dust plume no longer hid what was coming toward Spiral Town. There were big carts pulled by what must be chugs. Jemmy saw more than one cart, hard to tell how many. Children from farther up the Road were running alongside. Their voices carried a long way, but it was too far to make out words.

His siblings had filtered between the trees. They lined the Road, waiting. Jemmy looked toward the Warkan kids; looked back at Junior; saw her shake her head. He said. "Aw, Junior. What about class?"

"Wait." Junior said.

Of course there had been no serious thought of rushing to

class. Not with a caravan coming! They'd make up missed classes afterward. Computer programs would wait, and a human teacher was rarely needed.

Children began to separate at Junior's age. Boys spoke only to boys, girls to girls. Jemmy knew that much. Maybe he'd understand why, when he was older. Now he only knew that Junior would speak to him only to give orders. He missed his big sister, and Junior hadn't even *gone* anywhere.

If Junior went to join the Warkan girls, the Warkan boys would stare at her and rack their brains thinking of some excuse to talk to her. So Jemmy almost understood why the whole family simply waited by the elms while the wagons came near.

The wagons had flat roofs twice as high as a grown man's head. They moved at walking speed. You could hear the children who ran alongside carrying on shouted conversations with the merchants. There were deeper voices too: adults were negotiating with merchants in the wagons.

When the caravan reached the Warkan farm, the Warkans joined them, boys and girls together, it didn't matter. A few minutes later the troop had reached the Bloocher children.

It was Jemmy's first close view of a chug.

The beasts were small and compact. They forged ahead at a steady walking pace, twenty to a cart. They stood as high as Jemmy's short ribs. Their shells were the ocher of beach sand. Their wrinkled leather bellies were pale. Their beaks looked like wire cutters, dangerous, and each head was crowned by a flat cap of ocher shell. They showed no awareness of the world around them.

The wagons stood on tall wheels. Their sides dropped open to form shelves, and merchants grinned down from inside.

Jemmy let the first two wagons pass him by. Junior had already forgotten him; the rest of the children went with her, though Thonny looked back once. No eyes were on him when he reached out to stroke one of the chugs. The act seemed headily dangerous. The shell was paper-smooth.

The chug swiveled one eye to see him.

It was hard to tell who was what among the merchants,

because of their odd manner of dress. As far as Jemmy could tell, there were about two men for every woman. They enjoyed talking to children. A man and woman driving the third cart smiled down at him, and Jemmy walked alongside. He asked, "Can't you make them go faster?"

"Don't want to," the man said. "We buy and sell all along the Road. Why make the customers chase us?"

A golden-haired woman with a trace of a limp, Mom's age but dumpier, passed money up to a dark-skinned merchant on the twelfth and last cart. That was Ilyria Warkan. The merchant reached way down to hand her a speckles pouch.

It was transparent, big as a head of lettuce, with a child's handful of bright yellow dust in the corner. You never saw these pouches unless a merchant was selling speckles.

Jemmy ran his hand down a chug's flank. The skin was dry and papery. Belatedly he asked, "Do they bite?"

"No. They've got good noses, the chugs. They can smell you're Earthlife, and they won't eat that. Might bite you if you were a fisher."

The merchants seemed to like children, but nobody ever saw a child with the caravan. Did they keep their children hidden? Nobody knew.

The Road was beginning to curve. More children joined the caravan: Rachel Harness and her mother, Jael; and Gwillam Doakes, a burly boy Jemmy's age; and the very clannish Holmes girls. No more adults came, unless you counted Jael Harness, who hadn't got enough speckles as a child and was therefore a little simple. Jemmy could see people walking away, far down the straight arm of the Road.

The merchant woman caught him looking, and laughed. "Too many people now." Her words were just a bit skewed, with music in her voice. "Serious customers, they see the dust, they come to meet us. Give them more time to deal. Now we get no more till the hub. How far to the hub?"

"Twenty minutes . . . no, wait, you can't take cross streets. They're too narrow." The caravan would just have to go round and round, following the curve as the Road spiraled toward Civic Hall. "More like an hour and a half. You could get there faster without the wagons."

"No point," the merchant woman said. "I would miss the cemetery too, wouldn't I?"

"Don't go in there," Jemmy said reflexively.

"Oh, but I must! I've heard about the Spiral Town cemetery all my life. We follow the Road around by almost a turn? It's all Earthlife, they say."

"That's right," Jemmy said. "Spooky. Destiny life won't grow where the dead lie."

The merchant said, "I've never seen a place that was nothing but Earthlife."

She was strange and wonderful, swathed in layers of bright colors. It was a game, getting her to keep talking. Jemmy asked, "Have you seen City Hall? There's painted walls, really bright. *Acrylic,* Dad says."

She smiled indulgently. He knew: *She'd been there.*

He asked, "Where do speckles come from?"

"Don't know. Hundreds of klicks up the Road when we buy 'em."

Hundreds of klicks . . . kilometers. "Where did they come from before the Road was here?"

She frowned down at him. "Before the Road . . . ?"

"Sure. We learn about it in school, how James and Daryl Twerdahl and the rest took off in *Cavorite* and left the Road behind them. But that was eight years after Landing Day. So . . . "

The man was listening too. The woman said, "News to me, boy. The Road's always been here."

Jemmy would have accepted that, accepted her ignorance, if he hadn't seen the man's lips twitch in a smile. In his mind, for that instant, it was as if the world had betrayed him.

Then seven-year-old Ronny was beside him, saying, "I'm tired, Jemmy."

"Okay, kid. *Junjunjunior—*"

One wagon ahead, Junior stopped walking. So did Thonny and Brenda, and the Warkan girls that Junior had been talking to, and the Warkan boys, all without consulting each other. Sandy Warkan said, "Twerdahl Street's just ahead. We can stop for a squeeze of juice at Guilda's and wait for the caravan to come round again."

"School," Junior reminded them.

"Can wait."

The Road itself was magical.

Bloocher Farm was soft soil and living things and entropy. Plants grew from little to big, grew dry and withered, changed and died. Animals acted strangely, and presently gave birth to children like themselves. Tools rusted or broke down or rotted or ceased working for reasons of their own.

Closer to the hub, you saw less of life and more of entropy. The houses were old, losing their hard edges. New buildings were conspicuous, jarring. At night there were lines of city lights with gaps in them. Things that didn't work were as prevalent here as among the farms, but you noticed them more: they were closer together.

But the Road was hard and flat and not like anything else in the world. The Road was eternal.

The Road was a fantastic toy. Things rolled easily on its flat surface. Here, just short of Twerdahl Street and half a klick southeast of Bloocher Farm, was a favored dip used by the high-school kids. Sandy and Hal Warkan had showed Jemmy how to sweep the Road to get a *really* flat surface, so that balls or wheels could be rolled back and forth over the dip. They'd go forever.

No time for that today. They turned off at Twerdahl Street, and some of the merchants waved good-bye.

Rachel Harness chattered to Junior, pulling her mother along. Rachel's mother Jael seemed to listen, but answered rarely, and when she spoke her words had nothing to do with what she'd heard. Jemmy liked Jael Harness, but Junior and Brenda found her a little queer.

Children who didn't get enough speckles grew up like that.

But Rachel was a bright, active girl, Junior's age, who

treated her mother like a younger sister. Neighbors had helped to raise her, but speckles were expensive. Rachel must have had a steady source of speckles since her birth.

One wondered. Who was Rachel's father?

The Harness farm was to the right, and that was where Rachel was pointing, Junior looking and nodding. Jemmy couldn't hear them, but he looked. A silver bulge in the weeds . . . it was Killer!

The Council had sicced Varmint Killer on the Harness farm!

The old machine wasn't doing anything. Just sitting. Weeds and vegetation that had been crops ran riot here. It wasn't all Earthlife. Odd colors, odd shapes grew in wedge patterns, wider toward the southwest, toward the sea.

More than two hundred years ago, the great fusion-powered landers had hovered above Crab Island and burned the land sterile. This land was to serve Earthlife only. But the life of Destiny continued to try to retake the Crab.

Weeds tended to cluster, reaching tentatively from an occupied base, as if they did not like the fertilizer that made Earthlife grow. Black touched with bronze and yellow-green; branches that divided, divided, divided, until every tip was a thousand needles too fine to see. One could rip up an encroachment of Destiny weeds with a few passes of a tractor. One day the Harnesses' neighbors would do that.

But Destiny's animals were another matter. They lived among Destiny's encroaching plants, and some were dangerous. These were Killer's prey.

Killer squatted in the wild corn, a silver bulge the size and shape of a chug pulled in on itself. The children watched and waited. Older children bullied the youngers onto Warkan Farm's long porch, where Destiny creatures weren't likely to be hiding.

One would not want a child to come between Varmint Killer and its prey. They waited, waited . . .

Ssizzz!

Even looking, you might not see it. Jemmy just caught it: the line flicking out like a slender tongue, snapping back; a drop of blood drooling down beneath the little hatch cover.

Junior's hand was on his arm. He obeyed, remained seated, but *looked*. Something thrashed in the weeds. Killer's tongue lashed out again.

The caravan and the crowd were trickling away slowly but steadily, off down Twerdahl Street. The Bloocher family gathered itself. Junior called, "Sanity check. If we skip Guilda's now, we can get through school time and still beat the caravan to Guilda's. Vote!"

Reality sometimes called for hard choices. They looked at each other. . . .

THE RINGWORLD THRONE
EXCERPTED FROM THE NOVEL

This book started with a phone call from Barbara Hambly. She was working on a theme anthology, *Sisters of the Night.* All vampires, all women. Two of her contributors had dropped out. Could I oblige?

I don't normally write horror. I said so. "But we'll talk until one of us gets bored."

By and by, she said, "Ringworld vampires."

That's right, vampires are one of the hominid forms that evolved on the Ringworld. And they could rule a large piece of the environment if you put them under permanent cloud cover ... as Louis Wu had done at the end of *The Ringworld Engineers.* So began a novella, "The Vampire Nest."

The first part of "The Vampire Nest" appeared in *Sisters of the Night.* The middle appeared, with graphics, in Omni Comics. The whole story isn't likely to appear by itself, and I'm sorry for that. It's a neat little mystery.

I embedded it in a larger novel, and a larger mystery, a continuation of Louis Wu's exploration of the Ringworld.

A.D. 2882

The Hindmost danced.

They were dancing as far as the eye could see, beneath a ceiling that was a flat mirror. Tens of thousands of his kind moved in tight patterns that were great mutating curves, heads cocked high and low to keep their orientation. The clicking of their hooves was a part of the music, like a hundred thousand castanets.

Kick short, kick past, veer. One eye for your counterpartner. In this movement and the next, never glance toward the wall that hides the Brides. Never touch. For millions of years the competition dance, and a wide spectrum of other social vectors, had determined who would mate and who would not.

Beyond the illusion of the dance loomed the illusion of a window, distant and huge. The Hindmost's view of *Hidden Patriarch* was a distraction, a ground-rules hazard, an obstacle within the dance. *Extend a head; bow—*

The other three-legged dancers, the vast floor and ceiling, were projections from *Hot Needle of Inquiry*'s computer memory. Dancing maintained the Hindmost's skills, his reflexes, his health. This year had been a time for torpor, for recuperation and contemplation; but such states could change in an instant.

One Earthly year ago, or half of the puppeteer world's archaic year, or forty Ringworld rotations . . . the Hindmost and his alien thralls had found a mile-long sailing ship moored below the Map of Mars. They had named it *Hidden Patriarch* and set sail, leaving the Hindmost behind. The window in the Hindmost's dance was a real-time view from the webeye device in *Hidden Patriarch*'s fore crow's nest.

What the window showed was more real than the dancers.

Chmeee and Louis Wu lolled in the foreground. The Hindmost's servants-in-rebellion both looked a bit the worse for wear. The Hindmost's medical programs had restored them both to youth, not much more than two years ago. Young and healthy they still were, but soft and slothful, too.

Hind kick, touch hooves. Whirl, brush tongues.

The Great Ocean lay beneath a sea of fog. Wind-roiled fog made streamline patterns over the tremendous ship. At the shore the fog piled like a breaking wave. Only the crow's nests, six hundred feet tall, poked above the fog. Far inland, far across the white blanket, mountain peaks burst through, nearly black, with glittering peaks.

Hidden Patriarch had come home. The Hindmost was about to lose his alien companions.

The webeye picked up voices.

Louis Wu: "I'm pretty sure that's Mount Hood, and Mount Rainer there. *That* one I don't know, but if Mount St.

Helens hadn't blown her top near a thousand years ago, that might be it."

Chmeee: "A Ringworld mountain doesn't explode unless you hit it with a meteor."

"*Precisely* my point. I think we'll be passing the map of San Francisco Bay inside of ten hours. The kind of wind and waves that build up on the Great Ocean, you'll need a decent bay for your lander, Chmeee. You can start your invasion there, if you don't mind being conspicuous."

"I like conspicuous." The Kzin stood and stretched, claws extended. Eight feet of fur tipped everywhere with daggers, a vision out of nightmare. The Hindmost had to remind himself that he faced only a hologram. The Kzin and *Hidden Patriarch* were 300,000 miles distant from the spacecraft buried beneath the Map of Mars.

Whirl, forefeet glide left, step left. Ignore the distraction.

The Kzin sat again. "This ship is fated, don't you think? Built to invade the Map of Earth. Pirated by Teela after she became a protector, to invade the Map of Mars and the Repair Center. Now *Hidden Patriarch* returns to invade the Earth again."

Within the Hindmost's crippled interstellar spacecraft, a rising, cooling wind blew through the cabin. The dance moved faster now. Sweat soaked the Hindmost's elegantly coiffed mane and rolled down his legs.

The window gave him more than visible light. By radar he could see the great bay, south by the map's orientation, and a crust of cities the archaic kzinti had built around its shore. The curve of a planet would have hidden that from him.

Louis said, "I'm going to miss you."

For a few moments it might be that his companion hadn't heard. Then the great mass of orange fur spoke without turning. "Louis. Over there are lords I can defeat and mates to bear my children. *There* is my place. Not yours. Over there, hominids are slaves, and they're not quite your species, either. You should not come, I should not stay."

"Did I say different? You go, I stay. I'm going to miss you."

"But against your intellect."

"Eh."

Chmeee said, "Louis, I heard a tale of you, years ago. I must learn the truth of it."

"Say on."

"After we returned to our worlds, after we gave over the puppeteer ship to be studied by our respective governments, Chtarra-Ritt invited you to make free of the hunting park outside Blood-of-Chwarambr City. You were the first alien ever to enter that place other than to die. You spent two days and a night within the grounds. What was it like?"

Louis was still on his back. "Mostly I loved it. Mostly for the honor, I think, but every so often a man has to test his luck."

"We heard a tale, the next night at Chtarra-Ritt's banquet."

"What did you hear?"

"You were in the inner quadrant, among the imports. You found a valuable animal—"

Louis sat bolt upright. "A white Bengal tiger! I'd found this nice green forest nesting in all that red and orange kzinti plant life and I was feeling kind of safe and cozy and nostalgic. Then this—this lovely-but-oh-futz *man-eater* stepped out of the bushes and looked me over. Chmeee, he was your size, maybe eight hundred pounds, and underfed. Sorry, go on."

"What is it? Bengal tiger?"

"Something of ours, from Earth. An ancient enemy, you could say."

"We were told that you stepped briskly past it to pick up a branch. Confronted the tiger and brandished the branch like a weapon, and said, 'Do you remember?' The tiger turned away and left."

"Yah."

"Why did you do that? Do tigers talk?"

Louis laughed. "I thought he might go away if I didn't act like prey. If that didn't work, I thought I might whack him on the nose. There was this splintered tree, and a hardwood branch that looked just right for a club. And I talked to him because a Kzin might be listening. Being killed as an inept tourist in the Patriarch's hunting park would be bad enough. Dying as whimpering prey, *nyet.*"

"Did you know the Patriarch had set you a guard?"

"No. I thought there might be monitors, cameras. I watched the tiger go. Turned around and was nose to nose with an armed Kzin. I jumped half out of my skin. Thought he was another tiger."

"He said he almost had to stun you. You challenged him. You were ready to club him."

"He said stun?"

"He did."

Louis Wu laughed. "He had an ARM stunner with a built-up handle. Your Patriarchy never learned how to make mercy weapons, so they have to buy them from the United Nations, I guess. I set myself to swing the club. He *dropped* the gun and extended his claws, and I saw he was a Kzin, and I laughed."

"How?"

Louis threw his head back and laughed, mouth wide, all teeth showing. From a Kzin that would have been a direct challenge, and Chmeee's ears went quite flat.

"Hahahahah! I couldn't help it. I was tanj lucky. He *wasn't* about to stun me. He'd have killed me with one swipe of his claws, but he got himself under control."

"Either way, an interesting story."

"Chmeee, a notion has crossed my mind. If we could get off the Ringworld, you'd want to return as Chmeee, wouldn't you?"

"Little chance that I would be known. The Hindmost's rejuvenation treatment erased my scars, too. I would seem little older than my oldest son, who must now be managing my estates."

"Yah. And the Hindmost might not cooperate—"

"I would not ask!"

"Would you ask me?"

Chmeee said, "I would not need to."

"I hadn't quite realized that the Patriarch might accept the word of Louis Wu as to your identity. But he would, wouldn't he?"

"I believe he would, Speaker-to-Tigers. But you have chosen to die."

Louis snorted. "Oh, Chmeee, I'm dying no faster than you are! I've got another fifty years, likely enough, and Teela Brown *slagged* the Hindmost's magical medical widgetry."

That, the Hindmost thought, was quite enough of that!

"He must have his own medical facilities on the command deck," the Kzin said.

"We can't get to those."

"And the kitchen had medical programs, Louis."

"And I'd be begging from a puppeteer."

Yet an interruption might infuriate them. Perhaps a distraction?

The speech of the puppeteers was more concise and flexible than any human or kzinti tongue. The Hindmost whistlechirped a few phrases: *command [] dance [] drop one level in complexity [] again [] go to webeye six* Hidden Patriarch *[] transmit/receive [] send visual, sound, no smell, no texture, stunner off.* "Chmeee, Louis—"

They both jumped, then rolled to their feet, staring.

"Do I interrupt? I desire to show you certain pictures."

For a moment they simply watched the dance. The Hindmost could guess how silly he must look. Grins were spreading across both faces; though Louis's meant laughter and Chmeee's meant anger. "You've been spying," Chmeee said. "How?"

"Look up. Don't destroy it, Chmeee, but look above your head at the mast that supports the radio antenna. Just at the reach of your claws—"

The alien faces expanded hugely. Louis said, "Like a bronze spiderweb with a black spider at the center. Fractal pattern. Hard to see . . . hard to see where it stops, too. I thought some Ringworld insect was spinning these."

The Hindmost told them, "It's a camera, microphone, telescope, projector, and some other tools, too. It sprays on.

I've left them in various places, not just this ship. Louis, can you summon your guests?" Whistle: *command [] locate City Builders*. "I have something to show you. They should see this, too."

"What you're doing, it looks a little like Tae Kwan Do," Louis said.

Command [] Seek: Tae Kwan Do.

The information surfaced. A fighting style. Ridiculous: his species never fought. The Hindmost said, "I don't want to lose my muscle tone. The unexpected always comes at the most awkward times." A second window opened among the dancers: the City Builders were preparing a meal in the huge kitchen. "You must see—"

Chmeee's claws swiped at the puppeteer's eyes. Window Six blinked white and closed.

Kick. Weave past the Moment's Leader. Stand. Shift a millimeter; stand. Patience.

Avoid him they might. They had avoided him for ten hours now, and for half an archaic year before that; but they had to eat.

The wooden table was tremendous, the size of a kzinti banquet. A year ago the Hindmost had had to turn down the olfactory gain in the webeye, for the stench of old blood rising from the table. The smell was fainter now. Kzinti tapestries and crudely carved frescoes had been removed, too bloody for the hominids' taste. Some had been moved to Chmeee's cabin.

The smell of roasting fish was heavy on the air. Kawaresksenjajok and Harkabeeparolyn were doing things in the makeshift kitchen.

Their infant daughter seemed happy enough at one end of the table itself. At the other end, the raw half of a huge fish awaited the Kzin's pleasure.

Chmeee eyed the fish. "Your luck was good," he approved. His eyes roved the ceiling and walls. He found what he sought: a glittering fractal spiderweb just under the great orange bulb at the apex of the dome.

The City Builders entered, wiping their hands. Kawaresksenjajok, a boy not much past adolescence; Harkabeeparolyn, his mate, some years older; both quite bald across the crowns of their heads, their hair descending to cover their shoulder blades. Harkabeeparolyn picked up the baby and gave it suck. Kawaresksenjajok said, "We lose you soon."

Chmeee said, "We have a spy. I thought as much, but now we know it. The puppeteer placed cameras among us."

The boy laughed at his anger. "We would do the same to him. To seek knowledge is natural!"

"In less than a day I will be free of the eyes of the puppeteer. Kawa, Harkee, I will miss you greatly. Your company, your knowledge, your skewed wisdom. But my thought will be mine alone!"

I'm losing them all, the Hindmost thought. Survival suggests that I build a road to take them back to me. He said, "Folk, will you give me an hour to entertain you?"

The City Builders gaped. The Kzin grinned. Louis Wu said, "Entertain . . . sure."

"If you'll turn off the light?"

Louis did that. The puppeteer whistle-sang. He was looking through the display, watching their faces.

Where the webeye had been, now they saw a window: a view through blowing rain, down past the rim of a vast plate. Far below, pale humanoid shapes swarmed in their hundreds. They seemed gregarious enough. They rubbed against each other without hostility, and here and there they mated without seeking privacy.

"This is present time," the Hindmost said. "I've been monitoring this site since we restored the Ringworld's orbit."

Kawaresksenjajok said, "Vampires. Flup, Harkee, have you ever seen so many together?"

Louis asked, "Well?"

"Before I brought our probe back to the Great Ocean, I

used it to spray webeyes. You're seeing that region we first explored, on the highest structure I could find, to give me the best view. Alas for my view, rain and cloud have obscured it ever since. But, Louis, you can see that there is life here."

"Vampires."

"Kawaresksenjajok, Harkabeeparolyn, this is to port of where you lived. Can you see that life is thriving here? You could return."

The woman was waiting, postponing judgment. The boy was torn. He said a word in his own language, untranslatable.

"Don't promise what you can't deliver," said Louis Wu.

"Louis, you have evaded me ever since we saved the Ringworld. Always you speak as if we turned a blowtorch hundreds of thousands of miles across on inhabited terrain. I've questioned your numbers. You don't listen. See for yourself, they still live!"

"Wonderful," Louis said. "The vampires lived through it!"

"More than vampires. Watch." The Hindmost whistled; the view zoomed on distant mountains.

Thirty-odd hominids marched through a pass between peaks. Twenty-one vampires; six of the small red-skinned herders they'd seen on their last visit; five of a bigger, darker hominid creature; two of a small-headed variety, perhaps not sapient. All of the prey were naked, and none were trying to escape. They were tired but joyful. Each member of another species had a vampire companion. Only a few vampires wore clothing against the chill and the rain. The clothing was clearly borrowed, cut to fit something other than what wore it.

Vampires weren't sapient at all, or so the Hindmost had been told. He wondered if animals would keep slaves or livestock . . . but never mind. "Louis, Chmeee, do you see? Here are other species, also alive. I even saw a City Builder once."

Louis Wu said, "I don't see cancer and I don't see mutations, but they must be there. Hindmost, I got my information from Teela Brown. Teela was a protector, brighter than you and me. One and a half trillion deaths, she said."

The Hindmost said, "Teela was intelligent, but I see her as human, Louis. Even after her change: human. Humans don't look directly at danger. Puppeteers you call cowards, but not to look is cowardice—"

"Drop it. It's been a year. Cancers can take ten or twenty. Mutations take a whole generation."

"Protectors have their limits! Teela had no notion of the *power* of my computers. You left me to make the adjustments, Louis—"

"*Drop* it."

"I will continue to look," the puppeteer said.

The Hindmost danced. The marathon would continue until he made a mistake. He was pushing himself toward exhaustion; his body would heal and then grow strong.

He had not bothered to eavesdrop through the aliens' dinner. Chmeee had not slashed the webeye, but they would not speak secrets in its view.

They need not. A year past, while his motley crew was still trying to settle the matter of Teela Brown and the Ringworld's instability, the Hindmost's flying probe had sprayed webeyes all over *Hidden Patriarch*.

He would rather have been concentrating on the dance.

Time enough for that. Chmeee would be gone soon. Louis would revert to silence. In another year he, too, might leave the ship, leave the Hindmost's control. The City Builder librarians . . . work on them?

They were lost to him already, in a sense. The Hindmost controlled *Needle*'s medical facilities. If they saw that he used his power for extortion, they saw nothing but the truth. But he had been too direct. Chmeee and Louis had both refused medical attention.

They were walking briskly down a shadowed corridor, Louis Wu and Chmeee. Reception was poor in so little light, but they wouldn't see the web. The Hindmost caught only part of the dialogue. He played it back several times afterward.

Louis: "—dominance game. The Hindmost *has* to control us. We're too close to him, we could conceivably hurt him."

Chmeee: "I've tried to see a way."

Louis: "How hard? Never mind. He left us alone for a year, then interrupted himself in the middle of an exercise routine. Why bother? Nothing about that broadcast looked urgent."

Chmeee: "I know how *you* think. He overheard us, didn't he? If I can return to the Patriarchy, I won't need the Hindmost to recover my properties. I have you. You do not exact a price."

Louis: "Yah."

The Hindmost considered interrupting. To say what?

Chmeee: "By my lost lands he controlled me, but how did he control you? He had you by the wire, but you gave up your addiction. The autodoc in the lander was destroyed, but surely the kitchen has a program to make boosterspice?"

"Likely enough. For you, too."

Chmeee dismissed that with a wave. "But if you allow yourself to grow old, he has nothing."

Louis nodded.

"But would the Hindmost believe you? To a puppeteer . . . I do not insult you. I'm sure you speak the truth, Louis. But to a puppeteer, to let yourself grow old is suicide."

Louis nodded, silent.

"Is this justice for a trillion murders?"

Louis would have broken off conversation on another night. He said, "Justice for us both. I die of old age. The Hindmost loses his thralls . . . loses control of his environment."

"But if they lived?"

"If they lived. Yah. The Hindmost did the actual programming. I couldn't go into that section of the Repair Center. It was infested with tree-of-life. I made it possible for *him* to spray a plasma jet from the sun across 5 percent of the Ringworld. If he didn't do that, then *I* can . . . live. So the Hindmost owns me again. And that's important, if *I'm* the reason he doesn't own *you*."

"Exactly."

"So show Louis an old recording and say it's a live broadcast—"

The wind was rising, gusts drowning the voices. Chmeee: "What if . . . numbers . . ."

". . . Hindmost to drop it . . ."

". . . brain is aging faster than the rest of you!" The Kzin lost patience, dropped to all fours, and bounded away down the deck. It didn't matter. They were out of range.

The Hindmost screamed like the world's biggest espresso device tearing itself apart.

In his scream were pitches and overtones no creature of Earth or Kzin could hear, with harmonics that held considerable information. Lineages for two species barely out of the veldt, down from the trees. Designs for equipment that would cause a sun to flare, then cause the flare to lase, a cannon of Ringworld scale. Specs for computer equipment miniaturized to the quantum level, sprayed across the Hindmost's cabin like a coat of paint. Programs of vast resiliency and power.

You twisted rejects from half-savage, half-sapient breeds! Your pitiful protector, your luck-bred Teela, hadn't the flexibility or the understanding, but you don't even have the wit to listen. I saved them all! I, with software from my ship!

One shriek and the Hindmost was calm again. He hadn't missed a step. *Back one, bow, while the Moment's Leader engages the Brides in quadret: a chance to get a drink of water, badly needed.* One head lowered to suck, one raised to watch the dance: sometimes there were variations.

Was Louis Wu going senile? So quickly? He was well over two hundred years old. Boosterspice had kept some humans hale and sapient for half a thousand years, sometimes more. But without his medical benefits, Louis Wu might age fast.

And Chmeee would be gone.

No matter. The Hindmost was in the safest place imagin-

able. His ship was buried in cubic miles of cooled magma
near the center of the Ringworld Repair Center. Nothing was
urgent. He could wait. There were the librarians. Something
would change . . . and there was the dance.

THE WOMAN IN DEL REY CRATER

We were falling back toward the Moon. It's always an uneasy sensation, and in a lemmy I felt frail. A lemmy is a spacecraft, but a very small one; it won't even reach lunar orbit.

Lawman Bauer-Stanson set attitude jets popping. The lemmy rolled belly up to give us a view. "There, Hamilton," she said, waving at the bone white land above our heads. "With the old *verboten* sign across it."

It was four T-days past sunrise, and the shadows were long. Del Rey was well off to the side, six kilometers across, almost edge-on and flattening as we fell. There were dots of dulled silver everywhere inside the crater, clustering near the center. A crudely drawn gouge ran straight across the crater's center, deep and blackly shadowed. That line and the circle of rim formed the *verboten* sign.

I asked, "Aren't you going to take us across?"

"No." Lawman Bauer-Stanson floated at her ease while choppy moonscape drifted nearer. "I don't like radiation."

"We're shielded."

"Suuure."

The computer rolled us over and started the main motor. The lunie lawman tapped in a few instructions. The computer was doing all the work, but I let her land us before I spoke. She'd put us a good kilometer south of the crater rim.

I said, "Being cautious, are we?"

Bauer-Stanson looked at me over her shoulder. Narrow shoulders, long neck, pointed chin: she had the lunies' look of a Tolkien elf matriarch. Her bubble helmet cramped her long hair. It was black going white, and she wore it in a feathery crest, modified Belt style.

She said, "This is a scary place, Ubersleuth Hamilton. Damn few people come here on purpose."

"I was invited."

"We're lucky you were available. Ubersleuth Hamilton, the shield on a lemmy will stop a solar storm. The *wildest* solar storm. Thank God for the Shreveshield." The radiation signal pulled at Bauer-Stanson's eyes, and mine. No rads were getting through at all. "But Del Rey Crater is way different."

The Earth was a blue-white sickle ten degrees above the horizon. Through either window I could see classic moonscape, craters big and little, and the long rim of Del Rey. Wilderness.

"I'm just asking, but couldn't you have set us down closer to Del Rey? Or else near the processing plant?"

She leaned across me, our helmets brushing. "Look that way, the right edge of the crater. Now lots closer and a bit right. Look for wheel treads and a mound—"

"Ah." A kilometer out from the rim wall: a long low hill of lunar dust and coarser debris, with a gaping hole in one end.

"You should know by now, Hamilton. We bury everything. The sky is the enemy here. There's meteors, radiation . . . spacecraft, for that matter."

I was watching the mound, expecting some kind of minitractor to pop out.

She caught me looking. "We turned off the waldo tugs when we found the body. They've been off for twenty hours or so. *You* get to tell *us* when we can turn them on again. Shall we get to it?" Bauer-Stanson's fingers danced over pressure points on the panel. A whine wound down to profound silence as air was sucked from the cabin.

We were dressed alike, in skintight pressure suits under leaded armor, borrowed, that didn't fit well. I felt my belly band squeeze tight as vacuum enclosed us. Bauer-Stanson tapped again, and the roof lifted up and sideways.

We moved back into the cargo bay and positioned ourselves at either end of a device built along the lines of a lunar two-wheeled puffer. We lifted it out of the bay and dropped it overside.

The Mark 29's wheels were toroidal birdcages as tall as my shoulders, with little motors on the wheel hubs. In lunar gravity wheels don't have to be sturdy, but a vehicle needs a wide stance because weight won't hold it stable. The thing stood upright even without the kickstands. Low-slung between the wheels, a bulky plastic case and a heavy lock hid the works of Shreve Development's experimental radiation shield, power source, sensor devices, and other secrets, too, no doubt. A bucket seat was bolted to the case, cameras and more sensing devices behind that.

Bauer-Stanson scrambled after it. She pulled it several feet from the lemmy and turned on the shield.

I'd done spot repairs on the Shreveshield in my own ship, years ago when I was a Belt miner. The little version is a flat plate, twelve feet by twelve feet, with rounded corners, and a small secured housing at one corner. Fractal scrollwork covers it in frilly curves of superconductor, growing microscopically fine around the edges. You can bend it, not far. In my old ship it wrapped around the D-T tank, and the shield effect enclosed everything but the motor. In a police lemmy it wraps the tank twice around.

No Shreveshield could have been fitted into the Mark 29 puffer.

But a halo had formed around it, very like the nearly imperceptible violet glow around the lemmy itself. I'd never seen that glow before. The rad shield doesn't normally have to fight that hard.

Lawman Bauer-Stanson stood within the glow. She waved me over.

I crossed the space between one shield and the other in two bounces. Vacuum and hard bright stars and alien landscapes and falling don't scare me, but radiation is something else.

I asked, "Lawman, why did we only bring one of these puffers?"

"Ubersleuth Hamilton, there *is* only one." She sighed. "May I call you Gil?"

I'd been getting tired of this myself. "Sure. Hecate?"

"He-ca-*tee*," she said. Three syllables. "Gil, Shreve

Development makes active radiation shields. They only make the two kinds, and they're both for spacecraft—"

"We use them on Earth, too. Some of the old fusion plants are hotter'n hell. The Shreveshield was big news when I was, oh, eight years old. They used it to make a documentary on South-Central Los Angeles, but what got my attention was the spacecraft."

"*Tell* me about it. Thirty years ago a solar storm would have us marooned, huddling underground. We couldn't launch ships even as far as Earth."

The big shields came first, I remembered. They were used to protect cities. There was a Shreveshield on the first tremendous slowboat launched toward Alpha Centauri. The little shields, eight years later, were small enough for three-man ships, and that was enough for me. I lofted out to mine the Belt.

"I hope they got rich," I said.

"Yah. When nobody gets rich, they call that a recession," Hecate said. "They spend some of the money on research. They'd like to build a little man-size shield. They don't talk about the mistakes, but the Mark 29 is what they've got now."

"You must be persuasive as hell."

"Yonnie Kotani's my cousin's wife. She let us borrow it. Gil, whatever we learn about this is confidential. You are not to open that lock, ARM or no. *Puffer*," she said in fine disgust.

"Sorry."

"Yah. Well, this version works all the time, Yonnie said. It's still too expensive to market."

"Hecate, is it just conceivable," I wondered, "that Shreve would like me to test their Mark 29 active shield for them?"

She shook her head; the salt-and-pepper crest swirled inside the helmet. Amused. "Not *you*. A dead flatlander celebrity riding their Mark 29 Shreveshield? They could watch your death grin in every boob cube in the solar system! Shall I take the first ride?"

"I want a fresh look. I don't want to deal with your tire prints." I boarded the Mark 29 before she could object.

She made no move to stop me. I said, "Check the reception."

She was into the lemmy's cabin in a lovely graceful leap. She brought up the feed from my helmet camera. "You're on, nice and . . . actually the picture's jumping a little. Good enough, though."

"Keep your eye on me. You can coach." I kicked the Mark 29 into gear and rolled toward the rim.

I'd been wakened from a sound sleep by her call. They keep the same time over the whole Moon, so it was the middle of the night for Hecate Bauer-Stanson, too.

Ah, well. I had time to shower and get some breakfast while she landed and refueled, and that's never guaranteed. But it didn't sound like the intruder in Del Rey Crater needed *immediate* justice.

During the flight I'd had a chance to read about Del Rey Crater.

Just before the turn of the millenium, Boeing, then more or less an aircraft company, had done a survey. What kind of customer would pay how much for easy access to orbit?

The answers they got depended heavily on the cost of launch. A hundred and thirty years ago those costs were the stuff of fantasy. NASA's weird political spacecraft, the Shuttle, launched for $3000 per pound and up. At that price there would be no customers at all: nothing would fly without tax-financed kickbacks; and nothing did.

At $200 a pound (then considered marginally possible) the Net could afford to hold gladiatorial contests in orbit.

Intermediate prices would buy High Frontier anti-weapons, orbiting solar power, high-end tourism, hazardous waste disposal, funerals. . . .

Funerals. For $500/pound, an urnful of ashes could be launched frozen in a block of ice, for the solar wind to scatter to the stars. They launched from Florida in those days. Florida's funeral lobby must have *owned* the state. Florida passed a state law. No funeral procedure to be licensed in Florida unless grieving relatives could visit the grave . . . via a paved road!

Boeing also considered disposal of hazardous waste from fission plants.

You wouldn't just fire it off. First you'd separate the left-over uranium and/or plutonium, the fuel, to use again. Then you'd take out low-level radioactives and bury it in bricks. The truly noxious remainder, about 3 percent by mass, you would package to survive an unexpected reentry. Then you'd bomb a crater on the Moon with them.

Power plant technology would improve over decades to come. Our ancestors saw that far. In time that awful goo would once again be fuel. Future stockholders would want to find it.

Boeing had chosen Del Rey Crater with some care.

Del Rey was little but deep, just at the Moon's visible rim. Meteors massing 1.1 tonnes, slamming down at two kilometers per second, would raise dust plumes against the limb of the Moon. An amateur's telescope could find them. Lowell Observatory could get great pictures for the evening news: effective advertising, and free. The high rim would catch more of the dust . . . not all, but most.

My search program had turned up a Lester Del Rey with a half-century career in science fiction. The little crater had indeed been named for him. And he'd written an early story about an imaginary fission power plant: "Nerves."

To a man used to moonscapes, the view from the crater rim was quite strange. It's not unusual for craters to overlap craters. But they clustered in the center, so that the central peak had been battered flat, and *every crater was the same size*. Yet more twenty-meter craters shaped the line that made Del Rey into one huge FORBIDDEN sign.

Everything around me was covered in pairs of tractor tread marks a meter apart, often with a middle track as of something being dragged. A kilometer away, the tread marks thinned out and disappeared. There I began to see silvery beads at the centers of every crater.

And one a little shinier, the wrong color, off center. I used the *zoom* feature in my faceplate to expand the view.

A pressure suit lay facedown. It was a hardshell, not a skintight. I was looking at the top of its head.

Corrugated footprints ran away from the body, three and four yards apart. The intruder had been running toward the rim to my right, south-southeast, leaping like a Lunar Olympics runner.

"Still got me, Hecate?"

"Yes, Gil. Your camera's better than the one on the waldo tug, but I can't make out any markings on the suit."

"It's head-on to me. Okay, I'm setting a relay antenna. Now I'll get closer." I started the Mark 29 rolling into the crater. If the shield around me was glowing, I couldn't see it from inside.

"I think you were wrong. That isn't a flatlander's suit. It's just old."

"Gil, we went to some effort to get the ARM involved. That was *never* a lunie design. It's too square. The helmet's wrong. This fishbowl design we're wearing, we were already using it when we built Luna City!"

"Hecate, how did you find this thing? How long has it been lying here?"

Hesitation. "We don't send sputniki over Del Rey Crater very often. It's hard on the instruments. Nobody saw anything odd until the waldo tugs went in, then we got a nice view through a tug's camera."

Even if a few sputniki did cross over Del Rey, the suit wouldn't contrast with other silver dots around it. *How long has it been here?* "Hecate, divert a sputnik, or a ship with a camera. We need an overhead view. Do you have the authority, or do I have to play dominance games?"

"I'll find out."

"In a minute. These waldo tugs. What are you stockpiling? The Moon has helium-three fusion and solar power, too!"

"Those old impact tanks go off to the Helios plants."

"Why?"

Hecate sighed. "Beats the hell out of me. Maybe you can find out. You've got clout."

I saw a canister broken open and steered wide around it. Invisible death. I couldn't see any kind of glow around me: no evil blue Cherenkov radiation, and nothing from my own shield either.

What if my wheels broke down? I might trust the Shreveshield, but how careful had Shreve Development been with something as simple, as off-the-shelf, as a pair of power wheels? I couldn't leave the Mark 29 without frying. . . .

Dumb. I'd just carry it out. Hecate and I had picked it up easily. *Why* does radiation make people so nervous?

I stopped a little way from the downed suit. There were no tracks nearby, only the marks under the gloves and boots. The deader had clawed at the dust, leaving finger and toe marks. I ran the Mark 29 in a half circle, helmet camera running. Then I pulled as close as I could get and lowered the stand.

At that moment I still couldn't testify that it wasn't an empty suit. The only markings were the usual color-coded arrows, instructions for novices. They seemed faded.

I didn't much want to step down. Radioactive dust on my boots would be carried inside the Shreveshield. What I could do was lean far over, gripping the belly casing of the Mark 29 with legs and hands, and reach into the suit with my imaginary arm.

It's like reaching into water rich with weeds and scum. My fingers trail through varying texture. Yup, there's someone in there. It seems dehydrated. Corruption isn't obtrusive, and for this I'm grateful. Maybe the suit leaked. The chest . . . a woman?

I reach around to touch the face, lightly. Dry and ancient. I grimace and reach, trailing phantom fingers through chest and torso and abdomen.

"Gil, are you all right?"

"Sure, Hecate, I'm using my talent to see what I can feel out—"

"It's just that you didn't say anything for a while. What talent?"

I never know how someone will react. "Wild talent. I've got some PK and esper. It amounts to being able to feel around inside a locked box with an imaginary arm and hand. I can pick up things, little things. Okay?"

"Okay. What have you got?"

"She was a woman. Hecate, she's shorter than I am."

"Flatlander."

"Likely. No markings on the suit. Corruption isn't advanced, but she's dried out like a mummy. We should check the suit for a leak." I continued to search as I talked. "She's covered with medical telltales outside and in. Big, old-fashioned things. Maybe we can date them. Her face feels two hundred years old, but that's no sign of anything. Air tanks are dry, of course. Air pressure's near zero. I haven't found an injury yet. *Hel*-lo!"

"Gil?"

"Her oxygen flow is twisted right over, all the way up."

No comment.

I said, "Bet on a leak. Even money, a leak got her before the radiation did."

"But what the hell was she doing there?"

"Funny how that thought occurred to both of us. Hecate, shall I collect the body?"

"I sure don't want it in my cargo hold. —Gil, we *don't* want it on the Mark 29. If you let me start up the waldo tugs, I can guide one to the body and move it that way."

"Start 'em up."

I rolled past the dead woman. I stayed wide of the line of footprints leading north-northwest, but that was what I was following.

. . . Bounding across a crater that was the most radioactive spot in the Solar system, barring the Sun itself, and maybe Mercury. Frightened out of her mind? Even if there was no leak, it was a sane decision, giving herself maximum oxygen pressure, nothing left for later as she ran for the crater rim like a damned soul escaping Hell. But what was she doing *in* the crater?

I stopped. "Hecate?"

"Here. I've started the waldo tugs. Shall I send you one?"

"Yah. Hecate, do you see what I see? The footprints?"

". . . They just stop."

"In the middle of Del Rey Crater?"

"Well, what do *you* see?"

"They start here in the middle, already running. They get halfway to the rim. The way my rad sensor is losing its lunch, I'd say she made a good run of it."

I trundled back to where I'd left the corpse. There was a signal laser in the service pack on my back. I spent a few minutes cutting an outline in the rock around the corpse.

"Hecate, how fast are those tugs?"

"Not exactly built for speed. It's more important that they don't turn over, but they'll do 25 K on the flat. Gil, you'll have your tug in ten minutes. How's your shield holding?"

I looked at the rad counters. Hell raged around me, but almost nothing was getting inside the shield. "Whatever got through, I probably brought it in on my boots. From *outside* Del Rey at that. I'd still like to leave."

"Gil, give me a camera view of the boots."

I wheeled into place and leaned far over the corpse's boots. Without Hecate's mention I might never have noticed them. They were white. No decoration, no custom touches. Big boots with thick soles for lunar heat and cold, heavy treads for lunar dust. Built for the Moon. But of course they would be, even if they'd come straight from somewhere on Earth.

"Now the face. The sooner we find out who she was, the better."

"She's lying on her face."

"Don't touch her," Hecate said. "Wait for the tug."

I spent some of my waiting time easing a rope line under the body. Then I just waited.

A pair of arms on tractor treads was bumping toward me. It crossed crater after crater like it was bobbing on waves. It was making me queasy . . . if that wasn't the radiation . . . but the counters were quiet. I watched, and it came.

"I'll turn her over first," Hecate told me. Metal arms a little bigger than mine reached out. I lifted the rope. The arms went under and over the pressure suit, and rotated.

"Hold that," I said.

"Holding."

Three centimeters from her faceplate I still couldn't see through. Maybe the camera could, in one frequency or another. I said, "She's likely still got fingerprints, and we'll get her DNA, but not retina prints."

"Yah." The cargo tug backed and began moving away. "Get a view of where it was lying," Hecate said, but I already was. "Can you get closer? Okay, Gil, move out. You don't have to wait for the tug."

I passed another waldo tug as it was latching on to a canister. A third crawled over the crater rim ahead of me. I followed it over the rim and out.

I said, "I suppose nobody will disturb the scene of the crime? *If* there's a crime."

"We've got cameras on the waldo tugs. I'll set up a watch."

I watched the tug drag its canister toward the hole in the mound.

In my mind's eye that hill was an ancient British barrow, and all the ancient dead were pouring through the portal in its side, into the living world. But on this dead world what crawled out of the factory was only another set of arms riding tractor treads. Still, it was more deadly than any murderous old king's risen army.

Hecate Bauer-Stanson said, "Soon as we reach civilization, you start a search for missing flatlanders who could have wound up on the Moon, *and* a search for that model pressure suit. We've already ruled out anything manufactured here. It's got to be flatlander."

"Not Belter?"

"The boots, Gil. No magnets. No *fittings* for magnets."

Well, hell. I'd just lost serious sleuthing points to Lawman Hecate Bauer-Stanson.

"Come on, Gil. We'll let the waldo tug take the body back—"

"You can program it?"

"I can get it done from Helios Power One, which is where we're going. It'll be five hours en route. She's waited a long time, Gil, she'll wait a little longer. Come on."

"We taking the Mark 29?"

"It could go back by itself . . . no. If anything happened . . . no, I think we bloody have to."

Hecate directed me: we set the Mark 29 on a rock ridge. I didn't guess why until she went back to the lemmy for an oxygen tank.

I asked, "Can we spare that?"

"Sure, the whole lunar surface is lousy with bound oxygen. I have to get the dust off, don't I?" She pointed the tank and opened the stopcock. Dust flew from the Mark 29 and I stepped back.

"I mean, we wouldn't want to run out of breath."

"I packed plenty." She emptied the tank. Then we lifted the Mark 29 back into the lemmy's cargo hold. Hecate took us up and away.

How hard would she hit? Isaac Newton had it all worked out. I was trying to remember the equation, but it wouldn't come. Postulate a mass driver on the rim wall. Launch her in lunar gravity, three kilometers to the center. Up at forty-five degrees, down the same way, Sir Isaac had that straight, and land running. Keep running. Switch the oxygen to high and *run*, run for the far side of the rim, away from the RAP RAP RAP mad scientist who set her flying. "Gil?" RAP RAP RAP.

Knuckles on my helmet, an inch from my eye sockets. "Yah?" I opened my eyes.

We were falling toward a hole in the Moon, a vast glittering black patch with fine lines of orange and green scrolling across it. As we dropped—as the lemmy's thrust pulled me into my couch, creating a sudden scary sense of *down*—I could make out the shape of a rounded hill with a few tiny windows glittering in the black.

Hecate said, "I thought you might freak if thrust started while you were asleep."

The orange-and-black logo was upside down. Helios Power One was sheathed in Black Power™. I was amused, but it made sense: if the fusion plant went down, they'd still want lights, cooling, and the air recycler.

"What were you dreaming? Your legs were kicking."

I'd been dozing. What *had* I been dreaming? "Hecate, she turned the oxygen all the way up. Maybe there was no leak. Maybe it was to run better."

We settled into an orange-and-green mandala, Helios One's landing pad. Hecate eeled out of the cabin, then hustled me out. She said, "We'll see if her suit really has a leak. Anything else?"

"I was thinking a ship landed in the middle of Del Rey and left her there. A little ship, because you'd want the drive flame spashing into a crater, and those are little craters. Your lemmy could do that, couldn't it? And nothing would show—"

"Don't bet on that. It's always amazing what you can see from orbit. Anyway, *I'd* hate to ride *anything* into Del Rey Crater. Gil, I'm feeling a little warm."

"Just your imagination."

"Let's get to Decontamination."

Copernicus Dome was three hundred kilometers northeast of Del Rey. Helios Power One was only a hundred, in a different direction, but both would be just a hop in the lemmy.

Copernicus Dome certainly had medical facilities for rad poisoning. Any autodoc off Earth could treat us for that. Radiation treatment must date back to the end of the Second

World War! Near two centuries of improved techniques leave it difficult to die of radiation . . . but not impossible.

But *decontamination*, washing the radiation off something you want to live with afterward, is something else again. Only fission and fusion power plants would have decontamination facilities.

So far so good. But Helios One used He^3 fusion.

There's He^3 all over the Moon, adsorbed onto the rocks. The helium-three nucleus includes two protons and a neutron. It fuses nicely with simple hydrogen—which has to be imported—giving He^4 and energy, but only at ungodly temperatures. The wonderful thing about He^3 fusion is that it doesn't spit out neutrons. It's not radioactive.

Why would Helios Power One have decontamination rooms? It was another intelligence test, and I hadn't solved it yet. I could ask Hecate . . . eventually.

I have used decontamination procedures to get evidence off a corpse. At Helios Power One they were far more elaborate. There were rad counters everywhere. Still in my suit, I went through a magnetic tunnel, then air jets. I crawled out of my suit directly into a zippered bag. The suit went somewhere else. Instruments sniffed me. Ten showerheads gave me the first decent shower I'd had since leaving Earth.

Then on to a row of six giant coffins. They were Rydeen MedTek autodocs, built long for lunie height, and I wondered: why so many? They didn't look used. That was a relief. I lay down in the first and went to sleep.

I woke feeling sluggish and blurred.

Two hours had passed. I'd picked up less than two hundred millirem, but a red blinker on the readout was telling me to drink plenty of liquids and be back in the 'doc in twenty hours. I could picture Rydeen MedTek's funny molecules cruising my arteries, picking up stray radioactive particles, running my kidneys and urogenital system up to warp speed, shutting down half-dead cells that might turn cancerous. Clogging my circulation.

I used a phone to track Hecate Bauer-Stanson to the director's office.

She stood and turned as I came in, graceful as hell. When I try that, my feet always leave the floor. "Nunnally, this is Ubersleuth Gil Hamilton of the Amalgamated Regional Militia on Earth. Gil, Nunnally Sterne's the duty officer."

Sterne was a lunie, long-headed, very dark. When he stood to shake hands he looked eight feet tall, and maybe he was. "You've done us a great favor, Hamilton," he said. "We didn't like having the waldo tugs shut down. I'm sure Mr. Hodder will want to thank you in person."

"Hodder is—?"

"Everett Hodder is the director. He's home now."

"Is it still nighttime?"

Sterne smiled. "Past noon, officially."

I asked, "Sterne, what do you want with radioactive sludge?"

I'd heard that sigh everywhere on the Moon. *Flatlander. Talk slow.* Sterne said, "This isn't exactly a secret. It just wouldn't exactly be popular. The justification for these generators, on Earth and anywhere else, is that helium-three fusion isn't radioactive."

"Uh-huh."

"The flatlanders started lobbing these packages into Del Rey in . . . early last century. They—"

"Boeing Corporation, USA, A.D. 2003," I said. "Supposed to be 2001, but there was some kind of legal bickering. Makes it easy to remember."

"R-right. They kept it up for near fifty years. At the end the targeting was more accurate, and that's when they used the packages to paint that *verboten* sign across the crater. You must have—"

"We saw it."

"It could just have easily have been *Coca-Cola*. Well, deuterium-tritium fusion was better than fission, but it wasn't much cleaner. But when we finally got the helium-three plants going, it all turned around.

"We ship He^3 to Earth by the ton. When we had enough money we built four He^3 plants on the Moon, too. Del Rey Crater was out of business. And that held for another fifty years."

"Sure—"

"What's finally knocked the bottom out is this new solar-electric paint. Black Power™, they call it. It turns sunlight into electricity, just like any solar power converter, but you spray it on. Place your cables, then spray over them. All you need is sunlight and room.

"On Earth they're still buying He^3, and we can keep that up until your eighteen billion flatlanders start spraying the tops of their heads for power."

"You use it yourselves?"

"Stet, Black Power™ is a great invention, but it's so cheap that it's no longer feasible for us to build *new* He^3 fusion plants. You see? But running the old ones is still cheaper than the paint."

I nodded. Hecate was pretending she already knew all this.

"So my job is safe. Except that He^3 fusion has to be ten times hotter than D-T fusion. The plant is starting to leak heat. Fusion is running slow. We have to inject a catalyst, something to heat up the He^3. Something that fissions or fuses at a lower temperature."

Sterne was enjoying himself. "Wouldn't it be nice if there was something already measured out in standard units and uniform proportions, just lying around ready to pick up—"

"Stet, I see it."

"This radioactive goo from Del Rey Crater works fine. It hasn't lost much of its kick. The processor doesn't do much more than pop off the boosters and lift off the dust—"

"How?"

"Magnetically. We had to build an injector system, of course, with a neutron reflector chamber. We had to install these decontamination rooms and the autodocs and a human doctor on permanent call. Nothing is simple. But the canisters, we just pop them in and let them heat up until the stuff sprays out. We've been using them for two years. Eventually the waldo tugs moved enough canisters that we noticed the body. Hamilton, who was she?"

"We'll find out. Sterne, when this leaks out—" I saw his theatrical wince. "Sorry—"

"Don't say *leak*."

"Nothing gets attention like a murder. Then the media will all be looking at a fusion plant that was supposed to be radiation-free, that you guys have got running radioactive. We can keep that *half*-secret for a day or two while we thrash around, and you work on your story. If you'll do the same."

Sterne looked puzzled. "It was all fairly public, but . . . yes. Be glad to."

Hecate said, "We need phones."

We bought water bottles from a dispenser wall in the Technicians' Lounge. The Lounge had a recycler booth too. Hecate hadn't got nearly the dose I had, but we were both taking in water and funny molecules, and we'd be needing the recycler.

There were four phones. We settled ourselves under the eyes of curious techs and turned on privacy dampers. I called the Los Angeles ARM.

A message light was blinking on Hecate's phone. I watched her ignore it while she talked rapid fire in mime.

I waited.

It always takes forever to connect, and you never learn the problem. No satellite in place? Lightning sends its own signals? Someone left a switch point turned off? Muslim Sector is tapping ARM communications, badly? Sometimes a local government tries that—

But a perfect multiracial androgynous image was inviting me to speak my needs.

I tapped in Jackson Bera's code. I got Jackson explaining that he wasn't there.

"Got a locked room for you, Jackson," I told the hologram. "See if Garner has an interest. I need an ancient pressure suit identified. We think it was made on Earth. I can't send the suit itself, it's radioactive as hell." I faxed him the video I'd taken in Del Rey Crater, dead woman, footprints and all.

That should get their attention.

Hecate was still occupied. Given a free moment, I called Taffy in Hovestraydt City. "Hi, love, the lu—"

"I'm off performing surgery," the recording cried wildly. "The villagers say I'm mad, but this day I have created *life!* If you want the *heeheehee* patient to call back, leave your vital stats at the chime."

BONG! I said, "Love, the lunie law has me halfway around the Moon looking at something interesting. Sorry about tomorrow. I can't give you a time frame or a number. If the monster wants a mate, I'll look around."

Hecate had been watching me as she talked. Now she rang off grinning. "You'll get your view of Del Rey," she told me. "None of the sputniki are handy, but I got a Belt miner to do the job for a customs break. He'll do a low pass over Del Rey. Forty minutes from now."

"Good."

"And I've got another bugful of men coming here. We can send the Mark 29 back with one of them. Who was that?"

"My highly significant other."

She lifted an eyebrow. "You have others of lesser significance?"

I lied to keep things simple. "No, we're lockstepped."

"Ah. Next?"

"I sent what we've got on the suit to the ARM. If we're lucky, I'll get Luke Garner's attention. He's old enough to recognize that suit. And your message light's doing backflips."

She tapped *acknowledge*. A male head-and-shoulders spoke to her, then fizzed out. Hecate said, "Shreve Development wants to talk to me. Want in?"

"Is that the guy who loaned us—"

"I expect it's Yonnie's boss." She dialed and got a lunie computer construct who put her straight through.

He was a beanpole lunie, young but balding, his fringe of black hair a tightly coiled ruff. "Lawman Bauer-Stanson? I'm Hector Sanchez. Are you currently in possession of a piece of Shreve Development property?"

Hecate said, "Yes. We arranged the loan through Ms. Kotani, your chief of security, but I'm sure she—"

"Yes, of course, of course. She consulted my office, all most proper, and if I'd been available, I'd have done just what Ms. Kotani—but Mr. *Shreve* is extremely upset. We'd like the device back at once."

This was starting to feel peculiar. Hecate hesitated, looking at me. I opened the conference line, and said, "Shall we decontaminate the device first?"

Faced by two talking heads, he became flustered. "Decontaminate? For what?"

"I'm not at liberty—I'm Gil Hamilton, by the way, with the ARM. Happened to be available. I'm not at liberty to discuss details, but let's say that there was a spacecraft involved, and citizens of Earth, and—" I let a stutter develop. "I-if we hadn't had the, the *device*, it would have been an impossible situation. Im*poss*ible. But some r-radioactive material got tracked inside the S-shreveshield—Is that how you pronounce it?"

"Yes, perfect."

"So we need to know, Mr. Sanchez. We sprayed any dust off with an oxygen tank, but n-now what? Shall we run it through decontamination at Helios Power One? Or just return it as is? For that matter, may we turn it off? Or are there neutrons trapped in that field just waiting to be sprayed everywhere?"

Sanchez took a moment to collect himself. Thinking hard. Mr. Shreve, what would *he* want? It seemed their experiment had been used to clean up after a spacecraft accident involving celebrity flatlanders! Just as well that it was being hushed up. Witnesses might still remember a two-wheeled *thing* moving safely through radioactive debris. Meanwhile this ARM, this flatlander, seemed scared spitless by the Mark 29.

Ultimately Shreve Development would want the tale told. What they didn't want was noses poking into their experimental shield generator for details of construction.

Hector Sanchez said, "Turn it off. *That's* quite safe. We'll do our own decontamination."

"Police lemmy okay?"

"I . . . don't think so. We'll send a vehicle. Where are you?"

Hecate took over. "We'll bring it to Helios Power One. We're a bit busy now, so give us two or three hours to get it there."

She clicked off, and looked at me. " 'May we turn it off?' "

"Playing dumb."

"Convincing. The accent helps. Gil, what's on your mind?"

"Standard practice. Hold something back. It lets a perp display guilty knowledge."

"Uh-huh. You may find that's harder on the Moon. There aren't so many of us, and communications are sacred. You can be dead a thousand ways because someone didn't speak, or didn't listen, or couldn't. But be that as it may, *what's on your mind?* Is this another talent?"

"Hunch, Hecate. Something funny's going on. Sanchez doesn't seem to know what it is. He's just worried. But—this Mr. Shreve must be the Shreveshield Shreve, the inventor himself, the way Sanchez is acting. What does *he* want?"

"He's supposed to be retired, Gil. But if there was a radioactive spill somewhere—"

"*That's* what I mean. Something radioactive, he'd want the Mark 29, but he'd want it *right now*. He doesn't. He'd want it where the spill happened, but no, he doesn't. He'll come get it at Helios Power One. Maybe it's more a matter of where he *doesn't* want the Mark 29."

She mulled it. "Suppose his man gets here and the Mark 29 hasn't arrived yet?"

I liked it. "Somebody might get upset."

"I'll fix it. Next?"

I stretched. "It'll be a while before we have anything to look at. Let's see if there's a commissary."

"You scout out dinner," she said. "I'll make their widget vanish, then I want to check on the corpse."

There was no commissary, no restaurant either. There was a coin-operated dispenser wall in the Lounge. I glanced into the greenhouse: dead of night.

So we bought handmeals from the dispenser and took them into the greenhouse.

An artificial full Earth glowed overhead. The stars weren't flaming, but something about them . . . ah. They were color-coded. Deep red for Mars, brighter red for Aldebaran, violet for Sirius. . . .

Lunies try to turn their greenhouses into gardens, and there are always individual touches. There were fruits and vegetables to be picked as dark surprises, from a hill sculpted into a shadowy Sitting Buddha.

Hecate reported, "The body is en route. John Ling got us *two* waldo tugs. The second one is keeping the first in view. That way there's a camera watching the corpse at all times." She stopped to spit cherry seeds. "Good man. And Nunnally Sterne says he's set aside one of the handling rooms for an autopsy. We'll do it through leaded glass, with waldos."

I was carving a pear the size of a melon, partly by feel. "What do you think we'll find?"

"What am I offered?"

"Well, radiation, of course, or a leak. No gunshot or stab wounds or concussions, I'd have found that—"

"Psi powers are notoriously undependable," she said.

I didn't take offense, because of course she was right. I said, "I can generally count on mine. They've saved my life more than once. They're just limited."

"Tell me."

So I told her a story, and we ate the pear and the handmeals, and a quiet descended.

Taffy and I aren't exactly lockstepped. But Taffy and I and Harry McCavity, her lunie surgeon, and Laura Drury, my lunie cop, *are* lockstepped; and Taffy and I are affianced to become pregnant, someday. I used to like a complicated love life, but I've started to lose that. So the dark and quiet companionship began to feel ominous, and I said, just to be saying something, "She could have been poisoned."

Hecate laughed.

I persisted. "What if you murder someone, *then* freeze-dry her, then toss her three kilometers in lunar gravity? You don't expect anyone'll find her, not in Del Rey, but if someone did—"

"Tossed how? A little portable mass driver on the rim?"

"Damn."

"Would you have found bruising?"

"Maybe."

"And *then* she made the footprints?"

Double damn. "If we had specs on our mass driver, we'd know how accurate it was. Maybe the footprints were already there, and Killer just fired the body at where they ended. Then again, there aren't any portable mass drivers."

Hecate was laughing. "All right, who made the footprints?"

"Your turn."

"She walked in," Hecate said. "Trick was to erase any footprints that led in from the rim."

"Blast from an oxygen tank?"

"A lemmy doesn't carry *that* much oxygen. A serious spacecraft would. A spacecraft could just spray the whole area with the rocket motor, but . . . Gil, a ship could just land *in* the crater, push her out, and take off. You said so yourself."

I nodded. "That's starting to look like *it*. Besides, why would anyone walk into Del Rey Crater?"

"What if the killer persuaded her she was wearing a rad-shielded suit?"

Riiight. Still too many possibilities. "What if there was something valuable hidden in there? A bank heist. A dime disk with ARM secret weapons on it."

"A secret map of the vaults under the Face on Mars—"

"Down comes a lemmy to pick it up. Back goes a lemmy with the copilot left behind."

"How long ago? If it was forty or fifty years, say, your lemmy wouldn't even have a Shreveshield. It'd be a suicide mission."

Which narrowed the window a little. Hmm. . . .

"I never tried lockstepped," Hecate Bauer-Stanson said.

"Well, it's easier with four. And we're constantly being moved around, so getting together is a hobby in itself."

"Four?"

I stood. "Hecate, I need the recycler again."

"And I've probably got message lights."

The phones were signaling messages for both of us. Hecate punched hers up while I used the recycler. When I came out she was beckoning frantically. I moved to her shoulder.

"This is Lawman Bauer-Stanson," she said.

The construct said, "Please hold for Maxim Shreve."

Maxim Shreve was seated in a diagnostic chair, a reclining traveler with an extended neck rest for his greater length. Old and sick, I judged, holding himself together by little more than will. "Lawman Bauer-Stanson, we need the Mark 29 back at once. My associates tell me that it has *not* reached Helios Power One."

"Haven't they—? Will you hold while I try to find out?" Hecate punched HOLD and glared at me. "The Mark 29's under a tarp with dirt on it. We can't uncover it because Hector Sanchez has landed a cargo shell in plain view of it. What do I say *now*?"

I said, "It isn't loaded yet. Your man has a lemmy flying around the site looking for more casualties. Tell him that, but don't admit there's been a crash."

She mulled it for a moment, then put Shreve back on.

The old man was standing, dark and skeletally gaunt:

Baron Samedi. Travel chair or no, in lunar gravity he could *loom*. The instant Hecate appeared he was raging.

"Lawman Bauer-Stanson, Shreve Development has *never* been in trouble with the law. We're not only a *good* corporate citizen, we're one of Luna City's major sources of income! Ms. Kotani cooperated with your office when you expressed a need. I presume that need is over. What must I do to get the Mark 29 back quickly?"

I'd figured that out, but it wasn't a thing to be broadcast.

Hecate said, "Sir, the device hasn't even been loaded yet. My man on the spot is still searching for casualties, but her police vehicle is too big to get inside the, uh," Hecate allowed herself a bit of agitation. "Site. Sir, lives may depend on your device. Are lives at stake at your end?"

Shreve seemed to have recovered his aplomb. He floated back into his chair. "Lawman, the device is *experimental*. We've never put *any* test subject in an experimental Shreveshield without medical monitors, and I include whole herds of minipigs! What if the field hiccoughed with your man on it? Is she even a lunie citizen? Is her suit equipped with medical ports?"

"Yes, I see. I'll call Lawman Cervantes."

"Wait, Lawman. Did it work?"

Hecate frowned.

"Did the shield perform as it should? Is everyone all right? No radiation?"

Hecate said, "The, um, user tracked some radioactive material into the shield, but that certainly wasn't the Shreveshield's fault. It worked fine, far as we can tell—"

Maxim Shreve's eyes rolled up in his head and all his pain wrinkles smoothed out. In that instant it was as if his life was vindicated. Then he remembered us.

"I wish you could tell me more of the circumstances," he said briskly. "We will *certainly* want recordings if our device resolved a calamity. *Without* frying anyone!"

"We'll have the device back in your hands within hours, and of course we're very grateful," Hecate said. "I expect we'll be able to tell you the complete story within the week, but even then it may be confidential for a time."

"That's all right then. Good-bye, Lawman, ah, Bauer-Stanson." He was gone.

She didn't turn. "Now what?"

I said, "Tell your men to get the pilot inside."

"Pilots. Sanchez and a new voice heard from. Better if you invite them in, O Prince from a Foreign Land."

"All right."

"Cameras on their vehicle," she said.

"Um . . . stet. Hecate, what have you got to work with?"

"Six of my police. They've been setting up to examine the body. Two Helios personnel. They cooperated when we buried the Mark 29, so they'll cooperate when we uncover it. Two police lemmies—"

"Stet. Here's what we do. One lemmy takes off out of sight. Then the other hovers while the first one lands. We only want the dust cloud and a fast shuffle of police lemmies while your men uncover the Mark 29."

"This had better be worth the hassle." She got up and reached past me to connect my phone to the lunie cops outside. "Wylie, ARM Ubersleuth Hamilton wants to talk to your visitors. Then get back to me."

I waited.

Sanchez and a woman with short crisp blond hair fitted their heads into camera view. Bubble helmets still reflect light and hide a jawline. Sanchez said, "We came for the Mark 29, Hamilton—"

The woman edged him out. "Hamilton? I'm Geraldine Randall. We were told we could pick up the Shreveshield here. I hope it hasn't got itself lost."

Randall was in charge, very much so. I said, "No, no, not at all, but things are a bit complicated at present. Come in and wait, won't you?"

"I'll be right in," Randall said with a glowing smile.

She was going to leave Sanchez to watch the damn cargo shell. "Both of you, please. You may have to sit in. I don't know what authority I have here. Probably whatever nobody else wants." Just a touch of bitterness showing.

She frowned, nodded.

I switched off. Hecate was still miming. My own message light was blinking, but I waited. Presently Hecate sat back and blew hair out of her eyes.

I said, "Sanity check. When you gave him details, Shreve *calmed down*. Yes?"

She thought about it. "I guess he did."

"Uh-huh. But you didn't tell him anything reassuring. Device hasn't been loaded for return? It's sitting around the site of a disaster? involving spacecraft and extralunar celebrities? waiting for someone to use it? *again?*"

Hecate said, "Maybe his med chair doped him to stop a stroke. No, dammit, he was *lucid*. And who the hell is Geraldine Randall?"

"Bauer-Stanson? Hamilton? I'm Geraldine Randall." We stood, and my feet left the floor, and Randall reached up to shake hands with Hecate and down to shake hands with me. She was six-foot-five and lush, with short curls of buttery blond hair, full lips, and a wide smile. A short lunie in her forties, I judged her, carrying enough weight to round her out. "What news?"

"Cervantes says it's on the way," Hecate said. "Knowing Cervantes, it could mean he's almost ready to launch."

Sanchez looked miserable. Randall was losing her smile. "Hamilton, I hope you're using the device only for the purpose intended. Max Shreve is seriously worried about security."

I said, "Randall, I was pulled out of bed because there was flatlander politics involved, and I'm an ARM with the rank of Ubersleuth. If somebody's been high-handed, he'll have two governments on his tail, not just Shreve Inc."

"Persuasive," she said.

"Ms. Randall, it's all being recorded. Think of the movie rights!"

"Not persuasive. We may not hold those. The disaster

didn't take place on our turf. Hamilton, we want the device back."

"Are you with Shreve Inc. or the government?"

"Shreve," she said.

"In what capacity?"

"I'm on the board."

She didn't look that old. "For how long?"

"I was one of the original six."

"Six?"

Hecate was offering coffee. Randall took one and added sugar and cream. She said, "Thirty-five years ago Max Shreve came to five of us with the designs for an active shield against radiation. Everything he told us proved out. He made us rich. There's not a lot I wouldn't do for Max Shreve."

"He sent you? He wants it back that urgently?"

She ran a long-fingered hand through her short curls. "Max doesn't know I came, but he seemed very upset on the phone. I don't see it as that urgent, myself, but I'm starting to wonder. *How many* lunie police have left eye tracks and fingerprints on the Mark 29? And what do I have to do to get it back?"

Message light for Hecate. She picked up. I said, "It's probably incoming now. Randall, I suppose I'll sound naive, but I can't believe you're old enough—"

She laughed. "I was twenty-six. I'm sixty-one now. Lunar gravity is kind to human bodies."

"Would you try the same gamble again?"

She thought it over. "Maybe. I'm not sure a con man *could* have put together as good a package as Max had. He was a lunie, we could track him. He did very well at Luna City University. He could talk fast, too. Kandry Li wanted to go for a smaller version of the shield, and we watched Max talk her out of it. He made diagrams, charts, models, all on the spot. He played Kandry's own computer like a pipe organ. I think I could do his damn lecture myself."

"Do it."

She stared at me.

"I was just a kid when the Shreveshield came out. I wanted one just big enough for me. Why can't I have it?"

She laughed; trailed off. "Well. It doesn't scale up. You need a bigger template to retain the hysteresis effect that traps the neutrons. Otherwise, the shield effect just fades out on you. That's what the—" She caught herself.

"Right," I said.

Hecate Bauer-Stanson flicked off her privacy. "It's down," she said. "You can collect it anytime. Shall I give you some men to load it?"

"I'd be most grateful," Randall said to Hecate. She didn't have to tell Sanchez to see to it, because he was already leaving. To me she said, "We had to reconfigure the circuitry pattern. It's not the same fractal; it's not even related. Well, thank you both—" and she was gone too.

"Gil, you've got a message light."

Hecate watched over my shoulder as I played the message from the Los Angeles ARM. Split field, a computer composite of the dead woman's suit manifested next to Luke Garner in a travel chair.

Luke at 188 *was* paraplegic, had been for years, but he looked healthier than Maxim Shreve. Happier, too. He spoke rituals of courtesy, then, "We think your suit was customized from one of the pressure suits that came up with the first Moon colony. Thing is, those suits were returned to NASA for study. Your deader really did get it from Earth. It's ninety to a hundred years old.

"So right now you're probably wondering, 'Why didn't she just buy a new pressure suit?' And the answer might be *these*—" Luke's cursor highlighted points on the old suit. "Medical sensors. Those early suits didn't just keep an astronaut alive. NASA wanted to know what was happening to them. If they died, maybe the next one wouldn't.

"In the early space program the medical probes were invasive. You wince just reading about it. These later suits weren't so bad, but your deader may have upgraded them anyway. What she wanted was the medical ports on the suit. There are suits like that still being made, of course, but they're expensive, and the sale would be remembered. Take your choice, she was secretive or cheap.

"Let me know, will you? And remember, criminals don't *like* locked rooms. They're usually accidents."

I watched the empty space where Luke had been. "Hecate, didn't Shreve say that Shreve Development labs have pressure suits with medical ports? We might've guessed that—"

"I bet they're a lot less than a hundred years old, Gil. You want to see them anyway? I'll arrange that."

Four off-duty technicians had been watching our antics. Now they seemed to be losing interest. I didn't blame them. I got up and paced for a bit, wondering if there was anything more I could do.

Hecate said, "I've got your overhead view, Gil."

"Put it on."

A camera was panning slowly across a shrinking moonscape, tinted with violet from the fusion drive of a rising Belt trading ship. Del Rey Crater slid into view, shrinking. Little craters all the same size. Bits of silver in the little craters. Three bronze bugs . . . *four* crawling around near the southern rim. We watched until Del Rey was sliding off the edge of the field, shrunk too small to show detail.

Then Hecate replayed it, slowing it, slower yet. "See it?"

It's amazing what you can see from orbit.

Waldo tugs had made random tracks all across the southern quarter of Del Rey, like the tunnels in an ant farm. Down there they had obscured the flow lines. But from up here . . .

Something on the southern rim had sandblasted Del Rey Crater from the rim as far as the battered central peak.

Down there would be surfaces clean of dust, sharp crater rims slightly rounded, minicraters erased. Down there you would see only details. Close-up I had seen nothing of the overall fan-shaped pattern.

I didn't believe that had been done by a spacecraft's oxygen tanks. It was too intense. That smooth wash must have been made by the rocket motor itself.

"The footprints must have been made afterward," I speculated. "Anything earlier was washed out. I'm going to have to apologize to Luke."

"No. He called it," Hecate said. "Nobody sets out to make a locked room mystery. The perp was hiding something else. Now, he fired from the south rim? And prints made afterward lead from the center south-southeast. She ran *toward* the killer?"

"Right toward her only source of escape. And oxygen. And medical help."

"She was hoping for mercy," Hecate said.

I looked over at her. Hecate didn't seem unduly disturbed, only bemused. Whoever had set a woman down in that radioactive Hell would not offer mercy.

I said, "She might have begged. Who knows? I know people who would have been gasping curses. She might run to the center to leave a message, then run away from it to distract the killer."

"Did you see a message?"

"No." I wasn't even sure I liked the notion. "That rocket flame had to be erasing *something*. It looks like the killer didn't have the guts to go into the crater, but propping his lemmy right on the rim took *some* nerve. Why? To erase footprints?"

"Gil, only a madman would trudge out into the middle of Del Rey Crater unless he already knew something was there." She caught my smile. "Like you did. But someone *might* peek over an edge. The perp erased the bootprints that led in from the edge. The ones in the center, he left."

"Could have waited and got them all. And any later message."

"Your turn," she said.

The last time I read a murdered man's dying message, he'd been lying. But at least Otto Penzler hadn't erased it, then made me guess what it said!

"I need a nap," I said. "Give me a call when you know something."

It felt like I'd been asleep for some time. I was on the rug, totally comfortable in lunar gravity. I had a view of Lawman Hecate Bauer-Stanson's back. She was studying a diffuse rainbow glow. I couldn't see the hologram from down here.

I got to my feet.

Hecate had a split screen going. Through one holo window they were carving a woman like a statue of petrified wood. The band saw was running itself. I could see vague human shapes, out of focus behind a wall of thick glass.

One of the slices was passing through a second window. The view would zoom on some detail: arteries and sections through the liver and ribs. Details might fluoresce before the view backed off.

A third window showed the archaic suit.

"The damn trouble," I said, talking to myself because Hecate had her Privacy on, "is that there's nobody to pull in. No witnesses, no suspects . . . *millions* of suspects. With a proper leak in her suit she could have died yesterday. With no leak she could have been out there ten years. More."

What if her suit was *new* when she lay down?

No. Even sixty years ago the missiles were still falling in Del Rey Crater. "From ten to sixty years. Even on the Moon, that's a million suspects, and *nobody* has an alibi to cover a fifty-year span."

A fourth window blinked on, showing a fingerprint—another—another—something unidentified—"Retina," Hecate said without turning. "Completely degraded. But I got fingerprints and partial DNA. Maybe the ARM can match them."

I said, "Boot them over to me."

She did. I called the Los Angeles ARM. I left a message on Bera's personal code, then got through to a duty clerk. He showed signs of interest when he realized I was calling from the Moon. I gave him the dead woman to track down.

Hecate was looking at me when I clicked off. I said, "There are short lunies."

She said, "Bet?"

"What odds?"

She considered—and my phone blinked. I picked up.

Valerie Van Scopp Rhine. Height: 1.66 meters. Born A.D. 2038, Winnetka, North America. Mass: 62 KG. Gene type . . . allergies . . . medical . . . She was forty or so when the picture was taken, a lovely woman with high cheekbones and a delicately shaped skull under a golden crest of hair. *No children. Single. Full partner, Gabriel's Shield, Inc., A.D. 2083–2091. No felony convictions. WANTED on suspicion of 28.81, 9.00, 9.20—*

Hecate was reading over my shoulder.

I said, "The codes mean she's wanted on suspicion of embezzlement, flight to escape arrest, violation of political boundaries, misuse of vital resources, and some other stuff as of thirty-six years ago."

"Interesting. Vital resources?"

"It used to be the custom, you named every possible crime, then trimmed. Boundaries, that's an old law. Here it means they think she escaped to space."

"Interesting. Gil, her suit isn't leaking."

"Isn't it."

"There was a fair vacuum inside. We got traces of organics, of course, but it would have taken years—*decades* to lose *all* of her air and water."

I said, "Thirty-six years."

"All that time. In Del Rey Crater?"

"Hecate, at a distance her suit looked just like another of the Boeing packages, and nobody was looking anyway."

"Then we can guess why the body's in such good shape. Radiation," Hecate said. "What's she supposed to have embezzled?"

I scrolled through the file. "Looks like funds from Gabriel's Shield. And Gabriel's Shield turns out to be a research group. . . . Two partners: Valerie Van Scopp Rhine and Maxim Yeltzin Shreve."

"*Shreve.*"

"Bankrupt in A.D. 2091, when Rhine allegedly disappeared with the funds." I stood up. "Hecate, I've got to go sharpen my skates. You can study this, or you can summon up a dossier on Maxim Shreve."

She stared, then laughed. "I thought I'd heard every possible way to say that. Go. Then drink some more water."

I waited for a woman to step out of the recycler booth, then went in.

Hecate had a display up when I got back.

Maxim Yeltzin Shreve. Height: 2.23 meters. Born A.D. 2044, Outer Soviet, Moon. Mass: 101 KG. Gene type . . . allergies . . . medical . . . No felony convictions. Married Juliana Mary Krupp 2061, divorced 2080. Children: 1 girl, Marya Jenna. Single. A videoflat of his graduation, looking like a burly socker champ, *used with permission.* A holo taken at the launch of the fourth slowboat, the colony ship bound for Tau Ceti, bearing the larger model Shreveshield, in A.D. 2122. He didn't need a medical chair then, but he didn't look good. *Chairman of the board of Shreve Development 2091, retired November 2125.* Two years ago.

When your body gets sick enough, your mind starts to go, too. I could be putting too much weight on any oddities in this man's behavior.

I hit the key that got me the next dossier.

Geraldine Randall. Height: 2.08 meters. Born A.D. 2066, Clavius, Moon. Mass: 89 KG. Gene type . . . allergies . . . medical . . . She'd had a problem carrying a child, corrected by surgery. *No felony convictions. Married Charles Hastings Chan 2080.* She'd been at the launch of the fourth slowboat, too. *Member of the Board of Shreve Development 2091.*

Over Hecate's shoulder, they were still carving the dead woman. I understood why they were so casual about it. The remains of lunar dead become mulch, whatever can't be used as transplants. Hecate was listening to a running commentary, but if they'd found evidence of disease, she'd have told me.

Valerie Rhine hadn't rotted because radiation had fried all the bacteria in her body. She could have lasted a million years, a billion, without my hindrance.

I turned back to Maxim Shreve as he had been when he registered as Shreve Development, a lunar corporation, thirty-six years ago. He was posing with five others, and one was Geraldine Randall. A younger man, he already looked sick . . . or just worn down, working himself to death. It's one way to get rich. Give everything to your dream. Six years later, A.D. 2097 and looking a little better, he and his partners had an active shield up for patent.

Did lunies just get old quicker? I tapped Hecate's shoulder. She turned off Privacy, and I asked, "How old are you, Hecate?"

"I'm forty-two."

She met my stare. Older than me by one year, and healthy as a gymnast. The lunie doctor Taffy saw when I wasn't around was in his sixties. I said, "Shreve must be sick. He's less than ninety. What's his problem?"

"Doesn't it say?"

"I couldn't find it."

She slid into my spot and began diddling with the virtual keys. "The file's been edited. Citizens don't have to tell all their embarrassing secrets, Gil, but . . . he must be crazy. What if he needed medical help, and it wasn't in the records?"

"Crazy or guilty."

"You think he's hiding something?"

I said, "Call him."

"Now, Gil. Maxim Shreve is one of the most powerful men on the Moon, and I wasn't thinking of changing careers." She studied me, worried. "Are you just harrassing the man in the hope he'll tell us something?"

I said, "It seems pretty clear what happened, doesn't it?"

"You're thinking he killed her and took the money himself. Set down in Del Rey and pushed her out of the ship, still alive. But why not kill her first? Then there wouldn't be any footprints or dying messages."

"Nope, you've only got half of it."

She flapped her arms in exasperation. "Go for it."

"First: Mark 29. You said Shreve Development has been trying to build a little shield ever since they got the big ones. I believe it. Twenty-nine is a big number. Maybe a small version is the *first* thing he tried. That's what told him about the, what she said, hysteresis problem.

"Second: He didn't act like a thief running away with the money. When he founded Shreve Inc., he acted like a man who wants to build something and almost knows how. I think he and Rhine spent all they had on experiments.

"Third: Someone sprayed part of the crater from the rim, and I think that was Shreve. There's no sign he was in the crater, except for Rhine's footprints, and we already know *something* was erased.

"Fourth: Why Del Rey Crater? Why walk around in the most radioactive crater on the Moon?"

Hecate was looking blank. I said, "They were testing a prototype Shreveshield. That's why she walked in. I even know what he was hiding when he sprayed the crater."

She said, "I'll call him. Your theory, you talk."

Hecate looked around at me. "Mr. Shreve isn't taking calls. It says he's in physical therapy."

I asked, "Where's the Mark 29 now?"

"They took off almost an hour ago." It took her only a few seconds. "En route to Copernicus. That's the Shreve Inc labs. ETA ten minutes."

"Good enough. Luke Garner's travel chair has a sender in it, in case he needs a serious autodoc or even a doctor. What do you think, would a lunie's chair have one too?"

It took her longer (I got her coffee and a handmeal) to work her way through the lunar medical network. Finally, she sighed and looked up, and said, "He's in motion. Moving toward Del Rey Crater. I have a number for the phone in his chair, Gil."

"Futz! Always I get it almost right."

"Call him?"

"I'm inclined to wait for him to touch down."

She studied me. "He's going after the body?"

"Seems right. Any bets on what he might do with it?"

"It's a big Moon." She turned back. "He's crossing Del Rey. Slowing. Gil, he's going down."

"Phone him."

His phone must have been buzzing during the landing. When he answered it was by voice, no picture. "*What?*"

I said, "The thing about poetic justice is that it requires a poet. I'm Ubersleuth Gil Hamilton, with the ARM, Mr. Shreve. On the Moon by coincidence."

"I'm a *lunie* citizen, Hamilton."

"Valerie Rhine was of Earth."

"Hamilton, I'm supposed to run now. Let me set my headphones and get on the track."

I laughed. "You do that. Shall I tell you a story?"

I heard irregular puffing, less like a sick man running on an exercise track in low gravity than the same man climbing out of a spacecraft. No sound of fiddling with headphones: they'd be already in place inside his bubble helmet.

The puffing became much faster.

I said, "Shreve, I know you're not afraid of the organ banks. The hospitals wouldn't take anything you've got. Come in and tell your story."

"No. But I'll—tell *you* a story, Ubersleuth. Lawman.

"It's about two brilliant experimenters. One didn't have any money sense, so the other had to keep track of expenses when he'd rather have been working on the project. We were in love, but we were in love with an idea, too."

His breathing had become easier. "We developed the theory together. I *understood* the theory, but the prototypes kept burning out and blowing up. And every time something happened, Valerie knew exactly what went wrong and how to fix it. Warble the power source. More precision in the circuitry. I couldn't keep up. All I knew was that we were running out of money.

"Then one day we had it. It worked. She *swore* it worked.

We already had all the instruments we needed. I spent our last few marks on a video camera. *Stacks* of batteries. The— we called it the Maxival Shield—it ate power like there was no tomorrow.

"We went out to Del Rey Crater. Valerie's idea. Test the device and film the tests. Anyone who saw Valerie dance around in Del Rey Crater would throw funding at us with both hands."

"Gil, he's taking off."

Too fast. I suddenly realized why his breathing had eased. He'd left his Mark 20-odd sitting in the dust. Maybe it had quit working, maybe he stopped caring.

I asked, "Shreve, what went wrong?"

"She went out into Del Rey with the prototype. Just walking, turning to cross in front of the camera, then some gymnastics, staying within the shield effect, and all with that glow around her and her face shining in the bubble helmet. She was beautiful. Then she looked at the instruments and started screaming. I could see it on my own dials, the field was just gradually dying out.

"She was screaming, 'Oh my god, the shield's breaking down!' And she started running. 'I think I can get to the rim. Call Copernicus General Hospital.' "

"Running with the shield? Wasn't it too heavy?"

"How did you know that?"

Hecate said, "Gil, he's just cruising along the crater rim. Hovering."

I nodded to her. I told Shreve, "That was our biggest problem. What were you erasing when you sprayed rocket flame across the crater? I figure your shield generator was big. You had it on some sort of cart that Rhine could pull. She pulled a superconducting cable. She left her power source with you."

"That's right, and then she ran away and left it. If a hospital got her, every cop on the Moon would want to look into our alleged radiation shield. The doctors would have to know exactly what she was exposed to. We didn't have a tenthmark left. Nobody would believe we had anything, what with Valerie glowing in the dark, and if anyone did, he could get the designs on the Four O'Clock News."

"So you pulled it back."

"Hand over hand. Was I supposed to leave it sitting out on the Moon? But she saw me doing it. She—I don't know what she was thinking—she ran away, toward the center of the crater. I'd already had more radiation than I wanted, but those tracks . . . not just the footprints, but—"

"The tracks of the cable," I said. "All over the dust like a rattlesnake convention."

"Anyone could see them just by looking over the rim! So I moved the lemmy up onto the crater wall and turned it on its side and used the rocket. I don't know what Valerie was thinking by then. Did she write some kind of last message?"

Hecate said, "No."

"Even if she did, who would see it? But I picked up too much radiation. It's near killed me."

"Well, it kind of did," I said. "Rad sickness retired you early. It was part of what tipped me off."

"Hamilton, *where are you*?"

"*Wait*, Hecate! Shreve, it wouldn't be prudent to answer."

Hecate said edgily, "Gil, he's accelerating straight up. What was *that* all about?"

"Last gestures. Right, Shreve?"

"Right," he said, and turned off his phone.

I told Hecate, "When his Mark 20-odd shut down he had nothing left. He went looking for me. Spray my ship with rocket flame. I lied about being on the rim of Del Rey, but we don't know what he's flying, Hecate, and I don't want him to know where we are. Even a lemmy could do severe damage if you dropped it on Helios Power One at maximum. What's he doing now?"

"Coasting. I think . . . I think he's out of fuel. He burned up a lot, hovering."

"We should keep watching."

* * *

Two hours later Hecate said, "His travel chair just quit sending."

"Where did he come down?"

"Del Rey, near the center. I want to look at it before I assume anything."

"It could have been very messy. He was a hero, after all." I yawned and stretched. I could be back in Hovestraydt City by tomorrow morning.

LOKI

A story with no human characters is daunting. It's a tour de force, a demonstration of skill. Isaac Asimov did it well.

It's never a stunt. Never try this unless you have something to say, and no other way to say it.

As long ago as our memory runs, the witch wagon came crawling down out of the rippling silver sky. She brought a taste of chemicals and metals, but that went away over a crawler's generation. That was eighty generations ago.

Generations were shorter then. We were less careful at counting, too. Life changed rarely. Change came as disaster, as altered deep-sea currents, hordes of predators, water fouled by algae blooms. Only survival mattered then. Recording our history was not a high priority, before the witch wagon came.

The top of the witch wagon was a window to light and color, visible from any side. From above it was only a silver circle. The box underneath made sounds. She moved a little like a great angular snail. We hid from her for a time, but she never harmed any swimming or crawling thing.

She didn't eat. We thought she might be a free-moving plant, but she could not be eaten either.

Our oldest tales have been forgotten because they relied on memory. Teacher thought that we remembered what our ancestors had known, but that is not right. It is as if tracks were grooved in our minds before birth, so that we can more easily be taught what our ancestors knew.

We remember when the witch wagon came, but these early tales are vague. They were scrawled in sand and the pictures remembered from generation to generation.

The pictures she showed could be brilliant abstracts—black scattered with white and color-tinged dots and arabesques, green seabottoms shining as if a hotter sun were blazing just above the sky, or waters with far stranger creatures than ourselves. But the witch wagon learned to draw simpler sketches when she talked to us. The simplified pictures in the witch wagon's display window showed us that we could draw what we were shown. One of us must have thought of adding symbols for the sounds she thought went with the pictures.

There were no artists before the witch wagon.

The stories we crawlers tell are rich in detail, all sound and chemical cues and rippling fins and manipulators and the colors in our skins. But none of our language was made to describe anything so strange as what the witch wagon had to tell. Language did not have enough senses to play with. The witch wagon had far less, only pictures and sound. We took it for talk and tried to talk back.

We learned to draw in the sand where the sky is close and daylight pours through. Later tales were carved with the flint daggers the witch wagon taught us to make. We carved them wherever we could find vertical rock, and copied them before they faded.

Some of what she taught seemed nonsense.

Geometry was a matter of rigid shapes to hold and manipulate in one's mind, shapes made of straight lines and flat planes. There are no such shapes in our world! Rigid rock did poke through the soft land, or billowed up in boiling seawater and cooled into soft-looking pillow shapes that were hard to the touch. The shell of a dead dustman crab was hard and rigid. But nowhere were there straight lines or flat surfaces. None of us could understand. The witch wagon gave up on geometry.

But some lessons stuck.

Things need names, consistent names, and for more than poetry. Related things should have related names. Snark, leviathan, anvil jungle, dustman crab, crawler (ourselves). If we can name a thing's *kind*, we are a step toward understanding it.

Leviathan is huge, unstoppable, but slow to turn. Snarks are fast and agile. One could escape a snark by diving into an anvil jungle. A leviathan would just crash through and eat what flew out. Dustman crabs were not to be killed: they kept the environment clean even when the currents were quiet.

She told us of Teacher.

The witch wagon was the moving part of a larger entity. Her larger part . . . her mind . . . was above the silver sky, dry, where she could live a long time. The witch wagon was like a voice and hand turned loose to roam: Teacher's hand and voice, but tenuously connected, and stupid as a lost voice might be. She could crawl about where the sand was flat. Teacher could only squat where she fell, where the land poked through the sky, two days' crawl from where we then made our home.

We had been wanderers. Now too many of us gathered around the witch wagon, and stayed. We studied the witch wagon, and she studied us, for no more than seven generations. Then predators swam into our range and drove us away.

For twenty generations we dared not go near where the witch wagon must lie.

There was no way to lose that place. Where else did the land poke above the sky? We know four such places now—islands—but in that age, only one. It was twenty daywalks distant, and it seethed with snarks, leviathan, and a new predator we named *tractor crab*. The witch wagon lay a day's crawl sunsetward of the island. We never forgot.

Now we had nothing but memory and stories and speculation, and the flint daggers we used to carve rock.

We learned to fight with the daggers.

We'd given up on geometry, but we remembered that rigid things could be useful. We could tow rocks. Volcanic pillows are rigid after they cool, and porous: we could shape such stuff into refuges, imitating the hermit crab. We built barricade walls that would tear a leviathan's belly if it swooped to take one of us. We hunted the snarks from inside the barricades.

Our numbers grew. We took our territory back. We won our way to what had become half a memory, a children's tale, a metaphor, a myth. Back to the witch wagon.

The witch wagon waited, moving only when the mud had settled too thickly. Still, she paid a price in twenty generations of corrosion.

She showed us how to mount shards of flint on leviathan whiskers, for better weapons. We were taught how to fight in numbers, as a geometrical array. We did not die as prey any longer. We died battling what preyed on us. But some died in the enemy's teeth, and some died from exhaustion.

Then the witch wagon couldn't move any longer, and her ring of display window darkened and blurred. One day we saw nothing but a dulled silver cylinder.

Our language became sound alone, except that the witch wagon could see the pictures we drew. We grew better at talking, better at learning. In another ten generations we learned enough to change our kind forever. Our barricades were cities. There was not enough pillow lava to make our houses. Anyone could see that our numbers were grown too great; and then one of us saw the answer.

Civilization is partly what the witch wagon taught us. But how can we know what part? Think upon this matter of our numbers. The witch wagon told us that our tiny males who live in a crease behind the chin and are fed by dribblings from our mouths, reminded her of *sperm*, of the male seed of her kind. Another time she told us how sperm could be blocked from a parent. We saw the point: we need only kill all the males until our numbers are as they should be, then let them swarm again. But did Teacher think of that, or did we?

Counting generations used to be difficult, before we learned how to control our numbers.

She taught us things . . . but some things we learned because she taught us how to learn.

The witch wagon told us how to breed the life around us for traits we liked. We thinned the seaweed forests to be less benign to the snarks, while still housing the life that fed us. When leviathans were too rare to threaten us, we began shaping them, too.

The witch wagon told us of worlds beyond our worlds, seen as white points on black, but only from above the sky. She told us of melted-sand lenses that bend light but do not stop it, and how they can make the white points look larger. But she could not tell us how to make lenses out of sand.

But did she tell us to breed the high and low transparent jellyfish, to make our own telescopes and see the stars?

My parent is sure that Teacher was not crazy enough for that. Whatever madness our ancestors thought they'd found in her, her teachings proved out. Teacher never feels madness, divine or mundane. I've come to agree.

The witch wagon's voice grew rusty and stopped, thirty-eight generations before my own birth.

Teacher lived above the silver sky. Again we had to build from what we had learned; and again we knew our destiny, and never forgot.

After the witch wagon's voice stopped, we might perceive the next thirty-eight generations—long generations, because of what we have learned—as only my bottom-crawling kind learning how to reach Teacher.

We bred jellyfish as telescopes. The view grew clearer with each generation. Faith was not needed here. What we saw through them was no illusion: we saw seabirds as well as stars!

We destroyed the snarks that killed leviathans, and bred the leviathans for what we wanted, but that was hard. Leviathans live three generations. We had to invent governments stable over many lifetimes. But we did that.

Ultimately we butchered leviathans for their flotation bladders, filled them with water, and rolled up onto the land. Six generations ago our land rollers came out of the water to see Teacher face-to-face.

Two among those were my ancestors.

The witch wagon had told us of the world above the silver sky. Teacher spent effort analyzing what grew near her, and relayed what she knew to the witch wagon, though the relay failed early on.

We live through air dissolved in water. No walkers can survive on air alone, certainly no swimmer can, but some plants can grow above the sky. Endless generations of us have known how to find that strange place, how to find Teacher; but not how to survive up there. Teacher told us how her kind goes into worlds even less hospitable, into *vacuum*, wearing balloons made in the shape of her kind, that carry what they need. We have done the same. Gradually we get better at it.

Teacher looks like a rounded rock.

"This shape took me through the air without burning up," she said. "Motion is heat, and my voyage involved faster motion than I can easily describe." She would have demonstrated: "Put a pebble in this attitude jet, this hole under my spotlight. One blast, and I'll send it clear across the island!"

But my four-mother had no way to move a pebble. Even so, her balloon was much improved over her two-mother's. Those first air rollers nearly died when the water in their balloons went stale.

The balloons hold what we need: not air, but water. We learned to bubble air through it; there must be air in our water, or we die; but not too much, or we die. We learned to move the balloon by walking along its bottom, using our weight. It works better if we carry rocks.

In three generations we had a permanent base, an inland pond pointed out by Teacher and filled with seawater we carried in bladders. Underwater we built temporary homes, and pressure refuges, too, because rain changes the composition of seawater.

Teacher's voice carries not through thin air but through the rock. We began to learn again.

Teacher is the payload of an interstellar probe. Teacher was once far more powerful: one component of a personality greatly more complex than our own brains. The probe split to perform varied functions, a monotheistic God become a pantheon. There is an orbiter (moving so high and fast that it cannot fall) and a wanderer among the nearby worlds. Teacher is the lander. She was made to talk to whatever she found.

We must still take a good deal of this on faith.

"There are worlds like my world," Teacher told us, "covered three-quarters with water. Life shapes itself in water and eventually wants the land, too. But many worlds have too much water, just as some have too much air and some have too little of both. Your world is nearly all water. There's so little land that few living things want it."

"Why should we?" my three-mother asked.

"You've been building a civilization, but there are things you cannot build in water," Teacher said. "But you can't reach out of it, can you? How can you manipulate anything?"

"How do you?" we asked, and we listened to her answers.

I was born for this, trained for this. I was to be a land roller, whatever that might mean when I became mature. If we breed ourselves for special traits—as we do, but very cautiously—then I was bred not to fear the blinding sun or the dry air. So, I do not.

We were not sure what would work. Whatever we tried, some died. Whatever we tried, we became more capable.

This worked: a leviathan altered by radiation, genetic tampering, then natural selection.

I ride out of the sea where all before me walked. Leviathan hunches itself across the rocks, using stronger, thicker fins than its ancestors had. The skin of its back is thick, horny, armored against the sun. It still carries its bladder, but filled with water now, and the bladder protrudes through the beast's skin below its chin. Three of us ride inside. The view is a bit murky, a bit distorted.

I see our inland base below me. Tear this bladder apart, and we might wriggle to safety through the thin air. We have reached the highest point of the island, and Teacher.

"I could not see how you would reach me," Teacher said. "You have gone beyond me. I can make out your cities even from here, when the waves slacken. Still there are things I can teach. That plant in my spotlight, can you tear it up?" A tiny brilliant green dot blazes in a clump of dry-living plants. Raw daylight changes its color.

My companion manipulates nerve clumps. These land-based plants are tough, but Leviathan rips up a stalk thrice my length.

"It needs to dry," Teacher said. "Pull it to the top of that rock slope. Fetch seven or eight more. We'll see if the stuff is dry tomorrow. Then, can you recognize flint when it dries?"

The tiny green dot probes out. "That's flint. Pick up two chunks. Bigger." Twice the size of my head, these. I rap them against each other.

Teacher says, "You're not making knives now. Now we wait a day and hope it doesn't rain."

All the long generations have come to this. I asked, "What then?"

"Then I will teach you fire."

PROCRUSTES

I found Beowulf Shaeffer single and broke. His first story, "Neutron Star," got me my first Hugo Award. "The Borderland of Sol" got me my last. As I aged, he aged, until we find him settled and married, with children, though not yet his own.

Asleep, my mind plays it all back in fragments and dreams. From time to time a block of nerves wakes: *That's some kind of ARM weapon! Move it, move it, too late, BLAM. My head rolls loose on black sand. Bones shattered, ribs and spine. Fear worse than the agony. Agony fading* and I'm gone.

Legs try to kick. Nothing moves. Again, harder, *move! No go. The 'doc floats nicely on the lift plate, but its mass is resisting me. Push! Voice behind me, I turn, she's holding some kind of tube. BLAM. My head bounces on sand. Agony flaring, sensation fading. Try to hang on, stay lucid . . . but everything turns mellow.*

My balance swings wildly around my inner ear. *Where's the planet's axis? Fafnir doesn't have polar caps. The ancient lander is flying itself. Carlos looks worried, but Feather's having the time of her life.*

Sprawled across the planet's face, a hurricane flattened along one edge. Under the vast cloud-fingerprint a ruddy snake divides the blue of a world-girdling ocean. A long, narrow continent runs almost pole to pole.

The lander reenters over featureless ocean. Nothing down there seems to be looking at us. I'm taking us down fast. Larger islands have low, flat buildings on them. Pick a little one. Hover while flame digs the lamplighter pit wider and deeper, until the lander sinks into the hole with inches to spare. Plan A is right on track.

I remember how Plan A ended. The Surgeon program senses my distress and turns me off.

I'm in Carlos Wu's 'doc, in the Intensive Care Cavity. The Surgeon program prods my brain, running me through my memories, maintaining the patterns, lest they fuzz out to nothing while my brain and body heal.

I must be terribly damaged.

Waking was sudden. My eyes popped open and I was on my back, my nose two inches from glass. Sunlight glared through scattered clouds. Display lights glowed above my eyebrows. I felt fine, charged with energy.

Ye gods, how long had I slept? All those dreams . . . dream-memories.

I tried to move. I was shrink-wrapped in elastic. I wiggled my arm up across my chest, with considerable effort, and up to the displays. It took me a few seconds to figure them out.

Biomass tank: near empty. *Treatment:* pages of data, horrifying . . . terminated, successful. *Date:* Omygod. Four months! I was out for four months and eleven days! *Open*:

The dark glass lid retracted, sunlight flared, and I shut my eyes tight. After a while I pulled myself over the rim of the Intensive Care Cavity and rolled out.

My balance was all wrong. I landed like a lumpy sack, on sand, and managed not to yell or swear. Who might hear? Sat up, squinting painfully, and looked around.

I was still on the island.

It was weathered coral, nearly symmetrical, with a central peak. The air was sparkling clear, and the ocean went on forever, with another pair of tiny islands just touching the horizon.

I was stark naked and white as a bone, in the glare of a yellow-white dwarf sun. The air was salty and thick with organic life, sea life.

Where was everybody?

I tried to stand; wobbled; gave it up and crawled around into the shadow of the 'doc. I still felt an amazing sense of well-being, as if I could solve anything the universe could throw at me.

During moments of half wakefulness I'd somehow worked out where I must be. Here it stood, half coffin and half chemical lab, massive and abandoned on the narrow black sand beach. A vulnerable place to leave such a valuable thing; but this was where I'd last seen it, ready to be loaded into the boat.

Sunlight could damage me in minutes, kill me in hours; but Carlos Wu's wonderful 'doc was no ordinary Mall autodoctor. It' was state-of-the-art, smarter than me in some respects. It would cure anything the sun could do to me.

I pulled myself to my feet and took a few steps. Ouch! The coral cut my feet. The 'doc could cure that, too, but it hurt.

Standing, I could see most of the island. The center bulged up like a volcano. Fafnir coral builds a flat island with a shallow cone rising at the center, a housing for a symbiote, the lamplighter. I'd hovered the lander above the cone while belly jets scorched out the lamplighter nest, until it was big enough to hold the lander.

Just me and the 'doc and a dead island. I'd have to live in the 'doc. Come out at night, like a vampire. My chance of being found must be poor if no passing boat had found me in these past four-plus months.

I climbed. The coral cut my hands and feet, and knees. From the cone I'd be able to see the whole island.

The pit was two hundred feet across. The bottom was black and smooth, and seven or eight feet below me. Feather had set the lander to melt itself down, slowly, radiating not much heat over many hours. Several inches of rainwater now covered the slag, and something sprawled in the muck.

It might be a man . . . a tall man, possibly raised in low gravity. Too tall to be Carlos. Or Sharrol, or Feather, and who was left?

I jumped down. Landed clumsily on the smooth slag and splashed full length in the water. Picked myself up, unhurt. My toes could feel an oblong texture, lines and ridges, the shapes within the lander that wouldn't melt. Police could determine what this thing had been, if they ever looked; but why would they look?

The water felt good on my ruined feet. And on my skin. I was already burned. Albinos can't take yellow dwarf sunlight.

A corpse was no surprise, given what I remembered. I looked it over. It had been wearing local clothing for a man: boots, loose pants with a rope tie, a jacket encrusted with pockets. The jacket was pierced with a great ragged hole front and back. That could only have been made by Feather's horrible ARM weapon. This close, the head . . . I'd thought it must be under the water, but there was no head at all. There were clean white bones, and a neck vertebra cut smoothly in half.

I was hyperventilating. Dizzy. I sat down next to the skeleton so that I wouldn't fall.

These long bones looked more than four months dead. Years, decades . . . wait, now. We'd scorched the nest, but there would be lamplighter soldiers left outside. Those would have swarmed down and stripped the bones.

I found I was trying to push my back through a wall of fused coral. My empty stomach heaved. This was much worse than anything I'd imagined. I knew who this was.

Sunlight burned my back. My eyes were going wonky in the glare. Time was not on my side: I was going to be much sicker much quicker than I liked.

I made myself pull the boots loose, shook the bones out and put them on. They were too big.

The jacket was a sailor's survival jacket, local style. The shoulders looked padded: shoulder floats. The front and sides had been all pockets, well stuffed; but front and back had been torn to confetti.

I stripped it off him and began searching pockets.

No wallet, no ID. Tissue pack. The shrapnel remains of a hand computer. Several pockets were sealed: emergency gear, stuff you wouldn't want to open by accident; some of those had survived.

A knife of exquisite sharpness in a built-in holster. Pocket torch. A ration brick. I bit into the brick and chewed while I searched. Mag specs, one lens shattered, but I put them on anyway. Without dark glasses my pink albino eyes would go blind.

Sunblock spray, unharmed: good. A pill dispenser, broken, but in a pocket still airtight. Better! Tannin secretion pills!

The boots were shrinking, adapting to my feet. It felt friendly, reassuring. My most intimate friends on this island.

I was still dizzy. Better let the 'doc take care of me now; take the pills afterward. I shook broken ribs out of the jacket. Shook the pants empty. Balled the clothing and tossed it out of the hole. Tried to follow it.

My fingers wouldn't reach the rim.

"After all this, what a stupid way to die," I said to the memory of Sharrol Janz. "What do I do now? Build a ladder out of bones?" If I got out of this hole, I'd think it through before I ever did *anything*.

I knelt; I yelled and jumped. My fingers, palms, forearms gripped rough coral. I pulled myself out and lay panting, sweating, bleeding, crying.

I limped back to the 'doc, wearing boots now, holding the suit spread above me for a parasol. I was feverish with sunburn.

I couldn't take boots into the ICC. *Wait. Think. Wind? Waves?* I tied the clothes in a bundle around the boots and set it on the 'doc next to the faceplate. I climbed into the Intensive Care Cavity and pulled the lid down.

Sharrol would wait an hour longer, if she was still alive. And the kids. And Carlos.

I did not expect to fall asleep.

Asleep, feverish with sunburn. The Surgeon program tickles blocks of nerves, plays me like a complex toy. In my sleep I feel raging thirst, hear a thunderclap, taste cinnamon or coffee, clench a phantom fist.

My skin wakes. Piloerection runs in ripples along my

body, then a universal tickle, then pressure . . . like that feather-crested snakeskin Sharrol put me into for Carlos's party. . . .

Sharrol, sliding into her own rainbow-scaled bodysuit, stopped halfway. "You don't really want to do this, do you?"

"I'll tough it out. How do I look?" I'd never developed the least sense of flatlander style. Sharrol picked my clothes.

"Half man, half snake," she said. "Me?"

"Like this snake's fitting mate." She didn't really. No flatlander is as supple as a crashlander. Raised in Earth's gravity, Sharrol was a foot shorter than I, and weighed the same as I did. Stocky.

The apartment was already in child mode: rounded surfaces everywhere, and all storage was locked or raised to eyeball height (mine.) Tanya was five and Louis was four and both were agile as monkeys. I scanned for anything that might be dangerous within their reach.

Louis stared at us, solemn, awed. Tanya giggled. We must have looked odder than usual, though given flatlander styles, it's a wonder that any kid can recognize his parents. Why do they change their hair and skin color so often? When we hugged them good-bye Tanya made a game of tugging my hair out of shape and watching it flow back into a feathery crest. We set them down and turned on the Playmate program.

The lobby transfer booth jumped us three time zones east. We stepped out into a vestibule, facing an arc of picture window. A flock of rainbow-hued fish panicked at the awful sight and flicked away. A huge fish passed in some internal dream.

For an instant I felt the weight of all those tons of water. I looked to see how Sharrol was taking it. She was smiling, admiring.

"Carlos lives near the Great Barrier Reef, you said. You didn't say he lived *in* it."

"It's a great privilege," Sharrol told me. "I spent my first thirty years underwater, but not on the Reef. The Reef's too fragile. The UN protects it."

"You never told me that!"

She grinned at my surprise. "My dad had a lobster ranch near Boston. Later I worked for the Epcot-Atlantis police. The ecology isn't so fragile there, but—Bey, I should take you there."

I said, "Maybe it's why we think alike. I grew up underground. You can't build above ground on We Made It."

"You told me. The winds."

"Sharrol, this isn't *like* Carlos."

She'd known Carlos Wu years longer than I had. "Carlos gets an idea, and he follows it as far as it'll go. I don't know what he's onto now. Maybe he's always wanted to share me with you. And he brought a date for, um—"

"Ever met her?"

"—Balance. No, Carlos won't even talk about Feather Filip. He just smiles mysteriously. Maybe it's love."

The children! Protect the children! Where are the children? The Surgeon must be tickling my adrenal glands. I'm not awake, but I'm frantic, and a bit randy, too. Then the sensations ease off. *The Playmate program. It guards them and teaches them and plays with them. They'll be fine. Can't take them to Carlos's place . . . not tonight.*

Sharrol was their mother and Carlos Wu had been their father. Earth's Fertility Board won't let an albino have children. Carlos's gene pattern they judge perfect; he's one of 120 flatlanders who carry an unlimited birthright.

A man can love any child. That's hardwired into the brain. A man can raise another man's children. And accept their father as a friend . . . but there's a barrier. That's wired in too.

Sharrol knows. She's afraid I'll turn prickly and uncivilized. And *Carlos* knows. So why . . . ?

Tonight was billed as a foursome, sex and *tapas*. That was a developing custom: dinner strung out as a sequence of small dishes between bouts of recreational sex. Something inherited from the ancient Greeks or Italians, maybe. There's something lovers gain from feeding each other.

Feather—

The memory blurs. I wasn't afraid of her then, but I am now. When I remember Feather, the Surgeon puts me to sleep.

But the children! I've got to remember. We were down. Sharrol was out of the 'doc, but we left Louis and Tanya frozen. We floated their box into the boat. Feather and I disengaged the lift plate and slid it under the 'doc. Beneath that lumpy jacket she moved like a tigress. She spoke my name; I turned . . .

Feather.

Carlos's sleepfield enclosed most of the bedroom. He'd hosted bigger parties than this in here. Tonight we were down to four, and a floating chaos of dishes Carlos said were Mexican.

"She's an ARM," Carlos said.

Feather Filip and I were sharing a tamale too spicy for Sharrol. Feather caught me staring and grinned back. An ARM?

I'd expected Feather to be striking. She wasn't exactly beautiful. She was strong: lean, almost gaunt, with prominent tendons in her neck, lumps flexing at the corners of her jaws. You don't get strength like that without training in illegal martial arts.

The Amalgamated Regional Militia is the United Nations police, and the United Nations took a powerful interest in Carlos Wu. What was she, Carlos's bodyguard? Was that how they'd met?

But whenever one of us spoke of the ARM that afternoon, Feather changed the subject.

I'd have thought Carlos would orchestrate our sleepfield dance. Certified genius that he is, would he not be superb at that, too? But Feather had her own ideas, and Carlos let her lead. Her lovemaking was aggressive and acrobatic. I felt her strength, that afternoon. And my own lack, raised as I was in the lower gravity of We Made It.

And three hours passed in that fashion, while the wonderful colors of the reef darkened to light-amplified night.

And then Feather reached far out of the field, limber as a snake . . . reached inside her backpurse, and fiddled, and frowned, and rolled back, and said, "We're shielded."

Carlos said, "They'll know."

"They know *me*," Feather said. "They're thinking that I let them use their monitors because I'm showing off, but now we're going to try something a little kinky; or maybe I'm just putting them on. I've done it before—"

"Then—"

"—Find a glitch so I can block their gear with something new. Then they fix it. They'll fix this one too, but not tonight. It's just Feather coming down after a long week."

Carlos accepted that. "Stet. Sharrol, Beowulf, do you want to leave Earth? We'd be traveling as a group, Louis and Tanya and the four of us. This is for keeps."

Sharrol said, "I can't." Carlos *knew* that.

He said, "You can ride in cold sleep. Home's rotation period is six minutes shorter than Earth's. Mass the same, air about the same. Tectonic activity is higher, so it'll smell like there's just a trace of smog—"

"Carlos, we talked this to death a few years ago." Sharrol was annoyed. "Sure, I could live on Home. I don't like the notion of flying from world to world like a, a corpse, but I'd do it. But the UN doesn't want me emigrating, and Home won't take flat phobes!"

The flatlander phobia is a bone-deep dread of being cut off from the Earth. Fear of flying and/or falling is an extreme case, but no flat phobe can travel in space. You find few flat phobes off Earth; in fact, Earthborn are called flatlanders no matter how well they adjust to life elsewhere.

But Feather was grinning at Sharrol. "We go by way of Fafnir. We'll get to Home as Shashters. Home has already approved us for immigration—"

"Under the name *Graynor*. We're all married," Carlos amplified.

I said, "Carlos, you've *been* off Earth. You were on Jinx for a year."

"Yah. Bey, Sigmund Ausfaller and his gnomes never lost track of me. The United Nations thinks they own my genes. I'm supervised wherever I go."

But they keep you in luxury, I thought. And the grass is always greener. Feather had her own complaint. "What do you know about the ARM?" she asked us.

"We listen to the vid," Sharrol said.

"Sharrol, dear, we *vet* that stuff. The ARM decides what you don't get to know about us. Most of us take psychoactive chemicals to keep us in a properly paranoid mindframe during working hours. We stay that way four days, then go sane for the weekend. If it's making us too crazy, they retire us."

Feather was nervous and trying to restrain it, but now hard-edged muscles flexed, and her elbows and knees were pulling in protectively against her torso. "But some of us are born this way. We go *off* chemicals when we go to work. The 'doc doses us back to sanity Thursday afternoon. I've been an ARM schiz for thirty-five years. They're ready to retire me, but they'd never let me go to some other world, knowing what I know. And they don't want a schiz making babies."

I didn't say that I could see their point. I looked at Sharrol and saw hope in the set of her mouth, ready to smile but holding off. We were being brought into these plans *way* late. Rising hackles had pulled me right out of any postcoital glow.

Feather told me, "They'll never let you go either, Beowulf."

And *that* was nonsense. "Feather, I've been off Earth three times since I got here."

"Don't try for four. You know too much. You know about the Core explosion, and diplomatic matters involving alien races—"

"I've left Earth since—"

"—and Julian Forward's work." She gave it a dramatic pause. "We'll have some advanced weaponry out of that. We would not want the kzinti to know about that, or the trinocs, or certain human domains. That last trip, do you know how much *talking* you did while you were on Gummidgy and Jinx? You're a friendly, talkative guy with great stories, Beowulf!"

I shrugged. "So why trust me with this? Why didn't you and Carlos just go?"

She gestured at Carlos. He grinned and said, "I insisted."

"And we need a pilot," Feather said. "That's you, Beowulf. But I can bust us loose. I've set up something nobody but an ARM would ever dream of."

She told us about it.

To the kzinti the world was only a number. Kzinti don't like ocean sports. The continent was Shasht, "Burrowing Murder." Shasht was nearly lifeless, but the air was breathable and the mines were valuable. The kzinti had dredged up megatons of seabottom to fertilize a hunting jungle, and they got as far as seeding and planting before the Fourth Man-Kzin War.

After the war humankind took Shasht as reparations, and named the world Fafnir.

On Fafnir Feather's investigations found a family of six: two men, two women, two children. The Graynors were ready to emigrate. Local law would cause them to leave most of their wealth behind; but then, they'd lost most of it already, backing some kind of recreational facilities on the continent.

"I've recorded them twice. The Graynors'll find funding waiting for them at Wunderland. They won't talk. The *other* Graynor family will emigrate to Home—"

"That's us?"

Feather nodded. Carlos said, "But if you and the kids won't come, Feather'll have to find someone else."

I said, "Carlos, *you'll* be watched. I don't suppose Feather can protect you from that."

"No. Feather's taken a much bigger risk—"

"They'll never miss it." She turned to me. "I got hold of a little stealth lander, Fourth War vintage, with a cold sleep

box in back for you, Sharrol. We'll take that down to Fafnir.
I've got an inflatable boat to take us to the Shasht North
spaceport, and we'll get to Home on an Outbound Enter-
prises iceliner. Sharrol, you'll board the liner already frozen;
I know how to bypass that stage." Feather was excited now.
She gripped my arm and said, "We have to go get the lander,
Beowulf. It's on Mars."

Sharrol said, "Tanya's a flat phobe, too."

Feather's fingers closed with bruising force. I sensed that
the lady didn't like seeing her plans altered.

"Wait one," Carlos said. "We can fix that. We're taking
my 'doc, aren't we? It wouldn't be *plausible*, let alone intelligent, for Carlos Wu to go on vacation without his 'doc.
Feather, how big is the lander's freezebox?"

"Yeah. Right. It'll hold Tanya . . . better yet, both children. Sharrol can ride in your 'doc."

We talked it around. When we were satisfied, we went
home.

Three days out, three days returning, and a week on Mars
while the ARM team played with *Boy George*. It had to be us.
I'd familiarize myself with *Boy George*, Feather would super-
vise the ARM crews . . . and neither of us were flat phobes.

I brought a dime disk, a tourist's guide of Fafnir system,
and I studied it.

Kzinti and human planetologists call Fafnir a typical water
world in a system older than Sol. The system didn't actually
retain much more water than Earth did; that isn't the problem. But the core is low in radioactives. The lithosphere is
thick: no continental drift here. Shallow oceans cover 93
percent of the planet. The oceans seethe with life, five billion years evolved, twice as old as Earth's.

And, where the thick crust cracked in early days, magma
oozed through to build the world's single continent. Today a
wandering line of volcanoes and bare rock stretches from

the south pole nearly to the north. The continent's mass has been growing for billions of years.

On the opposite face of a lopsided planet, the ocean has grown shallow. Fafnir's life presently discovered the advantages of coral building. That side of the world is covered with tens of thousands of coral islands. Some stand up to twenty meters tall: relics of a deeper ocean.

The mines are all on Shasht. So also are all the industry, both spaceports, and the seat of government. But the life—recreation, housing, families are all on the islands.

Finding the old lander had indeed been a stroke of luck. It was an identical backup for the craft that set Sinbad Jabar down on Meerowsk in the Fourth War, where he invaded the harem of the Patriarch's Voice. The disgrace caused the balance of power among the local kzinti to become unstable. The human alliance took Meerowsk and renamed the planet, and it was Jabar's Prize until a later, pacifistic generation took power. Jabar's skin is displayed there still.

Somehow Feather had convinced the ARMs that (1) this twin of Jabar's lander was wanted for the Smithsonian Luna, and (2) the Belt peoples would raise hell if they knew it was to be removed from Mars. The project must be absolutely secret.

Ultimately the ARM crews grew tired of Feather's supervision, or else her company. Rapidly after that, Feather grew tired of watching me read. "We'll only *be* on Fafnir two days, Beowulf. What are you learning? It's a dull, dull, dull place. All the land life is Earth imports—"

"Their lifestyle is strange, Feather. They travel by transfer booths and dirigible balloons and boats, and almost nothing in between. A very laid-back society. Nobody's expected to be anywhere on time—"

"Nobody's watching us here. You don't have to play tourist."

"I know." If the ARM had *Boy George* bugged . . . but Feather would have thought of *that*.

Our ship was in the hands of ARM engineers, and that made for tension. But we were getting on each other's nerves. Not a good sign, with a three-week flight facing us.

Feather said, "You're not playing. You *are* a tourist!"

I admitted it. "And the first law of tourism is, *read everything*." But I switched the screen off, and said, in the spirit of compromise, "All right. Show me. What is there to see on Mars?"

She hated to admit it. "Nothing."

We left Mars with the little stealth lander in the fuel tank. The ARM was doing things the ARM didn't know about. And I continued reading. . . .

Fafnir's twenty-two-hour day has encouraged an active life. Couch potatoes court insomnia: it's easier to sleep if you're tired. But *hurrying* is something else. There are transfer booths, of course. You can jump instantly from a home on some coral extrusion to the bare rock of Shasht . . . and buy yourself an eleven-hour time lag.

Nobody's in a hurry to go home. They go by dirigible. Ultimately the floatliner companies wised up and began selling round-trip tickets for the same price as one-way.

"I do *know* all this, Beowulf."

"Mph? Oh, good."

"So what's the plan?" Feather asked. "Find an island with nothing near it and put down, right? Get out and dance around on the sand while we blow the boat up and load it and go. How do we hide the lander?"

"Sink it."

"Read about lamplighters," she said, so I did.

After the war and the settlement, UN Advance Forces landed on Shasht, took over the kzinti structures, then began to explore. Halfway around the planet were myriads of little round coral islands, each with a little peak at the center. At night the peaks glowed with a steady yellow light. Larger islands were chains of peaks, each with its yellow glow in the cup. Lamplighters were named before anyone knew what they were.

Close-up . . . well, they've been called piranha ant nests. The bioluminescence attracts scores of varieties of flying fish. Or, lured or just lost, a swimming thing may beach itself; then the lamplighter horde flows down to the beach and cleans it to the bones.

You can't build a home, or beach a boat, until the nest has been burned out. *Then* you have to wait another twelve days for the soldiers caught outside the nest to die. *Then* cover the nest. Use it for a basement, put your house on it. Otherwise, the sea may carry a queen to you, to use the nest again.

"You're ahead of me on this," I admitted. "What has this lander got for belly rockets?"

"Your basic hydrogen and oxygen," Feather said. "High heat and a water vapor exhaust. We'll burn the nest out."

"Good."

Yo! Boy, when Carlos's 'doc is finished with you, you know it!

Open.

The sky was a brilliant sprawl of stars, some of them moving—spacecraft, weather eyes, the wheel—and a single lopsided moon. The island was shadow-teeth cutting into the starscape. I slid out carefully, into a blackness like the inside of my empty belly, and yelled as I dropped into seawater.

The water was hip deep, with no current to speak of. I wasn't going to drown, or be washed away, or lost. Fafnir's moon was a little one, close in. Tides would be shallow.

Still I'd been lucky: I could have wakened underwater.

How did people feel about nudity here? But my bundle of clothes hadn't washed away. Now the boots clasped my feet like old friends. Until I rolled them up, the sleeves of the dead man's survival jacket trailed way past my hands, and, of course, the front and back were in shreds. The pants were better: too big, but with elastic ankle bands that I just pulled up to my knees. I swallowed a tannin secretion dose. I couldn't do that earlier. The 'doc would have read the albino gene in my DNA and "cured" me of an imposed tendency to tan.

There was nothing on all of Fafnir like Carlos's 'doc. I'd have to hide it before I could ever think about rescue.

"Our medical equipment," Carlos had called it; and Feather had answered, "Hardly ours."

Carlos was patient. "It's all we've got, Feather. Let me show you how to use it. First, the diagnostics—"

The thing was as massive as the inflatable boat that would carry us to Shasht. Carlos had a gravity lift to shove under it. The Intensive Care Cavity was tailored just for Carlos Wu, naturally, but any of us could be served by the tethers and sleeves and hypo-tipped tubes and readouts along one whole face of the thing: the service wall.

"—These hookups do your diagnostics and set the chemical feeds going. Feather, it'll rebalance body chemistry, in case I ever go schiz or someone poisons me or something. I've reprogrammed it to take care of you, too." I don't think Carlos noticed the way Feather looked at it, and him.

"Now the cavity. It's for the most serious injuries, but I've reprogrammed it for you, Sharrol my dear—"

"But it's exactly Carlos's size," Feather told us pointedly. "The UN thinks a lot of Carlos. *We* can't use it."

Sharrol said, "It looks small. I don't mean the ICC. I can get into that. But there's not much room for transplants in that storage space."

"Oh, no. This is advanced stuff. I had a hand in the design. One day we'll be able to use these techniques with everyone." Carlos patted the monster. "There's nothing in here in the way of cloned organs and such. There's the Surgeon program, and a reservoir of organic soup, and a googol of self-replicating machines a few hundred atoms long. If I lost a leg or an eye, they'd turn me off and rebuild it onto me. There's even . . . here, pay attention. You feed the organics reservoir through here, so the machine doesn't run out of material. You could even feed it Fafnir fish if you can catch them, but they're metal-deficient. . . ."

When he had us thoroughly familiar with the beast, he helped Sharrol into the cavity, waited to be sure she was hooked up, and closed it. That made me nervous as hell. She climbed out a day later claiming that she hadn't felt a thing, wasn't hungry, didn't even have to use the bathroom.

The 'doc was massive. I had to really heave against it to get it moving, then it wanted to move along the shore. I forced it to turn inland. The proper place to hide it was in the lamplighter nest, of course.

I was gasping like death itself, and the daylight had almost died, and I just couldn't push that mass uphill.

I left it on the beach. Maybe there was an answer. Let my hindbrain toy with it for a while.

I trudged across sand to rough coral and kept walking to the peak. We'd picked the island partly for its isolation. Two distant yellow lights, eastward, marked two islands I'd noted earlier. I ran my mag specs (the side that worked) up to 20X, scanned the whole horizon, and found nothing but the twin lamplighter glows.

And nothing to do but wait.

I sat with my back against the lip of the dead lamplighter pit. I pictured her: she looked serious, a touch worried, under a feather crest and undyed skin: pink shading to brown, an Anglo tanned as if by Fafnir's yellow-white sun.

I said, "Sharrol."

Like the dead she had slept, her face slack beneath the faceplate, like Sleeping Beauty. I'd taken to talking to her, wondering if some part of her heard. I'd never had the chance to ask.

"I never wondered why you loved me. Egotist, I am. But, you must have looked like me when you were younger. Thirty years underwater, no sunlight. Your uncles, your father, they must have looked a *lot* like me. Maybe even with white hair. How old *are* you? I never asked."

Her memory looked at me.

"Tanj that. *Where* are you? Where are Tanya and Louis? Where's Carlos? What happened after I was shot?"

Faint smile, shrug of eyebrows.

"You spent three weeks unconscious in the ICC followed by ten minutes on your feet. Wrong gravity, wrong air mix, wrong smells. We hit you with everything it might take to knock a flat phobe spinning. Then BLAM and your love interest is lying on the sand with a hole through him.

"Maybe you tried to kill her. I don't think you'd give her much trouble, but maybe Feather would kill you anyway. She'd still have the kids. . . ."

I slammed my fist on coral. "What did she *want*? That crazy woman. I never hurt her at all."

Talking to Sharrol: Lifeless as she was, maybe it wasn't quite as *crazy* as talking to myself. I couldn't talk to the others. They—"You remember that night we planned it all? Feather was lucid then. Comparatively. We were there for her as *people*. On the trip to Mars she was a lot wilder. She was a hell of an *active* lover, but I never really got the feeling that I was *there* for her."

We never talked about each other's lovers. In truth, it was easier to say these things to Sharrol when she wasn't here.

"But most of the way to Fafnir, Feather was fine. But she wasn't sleeping with me. Just Carlos. She could hold a conversation, no problem there, but I was *randy*, love, and frustrated. She liked that. I caught a *look* when Carlos wasn't looking. So I didn't want to talk to her. And she was always up against Carlos, and Carlos, he was a bit embarrassed about it all. We talked about plans, but for anything personal there was just you. Sleeping Beauty."

The night was warm and clear. By convention, boats would show any color except lamplighter yellow. I couldn't miss seeing a boat's lights.

"Then, fifteen hours out from the drop point, that night I found her floating in my sleeping plates. I suppose I could have sent her to her own room, I mean it was within the laws of physics, but I didn't. I acted like conversation was the last thing I'd be interested in. But so did Feather.

"And the next morning it was all business, and a frantic business it was. We came in in devious fashion, and got off behind the moon. *Boy George* went on alone, decelerating. Passed too close to an ARM base on Claim 226 that even Feather wasn't supposed to know about. Turned around and accelerated away in clear and obvious terror, heading off in the general direction of Hrooshpith—pithtcha—of another of those used-to-be-kzinti systems where they've never got the population records straightened out. No doubt the ARM is waiting for us there.

"And of course you missed the ride down . . . but my point is that nothing ever got *said*.

"Okay. This whole scheme was schemed by Feather, carried through by Feather. It—" I stared into the black night. "Oh." I really should have seen this earlier. Why did Feather need Carlos?

Through the ARM spy net Feather Filip had found a family of six Shashters ready to emigrate. Why not look for one or two? Where Carlos insisted on taking his children and Sharrol and me, another man might be more reasonable.

"She doesn't just want to be clear of Sol system. Doesn't just want to make babies. She wants *Carlos*. Carlos of the perfect genes. Hah! Carlos finally saw it. Maybe she told him. He must have let her know he didn't want children by an ARM schiz. Angry and randy, she took it out on me, and then . . ."

Then?

With my eyes open to the dark, entranced, I remembered that final night. *Yellow lights sprinkled on a black ocean. Some are the wrong color, too bright, too blue. Avoid those. They're houses. Pick one far from the rest. Hover. Organic matter burns lamplighter yellow below the drive flame, then fades. I sink us in, an egg in an egg cup. Feather blasts the roof loose, and we crawl out—*

We hadn't wanted to use artificial lights. When dawn gave us enough light, we inflated the boat. Feather and Carlos used the gravity lift to settle the freeze-box in the boat. They were arguing in whispers. I didn't want to hear that, I thought.

I turned off the doc's "Maintenance" sequence. A minute later Sharrol sat up, a flat phobe wakened suddenly on an alien world. Sniffed the air. Kissed me and let me lift her out, heavy in Fafnir's gravity. I set her on the sand. Her nerve seemed to be holding. Feather had procured local clothing; I pushed the bundle into her arms.

Feather came toward me, towing the gravity lift. She looked shapeless, with bulging pockets fore and aft. We slid the lift into place, and I pushed the 'doc toward Carlos and the boat. Feather called my name. I turned. BLAM. Agony and scrambled senses, but I saw Carlos leap for the boat, reflexes like a jackrabbit. My head hit the black sand.

Then?

"She wanted hostages. Our children, but *Carlos's* children. They're frozen, they won't give her any trouble. But me, why would she need me? Killing me lets Carlos know she means it. Maybe I told too many stories: maybe she thinks I'm dangerous. Maybe—"

For an instant I saw just *how* superfluous I was, from Feather Filip's psychotic viewpoint. Feather wanted Carlos. Carlos wanted the children. Sharrol came with the children. Beowulf Shaeffer was along because he was with Sharrol. If Feather shot Beowulf, how much would Carlos mind? BLAM.

Presently I said, "She shot me to prove she would. But it looked to me like Carlos just ran. There weren't any weapons in the boat, we'd only just inflated it. All he could do was start it and go. That takes—" When I thought about it, it was actually a good move. He'd gotten away with himself and Tanya and Louis, with both hostages. Protect them now, negotiate later.

And he'd left Feather in a killing rage, with that horrible tube and one living target. I stopped talking to Sharrol then, because it seemed to me she must be dead.

No! "Feather had you. She *had* to have *you.*" It could happen. It could. "What else can she threaten Carlos with? She has to keep you alive." I tried to believe it. "She certainly didn't kill you in the first minute. Somebody had to put me in the 'doc. Feather had no interest in doing that."

But she had no interest in letting Sharrol do that either. "Tanj dammit! Why did Feather let you put me in the 'doc? She even let you . . ." What about the biomass reserve?

My damaged body must have needed some major restructuring. The biomass reserve had been feeding Sharrol, and doing incidental repairs on us all, for the entire three-week trip. Healing me would take another . . . fifty kilograms? More? "She must have let you fill the biomass reserve with . . ." Fish?

Feather showing Carlos how reasonable she could be . . . too reasonable. It felt wrong, wrong. "The other body, the headless one. Why not just push *that* in the hopper? So much easier. Unless—"

Unless material was even closer to hand.

I felt no sudden inspiration. It was a matter of making myself believe. I tried to remember Sharrol . . . pulling her clothes on quickly, shivering and dancing on the sand, in the chilly dawn breeze. Hands brushing back through her hair, hair half grown out. A tiny grimace for the way the survival jacket made her look, bulges everywhere. Patting pockets, opening some of them.

The 'doc had snapped her out of a three-week sleep. Like me: awake, alert, ready.

It didn't go away, the answer. It just . . . I still didn't know where Sharrol was, or Carlos, or the children. What if I was wrong? Feather had mapped my route to Home, every step of the way. I knew exactly where Feather was now, if a line of logic could point my way. But—one wrong assumption, and Feather Filip could pop up behind my ear.

I could make myself safer, and Sharrol, too, if I mapped out a worst-case scenario.

Feather's Plan B: Kill Shaeffer. Take the rest prisoner, to impose her will on Carlos . . . but Carlos flees with the boat. So, Plan B-1: Feather holds Sharrol at gunpoint. (Alive.) Some days later she waves down a boat. BLAM, and a stolen boat sails toward Shasht. Or stops to stow Sharrol somewhere, maybe on another coral island, maybe imprisoned inside a plastic tent with a live lamplighter horde prowling outside.

And Carlos? He's had four months, now, to find Sharrol and

Feather. He's a genius, ask anyone. And Feather wants to get in touch . . . unless she's given up on Carlos, decided to kill him.

If I could trace Carlos's path, I would find Louis and Tanya and even Sharrol.

Carlos Plan B-1 follows Plan A as originally conceived by Feather. The kids would be stowed aboard the iceliner as if already registered. Carlos would register and be frozen. Feather could follow him to Home . . . maybe on the same ship, if she hustled. But—

No way could Feather get herself frozen with a gun in her hand. That would be the moment to take her, coming out of freeze on Home.

There, I had a target. On Shasht they could tell me who had boarded the *Zombie Queen* for Home. What did I have to do to get to Shasht?

"Feed myself, that's easy. Collect rainwater, too. Get off the island. . . ." That, at least, was not a puzzle. I couldn't build a raft. I couldn't swim to another island. But a sailor lost at sea will die if cast ashore; therefore, local tradition decrees that he *must* be rescued.

"Collect some money. Get to Shasht. Hide myself." Whatever else was lost to me, to *us*—whoever had died, whoever still lived—there was still the mission, and that was to be free of the United Nations and Earth.

And Carlos Wu's 'doc would finger me instantly. It was advanced nanotechnology: it screamed its Earthly origin. It might be the most valuable item on Fafnir, and I had no wealth at all, and I was going to have to abandon it.

Come daylight, I moved the 'doc. I still wanted to hide it in the lamplighter nest. The gravity lift would lift it but not push it uphill. But I solved it.

One of the secrets of life: know when and what to give up.

I waited for low tide, then pushed it out to sea and turned off the lift. The water came almost to the faceplate. Seven hours later it didn't show at all. And the next emergency might kill me unless it happened at low tide.

The nights were as warm as the days. As the tourist material had promised, it rained just before dawn. I set up my pants to funnel rainwater into a hole I chopped in the coral.

The tour guide had told me how to feed myself. It isn't that rare for a lamplighter nest to die. Sooner or later an unlit island will be discovered by any of several species of swimming things. Some ride the waves at night and spawn in the sand.

I spent the second night running through the shallows and scooping sunbunnies up in my jacket. Bigger flying fish came gliding off the crests of the breakers. They wanted the sunbunnies. Three or four wanted me, but I was able to dodge. One I had to gut in midair.

The tour guide hadn't told me how to clean sunbunnies. I had to fake that. I poached them in seawater, using my pocket torch on high; and I ate until I was bloated. I fed more of them into the biomass reservoir.

With some distaste, I fed those long human bones in, too. Fafnir fish meat was deficient in metals. Ultimately that might kill me; but the 'doc could compensate for a time.

There was nothing to build a boat with. The burned-out lamplighter nest didn't show by daylight, so any passing boat would be afraid to rescue me. I thought of swimming; I thought of riding away on the gravity lift, wherever the wind might carry me. But I couldn't feed myself at sea, and how could I approach another island?

On the fourth evening a great winged shape passed over the island, then dived into the sea. Later I heard a slapping sound as that flyer and a companion kicked themselves free of the water, soared, passed over the crater, and settled into it. They made a great deal of noise. Presently the big one glided down to the water and was gone.

At dawn I fed myself again, on the clutch of eggs that had been laid in the body of the smaller flyer: male or female, whichever. The dime disk hadn't told me about *this* creature. A pity I wouldn't have the chance to write it up.

At just past sunset on the eighth night I saw a light flicker blue-green-red.

My mag specs showed a boat that wasn't moving.

I fired a flare straight up, and watched it burn blue-white for twenty minutes. I fired another at midnight. Then I stuffed my boots partway into my biggest pockets, inflated my shoulder floats, and walked into the sea until I had to swim.

I couldn't see the boat with my eyes this close to water level. I fired another flare before dawn. One of those had to catch someone awake . . . and if not, I had three more. I kept swimming.

It was peaceful as a dream. Fafnir's ecology is very old, evolved on a placid world not prone to drifting continents and ice ages, where earthquakes and volcanoes know their place.

The sea had teeth, of course, but the carnivores were specialized; they knew the sounds of their prey. There were a few terrifying exceptions. Reason and logic weren't enough to wash out those memories, holograms of creatures the match for any white shark.

I grew tired fast. The air felt warm enough, the water did, too, but it was leeching the heat from my flesh and bones. I kept swimming.

A rescuer should have no way of knowing that I had been on an island. The farther I could get, the better. I did not want a rescuer to find Carlos Wu's 'doc.

At first I saw nothing more of the boat than the great white wings of its sails. I set the pocket torch on wide focus and high power, to compete with what was now broad daylight, and poured vivid green light on the sails.

And I waited for it to turn toward me, but for a long time it didn't. It came in a zigzag motion, aimed by the wind, never straight at me. It took forever to pull alongside.

A woman with fluffy golden hair studied me in some curiosity, then stripped in two quick motions and dived in.

I was numb with cold, hardly capable of wiggling a finger. This was the worst moment, and I couldn't muster strength to appreciate it. I passively let the woman noose me under the armpits, watched the man lift me aboard, utterly unable to protect myself.

Feather could have killed me before the 'doc released me. Why wait? I'd worked out what must have happened to her; it was almost plausible; but I couldn't shake the notion that Feather was waiting above me, watching me come aboard.

There was only a brawny golden man with slanted brown eyes and golden hair bleached nearly as white as mine. Tor, she'd called him, and she was Wil. He wrapped me in a silver bubble blanket and pushed a bulb of something hot into my hands.

My hands shook. A cup would have splashed everything out. I got the bulb to my lips and sucked. Strange taste, augmented with a splash of rum. The warmth went to the core of me like life itself.

The woman climbed up, dripping. She had eyes like his, a golden tan like his. He handed her a bulb. They looked me over amiably. I tried to say something; my teeth turned into castanets. I sucked and listened to them arguing over who and what I might be, and what could have torn up my jacket that way.

When I had my teeth under some kind of control, I said, "I'm Persial January Hebert, and I'm eternally in your debt."

Leaving all our Earthly wealth behind us was a pain. Feather could help: she contrived to divert a stream of ARM funds to Fafnir, replacing it from Carlos's wealth.

Riiight. But Sharrol and I would be sponging off Carlos . . . and maybe it wouldn't be Carlos. Feather controlled that wealth for now, and Feather liked control. She had not said that she expected to keep some for herself. That bothered me. It must have bothered Carlos, too, though we never found privacy to talk about it.

I wondered how Carlos would work it. Had he known Feather Filip before he reached Jinx? I could picture him designing something that would be useless on Earth: say, an upgraded version of the mass driver system that runs through the vacuum across Jinx's East Pole, replacing a more normal world's Pinwheel launcher. Design something, copyright it on Jinx under a pseudonym, form a company. Just in case he ever found the means to flee Sol system.

Me, I went to my oldest friend on Earth. General Products owed Elephant a considerable sum, and Elephant—Gregory Pelton—owed me. He got General Products to arrange for credit on Home and Fafnir. Feather wouldn't have approved the breach in secrecy, but the aliens who run General Products don't reveal secrets. We'd never even located their home world.

And Feather must have expected to control Carlos's funding and Carlos with it.

And Sharrol . . . was with me.

She'd trusted me. Now she was a flat phobe broke and stranded on an alien world, if she still lived, if she wasn't the prisoner of a homicidal maniac. Four months, going on five. Long enough to drive her crazy, I thought.

How could I hurry to her rescue? The word *hurry* was said to be forgotten on Fafnir; but perhaps I'd thought of a way.

They let me sleep. When I woke there was soup. I was ravenous. We talked while we ate.

The boat was *Gullfish*. The owners were Wilhelmin and Toranaga, brother and sister, both recently separated from mates and enjoying a certain freedom. Clean air, exercise, celibacy, before they returned to the mating dance, its embarrassments and frustrations and rewards.

There was a curious turn to their accents. I tagged it as Australian at first, then as Plateau softened by speech training, or by a generation or two in other company. This was said to be typical of Fafnir. There was no Fafnir accent. The planet had been settled too recently and from too many directions.

Wil finished her soup, went to a locker, and came back with a jacket. It was not quite like mine, and new, untouched. They helped me into it, and let me fish through the pockets of my own ragged garment before they tossed it in the locker.

They had given me my life. By Fafnir custom my response would be a gift expressing my value as perceived by myself . . . but Wil and Tor hadn't told me their full names. I hinted at this; they failed to understand. Hmm.

My dime disk hadn't spoken of this. It might be a new custom: the rescuer conceals data, so that an impoverished rescuee need not be embarrassed. He sends no life gift instead of a cheap one. But I was guessing. I couldn't follow the vibes yet.

As for my own history—

"I just gave up," I blurted. "It was so stupid. I hadn't—hadn't tried everything at all."

Toranaga said, "What kind of everything were you after?"

"I lost my wife four months ago. A rogue wave—you know how waves crossing can build into a mountain of water? It rolled our boat under. A trawler picked me up, the *Triton*." A civil being must be able to name his rescuer. Surely there must be a boat named *Triton*? "There's no record of anyone finding Milcenta. I bought another boat and searched. It's been four months. I was doing more drinking than looking lately, and three nights ago something rammed the boat. A torpedo ray, I think. I didn't sink, but my power was out, even my lights. I got tired of it all and just started swimming."

They looked at each other, then at their soup. Sympathy was there, with a trace of contempt beneath.

"Middle of the night, I was cold as the sea bottom, and it crossed my mind that maybe Mil was rescued under another name. We aren't registered as a partnership. If Mil was in a coma, they'd check her retina prints—"

"Use our caller," Wilhelmin said.

I thanked them. "With your permission, I'll establish some credit, too. I've run myself broke, but there's credit at Shasht."

They left me alone in the cabin.

* * *

The caller was set into a well in the cabin table. It was a portable—just a projector plate and a few keys that would get me a display of virtual keys and a screen—but a sailor's portable, with a watertight case and several small cleats. I found the master program unfamiliar but user-friendly.

I set up a search program for Milcenta Adelaide Graynor, in any combination. Milcenta was Sharrol and Adelaide was Feather, as determined by their iceliner tickets and retina prints. Milcenta's name popped up at once.

I bellowed out of the hatch. "They saved her!" Wil and Tor bolted into the cabin to read over my shoulder.

Hand of Allah, a fishing boat. Milcenta but not Adelaide! Sharrol had been picked up alone. I'd been at least half-right: she'd escaped from Feather. I realized I was crying.

And—"No life gift." That was the other side of it: if she sent a proper gift, the embarrassment of needing to be rescued at sea need never become public record. We'd drilled each other on such matters. "She must have been in bad shape."

"Yes, if she didn't call you," Wilhelmin said. "And she didn't go home either?"

I told Martin Graynor's story: "We sold our home. We were on one last cruise before boarding an iceliner. She could be anywhere by now, if she thought the wave killed me. I'll have to check."

I did something about money first. There was nothing aboard *Gullfish* that could read Persial January Hebert's retina prints, but I could at least establish that money was there.

I tried to summon passenger records from the iceliner *Zombie Queen*. This was disallowed. I showed disappointment and some impatience; but of course records wouldn't be shown to Hebert. They'd be opened to Martin Wallace Graynor.

They taught me to sail.

Gullfish was built for sails, not for people. The floors weren't flat. Ropes lay all over every surface. The mast stood upright through the middle of the cabin. You didn't walk in, you climbed. There were no lift plates; you slept in an odd-shaped box small enough to let you brace yourself in storms.

I had to learn a peculiar slang, as if I were learning to fly a spacecraft, and for the same reason. If a sailor hears a yell, he has to know what is meant, instantly.

I was working hard, and my body was adjusting to the shorter day. Sure I had insomnia; but nobody sleeps well on a small boat. The idea is to snap awake instantly, where any stimulus could mean trouble. The boat was giving my body time to adjust to Fafnir.

Once I passed a mirror, and froze. I barely knew myself.

That was all to the good. My skin was darkening and, despite sunblock, would darken further. But—when we landed, my hair had been cut to Fafnir styles. It had grown during four months in the 'doc. The 'doc had "cured" my depilation treatment: I had a beard too. I was far too conspicuous, a pink-eyed, pale-skinned man with long, wild, white hair.

My hosts hadn't said anything. They must have put it down to the pattern of neurosis that had me sailing like a zombie in search of my dead wife, until my love of life left me entirely. I went to Tor in some embarrassment and asked if they had anything like a styler aboard.

They had scissors. Riiight. Wil tried to shape my hair, laughed at the result, and suggested I finish the job at Booty Island.

So I tried to forget the rest of the world and just sail. It was what Wilhelmin and Toranaga were doing. One day at a time. Islands and boats grew more common as we neared the Central Isles. Another day for Feather to forget me, or lose me. Another day of safety for Sharrol, if Feather followed me to her. I'd have to watch for that.

And peace would have been mine, but that my ragged vest was in a locker that wouldn't open to my fingerprints.

Wil and Tor talked about themselves, a little, but I still didn't know their identities. They slept in a locked cabin. I noticed also an absence. Wil was a lovely woman, not unlike Sharrol herself; but her demeanor and body language showed no sign that she considered herself female, or me male, let alone that she might welcome a pass.

It might mean anything, in an alien culture: that my hair-style or shape of nose or skin color were distasteful, or I didn't know the local body language, or I lacked documentation for my gene pattern. But I wondered if they wanted no life gift, in any sense, from a man they might have to give to the police.

What would a police detective think of those holes? Why, he'd think some kinetic weapon had torn a hole through the occupant, killing him instantly, after which someone (the killer?) had stolen the vest for himself. And if Wil and Tor were thinking that way . . . What I did at the caller, might it be saved automatically?

Now *there* was a notion.

I borrowed the caller again. I summoned the encyclopedia and set a search for a creature with boneless arms. There were several on Fafnir, all small. I sought data on the biggest, particularly those local to the North Coral Quadrant. There were stories . . . no hard evidence. . . .

And another day passed, and I learned that I could cook while a kitchen was rolling randomly.

At dinner that night Wil got to talking about Fafnir sea life. She'd worked at Pacifica, which I gathered was a kind of underwater zoo; and had I ever heard of a Kdatlyno life-form like a blind squid?

"No," I said. "Would the kzinti bring one here?"

"I wouldn't think so. The kzinti aren't surfers," Tor said, and we laughed.

Wil didn't. She said, "They meant it for the hunting jungle. On Kdat the damn things can come ashore and drag big animals back into the ocean. But they've pretty well died out around Shasht, and we never managed to get one for Pacifica."

"Well," I said, and hesitated, and, "I think I was attacked by something like that. But huge. And it wasn't around Shasht, it was where you picked me up."

"Jan, you should report it."

"Wil, I can't. I was fast asleep and half-dead of cold, lost at sea at midnight. I woke up underwater. Something was squeezing my chest and back. I got my knife out and slashed. Slashed something rubbery. It pulled apart. It pulled my *jacket* apart. If it had ripped the shoulder floats, I'd still be down there. But I never saw a thing."

Thus are legends born.

Booty Island is several islands merged. I counted eight peaks coming in; there must have been more. We had been sailing for twelve days.

Buildings sat on each of the lamplighter nests. They looked like government buildings or museums. No two were alike. Houses were scattered across the flatlands between. A mile or so of shopping center ran like a suspension bridge between two peaks. On Earth this would have been a park. Here, a center of civilization.

A line of transfer booths in the mall bore the familiar flickering Pelton logo. They were all big cargo booths, and old. I didn't instantly see the significance.

We stopped in a hotel and used a coin caller. The system read my retina prints: Persial January Hebert, sure enough. Wil and Tor waited while I moved some money, collected some cash and a transfer booth card, and registered for a room. I tried again for records of Milcenta Adelaide Graynor. Sharrol's rescue was still there. Nothing for Feather.

Wil said, "Jan, she may have been recovering from a head injury. See if she's tried to find you."

I couldn't be Mart Graynor while Wil and Tor were watching. The net registered no messages for Jan Hebert. Feather didn't know that name. Sharrol did; but Sharrol thought I was dead.

Or maybe she was crazy, incapacitated. With Tor and Wil watching I tried two worst cases.

First: executions. A public 'doc can cure most varieties of madness. Madness is curable, therefore voluntary. Capital crimes committed during a period of madness have carried the death penalty for seven hundred years, on Earth and every world I knew.

It was true of Fafnir, too. But Sharrol had not been executed for any such crime, and neither, worse luck, had Feather.

Next: There are still centers for the study of madness. The best known is on Jinx. On Earth there are several, plus one secret branch of the ARM. There was only one mental institution to serve all of Fafnir, and that seemed to be half-empty. Neither Feather's nor Sharrol's retina prints showed on the records.

The third possibility would have to wait.

We all needed the hotel's styler, though I was worst off. The device left my hair long at the neck, and theirs, too, a local style to protect against sunburn. I let it tame my beard without baring my face. The sun had had its way with me: I looked like an older man.

I took Wil and Tor to lunch. I found "gullfish" on the menu and tried it. Like much of Fafnir sea life, it tasted like something that had almost managed to become red meat.

I worked some points casually into conversation, just checking. It was their last chance to probe me, too, and I had to improvise details of a childhood in the North Sea. Tor found me plausible; Wil was harder to read. Nothing was said of a vest or a great sea monster. In their minds I was already gone.

I was Schroedinger's cat: I had murdered and not murdered the owner of a shredded vest.

At the caller in my room I established myself as Martin Wallace Graynor. That gave me access to my wives' autodoc records. A public 'doc will correct any of the chemical imbalances we lump under the term *crazy*, but it also records such service.

Milcenta Graynor—Sharrol—had used a 'doc eight times in four-plus months, starting a week after our disastrous landing. The record showed much improvement over that period, beginning at a startling adrenaline level, acid indigestion, and some dangerous lesser symptoms. Eight times within the Central Islands . . . none on Shasht.

If she'd never reached the mainland, then she'd never tried to reach Outbound Enterprises. Never tried to find Carlos, or Louis and Tanya.

Adelaide Graynor—Feather—had no 'doc record on this world. The most obvious conclusion was that wherever she was, she must be mad as a March hare.

Boats named *Gullfish* were everywhere on Fafnir. Fifty-one registries. Twenty-nine had sail. Ten of those would sleep four. I scanned for first names: no Wilhelmin, no Toranaga. Maybe *Gullfish* belonged to a parent, or to one of the departed spouses.

I'd learned a term for *Gullfish*'s sail and mast configuration: *sloop rig*.

Every one of the ten candidates was a sloop rig!

Wait, now. Wil had worked at Pacifica?

I did some research. Pacifica wasn't just a zoo. It looked more like an underwater village, with listings for caterers, costume shops, subs, repair work, travel, hotels . . . but Wil had worked with sea life. Might that give me a handle?

I couldn't see how.

It wasn't that I didn't have an answer; I just didn't like it. Wil and Tor *had* to hand my vest to the cops. When Persial January Hebert was reported rescued, I would send them a gift.

Feather didn't know my alternate name. But if she had access to the Fafnir police, she'd tanj sure recognize that vest!

With the rest of the afternoon I bought survival gear: a backpurse, luggage, clothing.

On Earth I could have vanished behind a thousand shades of dyes. Here . . . I settled for a double dose of tannin secretion, an underdose of sunblock, a darkened pair of mag specs, my height, a local beard and hairstyle.

Arming myself was a problem.

The disk hadn't spoken of weapons on Fafnir. My safest guess was that Fafnir was like Earth: they didn't put weapons in the hands of civilians. Handguns, rifles, martial arts training belong to the police.

The good news: everyone on the islands carried knives. Those flying sharks that attacked me during the sunbunny run were one predator out of thousands.

Feather would arm herself somehow. She'd look through a sporting goods store, steal a hunting rifle . . . nope, no hunting rifles. No large prey on Fafnir, unless in the kzinti jungle, or *underwater.*

There were listings for scuba stores. I found a stun gun with a big parabolic reflector, big enough to knock out a one-gulp, too big for a pocket. I took it home, with more diving gear for versimilitude, and a little tool kit for repairing diving equipment. With that I removed the reflector.

Now I couldn't use it underwater; it would knock *me* out, because water conducts sound very well. But it would fit my pocket.

I took my time over a sushi dinner, quite strange. Sometime after sunset I stepped into a transfer booth, and stepped out into a brilliant dawn on Shasht.

Outbound Enterprises was open. I let a Ms. Machti take Martin Wallace Graynor's retina prints. "Your ticket is still good, Mr. Graynor," Ms. Machti said. "The service charge will be eight hundred stars. You're four months late!"

"I was shipwrecked," I told her. "Did my companions make it?"

Iceliner passengers are in no hurry. The ships keep prices down by launching when they're full. I learned that the *Zombie Queen* had departed a week after our landing, about as expected. I gave Ms. Machti the names. She set the phone system searching, and presently said, "Your husband and the children boarded and departed. Your wives' tickets are still outstanding."

"Both?"

"Yes." She did a double take. "Oh, good heavens, they must think you're dead!"

"That's what I'm afraid of. At least, John and Tweena and Nathan would. They were revived in good shape?"

"Yes, of course. But the women, could they have waited for you?"

Stet: Carlos, Tanya, and Louis were all safe on Home and had left the spaceport under their own power. Feather and Sharrol—"Waited? But they'd have left a message."

She was still looking at her screen. "Not for you, Mr. Graynor, but Mr. *John* Graynor has recorded a message for Mrs. Graynor . . . for Mrs. Adelaide Graynor."

For Feather. "But nothing for Milcenta? But they *both* stayed? How strange." Ms. Machti seemed the type of person who might wonder about other people's sexual arrangements. I wanted her curious, because this next question—"Can you show me what John had to say to Adelaide?"

She shook her head firmly. "I don't see how—"

"Now, John wouldn't have said anything someone else couldn't hear. You can watch it yourself—" Her head was still turning left, right, left. "In fact, you should. Then you can at least tell *me* if there's been, if, well. I have to know, don't I? If Milcenta's dead."

That stopped her. She nodded, barely, and tapped in the code to summon Carlos's message to Feather.

She read it all the way through. Her lip curled just a bit; but she showed only solemn pity when she turned the monitor to face me.

It was a posed scene. Carlos looked like a man hiding a sickness. The view behind him could have been a manor garden in England, a tamed wilderness. Tanya and Louis were playing in the distance, hide-and-seek in and out of some Earthly tree that dripped a cage of foliage. Alive. Ever since I first saw them frozen, I must have been thinking of them as dead.

Carlos looked earnestly out of the monitor screen. "Adelaide, you can see that the children and I arrived safely. I have an income. The plans we made together, half of us have carried out. Your own iceliner slots are still available.

"I know nothing of Mart. I hope you've heard from him, but he should never have gone sailing alone. I fear the worst.

"Addie, I can't pretend to understand how you've changed, how Mil changed, or why. I can only hope you'll both change your mind and come back to me. But understand me, Addie: you are not welcome without Milcenta. Your claim on family funds is void without Milcenta. And whatever relationship we can shape from these ashes, I would prefer to leave the children out of it."

He had the money!

Carlos stood and walked a half circle as he spoke. The camera followed him on automatic, and now it showed a huge, sprawling house of architectural coral, pink and slightly rounded everywhere. Carlos gestured. "I've waited. The house isn't finished because you and Milcenta will have your own tastes. But come soon.

"I've set credit with Outbound. Messages sent to Home by hyperwave will be charged to me. I'll get the service charges when you and Milcenta board. Call first. We can work this out."

The record began to repeat. I heard it through again, then turned the monitor around.

Ms. Machti asked, "You went sailing alone?"

She thought I'd tried to commit suicide after our wives changed parity and locked the men out: an implication Carlos had shaped with some skill. I made a brush-off gesture and said, "I've got to tell him I'm still alive."

"The credit he left doesn't apply—"

"I want to send a hyperwave message, my expense. Let's see . . . does Outbound Enterprises keep a camera around?"

"No."

"I'll fax it from the hotel. When's the next flight out?"

"At least two weeks, but we can suspend you any time."

I used a camera at the hotel. The first disk I made would go through Outbound Enterprises. "John, I'm all right. I was on a dead island eating fish for awhile." A slightly belligerent tone: "I haven't heard a word from Adelaide or Milcenta. I know Milcenta better than you do, and frankly, I believe they must have separated by now. Home looks like a new life, but I haven't given up on the old one. I'll let you know when I know myself." So much for the ears of Ms. Machti.

Time lag had me suddenly wiped out. I floated between the sleeping plates . . . exhausted but awake. What should I put in a *real* message?

Carlos's tape was a wonderful lesson in communication. He wants to talk to Feather. The children are not to be put at risk. Beowulf is presumed dead, *c'est la vie*, Carlos will not seek vengeance. But he wants Sharrol alive. Feather is not to come to Home without Sharrol. Carlos can enforce any agreement. He hadn't said so because it's too obvious. A frozen Feather, arriving at Home unaccompanied, need never wake.

And he had the money! Not just his own funds, but the money Feather knew about, "family funds": he must have reached civilization ahead of her and somehow sequestered what Feather funneled through the ARM. If Feather was loose on Fafnir, then she was also broke. She owned nothing but the credit that would get her a hyperwave call to Home, or herself and Sharrol shipped frozen. Though Carlos didn't know it, even Sharrol had escaped.

Nearly five months. How was Feather living? Did she have a job? Something I could track? With her training she might be better off as a thief.

Yah! I tumbled out of the sleepfield and tapped out my needs in some haste. She hadn't been caught at any capital crime, but any jail on Shasht would record Adelaide Graynor's retina prints. The caller ran its search. . . .

Nothing.

Okay, *job*. Feather needed something that would allow her time to take care of a prisoner. She had to have that if she had Sharrol, or in case she recaptured Sharrol, or captured *Beowulf*.

So I looked through some job listings, but nothing suggested itself. I turned off the caller and hoped for sleep. Perhaps I dozed a little.

Sometime in the night I realized that I had nothing more to say to Carlos.

Even Sharrol's escape wasn't information unless she stayed loose. Feather was a trained ARM. I was a self-trained tourist; I couldn't possibly hunt her down. There was only one way to hunt Feather.

It was still black outside, and I was wide-awake. The caller gave me a listing of all-night restaurants.

I ordered an elaborate breakfast, six kinds of fish eggs, gulper bacon, cappuccino. Five people at a table demanded I join them, so I did. They were fresh from the coral isles via dirigible, still time-lagged, looking for new jokes. I tried to oblige. And somewhere in there I forgot all about missing ladies.

We broke up at dawn. I walked back to the hotel alone. I had sidetracked my mind, hoping it would come up with something if I left it alone; but my answer hadn't changed. The way to hunt Feather was to pretend to be Feather, and hunt Sharrol.

Stet, I'm Feather Filip. What do I know about Sharrol? Feather must have researched her; she sure as tanj had researched me!

Back up. How did Sharrol get loose?

The simplest possible answer was that Sharrol dived into the water and swam away. Feather could beat her at most things, but a woman who lived beneath the ocean for thirty years would swim just fine.

Eventually a boat would find her.

Eventually, an island. Penniless. She needs work *now*. What kind of work is that? It has to suit a flat phobe. She's being hunted by a murderer, and the alien planet around her forces itself into her awareness every second. Dirigible stewardess is probably out. Hotel work would be better.

Feather, days behind her, seeks work for herself; but the listings will tell her Sharrol's choices, too. And now I was back in the room and scanning through work listings.

Qualifications—I couldn't remember what Milcenta Graynor was supposed to be able to do. Sharrol's skills wouldn't match anyway, any more than mine matched Mart Graynor's. So look for *unskilled*.

Low salaries, of course. Except here: *servant, kzinti embassy*. Was that a joke? No: here was *museum maintenance, must work with kzinti*. Some of them had stayed with the embassy, or even become citizens. Could Sharrol handle that? She got along with strangers . . . even near aliens, like me.

Fishing boats, period of training needed. Hotel work. Underwater porter work, unskilled labor in Pacifica.

Pacifica. Of course.

Briefly I considered putting in for the porter job. Sharrol and/or Feather must have done that, grabbed whatever was to be had . . . but I told myself that Feather thought I had no money. She'd never look for me in Pacifica's second-best . . . ah, *best* hotel.

The truth is, I prefer playing tourist.

I scanned price listings for hotels in Pacifica, called, and negotiated for a room at the Pequod. Then I left Shasht in untraditional fashion, via oversize transfer booth, still in early morning.

It was night in Pacifica. I checked in, crawled between sleeping plates, and zonked out, my time-lagged body back on track.

I woke late, fully rested for the first time in days. There was a little round window next to my nose. I gazed out, floating half-mesmerized, remembering the Great Barrier Reef outside Carlos Wu's apartment.

The strangeness and variety of Earth's sea life had

stunned me then. But these oceans were older. Evolution had filled ecological niches not yet dreamed on Earth.

It was shady out there, under a wonderful variety of seaweed growths, like a forest in fog. Life was everywhere. Here a school of transparent bell jars, nearly invisible, opened and closed to jet themselves along. Quasi-terrestrial fish glowed as if alien graffiti had been scrawled across them in Day-Glo ink to identify them to potential mates. Predators hid in the green treetops: torpedo shapes dived from cover and disappeared back into the foliage with prey wriggling in long jaws.

A boneless arm swept straight down from a floating seaweed island, toward the orange neon fish swimming just above the sandy bottom. Its stinger-armed hand flexed and fell like a net over its wriggling prey . . . and a great mouth flexed wider and closed over the wrist. The killer was dark and massive, shaped like a ray of Earth's sea. The smaller fish was painted on its back; it moved with the motion of the ray. The ray chewed, reeling the arm in, until a one-armed black oyster was ripped out of the seaweed-tree and pulled down to death.

One big beast, like a long dolphin with gills and great round eyes, stopped to look me over. Owl rams were said to be no brighter than a good dog, but Fafnir scientists had been hard put to demonstrate that, and Fafnir fishers still didn't believe it.

I waved solemnly. It bowed . . . well, bobbed in place before it flicked away.

My gear was arrayed in a tidy row, with the stunner nearest my hand. I'd put the reflector back on. I could reach it in an instant. Your Honor, *of course* it's for scuba swimming. Why else would I be in possession of a device that can knock Feather Filip into a coma before she can blow a great bloody hole through my torso?

I didn't actually want to go scuba swimming.

Sharrol swam like a fish; she could be out there right now. Still, at a distance and underwater, would I know her? And

Feather might know me, and Feather would certainly swim better than I, and I could hardly ignore Feather.

Sharrol had to be living underwater. It was the only way she could stay sane. Life beyond the glass was alien, stet, but the life of Earth's seas seems alien too. My slow wits hadn't seen that at first, but Feather's skills would solve *that* puzzle.

And Beowulf Shaeffer had to be underwater, to avoid sunlight. Feather could find me for the wrong reasons!

And the police of Fafnir, of whom I knew nothing at all, might well be studying me in bemused interest. *He's bought a weapon! But why, if he has the blaster that blew a hole through this vest? And it's a fishing weapon, and he's gone to Pacifica* . . . which might cause them to hold off a few hours longer.

So, with time breathing hot on my neck, I found the hotel restaurant and took my time over fruit, fish eggs in a baked potato, and cappuccino.

My time wasn't wasted. The window overlooked a main street of Pacifica's village-sized collection of bubbles. I saw swimsuits, and casually dressed people carrying diving or fishing gear. Almost nobody dressed formally. That would be for Shasht, for going to work. In the breakfast room itself I saw four business tunics in a crowd of a hundred. And two men in dark blue police uniforms that left arms and legs bare: you could swim in them.

And one long table, empty, with huge chairs widely spaced. I wondered how often kzinti came in. It was hard to believe they'd be numerous, two hundred years after mankind took over.

Back in the room, I fished out the little repair kit and set to work on my transfer booth card.

We learned this as kids. The idea is to make a bridge of superconductor wire across the central circuits. Transport companies charge citizens a quarterly fee to cover local jumps. The authorities don't get upset if you stay away from the borders of the card. The borders are area codes.

Well, it *looked* like the kind of card we'd used then. Fafnir's booth system served a small population that didn't use booths much. It could well be decades old, long due for replacement. So I'd try it.

I got into casuals. I rolled my wet suit around the rest of my scuba gear and stuffed the stunner into one end where I could grab it fast. Stuffed the bundle into my backpurse—it stuck way out—and left the room.

Elevators led to the roof. Admissions was here, and a line of the big transfer booths, and a transparent roof with an awesome view up into the sea forest. I stepped into a booth and inserted my card. The random walk began.

A shopping mall, high up above a central well. Booths in a line, just inside a big water lock. A restaurant; another; an apartment building. I was jumping every second and a half.

Nobody noticed me flicking in; would they notice how quickly I flicked out? Nobody gets upset at a random walk unless the kids do it often enough to tie up circuits. But they might remember an adult. How long before someone called the police?

A dozen kzinti, lying about in cool half darkness gnawing oddly shaped bones, rolled to a defensive four-footed crouch at the sight of me. I couldn't help it: I threw myself against the back wall. I must have looked crazed with terror when the random walk popped me into a Solarico Omni center. I was trying to straighten my face when the jump came. *Hey*— A travel terminal of some kind; I turned and saw the dirigible, like an underpressured planet, before the scene changed. —*Her!*

Beyond a thick glass wall, the seaweed forest swarmed with men and women wearing fins: farmers picking spheres that glowed softly in oil-slick colors. I waited my moment and snatched my card out of the slot. *Was it really*—I tapped quickly to get an instant billing, counted two back along the booth numbers. I couldn't use the jimmied card for this, so I'd picked up a handful of coins.—*Her?*

Solarico Omni, top floor. I stepped out of the booth, and saw the gates that would stop a shoplifter and a stack of lockers.

For the first time I had second thoughts about the way I

was dressed. Nothing wrong with the clothes, but I couldn't carry a mucking great package of diving gear into a shopping center, with a stunner so handy. I pushed my backpurse into a locker and stepped through the gates.

The whole complex was visible from the rim of the central well. It was darker down there than I was used to. Pacifica citizens must like their underwater gloom, I thought.

Two floors down, an open fast-food center: wasn't that where I'd seen her? She was gone now. I'd seen only a face, and I could have been wrong. At least she'd never spot *me*, not before I was much closer.

But where was she? Dressed how? Employee or customer? It was midmorning: she couldn't be on lunch break. Customer, then. Only, Shashters kept poor track of time.

Three floors down, the Sports Department. Good enough. I rode down the escalator. I'd buy a speargun or another stunner, shove everything into the bag that came with it. Then I could start window-shopping for faces.

The Sports Department aisles were pleasantly wide. Most of what it sold was fishing gear, a daunting variety. There was skiing equipment too. And hunting, it looked like: huge weapons built for hands bigger than a baseball mitt. The smallest was a fat tube as long as my forearm, with a grip no bigger than a kzinti kitten's hand. Oh, sure, kzinti just love going to humans for their weapons. Maybe the display was there to entertain human customers.

The clerks were leaving me alone to browse. Customs differ. *What the tanj was that?*

Two kzinti in the aisle, spaced three yards apart, hissing the Hero's Tongue at each other. A handful of human customers watched in some amusement. There didn't seem to be danger there. One wore what might be a loose dark blue swimsuit with a hole for the tail. The other (sleeveless brown tunic) took down four yards of disassembled fishing rod. A kzinti *clerk*?

The corner of my eye caught a clerk's hands (human) opening the case and reaching in for that smaller tube, with a grip built for a kzin child. Or a man—

My breath froze in my throat. I was looking into Feather's horrible ARM weapon. I looked up into the clerk's face.

It came out as a whisper. "No, Sharrol, no no no. It's me. It's Beowulf."

She didn't fire. But she was pale with terror, her jaw set like rock, and the black tube looked at the bridge of my nose.

I eased two inches to the right, very slowly, to put myself between the tube and the kzin cop. That wasn't just a swimsuit he was wearing: it was the same sleeveless, legless police uniform I'd seen at breakfast.

We were eye to eye. The whites showed wide around her irises. I said, "My face. Look at my face. Under the beard. It's Bey, love. I'm a foot shorter. Remember?"

She remembered. It terrified her.

"I wouldn't fit. The cavity was built for Carlos. My heart and lungs were shredded, my back was shattered, my brain was dying, and you had to get me into the cavity. But I wouldn't fit, remember? Sharrol, I have to know." I looked around quick. An aisle over, kzinti noses came up, smelling fear. "Did you kill Feather?"

"Kill Feather." She set the tube down carefully on the display case. Her brow wrinkled. "I was going through my pockets. It was distracting me, keeping me sane. I needed that. The light was wrong, the gravity was wrong, the Earth was so far away—"

"Shh."

"Survival gear, always know what you have, *you* taught me that." She began to tremble. "I heard a sonic boom. I looked up just as you were blown backward. I thought I must be c-crazy. I couldn't have seen that."

It was my back that felt vulnerable now. I felt all those floors behind and above me, all those eyes. The kzin cop had lost interest. If there was a moment for Feather Filip to take us both, this was it.

But the ARM weapon was in *Sharrol*'s hands—

"But Carlos jumped into the boat and roared off, and Feather screamed at him, and you were all blood and sprawled out like—like *dead*—and I, I can't remember.",

"Yes, dear," I took her hand, greatly daring, "but I have to know if she's still chasing us."

She shook her head violently. "I jumped on her back and cut her throat. She tried to point that tube at me. I held her arm down, she elbowed me in the ribs, I hung on, she fell down. I cut her head off. But Bey, there you were, and Carlos was gone and the kids were too, and what was I going to *do*?" She came around the counter and put her arms around me, and said, "We're the same height. Futz!"

I was starting to relax. Feather was nowhere. We were free of her. "I kept telling myself you *must* have killed her. A trained ARM psychotic, but she didn't take you seriously. She couldn't have guessed how quick you'd wake up."

"I fed her into the organics reservoir."

"Yah. There was nowhere else all that biomass could have come from. It had to be Feather—"

"And I couldn't lift your body, and you wouldn't fit anyway. I had to cut off your h-h-" She pulled close and tried to push her head under my jaw, but I wasn't tall enough any more. "Head. I cut as low as I could. Tanj, we're the same *height*. Did it work? Are you all right?"

"I'm fine. I'm just short. The 'doc rebuilt me from my DNA, from the throat down, but it built me in Fafnir gravity. Good thing, too, I guess."

"Yah." She was trying to laugh, gripping my arms as if I might disappear. "There wouldn't have been room for your feet. Bey, we shouldn't be talking here. That kzin is a cop, and nobody knows how good their hearing is. Bey, I get off at sixteen hundred."

"I'll shop. We're both overdue on life gifts."

"How do I look? How *should* I look?"

I had posed us on the roof of the Pequod, with the camera looking upward past us into the green seaweed forest. I said, "Just right. Pretty, cheerful, the kind of woman a man might drown himself for. A little bewildered. You didn't contact me because you got a blow to the head. You're only just healing. You ready? Take one, *now*." I keyed the vidcamera.

Me: "Wilhelmin, Toranaga, I hope you're feeling as good as we are. I had no trouble finding Milcenta once I got my head on straight—"

Sharrol, bubbling: "Hello! Thank you for Jan's life, and thank you for teaching him to sail. I never could show him how to do that. We're going to buy a boat as soon as we can afford it."

Me: "I'm ready to face the human race again. I hope you are, too. This may help." I turned the camera off.

"What are you giving them?" Sharrol asked.

"Silverware, service for a dozen. Now they'll *have* to develop a social life."

"Do you think they turned you in?"

"They had to. They did well by me, love. What bothers me is, they'll *never* be sure I'm not a murderer. Neither will the police. This is a wonderful planet for getting rid of a corpse. I'll be looking over my shoulder for that kzinti cop—"

"No, Bey—"

"He smelled our fear."

"They smell *everyone's* fear. They make wonderful police, but they can't react every time a kzin makes a human nervous. He may have pegged you as an outworlder, though."

"Oop. Why?"

"Bey, the kzinti are everywhere on Fafnir, mostly on the mainland, but they're on-site at the fishing sources, too. Fafnir sea life feeds the whole Patriarchy, and it's strictly a kzinti operation. Shashters are used to kzin. But kids and wimps and outworlders all get twitchy around them, and they're used to that."

He might have smelled more than our fear, I thought. Our genetic makeup, our diet . . . but we'd been eating Fafnir fish for over a month, and Fafnir's people are every breed of man.

"Stet. Shall we deal with the *Hand of Allah*?"

Now she looked nervous. "I must have driven them half

crazy. And worried them sick. It's a good gift, isn't it? Shorfy and Isfahan were constantly complaining about fish, fish, fish—"

"They'll love it. It's about five ounces of red meat per crewman—I suppose that's—"

"Free-range life-forms from the hunting parks."

"—and fresh vegetables to match. I bet the kzinti don't grow *those*. Okay, take *one*—"

Sharrol: "Captain Muh'mad, I was a long time recovering my memory. I expect the 'docs did more repair work every time I went under. My husband's found me, we both have jobs, and this is to entertain you and your crew in my absence."

Me: "For my wife's life, blessings and thanks." I turned it off. "Now Carlos."

Her hand stopped me. "I can't leave, you know," Sharrol said. "I'm not a coward—"

"Feather learned that!"

"It's just . . . overkill. I've been through too much."

"It's all right. Carlos has Louis and Tanya for a while, and that's fine, they love him. We're free of the UN. Everything went just as we planned it, more or less, except from Feather's viewpoint."

"Do you mind? Do you like it here?"

"There are transfer booths if I want to go anywhere. Sharrol, I was raised underground. It feels just like home if I don't look out a window. I wouldn't mind spending the rest of our lives here. Now, this is for Ms. Machti at Outbound, not to mention any watching ARMs. Ready? Take *one*."

Me: "Hi, John! Hello, kids! We've got a more or less happy ending here, brought to you with some effort."

Sharrol: "I'm pregnant. It happened yesterday morning. That's why we waited to call."

I was calling as Martin Wallace Graynor. Carlos/John could reach us the same way. We wanted no connection between Mart Graynor and Jan Hebert.

Visuals were important to the message. The undersea forest was behind us. I stood next to Sharrol, our eyes exactly level. That'd give him a jolt.

Me: "John, I know you were worried about Mil, and so was I, but she's recovered. Mil's a lot tougher than even Addie gave her credit for."

Sharrol: "Still, the situation was sticky at first. Messy." She rubbed her hands. "But that's all over. Bey's got a job working outside in the water orchards—"

Me: "It's just like working in free fall. I've got a real knack for it."

Sharrol: "We've got some money too, and after the baby's born I'll take Bey's job. It'll be just like I'm back in my teens."

Me: "You did the right thing, protecting the children first. It's worked out very well."

Sharrol: "We're happy here, John. This is a good place to raise a child, or several. Someday we'll come to you, I think, but not now. The changes in my life are too new. I couldn't take it. Mart is willing to indulge me."

Me: [sorrowfully] "Addie is gone, John. We never expect to see her again, and we're just as glad, but I feel she'll always be a part of me." I waved the camera off.

Now let's see Carlos figure *that* out. He does like puzzles.

MARS
WHO NEEDS IT?

There are minds that think as well as you do, but differently.

It's a matter of faith, the only thing that all of the science fiction field can agree on. Alien viewpoints and alien minds exist or will exist. What might they be able to teach us?

I grew up knowing that Mars was the home of intelligence.

But telescopes got better. When cameras replaced eyes, the canali went away. The more we learned, the less hospitable Mars became. I published my first stories in the days when human-built robots were sending data back from every world in the solar system. None of them showed signs of life.

It was becoming obvious: if we wish to learn of intelligent life in the universe, the taking of Mars will teach us only about ourselves.

We will learn our limits.

In those early stories I took an extreme position. Mars is not wanted. The wealth and the opportunities are all in the asteroids and outer moons. A planet is a gravity well: the bottom of a hole.

Extreme positions are more interesting than compromises. Still, why *do* we want Mars?

I

Knowledge is always of value, and the value is never predictable. This, at least, we are doing right. We are learning what we can of Mars, for its own sake. What will come of it we cannot know.

But a science fiction writer can guess. Try this:

Five billion years of water erosion is hell on the geological record. The geological history of Mars may be easier to read than Earth's. If Mars can tell us anything of ice ages, then we will have learned something of the behavior of the Sun. We may be able to predict our own next ice age . . . or heat age.

Then what? Freeman Dyson has said, "It's best not to limit our thinking. We can always air-condition the Earth."

II

We'll be sending more little wheeled robots. The ambition to put a tiny automated airplane on Mars hasn't died. VR sets get smaller, cheaper, more dependable. A Martian entertainment industry waits to be born.
We could all be flying or wheeling over the surface of Mars in virtual reality.

VR channels could pay for the space program.

III

There are better ways of reaching orbit than rockets. A teacher under the Czar, Konstantin Tsiolkovsky, described what we now call an orbital tower, or Beanstalk: a cable roughly a hundred thousand miles long, its lower end anchored on the Earth's equator, its center of mass in geosynchronous orbit. Use it as an elevator cable. Launch from the far end, you're beyond Mars or inward from Venus.

Half a dozen other devices exist, all still imaginary, each an attempt to design a rocket-free launching system.

Despite conceptual improvements, the Beanstalk is still the most costly, but also the most convenient. But each of these skyhooks would be very expensive to build and very cheap to run: a few dollars per kilogram to orbit. They have more in common:

Each requires materials we can't manufacture yet, though such materials are well within theoretical limits.

Each holds awesome energies imprisoned. After all, each was built to transfer awesome energies to a spacecraft and (in some cases) collect it again by decelerating the spacecraft. Any such device would be a disaster of awesome proportions, if its energies were accidentally released on Earth.

Most of these skyhooks depend on low gravity and high rotation. The Beanstalk, for instance, won't work at all on any world in the solar system, barring Earth and Mars. Mars is smaller and spins just as fast.

And each would be safer, smaller, cheaper, and require less robust materials if built on Mars. If something went wrong, no city would die, and Mars could bear the scars.

If we are to claim the solar system, we need Mars as a test bed for skyhooks.

Robert Forward had made an extensive study of orbital tethers. He intended to build and sell them. He started small, with a tether designed to drop a used-up satellite out of orbit.

IV

To take the universe, we must learn how to build habitats, and how to reshape worlds. By the time we set our feet on Mars, we will know a little about both.

The Apollo capsules weren't much of a habitat. There was no attempt at recycling. There wasn't room for the kind of exercise that could keep a human being human during years in free fall. Artificial gravity wasn't even considered. A mission to Mars would need all of that. A habitat on Mars would benefit from all we will have learned from the taking of the Moon.

V

We're already learning how to reshape a world: the Earth.

We speculate that Mars could be made habitable by releasing buried water or water in hydration, by warming the planet, or by bashing it with comets. (The skyhooks come first. To reach the comets, bringing enough horsepower to hurl them into the inner solar system, we will need easy access to orbit.)

VI

It bothers me a little to be so treating a *planet* as raw material. Arrogance may come naturally to me, but I remember wanting Mars because it was . . . well, Mars.

If I've slighted your own reasons for claiming Mars, forgive me. My viewpoint may be peculiar. I've wanted to walk the surfaces of other worlds ever since I found Heinlein. Any excuse will do.

VII

A successful species evolves in many directions. Species that follow one line of development, like humans or horses, are unusual, and it isn't a mark of success. Where did *Homo erectus* go, anyway?

If we do not first destroy ourselves, we will make our own aliens.

If we intend to take the universe for ourselves, we will need Mars. Our selves will change in the process. The Martians may not remain human. The entities that reach the nearest star may be beyond imagination. The trick is to remain adaptable.

HOW TO SAVE CIVILIZATION
AND MAKE A LITTLE MONEY

Jerry Pournelle and I were gearing up to write about parasite control. We'd have set a novel on the Moon and built it around a concept I've been revising since (I think) high school.

Parasite control is needed to keep any enterprise from ballooning into something unaffordable, particularly any government project. It's terribly important to achieving orbit. Nothing lifts from the ground unless you can keep people from piling their own projects on it. That was what made the X-plane program work: build one device to test one concept. Build and launch it quick, before the parasites notice.

X-33? X-34?

So there we were, rewriting the space program yet again . . . and I realized that the books stacked all around my office, some published, some just manuscripts, were all rewriting the space program. They're all over the bookstores too: Baxter's *Titan* and *Voyage*; Greg Benford's *The Martian Race*; Victor Koman's *Kings of the High Frontier*; Michael Flynn's *Star* series. The website <larryniven-l@buckness.edu> is currently jammed with speculation on how to make space enterprises work better.

I told Jerry that that ecological slot is full.

But it continued to worry me. In my own recent novels I have often rebuilt the space program. Delta Clipper-like craft flew in the background in *Destiny's Road*. *Rainbow Mars* is a fantasy set eleven hundred years from now and based in *time travel*, but the Space Bureau *still* has to lie about their accomplishments; they reach Mars via an underfunded version of Robert Zubrin's "Mars Direct" scheme.

If I wanted to write the same novel over and over again, I'd do romances.

What's going on here? A. E. Van Vogt never worried about what a spacecraft cost. I don't think Isaac Asimov did either.

Nobody ever did until, in the 1950s, Robert Heinlein published *The Man Who Sold the Moon*. And nobody did again for a long time. Imitating Heinlein used to be normal, but the science fiction writers of the day couldn't imitate *this*. None of us had trained for it. The excitement of travel to other worlds is in our nerves and bones, but where is the excitement in *economics*?

Then we watched mankind set twelve human beings on the moon for a few days at a time, come home, and *stop*.

We saw our space station built in Houston, orbiting too low and too slow, at ten times the cost.

Thirtieth anniversary of the first man on the Moon, celebrated by grumbling.

My T-shirt bears an obsolete picture of Freedom space station and the legend, "Nine years, nine billion dollars, and all we got was this lousy shirt," and it's years old and wearing out.

Now is economics interesting?

Heinlein's D. D. Harriman used his own major fortune and every possible confidence trick to fund the three-stage spacecraft needed to set a human being (a midget: much cheaper) on the Moon. Heinlein showed the way, and the rest of us began to see the problems. Forty-odd years later, the science fiction community has caught up.

You could persuade yourself that that's the answer. One of Randall Garrett's pseudonyms built the economic foundation for an asteroid belt civilization (and I found it so convincing that I borrowed it). Gerard O'Neill and his students designed huge orbiting habitats, and it all began as an economics exercise. Meanwhile NASA destroyed our last working moonship, laying it out as a lawn ornament, and tried to burn the blueprints too, in a wonderful demonstration of what you can do in space when money is no object.

In 1980, when it seemed sure that Ronald Reagan would be president and his science advisor would be one of Jerry's brighter students, Jerry Pournelle gathered about fifty people at my house for an intense weekend. We called ourselves the Citizens Advisory Council for a National Space Policy. We were from every profession that deals with achieving orbit. Our assignment: to create a space program with costs and schedules.

We met four times during Reagan's eight years, and twice afterward. We generated the Space Defense Initiative and the renewal of the X-plane program.

The addition of a few science fiction writers was stunningly effective. We can translate for these guys! Lawyers, corporation heads, plasma physicists, NASA honchos, rocket engineers: they don't talk like normal people, but they can explain it to *me*. I myself translated one of our committee papers from lawyerese to English, with Art Dula (the author, a lawyer) hovering at my shoulder, while a party was going on downstairs. It was damn weird, but it came out readable. It's in *N-Space* under my title, which they kept:

"How to Save Civilization and Make a Little Money."

The science and engineering communities have also indulged in economics. "Faster, better, cheaper." Where else would we writers of fiction get our data? The movie *Mission to Mars*, just out, opened with technology straight from Robert Zubrin's "Mars Direct."

Then it went transcendental.

"*2001: A Space Odyssey*" did that too. It started with well-designed technology and sociology. Convincing, realistic. No insane clusters of whizzing asteroids; you can barely spot them. No noises in vacuum, not with Arthur Clarke in charge. Even the worst of today's movies at least try to match that ideal. And then the movie went transcendental.

Is there some reason you can't tell a story that big, and still find an ending?

I think I'm onto something here. *When you're out to take the universe, there is no proper ending.*

The conquest of the universe is *never* where you want it to be. How could it be otherwise? There's always something more, something next. Sputnik is in orbit? Put up a dog. Television from Mars? Put a camera on a rover! And always and forever, now we send a science fiction writer, or at least a human being, to look around, and touch.

In reality or in our minds, we will always be rebuilding the space program.

The Burning City took six years to write and was damned hard work in spots, but—a fantasy set in Los Angeles fourteen thousand years ago—at least it wasn't rebuilding the space program. I deserve a break today.

Now I'll try to turn "The Moon Bowl" into a novelette.

THE BURNING CITY
COLLABORATION WITH JERRY POURNELLE

In 1992 there were riots. My city of Los Angeles was partly burned. Friends were endangered.

What does a writer do when he's pissed off?

I started a story set fourteen thousand years ago, in the fantasy universe of *The Magic Goes Away*. There was a city they burned down every few years to placate the fire god . . .

It went slowly. It was a hard story to write, with a main character who grows up as a gangland thug and evolves into . . . something else.

I hike with Jerry Pournelle and his dog on the hill behind his house. We talk of many things. We talked about *The Burning City* until it became obvious that I needed him as collaborator.

And so Jerry (the sane one) came to write his first fantasy. It was his suggestion that the California chaparral as of fourteen thousand years ago was *really* malevolent.

We're working on a sequel, a tale of Whandall Feathersnake's daughter, *Burning Tower*.

They burned the city when Whandall Placehold was two years old and again when he was seven.

At seven he saw and understood more. The women waited with the children in the courtyard through a day and a night and another day. The day sky was black and red. The night sky glowed red and orange, dazzling and strange. Across the street a granary burned like a huge torch. Strangers trying to fight the fire made shadow pictures.

The Placehold men came home with what they'd gathered: shells, clothing, cookware, furniture, jewelry, magical items, a cauldron that would heat up by itself. The excitement was infectious. Men and women paired off and fought over the pairings.

And Pothefit went out with Resalet, but only Resalet came back.

Afterward Whandall went with the other boys to watch the loggers cutting redwoods for the rebuilding.

The forest cupped Tep's Town like a hand. There were stories, but nobody could tell Whandall what was beyond the forest where redwoods were pillars big enough to support the sky, big enough to replace a dozen houses. The great trees stood well apart, each guarding its turf. Lesser vegetation gathered around the base of each redwood like a malevolent army.

The army had many weapons. Some plants bristled with daggers; some had burrs to anchor seeds in hair or flesh; some secreted poison; some would whip a child across the face with their branches.

Loggers carried axes, and long poles with blades at the ends. Leather armor and wooden masks made them hard to recognize as men. With the poles they could reach out and under to cut the roots of the spiked or poisoned lesser plants and push them aside, until one tall redwood was left defenseless.

Then they bowed to it.

Then they chopped at the base until, in tremendous majesty and with a sound like the end of the world, it fell.

They never seemed to notice that they were being watched from cover by a swarm of children. The forest had dangers for city children, but being caught was not one of them. If you were caught spying in town, you would be lucky to escape without broken bones. It was safer to spy on the loggers.

One morning Bansh and Ilther brushed a vine.

Bansh began scratching, and then Ilther; then thousands of bumps sprouted over Ilther's arm, and almost suddenly it was bigger than his leg. Bansh's hand and the ear he'd scratched were swelling like nightmares, and Ilther was on the ground, swelling everywhere and fighting hard to breathe.

Shastern wailed and ran before Whandall could catch him. He brushed past leaves like a bouquet of blades and was several paces beyond before he slowed, stopped, and turned to look at Whandall. *What should I do now?* His leathers were cut to ribbons across his chest and left arm, the blood spilling scarlet through the slashes.

The forest was not impenetrable. There were thorns and poison plants, but also open spaces. Stick with those, you could get through . . . it *looked* like you could get through without touching anything . . . almost. And the children were doing that, scattering, finding their own paths out.

But Whandall caught the screaming Shastern by his bloody wrist and towed him toward the loggers, because Shastern was his younger brother, because the loggers were close, because somebody would help a screaming child.

The woodsmen saw them—saw them and turned away. But one dropped his ax and jogged toward the child in zigzag fashion, avoiding . . . what? Armory plants, a wild-flower bed—

Shastern went quiet under the woodsman's intense gaze. The woodsman pulled the leather armor away and wrapped Shastern's wounds in strips of clean cloth, pulling it tight. Whandall was trying to tell him about the other children.

The woodsman looked up. "Who are you, boy?"

"I'm Whandall of Serpent's Walk." Nobody gave his family name.

"I'm Kreeg Miller. How many—"

Whandall barely hesitated. "Two tens of us."

"Have they all got"—he patted Shastern's armor—"leathers?"

"Some."

Kreeg picked up cloth, a leather bottle, some other things. Now one of the others was shouting angrily while trying not to look at the children. "Kreeg, what do you want with those candlestubs? We've got work to do!" Kreeg ignored him and followed the path as Whandall pointed it out.

There were hurt children, widely scattered. Kreeg dealt with them. Whandall didn't understand, until a long time later, why other loggers wouldn't help.

Whandall took Shastern home through Dirty Birds to avoid Bull Pizzles. In Dirty Birds a pair of adolescent Lordkin would not let them pass.

Whandall showed them three gaudy white blossoms bound up in a scrap of cloth. Careful not to touch them himself, he gave one to each of the boys and put the third away.

The boys sniffed the womanflowers' deep fragrance. "Way nice. What else have you got?"

"Nothing, Falcon brother." Dirty Birds liked to be called Falcons, so you did that. "Now go and wash your hands and face. Wash hard, or you'll swell up like melons. We have to go."

The Falcons affected to be amused, but they went off toward the fountain. Whandall and Shastern ran through Dirty Birds into Serpent's Walk. Marks and signs showed when you passed from another district to Serpent's Walk, but Whandall would have known Serpent's Walk without them. There weren't as many trash piles, and burned-out houses were rebuilt faster.

The Placehold stood alone in its block, three stories of gray stone. Two older boys played with knives just outside the door. Inside, Uncle Totto lay asleep in the corridor, where you had to step over him to get in. Whandall tried to creep past him.

"Huh? Whandall, my lad. What's going on here?" He looked at Shastern, saw bloody bandages, and shook his head. "Bad business. What's going on?"

"Shastern needs help!"

"I see that. What happened?"

Whandall tried to get past, but it was no use. Uncle Totto wanted to hear the whole story, and Shastern had been bleeding too long. Whandall started screaming. Totto raised his fist. Whandall pulled his brother upstairs. A sister was washing vegetables for dinner, and she shouted, too. Women came yelling. Totto cursed and retreated.

Mother wasn't home that night. Mother's mother—Dargramnet, if you were speaking to strangers—sent Wanshig to tell Bansh's family. She put Shastern in Mother's room and sat with him until he fell asleep. Then she came into the big second-floor Placehold room and sat in her big chair. Often that room was full of Placehold men, usually playful, but sometimes they shouted and fought. Children learned to hide in the smaller rooms, cling to women's skirts, or find errands to do. Tonight Dargramnet asked the men to help with the injured children, and they all left so that she was alone with Whandall. She held Whandall in her lap.

"They wouldn't help," he sobbed. "Only the one. Kreeg Miller. We could have saved Ilther—it was too late for Bansh, but we could have saved Ilther, only they wouldn't help."

Mother's mother nodded and petted him. "No, of course they wouldn't," she said. "Not now. When I was a girl, we helped each other. Not just kin, not just Lordkin." She had a faint smile, as if she saw things Whandall would never see, and liked them. "Men stayed home. Mothers taught girls and men taught boys, and there wasn't all this fighting."

"Not even in the Burnings?"

"Bonfires. We made bonfires for Yangin-Atep, and he helped us. Houses of ill luck, places of illness or murder, we burned those, too. We knew how to serve Yangin-Atep then. When I was a girl there were wizards, real wizards."

"A wizard killed Pothefit," Whandall said gravely.

"Hush," Mother's mother said. "What's done is done. It won't do to think about Burnings."

"The fire god," Whandall said.

"Yangin-Atep sleeps," Mother's mother said. "The fire god was stronger when I was a girl. In those days there were real wizards in Lord's Town, and they did real magic."

"Is that where Lords live?"

"No, Lords don't live there. Lords live in Lordshills. Over the hills, past the Black Pit, nearly all the way to the sea," Mother's mother said, and smiled again. "And yes, it's beautiful. We used to go there sometimes."

He thought about the prettiest places he had seen. Peacegiven Square, when the kinless had swept it clean and set up their tents. The Flower Market, which he wasn't supposed to go to. Most of the town was dirty, with winding streets, houses falling down, and big houses that had been well built but were going to ruin. Not like Placehold. Placehold was stone, big, orderly, with roof gardens. Dargramnet made the women and children work to keep it clean, even bullied the men until they fixed the roof or broken stairs. Placehold was orderly, and that made it pretty to Whandall.

He tried to imagine another place of order, bigger than Placehold. It would have to be a long way, he thought. "Didn't that take a long time?"

"No, we'd go in a wagon in the morning. We'd be home that same night. Or sometimes the Lords came to our city. They'd come and sit in Peacegiven Square and listen to us."

"What's a Lord, Mother's mother?"

"You always were the curious one. Brave too," she said, and petted him again. "The Lords showed us how to come here when my grandfather's father was young. Before that, our people were wanderers. My grandfather told me stories about living in wagons, always moving on."

"Grandfather?" Whandall asked.

"Your mother's father."

"But—how could she know?" Whandall demanded. He thought that Pothefit had been his father, but he was never sure. Not *sure* the way Mother's mother seemed to be.

Mother's mother looked angry for a moment, but then her expression softened. "She knows because I know," Mother's mother said. "Your grandfather and I were together a long time, years and years, until he was killed, and he was the father of all my children."

Whandall wanted to ask how she knew that, but he'd seen

her angry look, and he was afraid. There were many things you didn't talk about. He asked, "Did he live in a wagon?"

"Maybe," Mother's mother said. "Or maybe it was his grandfather. I've forgotten most of those stories now. I told them to your mother, but she didn't listen."

"I'll listen, Mother's mother," Whandall said.

She brushed her fingers through his freshly washed hair. She'd used three days' water to wash Whandall and Shastern, and when Resalet said something about it she had shouted at him until he ran out of the Placehold. "Good," she said. "Someone ought to remember."

"What do Lords do?"

"They show us things, give us things, tell us what the law is," Mother's mother said. "You don't see them much anymore. They used to come to Tep's Town. I remember when we were both young—they chose your grandfather to talk to the Lords for the Placehold. I was so proud. And the Lords brought wizards with them, and made rain, and put a spell on our roof gardens so everything grew better." The dreamy smile came back. "Everything grew better; everyone helped each other. I'm so proud of you, Whandall; you didn't run and leave your brother—you stayed to help." She stroked him, petting him the way his sisters petted the cat. Whandall almost purred.

She dozed off soon after. He thought about her stories and wondered how much was true. He couldn't remember when anyone helped anyone who wasn't close kin. Why would it have been different when Mother's mother was young? And could it be that way again?

But he was seven, and the cat was playing with a ball of string. Whandall climbed off Mother's mother's lap to watch.

Bansh and Ilther died. Shastern lived, but he kept the scars. In later years they passed for fighting scars.

Whandall watched them rebuild the city after the Burning. Stores and offices rose again, cheap wooden structures on winding streets. The kinless never seemed to work hard on rebuilding.

Smashed watercourses were rebuilt. The places where people died—kicked to death or burned or cut down with the long Lordkin knives—remained empty for a time. Everybody was hungry until the Lords and the kinless could get food flowing in again.

None of the other children would return to the forest. They took to spying on strangers, ready to risk broken bones rather than the terrible plants. But the forest fascinated Whandall. He returned again and again. Mother didn't want him to go, but Mother wasn't there much. Mother's mother only told him to be careful.

Old Resalet heard her. Now he laughed every time Whandall left the Placehold with leathers and mask.

Whandall went alone. He always followed the path of the logging, and that protected him a little. The forest became less dangerous as Kreeg Miller taught him more.

All the chaparral was dangerous, but the scrub that gathered round the redwoods was actively malevolent. Kreeg's father had told him that it was worse in his day: the generations had tamed these plants. There were blade-covered morningstars and armory plants, and lordkin's-kiss, and lordkiss with longer blades, and harmless-looking vines and flower beds and bushes all called touch-me and marked by five-bladed red or red-and-green leaves.

Poison plants came in other forms than touch-me. Any plant might take a whim to cover itself with daggers and poison them too. Nettles covered their leaves with thousands of needles that would burrow into flesh. Loggers cut under the morningstar bushes and touch-me flower beds with the bladed poles they called severs. Against lordwhips the only defense was a mask.

The foresters knew fruit trees the children hadn't found. "These yellow apples *want* to be eaten," Kreeg said, "seeds and all, so in a day or two the seeds are somewhere else, making more plants. If you don't eat the core, at least throw it as far as you can. But these red death bushes you stay away from—far away—because if you get close you'll eat the berries."

"Magic?"

"Right. And they're poison. They want their seeds in your belly when you die, for fertilizer."

One wet morning after a lightning storm, loggers saw smoke reaching into the sky.

"Is that the city?" Whandall asked.

"No, that's part of the forest. Over by Wolverine territory. It'll go out." Kreeg assured the boy. "They always do. You find black patches here and there, big as a city block."

"The fire wakes Yangin-Atep." the boy surmised. "Then Yangin-Atep takes the fire for himself? So it goes out . . ." But instead of confirming, Kreeg only smiled indulgently. Whandall heard snickering.

The other loggers didn't believe, but . . . "Kreeg, don't you believe in Yangin-Atep either?"

"Not really," Kreeg said. "Some magic works, out here in the woods, but in town? Gods and magic, you hear a lot about them, but you see damn little."

"A magician killed Pothefit!"

Kreeg Miller shrugged.

Whandall was near tears. Pothefit had vanished during the Burning, just ten weeks ago. Pothefit was his father! But you didn't say that outside the family. Whandall cast about for better arguments, then said. "You *bow* to the redwood before you cut it. I've seen you. Isn't that magic?"

"Yeah, well . . . why take chances? Why do the morningstars and laurel whips and touch-me and creepy-julia all protect the redwoods?"

"Like house guards." Whandall said, remembering that there were always men and boys on guard at Placehold.

"Maybe. Like the plants made some kind of bargain," Kreeg said, and laughed.

Mother's mother had told him. Yangin-Atep led Whandall's ancestors to the Lords, and the Lords had led Whandall's ancestors through the forest to the Valley of Smokes, where they defeated the kinless and built Tep's Town. Redwood seeds and firewands didn't sprout unless fire had passed through. Surely these woods belonged to the fire god!

But Kreeg Miller just couldn't see it.

They worked half the morning, hacking at the base of a vast redwood, ignoring the smoke that still rose northeast of them. Whandall carried water to them from a nearby stream. The other loggers were almost used to him now. They called him Candlestub.

When the sun was overhead, they broke for lunch.

Kreeg Miller had taken to sharing lunch with him. Whandall had managed to gather some cheese from the Placehold kitchen. Kreeg had a smoked rabbit from yesterday.

Whandall asked, "How many trees does it take to build the city back?"

Two loggers overheard and laughed. "They never burn the whole city," Kreeg told him. "Nobody could live through that, Whandall. Twenty or thirty stores and houses, a few blocks solid and some other places scattered, then they break off."

The Placehold men said that they'd burned down the whole city, and all of the children believed them.

A logger said, "We'll cut another tree after this one. We wouldn't need all four if Lord Qirinty didn't want a wing on his palace. Boy, do you remember your first Burning?"

"Some. I was only two years old." Whandall cast back in his mind. "The men were acting funny. They'd lash out if any children got too close. They yelled a lot, and the women yelled back. The women tried to keep the men away from us.

"Then one afternoon it all got very scary and confusing. There was shouting and whooping and heat and smoke and light. The women all huddled with us on the second floor. There were smells—not just smoke, but stuff that made you gag, like an alchemist's shop. The men came in with things they'd gathered. Blankets, furniture, heaps of shells, stacks of cups and plates, odd things to eat.

"And afterward everyone seemed to calm down." Whandall's voice trailed off. The other woodsmen were looking at him like . . . like an enemy. Kreeg wouldn't look at him at all.

SATURN'S RACE
COLLABORATION WITH STEVEN BARNES

LARRY'S TAKE—

I tossed a phrase into an early story, long before I ever met Steven Barnes. It was just a bit of a story's back history; it didn't mean anything at the time. *The One Race War.*

Over the years my mind toyed with that phrase, elaborating it. Not so long ago, racism didn't even have a name; it was just a universal way of thinking.

Everyone on the far side of the hill is demons. We are the one race, the Platonic ideal of *race*, and we must be protected.

Despite the courts, despite the media, despite all the yelling of victims and "victims," people continue to color-code people. That perfectly normal line of thinking would lead to a horror, sometime in our future. I needed to *see* it.

With *Saturn's Race*, with Steven's help, I finally got to write about the One Race War. Let the story speak for me.

(And I've added some notes to Steven's.)

STEVEN'S TAKE—

Over the twenty-plus years that Larry Niven and I have collaborated, we've covered a lot of odd territory. From high-tech gaming to a future Olympics, from monster-haunted planets to stranded space shuttles, it's been a wild ride indeed.

We wanted our latest work to be something special. Because I had moved to Washington state from my native Los Angeles in 1994, it was growing more difficult to find the kind of relaxed time that leads to the generation of ideas and the meshing of creative gears. We had the Internet to link us, but we hadn't tested that. There was a real possibility that this might be the last book we wrote together.

(As of this writing, there lurks on the horizon a terrific

Niven idea involving asteroid mining and nanotech . . . so who knows?)

At any rate, if this was our valedictory, I wanted to be very certain that it was a good one. So we batted ideas around for months.

We chose to write a prequel to *Achilles' Choice*.

This was attractive for a number of reasons. *Achilles' Choice* was actually a novella expanded with wonderful art by Boris Vallejo. I feared our readers might feel a bit cheated by its length; but they've been gracious (as SF readers tend to be), and reviews and comments were positive. Nonetheless, we've wanted to tell more of the story.

We could further explore the destiny of Jillian, the woman who bet her life in an Olympiad which promises extended life and vast power to the winners, and death to the losers. Perhaps we could go sideways: tell another story set in the same world.

But first we've gone backward to explore the history of the mysterious entity called Saturn.

Achilles' Choice was a parable about the price ultracompetitive type A people pay to achieve their goals. Remember Achilles, the invulnerable Greek hero? The gods gave him a choice: a long, dull life or a short glorious one. It has been said that if world-class athletes were offered a drug that would guarantee gold medals and fame, but kill them within five years, 80 percent of them would say "yes." This is something that many people cannot understand. They look at a Muhammad Ali, stricken by Parkinson's, and think boxing should be outlawed. "Poor man," they say, certain that he regrets the day he stepped into the ring. Nothing could be further from the truth. The truth is that all men and women die, and too many of us die without even distantly reaching our potential. In the overall life of the universe, whether you live to 30 or 90 or 120 means little. What might mean something is the degree to which you tap every last bit of potential within you: physical, mental, emotional, and spiritual. And if you do that, during the moments you are in that space of total awareness, psychological time does not exist. These moments (sometimes referred to as the flow state) are so precious that mankind has pursued them in every form, even where such pursuit is risky or lethal.

It was easy to tell the story of Olympic hopeful Jillian. So strong, so smart, so basically decent, and doomed but for the intercession of the mysterious Saturn.

So, then: who was Saturn? That is the story we set out to tell next.

Larry and I had spoken of that time, in the not-too-distant future, when corporations would grow stronger than governments. Some would argue this has already happened (though William Gates wouldn't. LN). Seen from this point of view governments, as geopolitical entities, might seem to be dinosaurs stumbling blindly toward the nearest tar pit. But if they are eventually supplanted, they won't go without a fight.

Saturn's Race grew around this idea nucleus, adding a few more: life extension, a radical approach to overpopulation, the enhancement of intelligence by means ranging from surgical to electronic, the "Millennial Project" approach to privatization of space conquest, and a few other surprises.

And because we were touching so many bases, and ranging so far, we wanted the story to wrenchingly affect the lives of four extraordinary characters: Chaz Kato, survivor of the infamous Manzanar "relocation" camps and citizen of the floating island Xanadu. Clarise Maibang, security officer, and a woman walking a tightrope between two cultures: one virtually stone-age, and one already halfway to the stars. Arvad Minsky, master and victim of augmentation technology. And Lenore Myles, the beautiful, brilliant young woman who stumbles onto a terrible secret and pays a horrific price

Not all of these characters survive the book, but we fell in love with them anyway. Each has needs, drives, emotions. Each watched over our shoulders as the act of creation proceeded. Occasionally, they broke our hearts.

Don't get us wrong. We and they had fun along the way, playing with intelligent dolphins and sharks, a few asides at Hollywood's foibles, speculation on the future of Ninjutsu, and a dollop of virtual reality. Because there were a number of serious concerns in *Saturn*, the book had the potential to become didactic, and nothing kills a good read faster than a lecture. Our basic philosophy became: if we're having a good time, so will the readers! Judging by our initial feedback, it was the right way to proceed.

If *Achilles' Choice* had a basic theme about the hazardous peaks our best and brightest will climb on the way to the heights, *Saturn's Race*'s theme had to do with change and identity and the value of life itself. At what price is life extended? What enhances it best? Love? Intelligence? Wealth? Power? Under what pretext can it be taken from others legitimately? Given the power to impose change from without, without consent, how much change constitutes murder? When is mass murder not murder at all? And ultimately, who has the right to make these decisions, and how will we select them?

One thing is crystal clear: no matter what system we have, someone is going to end up on the top. In the past, status has been relegated based on inheritance, brute strength, political savvy, leadership capacity, "divine right," or a dozen other values. In *Saturn's Race* we propose another model. You may or may not like it. But you had better believe it is possible, and it may be our immediate future.

For now, be happy it's just a book.

Hey Steven! Hi, Tananareve!

Bob and I spent an hour in a deli talking about Saturn's Race. This is what emerged—and a lot of it is my notes made at his instigation and sanity-checked with him.

What I'm doing right now is writing very slowly and meticulously. I left the first chunks alone; I'll get there on another pass, once I've become more familiar with the characters, background, etc. Going into the meet with Bob Gleason, I was (and am) watching Chaz recover from the Barrister attack.

Here's what I wrote—

1. Don't panic if you see a check for only part of the on-acceptance payment. Bob is putting the whole sum through.

2. *Basic problem is not enough development of Saturn . . . that is Saturn himself, the villain. That's my job; I said you'd largely left slots for me to work. I told Bob it was going to be wonderful, and gave details.*

3. *He had some detailed suggestions, too. If what follows sparks any ideas, tell me what they are. I'm planning to do a lot with Saturn!*

4. *How does Saturn react (throughout) to Lenore?*

5. *To Chaz?*

6. *To Needles rescuing Chaz at the cost of being bitten by Barrister?*

7. *Saturn's opinion of Needles? Of Barrister? Of the linking program? Remember, all of these relationships and entities are evolving.*

8. *To heroes? Some minds can't see a hero or archetype. To others, there's a favorite. Who would Saturn be imitating? (This too evolves!)*

9. *To Poetry? Is there poetry that obsesses Saturn, that he can't figure out?*

10. *To fiction? If Saturn retrieves it from "memory," he never had the experience of reading it . . . only of having read it!*

11. *To the planet Saturn, or the Zodiac Saturn? Would these have meaning to such an entity? (The entity Saturn is not saturnine but mercurial!) (We can put permanent probes around planet Saturn.) (I noticed years ago that Saturn never disappointed anyone. Though a telescope Mars can be just a jumpy pink blur, but Saturn is always spectacular.)*

12. *Saturn is superintelligent and mad. Bob saw that much . . . but I find it more interesting that Saturn is evolving. His motives, his abilities, everything is changing. By the time Chaz confronts him—for instance—*

13. *He may have decided the attack on Lenore was a horrible mistake. He certainly knows (by now) how to chop off a few hours of Lenore's memory and seal it*

off without spreading damage. He can see how much more malleable Chaz would have been with a happy Lenore in his company. She must still be persuaded that any paranoid remnants are false . . . a challenge, at least . . . but sharks aren't herders.

14. *Saturn is always hungry. There's no on/off switch for a shark's hunger.*
   So much for Saturn. There is more to fix . . . . . .

15. *We need a better setup for the state in which we find Lenore after the jump. I can insert data: Confused and frightened and damaged, she thought of no better plan than to go on to where she had contracted to work. We find her there. (I haven't even noticed if that's already in place. It needs pointing out!)*

16. *Pg. 309–311: set up those global riots better. (I don't know how. Something will suggest itself. Maybe Nero spots something anomalous that Chaz ignores.)*

17. *Bob says: set up the meet between Lenore and Chaz. I thought you'd done that well, but I'll look again.*

18. *Life on Java. Give it detail or cut it, Bob suggests. I'll leave it in, Steve, for your next pass. If I don't see it get better, I'll chop it then.*

19. *Pg. 314—riots are described after the fact! I don't know of an editor who wouldn't flinch at that. I'll try adding immediacy before you see it again.*

20. *The best writing in here, says Bob, is Chaz and Lenore falling in love. After that Chaz turns shallow. He's right. I noticed it myself. I expect you're better at fixing that than I am, but I'll give it a shot . . . when I start my second run.*

21. *THEME: Privacy. Chaz spies on Lenore. Chaz's medical interface plug spies on him. Clarise of Security spies on everyone . . . spies on her husband, then ex . . . She may have seen him mooning over Lenore.*

22. *THEME: Mutability. The Chaz, the Saturn, the Lenore who end the book are not the same as those who began it.*

23. *Nail down the ending for Chaz! It's Shane! He goes off alone. Triumph amid the ashes. Chaz intends to use the Saturn power for good . . . but as we leave him, that power is all bluff! Bluff, and a fantastic plug that will interface with hardware and software that the Ninjas were able to duplicate.*

24. *Saturn knew how to use this. Chaz doesn't. But the Ninjas don't know how it works either, so they can't catch him being inept. He can grow into the role of Saturn.*

25. *"His servant he made me and thereby I knew him, But later betrayed me and therefore I slew him." It was scripted on an old dagger.*

The ninjas see Saturn (though they never have seen him!) as a man of honor. No crime of Saturn's will ever persuade them otherwise; because they commit horrors too. They would have to see Saturn betray what they see as his motivation; and must then persuade themselves that it's a trick.

Can we foreshadow this?

So Chaz is almost safe.

And we have seen what he became in Achilles' Choice.

STEVE—

YOU'RE RIGHT: Lenora MUST think like a very high quality mind. You keep writing and I'll work to make her lectures more lucid. Some will become dialogue, Lenora to Tooley.

This all hangs together better than before; the background details are clearer and fit better. It still feels like I'm butting my head against a wall. I can't get into it.

I've figured out some of the reasons. Lenora is badly flawed. Chaz is a little strange too.

Here's what has to happen—

We need to work together. We need a week.

I can't tell when you were trying to get at something. Some of this only needs to be said better, but some is blind alleys. I can't tell which.

So: for the moment I'm talking to an imaginary Steve. I can only go so far with that . . .

What we need is an outline. The outline we carved out together is likely to be obsolete. Do another, or rewrite the old outline thoroughly. Tell me where you're going, tell me what's on the way. I'm lost because I don't have a map!

First scenes: Lenora has been indulging in telemetrically operated thermal gliding. You said so later. Say so at the opening! Maybe she fled the setting sun and oncoming dark, just in time for the show. That would leave her fizzing with adrenalin, aware of every breeze . . . ?

Place her! There's lots of detail and no integration. It might help you see Lenora better.

Lenora is a basket case. There's absolutely no reason why she should be.

That night, she was alert for a chance to get laid. She wanted a job offer, too. But when Chaz made an offer, she went into full paranoia!

I can see her carefully considering pros and cons. Shying back from mixing business with pleasure, from screwing a boss or co-worker; I was warned about that when I was young, because an uncle did it. But that isn't what I see.

Everything's coming together in her life. I can see her reason pulling hard on the reins of her joy; but the joy isn't even there!

More: Her thoughts, her motives, her train of thought are all fragmented. She's using textbook philosophy to try to pull it together; integrated personalities don't do that. Lenora is crazy. If they looked at her hard enough to see that, they would have looked further, and seen her political alliances.

Why was she allowed at Xanadu in the first place?

This is bad narration too. Why shouldn't Lenora remain ecstatic and triumphant until she finds a dead nympho humping her roommate in the hall?

Chaz's studies: we need to talk. We need to winnow!

The spare ribs: is this so important as to deserve all this volume? I can't fix it without knowing what you wanted from it.

ALIENS. Yes, I'm good with aliens. I get that way one alien at a time. I practice with the individual alien until I understand it, until I know it.

I'm way behind with the squarks. . . . And I still need to talk about them with you. What they are is too nebulous; I can't work with them yet.

(By the way, if you dropped dead of sexual excess, I'd just go ahead and suck it out through my fingers. The book wouldn't be as good, but it would happen.)

MAKE A MAP. We'll trade it back and forth until it's right.

It's not my style to do the map first. I normally let the story evolve until I feel cramped . . . but I don't think we're jumping the gun here either! It's time.

Subj: proofs
Date: 2/1/00

I got a certain distance with this proofing job, but now I need help. And I've reached page 275.

The proofreader couldn't stand it and wants all Scaliens and Squarks in lower case. I can't stand it either so I gave in.

You left boldface crap throughout. Most were just for each other's attention, can be romanized. One was a note, me to you, excised.

"Schatoma." I took your word for this word. Proofreader can't find it. Is it real?

Planet Hollywood: disappeared? Is it a problem? I said, "STET, they might rebuild it." This scene is all nostalgia anyway.

Belsen becomes Bergen-Belsen?

"Zarathushtra" is old Iranian for Zoroaster. Make a decision: which?

Proofreader quarrels with your interpretation of Bombay history:

Ref Encyclopaedia Britannica on-line, in 1661 Bombay came under British control as part of marriage settlement between King Charles II and Catherine of Braganza, daughter of King of Portugal. I never checked any of this. What happened? What should our characters think happened?

I'll keep going. Get back to me soonest. They put a close deadline on us.

                                                                    Larry

Subj: Re: proofs

Date: 2/2/00

Good. (I've left "bought." Alternatives were awkward.)

Now tell me, so I don't have to read half the damn manuscript: is Pak Jute the Lurah?

Proofreader Brian Callaghan says "Mindy" pops up from nowhere. Wasn't on the 'cat. Suggests Crystal or Nadine?

Larry

Subj: proofs

Date: 2/2/00

We should have done a global search for <miles, feet, tons>, to turn English to Metric. Too late now. It's driving our reader crazy. I'm following his notes and using it to characterize: Chaz tries to use Metric but lapses into English; Levar won't even try. But the numbers are going to be loose and sloppy. We'll get letters.

Is Bay of Bengal a thousand miles (1600 kilometers) across?

Mitsubishi Wetcat, how many tonnes (kilotons)?

Subj: Re: Fw: Casimir effect

Date: 10/20/99

message dated 10/20/99 12:56:10 PM Pacific Daylight Time, Original Message—

Date: Re: Wednesday, October 20, 1999 1:00 PM

Subj: Casimir effect

I vaguely remember something about placing two plates very close together and being able to measure some force holding them together (?) due to particles being created and immediately annihilating each other with no net energy input or output. There isn't room between the plates for these particles to come into being to exert any pressure, but the particles on the out-sides of the plates do exert pressure. At least, that is my vague recollection of it. I have no idea how hard it is to do the experiment.

Peter

Without my actually checking, that seems to fit. There might be room in the story to embed that description . . . but not much else.

(Stories come in ideal lengths. I wrote a looong Draco Tavern story once, because I had to. I prefer vignette size.)

Larry

Title: Re: Greg Benford
Subj: hydrogen wall
Date: 1/19/00

Great! It's a good story. It's faithful to the original premise, and builds on it. You may have beat the rest of the field into print with another clever way to destroy human civilization.

The file transfered badly: O-with-accent for quotes, and unexplained gaps.

There were lots of typos too. You need to take another proofread. (If you leave him too much to do, a proofreader will keep fixing things after he's run out of mistakes. My theory.)

When you publish, I want a copy.

Larry Niven

Subj: My Soul To Keep
Date: 2/23/00
Steve

This is for Tananareve. If you'll send me her email address, I can go directly.
Tananareve:

I said I'd read your second book and get back to you with impressions, with an eye toward a sequel. I am to pay special attention to the immortals' culture we only glimpsed.

I didn't want you to think I'd forgotten my promise. I've read the book, but nothing is happening.

The problem, from my viewpoint, is that there's not enough of the culture showing to even suggest implications. But let's get together, whenever, and start a conversation. Maybe something will emerge. You may know more about these people than ever showed in the book.

Subj: Re: "Ringworld" rights and Mandell
Date: 12/11/99

Robert Mandell took an option on RINGWORLD, then exercised it. He holds all rights involved in making a movie, plus sub rights plus nonexclusive rights related to use of characters. I signed the wrong papers at least three times here, in my eagerness to get a movie made. If you can deal with him, buy his rights or get them legally discontinued, you can make a Ringworld movie.

Larry Niven

SATURN'S RACE

Taking the elevator back to his apartment, Chaz was caught three times by various Xanadu folk seeking audiences.

In the last year he had steadily and surely felt the hand of discipline closing around him. There seemed to be endless demands for his services, and it would have been impolite and impolitic for him to refuse.

There were standard linking questions: amplification and modifications to installed equipment bases. New equipment to be tested and installed in Xanadu and abroad. The operation of telemetrical systems around the planet and beyond. Interpretations of data from subjects like Barrister, questions about whether this or that action or reply could possibly indicate true intelligence or awareness.

Then there was the arena of finance. As little as it might mean to him, his money continued to amass, and there was a call from a broker. . . .

"Chaz?"

"Van Buren. How's the weather in Geneva?"

"Fine, thank you." Sober banker the fellow might well have been, but Chaz still remembered Van Buren's last visit to Xanadu, when Chaz had talked him into a descent to Squark City. It was hard to forget the image of Van Buren in full rebreather gear, goggle-eyed and incoherent at the sight of the first Squark dome ever shown to an outsider and fourteen armed and dangerous squarks juggling steel rods underwater.

Today: "I want to discuss the disbursement of funds for the month. You have a standing order for the purchase of Synaptech. We know that there will be a new offering soon and wished to be certain that you hadn't changed your mind."

"It's been awhile, hasn't it?"

"Yes, and frankly, we feel that there are some better opportunities available."

"I'm sure. Keep me there, Carter."

Pause. Van Buren didn't like it, but then there was no reason for him to. Chaz's motivations were not shaped by money here.

The image winked off.

The last call requested that he attend a board meeting in the afternoon. Decisions had to be made about copyright piracy in India. He made useful noises and signed off just as the elevator reached his apartment.

The door opened and closed behind him, and the new security systems went into operation.

Chaz entered his library.

He loved his collection of computers. It was hard to recall his enthusiasm over the Sinclair's membrane keyboard, or that he had once been involved in a lively debate defending the minuscule CRT screen on the Osborne as "Almost exactly the size of a paperback book held at arm's length," as if anyone read that way.

No outsider knew, or could know, that he had personally purchased every one of these at retail. But any citizen of Xanadu would understand.

And it was hard to believe that the Macintosh computer case had once looked so strange, or that its sealed system had once caused so much frustration to its devoted fans. If he used the special tool and took the case apart, there, engraved on the inside of the composition plastic, would be the names of the original design team. Flush against the right edge, halfway down the list, was the name Chadwick Kato.

Ten months ago he had waited until his standard meditation time and placed his apartment under full security seal. He'd established that habit long before the Lenore incident. It wouldn't attract unwanted attention. Chaz had disassembled the Mac case, and not merely to view the name of the young man he had been so many years before. He had rebuilt its innards.

* * *

He knew nothing of Saturn. How could he outguess an opponent of unknown intelligence, unknown experience, unknown background? But even the most basic understanding of human psychology would suffice to warn Saturn that Chaz would be disturbed by what had happened eleven months before. Chaz Kato could not be expected to leave this alone.

His apartment could be, *would* be, searched or bugged. Saturn was watching.

Chaz must be seen to react.

Publicly if quietly, Chaz had engaged the services of a detective agency to keep a steady, long-distance check on Lenore and her roommate, Tooley Wells. It was only after the terrible duel with "Saturn" that he realized that anyone who had been in close contact with Lenore might have been entrusted with dangerous knowledge.

He only guarded her. He had never approached Tooley Wells in any way.

Lenore had been targeted for death. Why? Lenore the thief and spy was a fiction, but what was the truth? Had she learned something? There were too many factors, and too much information, to sort through with his unaugmented mind. He could not even be seen asking the right questions. He did not believe that any level of security could protect him from Saturn.

He couldn't rely upon Clarise. He dare not even question her directly. But he needed to search.

This was his current solution.

Chaz lifted the ancient Macintosh down from the shelf and plugged it in. He touched the switch on the back, and the little "Mac" icon smiled at him from the middle of the screen.

Under routine security seal, sealed into a womb of privacy and silence, Chaz had, for the next half hour, a window of opportunity.

The screen blinked. "PLAY BLACK DOG?"

"N. PLAY PONG," he typed.

The screen lit up in black and white. A little white ball bounced from one side to another at moderate speed. It was difficult to believe that the game had ever been anything but a child's toy, but the simple blip-blip of it, called Pong, had once been the most popular computer game in the world.

Simpler, happier days. He was well practiced in the game, his coordination perfectly synced so that the minutes passed fluidly, his wrist flipping and flipping, catching the little ball of light as it zipped to and fro, until the score read 83101021—Chaz's age, plus the date.

He let the ball dance past his paddle. "Now Quest Gold," he said.

Inside the innocuous case was the most advanced processor that Chaz had been able to obtain secretly. Knowing that all of his accounts could be monitored, and most of his movements as well, he had done the only thing he could. He had stolen the parts. He needed a processor and an independent power source, so that Archie (the hardware) and NERO (the program) could sit in their shielded box and work even when the plug was pulled.

He took the VR headset from the machine at the far end. It was a standard Dream Park rental; hundreds were stolen out of the park every year. He rotated a component inside Archie and plugged the headset in and put it on.

A street scene formed, foggy, then sharp. Tall buildings and long shadows and a three-story brownstone dark with age. Sudden sounds: blatting horns, a prolonged shriek of bad brakes. Three antique cars danced with each other and the parked cars and dirty brick walls along the street. Chaz escaped a swinging chrome fender by jumping his character onto a parked car. All three cars somehow escaped with no more than dents and roared off in a wave of faintly heard curses.

The brownstone's front door emitted a tall, brawny, actor-handsome white man. He looked up at Chaz perched on the Heron's hood.

He said, "Dr. Kato, a problem. I can't let you in. I don't work here any longer."

This was new. "Some argument?"

"Resolved. But if you want him, you'll have to ring." He walked off down the street.

Chaz pushed the doorbell button. Waited. Would a program adapted from a detective puzzle game waste his time this way?

He tried the door handle. It opened. He walked in.

The office was locked. The front room was empty of life, barring a few *Polystachya* and donkey orchids. A clock above the sofas matched Chaz's wristwatch at just past six in the evening. At this time of day he wouldn't be on the top floor with the orchids. Chaz wouldn't consider invading the bedrooms and such, but . . . what would the game show? It might just kick him out.

Chaz was still exploring. The dining room was set with dinner for two, half-eaten. Small birds—squabs—tiny potatoes, a vividly orange tart. Squash? Carrot?

Chaz rapped on the kitchen door and went in.

Both men were massively overweight, though it didn't seem to bother either. Lupus Nero snapped, "Who the devil—! Oh, it's Dr. Kato. Doctor, I must apologize. Ritchie is in a snit, and of course we don't hear the doorbell in here. Have you eaten?"

The NERO game had featured a first attempt at full sensory input. In 2001 c.e. it had not worked well. Chaz Kato Senior had fiddled with it. This version would be upgraded one day when it was safe. For now there was only sight, sound, touch. Chaz couldn't smell the stench of cars outside, nor Nero's orchids, and what was the point of eating at Lupus Nero's table if he couldn't smell or taste anything?

Chaz said, "I've eaten, thank you."

Nero said, "Dinner is ruined in any event. Shall we continue in my office? Yes, Fritz, I'll tell him."

* * *

Chaz loved MAD MASTER. He'd grown ever fonder of it over the years. A kind of playful AI program designed to evolve varying answers and interpretations from a given set of data, this type of metaphor provided scenarios based on what it thought the programmed personality would have said or done had he been present. Companies used it to get virtual answers from absent bosses. Sons used it to figure out how a deceased parent might have dealt with a family emergency.

But there was fun and mischief in it as well. One could interact with a virtual Napoleon, or Attila the Hun or Jefferson or Robert Frost or Heinlein, or any number of fictional characters. All of this was originally in the spirit of determining how a computerized personality might react. What was awareness or creativity, what was mere information sorting?

And who wouldn't burn a library of books in exchange for the chance to be taught political science by Lincoln, physics by Hawking, American literature by Twain, or gender relationships by Hugh Hefner and Dr. Ruth?

The Y2K panic in January 2000 c.e. had driven good software companies out of business. Chaz had acquired a batch of commercial computer games nearly ready for market.

NERO, from Low Road Games, showed signs of haste: a bit too intellectual, and the sensory input needed more work. Instead of buying rights to the Rex Stout characters, Low Road had just made up new names. Chaz toyed with the game, then lost interest when his wife died . . . and no other living human being knew that NERO had ever been.

Chaz had written NERO into the character template in MAD MASTER. Over the past year, he had fed NERO random communications from members of the Council.

NERO couldn't have complete data access. Chaz could provide his desktop detective with all of the usual news feeds. He could carry copies of files for Nero to chew through. But he daren't allow his spy to make direct inquiries, or even draw a suspicious level of power.

One thing they could do was search for Saturn's "fist."

"Fist" was a nineteenth-century term used to describe the eccentric patterns of rhythm that would identify a telegraph specialist by the way he used the key. Programmers had individual "fists." Saturn's communications had been an impeccable weave of fabrication and disguise, but what Saturn had done, how he had done it, would suggest things about the man behind the curtain. Comparing Lenore's true metaphor patterns with Saturn's counterfeit might yield additional clues.

There was no way for Chaz to sort through possible variations. He wasn't even certain what he was looking for. NERO worked at it full-time.

Lupus Nero glared at what had been Ritchie's desk, cruised around it, and dropped into a chair big enough to hold him. He was Nero Wolfe exaggerated to four hundred pounds, and tall enough to loom. The green blackboard behind him nearly covered the wall.

He was holding his temper, but the effort showed. "Fritz would want me to tell you," he said, "that nobody enters my kitchen without Fritz's permission. Don't consider yourself unwelcome on that account, Dr. Kato. Without invitation I don't enter either."

"I'll be more careful in future," Chaz apologized. "Have you had the opportunity to look over the other material?"

"Indeed, Doctor. Eight months is a much longer time for me than for you. You have also increased the . . . ah . . . clarity of my thought through additions to the speed, depth, and number of the processors available to me."

"I hope they've been sufficient."

"No."

"Can you suggest—"

"Upgrades? The problem is not with my intelligence! Input may be the problem. My latest news feed came from Entertainment at six-twenty today, and I have a fax from Transportation concerning the proposed Ecuador Beanstalk." The blackboard was a window: it flashed displays to match Nero's words. "Both purported to be direct communications from their respective department heads, Yamato of Japan and the Nigerian who calls himself El Cid. Plausible?"

"I'd say so."

"I know everything you've learned in this matter, everything that makes its way into the media, and proprietary information gained from various sources through security lapses and carelessness, though you've restricted me to passive observation. If that were sufficient, I would have answers! This is the core of what we know."

The blackboard was running two windows now. One was a voiceprint of Saturn as he traded threats and bargains with Chaz Kato over dying Lenore. In the other, Lenore's cartoon animals ate into Xanadu's airport programs. The beasts looked odd; they were too agile; their legs didn't move right and didn't move often enough.

Nero said, "Is it clear that Saturn's metaphors are sea life? The pictures are Myles's, but they are imposed on fish." Certain animals flashed green borders: gazelles, giraffes, zebras. "These two—" Borders blinked on zebra unicorns. "—match very well with swordfish. The elephant is too supple," yellow flash. "Giant squid, I think.

"There are many marine biologists on Xanadu, but few have Saturn's abilities. I eliminated them first. I consider them again because *every* approach has failed.

"Doctor, let us examine what we think we know.

"First, what did Lenore Myles know? She may know that three equals one, as Saturn said. Chaz Kato the Third is Chaz Senior. Saturn is not trustworthy, but this would explain why she left you so abruptly. She spent all night and the next afternoon in the bed of an eighty-three-year-old roué."

Chaz winced; but these were his own suggestions.

"But this is not a killing matter! There are other ancients in Xanadu. A good publicist—spin doctor?—might sell you as a mere freak. People have often lived longer than a century."

"They couldn't do handstands," Chaz said bitterly.

"Don't do handstands in public, Doctor. Or join a circus! Brag of your abilities. Let the story fly free, fodder for the tabloids. Radical experiments done in secret. Ten die for every survivor. *You* would be exposed, but Xanadu's secret would be safe. Killing a witness would only make the secret more interesting. Dr. Kato, if you hadn't been suffering from sixteen years of survivor guilt, you would never—"

Chaz barked, "*Survivor guilt?*"

Nero shrugged theatrically; his flesh rippled. "You abandoned them all. Friends, business allies, and partners and rivals, the factories you founded, the people you hired and trained. Ako Kato's grave. Saturn's transparent justifications triggered your password, Dr. Kato!"

"Triggered my password." Chaz swallowed his fury. Only fools get angry at a computer program . . . and the damn thing was right. Saturn had pushed the buttons that turned off Chaz Kato's defenses.

"Where was Myles during her hours at Xanadu? What did she learn? The attempt to kill her in Sri Lanka suggests time pressure. If she committed some criminal act, there would be no need to fabricate evidence . . . unless her crime exposed or revealed some secret of Saturn's."

"If Saturn's a Councilor," Chaz objected, "why a crime? They make the law."

"Crimes against other Councilors, or against world opinion. We seek evidence of a wrongdoing that would force a member of the Council to act as swiftly and ruthlessly as Saturn has. How can I investigate such a thing? I am restricted to news feeds." The blackboard was flashing a stream of headlines. "I must be a passive listener. I dare not make direct inquiries, or even draw a suspicious level of power, lest Saturn track me to my virtual lair. Over eight months I've turned up nothing.

"I have eight months of computer activity from the twelve major and five minor members of the Council, and from every major power here on the island. The exception was Medusa, the cosmetics and beauty care magnate. Born Helena Schwartz—"

"You got *that*?"

"That and little more. Her security is better than the tools available to me. That might suggest something to hide, or merely a love of privacy."

Chaz liked Medusa, her public persona, but he'd never met Helena Schwartz. "Can she be Saturn?"

Nero said, "No. Ten days ago . . . Do you recall the crash of Continental LEO-33? I have two minutes of Schwartz unloading stock before the news broke. She was conference-linked to four cities in real time, and Ritchie picked it up. She does not have Saturn's fist. I spent some effort trying to falsify the source. Do you understand this term *falsify*?"

"You tried to show that the input isn't to be trusted."

"Yes. I could not falsify. It was Helena Schwartz, not a computer persona or an agent, and she is not Saturn."

"One down. Anyone else?"

"Yes. Saturn knows you well, perhaps through research, perhaps not. A Council member resides here openly, and he knows you. I have been able to observe behavioral aspects that might have been impossible at a distance."

"Arvad," Chaz said.

"Quite. Arvad Minsky is not Saturn either. His fist clears him."

"Who else? Wayne and Shannon Halifax? Diva?"

"Diva the Brahman, racist from a nation of racists. Her fist clears her, but she might be Saturn's ally or minion or master. What then? I know no way to question her. Shannon Halifax the former Playmate of the Year is too public to hide secrets, and I think her husband is too."

"Right. Joe Blaze?"

"Energy? That is Yamato. His fist clears him. Why, Doctor?"

"Country club white. Yamato's joke, I suppose." Hating himself, Chaz asked, "Did you consider Clarise?"

"Pfui. Clarise Maibang, second in Security, briefly your wife? Am I a witling? She might want Lenore dead for reasons of jealousy, but she has no legitimate access to the kind of power Saturn displayed, and how could she act under Whittlesea's eye? But I have her fist," and the blackboard showed the graphs. "Maibang plods. The woman is wary of errors, and she learned to read and write late in life. Her style is superficial."

Chaz's cheeks burned. Clarise deserved better than that! "Of course you're only judging her by how she uses a computer."

"I considered Whittlesea. I considered Tooley Wells, who came as Lenore's companion." More graphs. "Wells types very fast, then backs up to fill in the mistakes. Whittlesea's education and programming style are classical British. Paul Bunyon's fist is artificially generated, with a delay of five seconds while a human input is rewritten. His real name is Valentine Antonelli, and he was in a frenzy of strike negotiations over a conference network while you and Saturn were dicing for Myles's life.

"But Saturn's fist is highly skilled, methodical in his approach, brilliant in basic programming, and I cannot identify the source of his education. I wondered if he might have been taught to program before he learned mathematics."

"That's not so strange. Children do that."

"Not to such an extreme as Saturn."

"Who's left?"

"Nobody, Doctor."

Chaz said, "Damn."

"Regarding your interface plug—"

"Yes, I tested it. You were right. After I wasn't sick enough to need supervision, they told me they turned off the finder feature. It was a lie. The thing is still sending my location. Saturn always knows where I am."

"Only that?"

"No, it's reading my pulse and temperature too. It's a decent lie detector."

"Whether Saturn arranged that or not, we must assume he has access. You left it still sending?"

"I did. *Who is he?*"

"Shall we reexamine our assumptions? First postulate: only a Council member could intrude into your communication line at will. You may be better able to judge the truth of this than I. Can you think of a technique someone else might use?"

"No. I've tried. It wasn't some visitor, and we check the service people down to their DNA. I might still think of something." Chaz Kato, hacker. He'd never done that, never, and now it might cripple him. He'd known enough to protect his companies against hackers . . . sixteen years ago.

"Second postulate: only a Council member, or one directly empowered to act in his service, could have blocked communications to Sri Lanka and implemented the lethal procedures used against Miss Myles. Dr. Kato, I know exactly how all of that was done. Only a Council member could pacify Security here and at Sri Lanka while monitoring the Napcap system too."

"One or more."

"Worth noting, but our only avenue is to Saturn. We find his allies by finding the individual who announced himself to you. Third postulate: Miss Myles attracted lethal attention because of something that happened on Xanadu. Fourth, Miss Myles is essentially innocent. Her attempt to penetrate the air traffic control network is fiction. I have analyzed her fist; you were certainly right. She discovered something dangerous to Saturn. But was she innocent?"

"Have you—?"

"Lenore Myles did indeed share Levar Rusch's life and bed for nearly a year. She was faithful, and very busy at her studies. As for Rusch, he certainly organized the attack on Sandefjord. He procured the virus and arranged to move it to Antarctica."

"God! Could he have done it without Lenore's help?"

"Oh, yes, he certainly has that range of skills. Further, it was never Rusch's habit to confide in a lover."

"Where is he now?"

"That I could not learn. He vanished after the Antarctica incident. He may be dead. If not, he'll survive in some English-speaking region where his accent will not mark him. My estimate is that Lenore Myles did not share in his crimes and could not locate him now."

"Good!"

"Very well. Fifth," Lupus Nero said, and stopped to drink deeply from a quart-size glass of beer. "Ah. Miss Myles herself cannot help us unravel this mystery. Her memory of pertinent events was completely erased. Her mind has since deteriorated further—"

"Oh, God."

"Doctor, a cup of tea? Beer? A Calvados?"

"No, let's go on."

"Sixth, Saturn noticed Myles only after you gave her access to secured areas."

"Why?"

"She indulged in a dangerous sport, telemetrically operated thermal gliding, hours before you met. Saturn could have hurled her at a building, killed her or put her in a Xanadu hospital where he could work on her. Nobody's curiosity would have been roused, not even yours. And it was through you that she gained access to possible secrets. Elementary."

Chaz had to smile. "Good. So. What are your conclusions?"

"We know nothing of Saturn beyond what you learned during his attempt to kill Myles. The image 'Saturn' projected to you then matches no registered trademark, nor do its component parts suggest anything other than a carefully randomized ethnic and gender composite. I cannot match it to any member of the Council, nor to anyone directly connected to Council members, where such information is available. We have at this point examined the programming style of all persons who could possibly have access to such power."

Chaz said, " 'Saturn' was satisfied to let her live after wiping a portion of her memory. It couldn't have been a vengeance killing. It was preventive."

"It is suggestive that Saturn altered the record of her last research session."

Chaz nodded.

"She was not attacking an airport, but she was using a workstation. What *was* she doing? We can't read the record because Saturn wrote over it. What triggered her inquiry? Some conclusions might be reached if I had more access to the security tapes, all the comings and goings for Medical section for the hour before she began her research."

Chaz shook his head. "I can't do that."

Nero's simulacrum studied Chaz. "Do what you can. I have gone as far as I can with the present course of inquiry. Saturn's kinesthetic signature is no fiction, unlike Lenore's airport attack, but it doesn't match anyone with a legitimate, logical access to such power. I seem to be looking for the wrong 'Saturn.' "

"Suggestion?"

"The invisible postulate. We've assumed that the Saturn who confronted you is still waiting to be confronted."

"What?"

"You people alter yourselves in many ways," said the Nero persona. "You, Doctor, your knees have been replaced, you take chemicals to alter the behavior of the nerves in your brain, your exercise programs play you like a toy robot, and while you design and program computers, *they* shape *you*. Any Council member may have shaped himself into something beyond my grasp, by these means or by others known to you. Dr. Kato, this question wriggles in my mind like a double handful of fer-de-lances. Here am I, a mock-up of a fictional character from a line of puzzle stories. To know this is hard on my self-esteem. Here are you as you wish to be seen, and that too might be a matter of self-esteem. Here is Saturn, but is he human? Or a computer persona with an operator behind it, or a program running on its own? Or has he changed his intelligence and abilities until his programming technique is changed too? The Saturn we are investigating may be long gone. These are all possibilities, aren't they, Dr. Kato? I cannot explore them."

Chaz nodded. "But these suggestions lie squarely in my own line of research."

"A security officer could tell you much about the needs and fears and abilities of any Council member. Clarise Maibang is not Saturn. You have been intimate in the past. Try to pry something out of her."

Chaz logged off early. He should have time to exercise, to wear himself out. These sessions always left him twitchy, but this time he was in a rage. His mood might be noticed.

He stripped and chose a jump rope from his closet, a pulse-rate monitor built into the handles. "Sprint routine," he said loudly, and a hologram blossomed in front of him, an idealized version of his own body, dressed only in shorts, muscles rippling in shoulders and back. He'd never looked that good in his life.

The image took him through four minutes of sweaty warm-up followed by twenty wind sprints: ten seconds of all-out action followed by a minute of slower-paced work. Ten cycles of this and his body was so filled with lactic acid, he was so oxygen starved, that all tensions were blotted out by pain and exertion. Five minutes of cool-down. Three minutes of stretches. A shower.

He felt human again. As he showered, he felt the muscles in his arms twitching a bit. He was still angry, but at least he was in control now.

All right. He remembered the computer's words:

Try to pry something out of her.

Such cynicism was very like Nero. Chaz had bottled his rage then. He already knew that he was going to have to involve Clarise.

He had been lonely. He'd spent a year letting go, mourning his fantasy Lenore. Now he needed the woman he had pushed aside. But—he flinched. Clarise would be easy to hurt, and he'd *seen* the depths of her anger.

ICE AND MIRRORS
COLLABORATION WITH BRENDA COOPER

Ice crunched under her boots, loud in the silence. Trine's harsh sunlight reflected from a world of multifaceted ice and mineral crystals, surrounding her with rainbows. She was too exhausted to appreciate the display . . . but hey, it was pretty. Dark blue sky, brilliant sun, even through her blue blockers: awesome. What would it really take to warm this world?

She shivered. Hunger was finally getting to her. She hadn't been so cold the first few nights. Just alone. She was the only human on a planet surrounded by enemies; it left her very small and far away from home. She felt daggers of ice on her neck; the scarf and the parka's collar kept shifting. Should she have kept the pressure suit?

The blazing sun touched the horizon and was gone.

Kimber tilted her head to the darkening sky. The lights of the Thray starship should be visible soon. She leaned back against a slab of rock rising out of the ice. After a moment, she settled her backpack between her feet. It had to be kept close. She would die for what was in it, unless Eric found her first.

Would that surprise the Thray? They'd certainly surprised *her!* What had these aliens known of Kimber Walker when they chose her to bring to Trine?

The cafeteria at the Institute for Planetary Ecological Surveys was completely full. Graduating students milled about, competed for seats, shared laps when there were none, and moved nervously between groups. Kimber struggled to wait quietly with her best friends. There were four off-planet assignments available to a graduating class of over thirty students. Kimber feared getting stuck at the Institute as a teaching assistant or grant grunt. The last year had been *hard*; she'd fallen from third place to middle of the class.

Competing students had turned in psych profiles and agonized over résumés. They could have waited anywhere on campus. Most of them chose company and coffee.

Two of the three open surveys would take one student each. Those students would join groups of more experienced human surveyors doing spot checks on inhabited planets. One was a water world; the other was held by entities who lived beneath desert sand. The third survey would take two students as the only human members of a joint expedition with the Thray, an older star-faring race. The Thray planned to terraform and then inhabit Trine, a currently unclaimed world.

There was a hierarchy among species with interstellar capability. The United Nations was trying hard to buy or lease the secret of the Shift Trick, but none of Earth's visitors would even discuss the subject. Humans might join alien enterprises, riding spacecraft with interstellar capability. The Thray had ships that used the Shift Trick; but somewhere above them were unseen entities who enforced interstellar law.

The Thray could not approve their own occupation of a new planet. A neutral race must support any new planetary real estate deals. The Thray had drawn humans by lot. They would choose a survey leader and assistant surveyor from the graduating class.

Look the place over, then sign off on the Thray occupation. It sounded simple enough, but *interstellar flight!* A *whole new world!*

A frozen world to be reshaped. Thray had played tourist on Earth, always under wide-brimmed hats, with a dark glass hemisphere over each eye, except when they were exploring Earth's caverns. They would want a world like Earth. How would they go about making it?

One day humanity would be doing this.

Kimber's heart was set on the assistant job. It was the least of the off-planet assignments, but better by far than staying home. After six years she was desperate to test herself in the field.

The room was silent as results were read. The water planet went to Aaron Hunter of Hawaii. He groaned. Aaron was an amazing diver and swimmer, but he had developed a surfer's ear problem: mushy hearing, loss of balance. The sophonts were sea dwellers. Aaron would be living underwater . . . but Kimber knew he'd take the job.

The sand dwellers went to Wendy Lillian, the best of them at languages. Eric Keenen got the assistant position for the coveted job with the Thray, and actually had the bad grace to look disappointed. First in the class all the way through, he had been expecting the lead on that team.

Kimber's heart sank. She twisted her black hair around her index finger, grimaced as some of it caught in her rings. She stood up to leave, hoping her disappointment didn't show. She almost tripped at the sound of her name.

"Kimber Walker, Trine, Chief Surveyor."

She jumped, somehow tangling her hand further in her hair so she yelped. It was only when her friends Julia and Rick congratulated her that the job began to seem real.

Eric Keenen glared at her.

She'd be going down to the surface of a new world. Eric would fly between the stars, but it was unlikely he'd make planetfall. He wasn't the type to take that with good grace. She and Eric had fought each other throughout school after a bad relationship in her freshman year, but she had hardly seen him all semester.

It was a problem, but not enough to ruin her elation. That night, far from sleep, she watched the stars from her window until they faded to dawn.

The next month passed quickly, filled with finals and ceremonies, good-byes, and planning for the survey. She and Eric saw each other regularly as they completed plans, but always in the company of the advisor, Dr. Janice Richardson.

Star Surveyor II was the cabin and cargo section of a Space Shuttle affixed to the flat face of a massive silver cylinder with no breaks in it at all, no rocket nozzles, air-locks or access hatches, no windows or antennae or sensing devices, *nothing*. The Shuttle overlapped the edges a bit, like a cat fallen asleep on a hatbox. Dr. Richardson's office had a display wall, and the Shuttle/Wayfarer Basic assembly lived there for two weeks. Richardson could pull close-ups; she could set the pilot's display as a virtual flight test.

Kimber believed that *Star Surveyor II* was an embarrassment to Dr. Richardson.

"We can't get into the Wayfarer Basic module. Contract says we don't even think about it," she said. "We didn't even link up the Shuttle components. The Pillbugs did that, and they build the Wayfarer Basic too. But we can fly it."

"Show me," Eric said. And as she lectured, he questioned, argued, speculated, demanded. In Janice Richardson's presence Eric was loquacious. He never addressed Kimber directly.

"Communications. Are we talking just to the Thray?"

"By no means! Eventually, you'll send your results." A view of the lower floor of the Shuttle cabin. "We fitted the Verification Link module into two of the locker spaces. It connects to the Wayfarer Basic—the hatbox. You'll have a variety of sensing devices; we've labeled the sockets.

"But you, Eric, *you* don't communicate results. I was told there's no clear limit on what data you can store or request, so record *everything* in *every* interesting frequency. Make notes and speculations and complaints. You'll keep and organize the samples and data Kimber gathers from Trine, what both of you discover using the VL. The Link gives you access to the libraries of a hundred species, instantaneous information, if you can learn to use it. But you're barred from sending messages except library search queries."

Eric looked away, dark eyes fixed pointlessly on a spot where two struts joined. Kimber watched his rigid back while Dr. Richardson ignored him and continued.

"Kimber, you're the Chief Surveyor. Listen to Eric, but keep the decision yours. Only you can send results via the VL, and you only send *once*. You send all the data that might be pertinent, and your own verdict. *Go* or *No Go*. If you don't get a response, the only thing you can do is send the same message again." Dr. Richardson paused, looked them both in the eye. "Or a standard low-level SOS."

Eric asked, "They don't like to be bothered?"

Shrug. "Traffic across a galaxy, individuals in the trillions or higher . . . Eric, Kimber, how easy is it for a novice or a hacker to mess up just the Internet? You've the regular low-level access to query the libraries and can talk to the Thray all you want, but no other traffic, not even with us. We asked. There's a special onetime code that lets you send survey results. Now, we don't know where that message goes, or how. The Pillbugs, you've seen them, right? They're the source of the VL and the Wayfarer modules and a lot more. We think they're working for some other entity, some species at the Dyson Sphere level . . . but that's not my field."

Pillbugs were two and a half feet long and always came in groups. The workers she'd seen had hard-shelled back plates of silver armor that would lock when they rolled up. Any drop in pressure, a Pillbug could seal itself against vacuum and await rescue. Kimber had seen a dozen Pillbug workers do that at a loud noise.

While Richardson was instructing him on how to fly, Eric glanced aside just once. *Kimber, are you picking up on this?* But he still wouldn't speak to Kimber. In later days he flew the virtual controls whenever Dr. Richardson was out of the office. If Kimber wanted to fly, he gave her the pilot's seat and went elsewhere.

The day before take off, it changed. He became so insistent about little things in the supply-loading process that Kimber had to pull rank to make the final choices. The ensuing argument caused Professor Richardson to step in and deliver a lecture on chain of command and respect for commanders.

*   *   *

Star Surveyor II did not quite belong to Freedom Station. The aliens called Pillbugs *leased* them the Wayfarer Basic. They could reclaim it with ten months' notice. Without it the partial Shuttle was junk.

But Kimber had flown it virtually, and Eric flew it better. Let the politicians worry about contracts with civilizations they didn't understand yet—Kimber wanted stars and space.

They didn't bother with gravity assists, complicated orbits, or finicky burns. Those days were gone. Eric just aimed away from the sun and *left*. The greatest moment of her life, *their* lives, passed in choppy formalisms and silence.

The second morning they sat together on the flight deck under half a gravity of thrust, with a glorious view of stars and two tiny crescents. Eric presently made coffee—a complicated procedure because the coffeemaker was designed to work in microgravity—and brought Kimber a cup. He said, "Captain?"

"I thought I'd have your job, not mine," Kimber said.

"I know. So did I. After all, Kimber, what jobs have you been responsible for?"

"You could look it up." He had done that, of course. None.

"Doc Richardson thought I might manage this too, but the last night she reminded me Thray aren't human. They might look at different characteristics than we would when choosing leaders."

"Or teams." Kimber reached for the right words. "It's not like we got along in school. I hated it when you dumped Julie last year. It hurt her feelings a lot—"

"She pretend—"

"—Or me, years ago."

"Didn't you—"

"But that aside, whether I expected to lead or not, I've got to now. Eric, if you were me, you wouldn't turn it down, you'd do your best. As yesterday's grads, we've all got names to make. Reputations. I intend to succeed."

"I'm behind you, Captain. Mission-oriented. But Kimber, something doesn't feel right."

"Besides me having the lead?"

"That too."

"Well, all I feel is excited." She sat at the small table and sipped carefully at the hot coffee: a major concession on his part, and she'd better drink it! "Now, let's review today's task list and see if it changes as we talk."

For nine days *Star Surveyor II* was under thrust. The ship didn't require much of Eric's attention. Accommodations were roomy, and over the years students had added some modern amenities.

They played with the alien telescope, getting used to it, zooming on a handful of known asteroids, then amazing views of Saturn, Io, the tiny base on Titan.

Eric didn't talk much. Kimber knew why. She wouldn't raise *that* subject again.

The Verification Link filled two locker spaces on the Shuttle's lower floor. It was an almost-cube with a big hole in the middle. Filigree ran along the rims. Some of that was plugs for cameras and recorders and such. Some was hardwired buttons that would summon a variety of virtual keyboards. Some might be only decoration.

The hole in the middle was half a meter across. It bore the curled DON'T TOUCH symbol that all the interstellar species seemed to use, that looked *just* enough like a proofreader's takeout sign. There was a sense of optical illusion to the hole, as if it were deeper than the Shuttle hull. "Resonance cavity," Dr. Richardson had called it, for no obvious reason. "*Sure* it's been investigated. *No*, I don't know what was done or what was found. You don't touch the RC." Or BH (Big Hole, Eric's term).

Eric played obsessively with the Verification Link. Kimber had seen him in this state. In his freshman year, computer games had dropped him a full grade point before she talked him around. Now he was playing for higher stakes, for all the knowledge in the universe.

When Eric could tear himself away, Kimber took his place.

The VL set connected to a number of "libraries." One was the Smithsonian Institution in Washington, DC. Others circled other stars. She found translation errors, misaddresses, and when she finally got something right there were floods of information more likely to drown her than inform her. How did Eric stand it?

She found she could connect to the Thray ship *Thembrlish*. Kimber used the Verification Link to exchange pleasantries with Althared. Althared had served as an ambassador's aide to the United Nations; he had been at the Institute to choose the Trine verification team; but *Thembrlish* had never been near Sol system. The ship would meet them at Trinestar. It was currently light-years away.

Althared gave her an access code to the Thray home world library. Eric watched over her shoulder as she tried it out. It was murderously difficult. Thray had evolved as cave dwellers, and learned to expand and brace and carve their caves into vast city-sized networks. It affected every aspect of the way they thought. They loved the underground warrens of the Mars colony; they'd offered to help out. They'd terraformed a world in their own system. Trine would be their first interstellar project.

There was no way to test her link to the Overlord . . . or Overlord species, or Council of Species, or Overlord artificial intelligence program . . . the source of laws that even interstellar civilizations must obey. Kimber was to use the VL to reach that level only once. So much isolation made her uneasy.

Around Uranus's orbital distance, but nowhere near Uranus, Eric prepared to do the Shift Trick. Kimber made him wait until she could use the Verification Link to speak to Althared. She was in conversation with the alien when Eric made his move. When the stars around *Star Surveyor II*

swirled and vanished, Althared's display—and Althared—
never even blinked.

Kimber waited for the stars' return. If she was tense, Eric
looked ready to *lunge* at his instruments. He didn't move, he
didn't *breathe*. And there they were, a billion white dots
sprayed across the Shuttle windows, one very bright. Trinestar, Trine's sun.

Eric said, "I'd sell myself into slavery to know how that
works."

Then it was only a matter of moving inward, shedding velocity at half a G, staying above Trinestar's ecliptic plane.
Trinestar kept a dense, dangerous asteroid belt. Those resources would make Trine more valuable, and maybe easier
to terraform.

Trine was a frozen world, a white dot becoming a white
pearl. *Star Surveyor II* was in orbit before texture began to
show. Heights and depths, a topography as rough as Earth's
done in glare white and black shadow. The tops of mountains thrust through icy swirls of white like dark pearls on a
linen cloth. A gaudy egg-shaped Christmas ornament passed
below, painted in fractals, white and iridescent red with huge
curved windows in odd shapes. The *Thembrlish*. Drifting,
gone.

Free fall didn't bother Kimber when she could hold the
right mind-set. She was not falling, she told herself. She was
floating. Floating, looking down like a goddess on her
world; and her world was good. Fifteen minutes passed before she stretched and reached for her pocket sec' to dictate
some subvocal notes.

Eric drifted forward. Kimber didn't stop him, didn't even
speak to him. She was bored with his reserved distance.

The Thray ship drifted back . . . oh, of course. Eric was
matching course. A tube snaked out of the white-and-
crimson sphere and fumbled about until it lipped the Shuttle
airlock.

Regulations required one of them to stay on board. Eric looked resentful as Kimber left him and went into the Thray ship.

She walked through a maze of twisty passages not much wider than her outspread arms, keeping to the gold carpet. Gold marked her path, and marked out gravity. If she left that path she'd be falling. Thray drifted past her, facile in free fall, ignoring her but never brushing her. Armor covered them, not pressure suits, just protection. Their joints bent oddly; otherwise, they might almost have been human. She saw only half a dozen crew before the corridor suddenly ballooned out.

Thembrlish's viewing deck was so huge that *Star Surveyor II* would fit inside and leave room for seats along the wall. She followed the golden strip around and bowed to her Thray contact.

Althared's face glowed with a milky white translucence. Veins of blue liquid moved just under the skin and pulsed through the darker blue of his mouth. Large almond-shaped eyes were inset deeply on each side of his head. When he bowed, he turned his head left, his right eye holding hers. Then he stepped forward, took her hand, placed his other hand on the small of her back and turned her and jumped.

He had big hands, long and fragile fingers. His hand covered most of her back. She couldn't help thinking of a tarantula, and falling distracted her. She flinched violently before she got herself under control.

Althared didn't seem to notice. He turned her so they looked out on the patterned whites and grays of Trine in a floor-to-ceiling window. Althared spoke softly, his voice audible only through the translator at his throat.

"It was once a green planet. We intend to make it so again."

"How?"

"It would warm itself in a million years. We will not wait. We will reflect sunlight down onto the surface from a hundred thousand klicks around. We will pour heat onto the planet until the ice melts. Even as little as we like cold, we believe we can live near the equator in less than a hundred years. Most of the landmass is there. We will begin as soon as we get your positive report." He gestured, and a hologram of Trine appeared in front of them, superimposed on the image of the real planet in the window. As it rotated, she saw the ice pull back slowly, then faster, until continents and seas emerged between two great caps of ice. "This, Kimber, is our goal. Your survey will clear us to start down that road. A base camp has been prepared. We made maps in anticipation of your arrival."

"My world has been like this," Kimber said. "Twice." Eric had told her that. Suddenly she wished she had listened more carefully.

"Early in its evolution, I expect." Althared wasn't interested.

The map was still up. The roughness under Trine's white blanket, lines of mountain ridge, clearly shaped a large and two smaller landmasses, all near the equator, leaving vast white curves north and south.

Her thoughts caught up. Training told Kimber to choose the base camp. She grimaced, then asked, "Where did you put us?"

She didn't see Althared's hand move, but the map zoomed on a white nothing, well north of the equator. Two red dots became domes painted red and black, like the pattern that marked *Thembrlish* itself. They squatted in a sprawl of temporary roads, white on white. Kimber blinked.

"Althared? Did you put the base camp on an *ocean?*"

"Yes, that must once have been an ocean. It made an easy landing field."

"But what can you possibly expect us to *learn* there?"

"Here and here are islands not far below the ice. Peaks protrude here. No? Then choose a place. We will move the camp."

Irregularities sprawled along the equator, touches of shadow under the ice. Two big continental masses, narrowly separated, reaching no more than fifteen degrees north and twenty south. A third mass, far west and much smaller, still equatorial. A handful of islands farther north. They'd have Thray names . . . would they? Kimber tagged them. Blotch was the size of Asia or larger. Internal magma flows had stretched the next largest mass like taffy, she thought, giving it the curve of an integral sign. Black mountain peaks followed the spine. Integra, she called it. The shadow shaped like nothing in particular, she called Iceland. What the hell, she could change it later.

Kimber pointed at near random, below a black ridge of mountain peaks, Integra's spine. "There."

"Direct overhead sunlight on such a vastness of ice might hurt your vision. Too much of this world's atmosphere has frozen out. The sunlight is not thinned."

She looked at Althared's profile. It never showed anything at all. She'd been told that the human face evolved to convey messages; it was not so for other species.

"I brought blue blocker glasses," she said.

"Moving camp will cost us perhaps thirty hours. Return to your ship."

"You're back?"

Kimber sounded defensive even to herself. "They put our base camp in the middle of an ocean!"

"Show me."

"What was I supposed to *find*?"

"Mmm."

"So they're moving the camp."

"Where? Show me." He'd forgotten who was in charge again, but at least he was talking. "That looks mountainous. Was it your pick?"

"Yes. Why?"

"Oh, I'd have . . . here." He pointed at the center of a sketchy Y, white on white, hard to see. "Might be two rivers converging. The point is, you picked it."

"Eric, I told Althared that the Earth has been frozen twice. *You* told me that, didn't you? Years ago? Frozen right across the equator, pole to pole, you said."

He grinned. "I thought you'd stopped listening."

"I didn't stop listening. I stopped helping you do your

homework when I had my own courses. But is it still true? Since the aliens came, the facts change pretty fast."

"They sure do. Captain, do you see where the continents lie? Right along the equator?"

"Yes."

"What we used to know, what *every* geologist *knew,* was that the Earth has a stable state. Ice ages come and ice ages go, but if we ever froze all the way, the albedo, the Earth's reflective index, would shoot up near a hundred percent. We'd still be getting sunlight, but it would all bounce off the ice, right back to space. We'd be frozen forever."

"Uh-huh."

"We *knew* this, like we once knew that continents don't move. Then some geologists found evidence that Earth *was* frozen. Twice. The record is in the rocks, but what they knew was crazy. If the Earth was all one glittering icy pearl, how would it ever warm up?"

Kimber speculated. "The sun could flare, if you wait long enough. Or a giant meteoroid impact?"

"Twice? Oh, all right, but try this. You know that carbon dioxide is a greenhouse gas?"

"Sure, and water vapor too."

He waved it off. "Water vapor freezes out in an ice age. Rock absorbs carbon dioxide by making limestone. But if you cover whole continents with ice, you've covered the rocks. Limestone formation stops, carbon dioxide builds up, heat gets trapped, and that's how an ice age ends."

"Oh. *Oh.* What if the continents are all on the equator?"

"Yes! Yes, Captain." Was it *that* startling, that she should have an insight? "On Earth it was all one continent then, but it's the same with Trine, the ice cover is nearly complete before limestone production slows down. Now the only question is, how are the Thray going to warm it?"

"Sunlight," she said. "Mirrors. From a hundred thousand kilometers around, Althared said."

"Ten-to-the-fifth klicks radius? That's . . . Kimber, it's pi times ten-to-the-tenth, that's thirty billion square klicks of mirror."

She shrugged.

"Kimber, how do you talk to a Thray?"

"Althared is the one who talks. I don't know their language at all. There are heat flashes in it, and some fine muscle structure around the breathing orifice—"

"I meant, he looks so fragile."

"Fragile. Right. Think about what we'd look like to a gorilla." Ugly? Had Eric been about to say *ugly*? That was the first thing any student unlearned.

Eagle was a Wayfarer Minim, Pillbug built, a sealed hockey puck with a small cabin and cargo lashings bolted on. It rode in the bay of *Star Surveyor II*. There were four seats, one built for Thray. Two were folded down.

Althared was wearing a full EVA pressure suit. He looked like a cluster of clear balloons and took up a lot of room. At Althared's insistence, Kimber too was in "Moonwalker" pressure gear. She'd packed a wealth of skiing and cold weather equipment in the cargo hold, but in Althared's view this world was nowhere near that friendly. She'd try it his way.

Althared pointed out the base camp, two big domes dropped by the Thray's heavy lifter. When they got close enough she saw four of the large slow insulated vehicles called Skidders. Reflectors marking the survey boundaries bounced the midday sun in multiple directions. From the sky, the reflections looked as bright as artificial lights. As they climbed out of the Shuttle, Althared darkened his faceplate against ice blindness. Kimber flipped her filter down.

Now it begins. Sweat trickled down the back of Kimber's neck.

By strict Bio/Geological Survey doctrine, Kimber was supposed to be neutral. Still, the Thray were powerful galactic citizens, and she felt like a small child wanting to please a parent. Humans were so new at this, how else was she supposed to be?

Luckily, all she had to do was use what she'd learned in

school, prove Trine had not been recently inhabited by a sentient species that might have a valid right to it, and that the planet held no insurmountable intrinsic threats to life. It should be easy. The Thray had already done the preparatory work. She would review their notes and do her own independent survey, and the Institute would grant their claim. Kimber and Eric would have real jobs well-done for their résumés.

Thray biology required heavy insulation against the constant cold. Althared worked with her for three days, but she could see his discomfort. He showed her how to read Thray maps and made sure she knew how to operate the ice Skidder that would be her transportation. She looked forward to every morning, even though she still felt like a child compared to the solemn and brilliant Thray she worked beside. Althared shared information with her about Trine's dry, cold climate and ferocious windstorms. He'd made sonar maps of the layers of ice around the base camp. He was willing to discuss the terraforming process they would use. He asked numerous questions about Earth and humans, but he already knew a lot about human history.

Kimber fell into bed too tired to undress each night. The fourth morning, she found the courage to announce she would begin going about on her own.

Althared politely withdrew, and Kimber finally felt in charge and free to start work. She would be in constant instrument contact with Eric, working almost side by side if not in the same physical space. She hoped it would strengthen their working relationship.

The next morning she went out without a pressure suit.

It was no-kidding *cold*. Kimber was geared up for skiing in Nevada or Vermont: two layers of everything, more than that under her parka, a ski mask and fake fur hat with a brim, Blue Blockers, real cross-country skis . . . it was enough. She'd wondered if scents in the air would tell her anything. She smelled nothing but the cold. But she could move more freely, she could snack as she moved . . . and she felt closer to Trine.

She spent two weeks following the Thray maps. Hundreds of detailed readings were beamed between her Skidder and the ship daily using straight sight, handheld tools, and the instruments in *Star Surveyor II*. It would all go to Eric and into the Verification Link.

Where she could reach rock, she found fossils of long-dead plants. The Thray already had an extensive collection; but some of the species she found weren't in their records. She named them. Now they were hers.

She traveled alone except for her link to Eric. She must be extremely visible to the orbiting Thray ship, neon orange parka on glittering white; but she saw Althared only periodically, and always at base camp.

Kimber shuttled samples up to Eric. He did not discuss interpretations of her finds. They talked daily, but only briefly unless they were calibrating instruments on the ships.

She remembered that they'd had the same interests when they moved in together. It was wonderful. They talked . . . *he* talked, mostly, but she learned. That was when their studies were the same. Going into their junior years, their courses had changed. He would still talk about what interested him, but now it was a distraction she couldn't afford. Finally, she'd said so. For a long time, he hardly said a word to her.

Now he'd become the talker again, losing a touch of the reserve. Shutting a man up was supposed to be easy. Dammit.

She tried. "The winds are ferocious. I'd guess there's nothing to stop it, no barriers, just flat ice across most of the planet."

"Mmm."

"The carbon dioxide, did you notice? Three percent."

"Yeah. Strange. No variation?"

"About a percent. The wind mixes the air up pretty good. The continents are all under tons of ice, right? No limestone formation. Where's all the carbon dioxide?"

". . . Right. Can you spare me for half a day? I can do a pole-to-pole orbit and see if the CO_2 is freezing out."

"Go for it."

The next morning Kimber took her Skidder farther out than before. Althared had indirectly requested she stay inside the survey boundaries, and she had until now. But the sonar map showed greater area, the winds had eased off, she was on schedule, and she had legal access to the whole planet. She left quietly after filing a vague plan with the base camp computer.

Kimber drove out toward a simple sector between mountains and probable ocean, colored yellow on the map to represent tundra fields. Her hope was to get a horizon view and maybe dig into the permafrost looking for evidence of past warmth. The first hour she rode across bare flat fields of ice. Dips and rises in the terrain made the horizon line elusive, and she traveled fast without stopping for samples. In two hours she'd gone twice the distance her filed plans called for.

She came over the top of a low hill and found herself dropping fast, manhandling the Skidder through ravines of sharp clear ice punctuated with dark gray and black upthrust rock. Twice she could only move forward by using the Skidder's weight to push through thin walls of ice: running water frozen in bright sheets, like waterfalls trapped by winter back home. She emerged from the twisted chasms into a narrow white valley, and stopped to check her map. Getting lost now would be *bad*.

She hadn't made a mistake: the coordinates she showed were marked as tundra. Surprising . . . but the most extensive Thray mapping had been done elsewhere, on a frozen ocean.

"Eric?" she called.

"I'm back. Where are you? You just lost three hundred meters of elevation."

"I'm in a canyon. It's not on the Thray map, but it's big. Different too—I can see more rocks and less ice."

"Glad you're OK. Kimber—the poles are too warm to freeze carbon dioxide. *I* don't know where it's going."

"OK. Later. Please scan the area south and east of me."

"*Oui, mon Capitaine!*"

She sent him up a few still pictures to give him her

viewpoint, and to show him the canyon's stark beauty. Then she flicked the Skidder back into forward gear. Traction was good and she relaxed and watched the scenery. Tall spires of rock stuck up in the canyon wall, encased in ice. It was a strange formation—usually a long freeze like this would not make such straight walls, but maybe a river had run through here at some point, cutting the ice down and leaving the flat valley she was traveling through.

Eric's voice sounded in her ear. "OK. I can see where you are. The canyon goes for two miles. Scanning. Hey—some of that looks like cavities. You might be above water."

"Not water. At these temps, it would freeze anywhere near the surface. Air pockets?"

"They'd be *big*."

She looked carefully at the ice ahead of her but it seemed to be all the usual shades of white. Then she had to push the Skidder through another thin sheet of frozen ice. She found herself staring at thick ice over a rock overhang. Below, the distinction between ice and rock faded into deep shadows.

"Eric," she called, "I've found a cave."

No answer.

She clambered backward to stand by the shattered hole she and the Skidder had made in the ice curtain. "Eric?"

"Here."

"Good. I found a cave. I'm going to explore. I don't think we have good com, so expect to hear from me in about an hour."

Kimber belted tools around her waist and turned her headlamp on before heading toward the back of the cave. The light bobbed up and down as she walked, making it hard to focus clearly on what was ahead of her. The cave wall appeared to be unnaturally smooth and to turn right near the back. She traced the wall with a gloved index finger for balance in the choppy light, and found herself passing through a natural doorway. She stood still, flicking on her handheld light to augment the headlamp. Her breathing stopped, and then started again jerkily. As the light traveled around the small room, she stopped it multiple times to highlight crude drawings on the walls. Finally, she rested the light on a fig-ure huddled in the far back.

The frozen bones were large. Whatever wore them in life was more than twice as tall as Kimber, and it sure as hell wasn't a Thray. The hollow bones reminded her of birds; the joints suggested the artist Escher. They differed greatly from Earthly designs. There was an elongated spine—twelve-centimeter-long vertebrae, oddly interlocked—and long bones that could have supported wings. She found scraps of leftover flesh frozen in strange shapes on the bones, like a mummified Andes sacrifice. How could the Thray have missed this in their survey? It couldn't be the only accessible example of the species.

This might be just a cave-nesting bird, she thought. Thray would explore caves; the artist might have been a bored Thray surveyor.

Bored, during a thirty-hour survey? She didn't believe it. Still . . . aliens . . .

She looked for more.

The angular drawings had been hacked and gouged into the ice. She found the tools: four flint fist-axes repeatedly dulled and flaked sharp again. The tools would have been too small for Althared's hand. Would have hurt him, too. But the birdman's fist was its foot: powerful, with toes become short fingers. She held the frozen bones near a fist-ax and saw a plausible grip.

She took pictures. She set up a light for a central piece as big as all the rest. The rest had been just practice, she thought. A maze . . . or an abstract . . . but the shape teased her mind. Suddenly she saw it, a bird in flight, a match for the bones she'd found.

She stepped outside and beamed the pictures up to Eric. Then she returned to carefully add some tissue samples and artifacts to her backpack. She'd see what he'd have to say about *this*.

It was late. Safer to camp by the cave than to head back. She sent her coordinates at *Star Surveyor II*, then set up her tent under a ribbon of starlight between the canyon walls. As she rolled off to sleep, questions nagged at her. What if the Thray hadn't missed this? What if they knew about it and mapped it as tundra on purpose? Why hide it at all?

As the brilliance of the stars faded in the pale morning light, her suspicions of the previous night felt like unnecessary ghosts. *Of course* she'd find things the Thray had missed. She'd given them less than thirty hours to survey *this* region.

The unprotected surface of Trine was a cold place to sleep. Kimber packed up hurriedly and drove as quickly as she could safely navigate back to the Thray base. Two Thray looked up from the mouth of the cavern they'd been digging. Neither was Althared, so they couldn't talk, but one helped her lift bags into *Eagle*.

At *Star Surveyor II* she crawled through the hatch (flying, not falling) and called out, "Eric! Help unload."

He came, flight deck to lower deck, kicking once at the wall. He'd grown skilled in free fall. "I come, O my Captain!" He eeled past her without stopping.

She didn't like his tone. She didn't like her own either: too commanding. Then again, she wasn't particularly happy with him. "Eric, why haven't I gotten any compiled results back? It's been like sending stuff up into a black hole."

He wiggled out of the hatch, pulling a padded stow bag behind him. The massive bag must have massed as much as he did. He set it coasting, then got behind it and pushed it toward the lab.

Kimber followed him with another bag. He helped her stow it. When he finally spoke his tone was reasonable. "I haven't got anything intelligent to say yet. I've been looking for cross-reference material in the Link libraries. Besides, what you sent last night changes everything."

"We only have two more weeks here."

"I know," he said.

"I need to compare what I sent so far with the new data.

There might be clues we missed in the early analysis. I feel like I've been in a sanitized zone all along, and picked up only lies."

"We have the Link libraries. I've been learning how to access them. Kimber, doesn't it bother you? They *know*. They all know the answers to all of these questions, everything we want to learn. We're still guessing."

"Eric, what is this? I've never seen you quit."

"Who said anything about quitting? I'm just not interested in dying. Let's see what you brought, Captain."

Dying? Kimber laid out samples and photographs for his review, backed against the Velcro display wall. "Any ideas?"

Eric shook his head.

"Come on," she chided. "You scored A's in xenobiology. What is this thing? Is it something we know about?"

"I've never seen it. Is it a tool user?"

"Yes. Cave drawings . . . friezes, really. Rocks to carve them. This bit of skin, I thought it might not be *his* skin, but *this* came off its skull, so it is. We'll compare the genetic coding. See if it wore clothing."

"Did you tell Althared about it?"

"No. I want to learn more. But I also don't want to insult Althared. I just want to know more and then tell him."

"I think it's gone beyond insult, Kimber. You think you were in a sanitized zone? With *this* in it? They *had* a sanitized zone all ready for you, out on a frozen ocean! You wouldn't have that. *Don't* tell Althared anything."

"Eric," she said carefully, "when I talk to Althared, you're never in front of the camera. Am I wrong?"

"I didn't think you'd noticed. I can't look at an . . . at some kinds of handicapped people either."

"He's ugly?"

"Hideous."

"Are all aliens ugly?"

"Oh, no. Pillbugs are wonderful. This thing, *look* at that wingspan. Birds are beautiful."

"Buzzards aren't."

"Have you seen buzzards fly? Damn right they're beautiful. Are you accusing me of making villains out of the Thray? By reflex?"

"I think it's worth looking at."

"How could the Thray not know about these creatures?" Eric swept his hand above the neat piles laid out on the Velcro. "And if they knew, why hide them? A world freezes. All life dies above the one-celled level. By and by the Thray come along. It's tragic, but what's the problem?"

"Eric, what *is* the problem?"

"The problem is that you and I might keep looking. Might find something more. I think we both win if we live through this survey."

Paranoia.

Kimber started punching up biological species records looking for matches with large birdlike species. Even if it was sentient, it didn't have to be a starfarer. Maybe it had never been cataloged. She didn't find anything that looked right in the databases, and that increased the odds that it evolved here.

"Kimber," Eric said, "while you were gone I found a reference that indicates the Thray may have been here about a thousand years ago. That was *before* this thing died."

"That's not possible, the first survey was less than a hundred years ago," she said.

"Remember, the Thray prepared our briefings. I went looking in other libraries until I found an archived reference. They didn't call it Trine, and it wasn't ice, but the coordinates fit."

"Why hide it?"

"Carbon dioxide. Maybe Trine froze recently." He looked at her stony expression. "The poles are too warm. The CO_2 isn't freezing out. If the continents haven't been covered for more than a thousand years, then that's when limestone formation stopped—"

"Then the Thray froze the planet? Damn it, Eric! You're accusing a whole species of premeditated genocide! If we're wrong, if we accuse the Thray of a crime this big and we're *wrong,* we'd be lucky to be teacher's assistants in some backwater for the rest of our lives, and not in prison, or extradited to some Thray cavern to face their judgment! Of which we know nothing." She hadn't planned to say any of that. She hadn't quite known it was in her head.

Eric asked, "Did you ever wonder, Kimber, why they chose you? Your psych profile was the most compliant of all of us, at least with authority figures. I know, I looked it up when I lost the job to you."

"And if we're right, if they even guess at what we're thinking, they'll swat us like two flies," Kimber said. "But they have not done anything threatening. Althared is always friendly. He's given in on several points."

Eric silently pointed at her photographs of the flyer's bones.

Damn him anyway. She turned her searches to planetary magnetism and technology. The silence settled again.

Kimber worked through the night while Eric slept. In the morning she packed for four days down. Her eyes were swollen from staring at search screens and her whole body was tired. All her muscles knotted up when she slept in free fall.

Eric bounced down from the flight deck. "Kimber, I think you should stay here for a few extra days."

Kimber sighed. The fears that drove her from sleep the previous night floated near the surface. She was truly scared now: scared of what she had found, and of what she had not found yet. Scared that she was seeing ghosts where there were none. The safest thing to do was to finish the survey. Act normal. They were already behind schedule. And *Star Surveyor II* was a fragile egg with no more protection than the distant Institute could offer.

Eric said, "Look, I think the Thray were here before the planet froze. They're hiding that much anyway. I had to dig for days to find a reference, and there's none in the survey prep documents. They're pulling a fast one."

"If they wanted to run a scam, why pick you?" she asked reasonably.

"I'm the top student. They had to pick me, or someone would ask why not. But why you?"

She could feel herself blushing. "We were lovers. *Mated.* To an alien it must be clear we get along."

"That's an interesting take," he said slowly. "I hadn't thought of it. The Thray could have got that off our e-mail, right?"

"That would be . . ." Illegal, of course; but they'd had a bitter flame war on-line, too, and then three years of silence. "More likely they looked at our psych testing," she said. "They might misinterpret what they found."

"They might have got it right," he said.

"Oh, God. You're a xenophobe, aren't you? And you try to give me orders, and then I do whatever you tell me not to. They put *me* in charge. If you tell me it's *No Go* on the Thray project, I'll do the opposite."

Eric had that *verbal minefield* look. Cautiously he said, "An alien might think we're that simplistic."

"Eric, I'm scared," she admitted. "But I can't do anything obviously different. If they are dangerous, and they think we know it, we're in a lot of trouble. We'd best play stupid."

He looked at her appraisingly for what felt like forever. "Kimber, are we thinking the same thing? This world froze *fast,* and recently. Worlds this near to Earthlike are scarce. If a world evolves anything intelligent, the Overlords protect it. Terraforming . . . it rolls in your mouth, it's such an easy word, but . . . shaping a planet. The closer we look, the harder it gets. What if you started with a world that was already inhabited? It would be so much easier."

"They're burrowers. It must be easy for a burrower to hate birds," Kimber said.

"What if the Thray found this place and *made* it cold?"

"Froze a whole world?"

He flared, "Well, they plan to warm one!"

"I guess so. How?"

"I think they blocked the sun. Changed the insolation—the amount of the sun's warmth that gets through to the surface."

"Same question."

"Don't laugh yet. They'd need a mirror bigger than whole planets. When Althared was talking about warming Trine, he said . . . what? Sunlight from a hundred thousand klicks around Trine? That's ten to the sixteenth square meters. Three hundred thousand trillion. A mirror bigger than whole planets. Now laugh."

Kimber didn't feel like laughing.

"Right. *That* part's plausible because they already need the mirror for the warming phase!"

"A mirror that big, would it be hard to hide?"

"Hah! I'm still working on that."

"But it's only engineering. We picked a killer and now we're working on the locked room. Eric, why haven't they swatted us?"

"Plausibility. Got to make it look like an accident."

"Or maybe a murder-suicide. What if you could roll it up?"

"Or fold it? Make the mirror a few atoms thick, you could fold it into something the size of a . . . city? Aw, Kimber. Have you ever tried to refold a map?"

"Say it's gone. They destroyed it, dropped it into the sun. How can we prove anything? There'd be no trace of what they did on the surface, barring the ice itself."

He said nothing.

"Eric, how do you make coffee? Show me."

He showed her, carefully. It took fifteen minutes. Neither referred to anything outside their ship. Kimber was hours late at Trine Base; she didn't mention that either.

They went up to the flight deck and sipped coffee from squeezebulbs. By and by Eric said, "Give me a sanity check here: they *didn't* destroy the mirror. They need it for the warming phase."

"You're sane."

"Permission to run an errand?"

"Where?"

"I want to look in the L1 point. I'll be back in a few days." He saw her go blank and said, "The first Lagrange point, between Trine and the star. It's around a million klicks inward from the planet. It's an equilibrium point. Whatever you put in a Lagrange point, it stays if you don't nudge it. *Metastable* equilibrium. We've been thinking about a big, big mirror, but what if they used a lot of little ones? We'd—"

"They'll see the ship move! What do we tell them?"

Eric glared at her. "I think we're running out of time."

"But what do we *tell* them?"

She waited while he thought it through.

"I wouldn't say anything," he said. "If they've left something—doesn't have to be a mirror—*any* bit of evidence anywhere around Trine, then as soon as I start searching . . . they don't have to know what I think I'm after. Why bother to tell them a lie? They only have to decide if I live to talk. My best chance is, I *can't* deliver the verdict. Only you can talk."

"And I'll be down there."

"A hostage!"

She blinked back tears and turned away from Eric so he wouldn't see. She told herself she was tired and stressed, but it was more than that. They were in a box. If they played nice, they'd be let loose. And they'd be liars.

Or Eric was crazy, and so was Kimber.

She turned to him. "Eric. I want to dazzle them with footwork."

They talked it through. At one point Eric said, "Skis? You are nuts! The ice on this planet has been settling for hundreds of years. It's a sedimentary rock, *not* the snow you're used to."

And again, "This isn't pretend danger. It's *real*. If you *really* got killed by accident, then there's only me to worry about, and I'm *mute*!"

"No," she said. "Thray can't take cold. They don't like snow. They might not like *any* kind of surface conditions. Althared will think I'm committing suicide when I'm only out cross-country skiing. And we'll have one more thing going for us."

She explained. He listened. He said, "I can sure use the distraction. Next question. Why are you late going down?"

"Maybe we kissed and made up and indulged in"—she

glanced at the computer's clock—"three hours of mating practices. Or maybe we fought about this, this snow trek."

He didn't leer; his lips didn't even twitch. He said, "Okay. Any way it breaks, they'll be watching *you*. If Althared asks, *I* wanted an unblocked view of the sun . . . and a chance to get away from you, because we had a fight. Good call, Kimber."

"*Is* there a touch of that?"

"Not bloody funny. It's *plausible*. Make your call."

Althared wiggled his head rapidly, then settled on a left profile. He waited.

Kimber said, "I expect to complete my exploration in two weeks."

"Acceptable."

"Please access your map."

"Pause. Done."

Kimber's map was already displayed. She zoomed on Integra Continent. At her direction the Thray had set their base near the midcontinent, a mile below the peaks. Kimber popped up a green dot where a trailing end of Integra curled into a bay.

"I want to drop *here*. Over the next ten days I'll make my way back to Trine Base. That gives me four days leeway, to get lost or to take a closer look at anything I find. I want you to arrange to drop a Skidder for me and take the *Eagle* back to Trine Base to wait."

Althared turned his left eye full on her, then the right, then left again. "Kimber, have you lost your sanity?"

She glared off-screen, and Eric grinned back. She exploded, "Do you *all* think like that? If I start and end at the Base, I have to loop. This way I can go twice as far! Thus far I've only seen the midcontinent. Now I'll go through terrain none of us has explored."

"You take a fearful risk for no clear profit."

"You built the skidders. Aren't they safe? A skidder does fifty on the flat, but call it twenty; that's plenty of leeway. I can drive for ten hours a day. If I lose ground, I'll drop back to sea level. In ten days I'll cover two thousand miles and be back at Base."

"Chief Surveyor, it would be tragic if you went mad during your investigation. If you disappear into the ice, tragic also. We must return our legal dance to the beginning, our destiny delayed by twenty years."

"I'll be careful." She waited.

"I will make arrangements. Come for me in two hours."

There was no pomp and circumstance this time, and no return to the great viewing port. When she docked, Althared simply climbed into the *Eagle*'s cabin and signaled for her to head down. Kimber left the communications port open so that Eric could hear them. Knowing Eric was listening felt like spying, but it was comforting as well.

Althared said, "I had hoped to see a draft of your report on the first half of your work."

How should she answer? "My notes are half-digested. I'll organize them during the trek."

"May I help? Our translator program has software to collate such material."

She stared. Let the *Thray* organize her evidence? She asked, "If I don't follow the regulations, who gets upset?" She intended to suggest danger, but . . . might he really answer? *Who are the Overlords?*

He said, "Your answer is proper. Of course we must obey the code. I had forgotten that this is your first survey. Perhaps you need more time?"

Kimber doubted he had forgotten. His greatly inflated shape, the unearthly features within his fishbowl helm, seemed more alien, more intimidating . . . and Kimber suddenly remembered his big, spidery hands on her, turning her in free fall to face a window. Had he *meant* to intimidate?

She was long past that! "In ten days I'll be ready, fourteen at the outside."

Blotch raced beneath them: the major continent, its

edges blurred by a kilometer's thickness of ice. Now the terrain flattened over what had been ocean. Here came the western peninsula of Integra, seen through an orange glow of reentry—

"Althared, when did your people first visit Trine?"

"Why do you ask?"

Damn, she thought, how subtle. "I'm trying to determine how long the ice has been in place. The air is so dry it's hard to imagine any running water, but I found a plant that looks like it was alive recently." There were plant fossils in her samples. And—"Althared, where did all the carbon dioxide go?" She *had* to ask that, didn't she? Earth itself had twice been frozen, and the alien knew that *Kimber* knew—

Althared looked directly at her. "We saw that too. We think the ice spread over time; the last of the bare ground was covered a thousand years ago, more or less. There may have been a geologic event to hasten it. Smoke from volcanoes. A major meteoroid impact.

"That is enough of geology. Please tell me about the plants you found."

"I have a dozen new species. Take over?"

Althared took the flight controls. Kimber popped up a display. She ran through her records with some care: rock formations, traces of plants, threads that had to be a root network, plant genetic material—not DNA, but a related chemical. She avoided showing hollow bones or wall friezes.

The feeling that she had trusted Althared too much was getting stronger, fluttering in her stomach. She ran through video of her travels, the digs, plants, and her classifications. She let her pride show; she burbled; she wished aloud that Eric had completed his notes and addenda, and let anger leak through.

The Thray made no comments, had no expression to give back; he watched her and her displays with his left eye, flew with his right. The continent's midrange passed below, white on white and two red-and-black dots for Trine Base. More white ice, growing close. There! Black and red, a tent, a Skidder, and two pressure-suited Thray.

The Thray helped her get her gear from *Eagle* into the Skidder. Althared stared left-eye, right-eye at a pair of broad skis. He didn't seem familiar with them, but he didn't ask. The three let her test the Skidder, let her set it moving, before they took off.

Red-and-black *Thembrlish* passed overhead every two hours, close enough to show like a baroque moon. *Star Surveyor II* was, of course, gone.

She kept the mountains on her left. The ice was rough, sometimes a jumble of boulders, sometimes great splits. Surprise crevasses scared her twice. At night she put up her tent, but she slept the way she'd traveled, in her pressure suit.

In the morning's brilliant light that seemed excessive. She changed in the tent, into gear that would have looked familiar on Everest. Three percent carbon dioxide had her puffing, but the air was thick, with enough oxygen at these low altitudes.

By the fourth day she was inside-out cold and tired of camping without the warmth of the base camp. She'd found nothing but ice. She wondered if she'd gone the wrong way: the continent's curling tip would make a good bay, if Trine's Flyers sailed ships.

The morning of the fifth day the easiest path descended gently for several hours. She spotted a large cave opening and headed the Skidder into it. Its lights illuminated a long tunnel that was mostly rock with very little ice. The tunnel narrowed abruptly and she had to park the Skidder. The edges of the constriction were unnaturally smooth, like sand fused to glass. She resisted taking a glove off to feel the smoothed edges. It was cold enough that she'd leave skin behind.

Cautiously, she stepped through. There was a short hallway, then a huge cavern. The Skidder's lights illuminated the back wall faintly. Bright colors showed in the circles of light. She took a few steps forward, added the illumination of her handheld light.

It was a painted frieze. She ran her flashlight over the shadows around the headlamps. There were the flyers—long feathered wings and thin bodies. They were fantastic images—almost angels but in no way human. She walked backward, entranced, and took a floor light from the Skidder with shaking fingers.

The additional illumination brought colors and shapes out more clearly. She could see the ceiling now, and carved into it was the unmistakable image of an egg painted in red and white fractals: a Thray ship.

Kimber turned slowly in the new light and her eyes found a ledge with the bodies of three more flyers, complete and frozen. They were different sizes. Family group? She closed her eyes and struggled to control her breath.

This *didn't* prove that the Thray had frozen the planet or even caused harm to the flyers. But the flyers were sentient, and the Thray had been here when they were.

She carefully videoed the cave, twice, and checked her disks to be sure they showed the most damaging evidence, then tucked equipment and disks in her backpack.

The Skidder had to be backed through the cave. By the time she was free of it, she was shaking from the effort. The slopes were smooth ahead; the sun gave at least an illusion of warmth. Kimber ran the Skidder up to fifty and it died.

Dead as a stone. The DON'T TOUCH mark was on the motor housing. Kimber began to smile. She wasn't crazy. It was all real. She had to live to tell Eric!

She'd have to be selective now.

Tent. Clothes: she'd better leave the pressure suit, rather than depend on the air recycler or temp control. Ski mask and a scarf to breath through. Wear everything. Zippers in the orange parka for temp control.

Her data: video disks, notes, instrument recordings. The main camera was too heavy: she left it. She kept what she thought were the skull and wing of a child, and a fist-ax drawing tool.

Food. She rethought that, set up her tent and the stove and spent a few hours eating herself stupid. Going hungry for a

few days wouldn't hurt her if she remembered to drink . . .
thaw and drink a lot of water. She packed what was freeze-
dried and left everything that wasn't.

Skis.

She made three hours, perhaps twenty-five klicks, before
she quit for the night.

At full dawn she was on her way again. She grinned up at
Thembrlish drifting across the sky. Her parka was neon orange and her ski tracks would show too, but would they
look? Next to the ruined/sabotaged Skidder she had left her
pressure suit splayed out on its back in *savasana* pose, faceplate closed.

She spent the seventh day striving for altitude, not distance.
She knew too little; she must see more of what might save
her or kill her.

There was nothing wrong with her timing.

She settled on the local crest, comfortable in full sunlight,
her back to a flat boulder, and set up her stove. Presently she
used binoc specs to look around. In a glare white world, a
red double dot, a colon mark, was wobbling at the jagged
eastern horizon.

It rose slowly.

Another red colon rose behind it.

It dawned on her that she was watching heavy lifters
move Trine Base.

She watched her lifeline being pulled into the sky. The
Base wouldn't just disappear, she thought. It would be set
somewhere else. The implication: the Chief Surveyor knew
where it was and got herself lost anyway.

What would they expect of her now? Bereft of rescue,
robbed of even a goal, Kimber Walker had nothing left.
When the cold became overpowering, as it must, she would
dig. Whoever found her later would find her hidden from her
Thray rescuers and dead of starvation.

Of course she wouldn't be where Althared expected her.

Skis were moving her faster than that. Still, unless Eric came for her, that was how she'd end up.

Keep moving. Stay high. There was one more thing the Thray didn't know.

Darkness deepened the cold. Kimber pulled a lightweight reflective covering from the backpack. It was torn. She settled it around her, tucking it carefully between her and the frozen rock. At least it would be warmer than stopping on bare ice. The rock had collected some of the sun's tepid warmth.

The Thray ship rose above the glaciated eastward peaks. Seeing it brought tears and anger. How could she have let Althared use her so?

But Eric the cynic would be asking: why the mind games?

Leaving the pressure suit splayed like a dead woman, that was fun, but it was a message to Althared. *Kimber knows.* Althared knew she knew. Why not just kill the Chief Surveyor and have done with it?

Kimber knew people who would have trouble doing that. She might be one herself. But why choose such a one for such a mission? Unless . . .

Unless the sons of bitches were just *nicer* than characters in *James Bond* movies and *The Godfather*.

Every muscle ached. She'd ripped her pants at ankle and knee; cold needled in to rob tiny parts of her of any sensation. She imagined ending up frozen forever behind a water curtain. Not today . . . but she didn't have the energy to erect the tent. This was good enough. She slept.

As light started to spill onto the ice, Kimber pushed up and looked around approvingly. A good last morning, if that's what it became. There were blue skies above pearl drops of rock on ice. She recalled how soft and simple Trine had looked from the great viewing deck while Althared stood beside her and talked about warming the planet.

Inhabitable galactic real estate was valuable, but nowhere in her studies or the stories of other surveyors in the bars by the Institute had she heard of anything so proud and horrible as the freezing of a world.

She climbed. Sweat chilled to an uncomfortable dampness against her skin whenever she rested. It couldn't matter. It wasn't like she had enough time left to die of a cold. Such a simple thought. She knew she could think more complex thoughts once. She knew that there was a time when she didn't expect to die. And another time when she was warm, and didn't have to gasp for air.

Halfway up, she let herself rest. The late-morning sun reflected from icy rock faces and turned the light into dappled rainbows. Kimber was grateful for the display, for something, however small, to smile at. The Thray had done this world no favors. She imagined a green world with flying beings, and the anger set her climbing again. Althared had joked with her and had been gentle when he taught her to drive the Skidder and work the maps the Thray had made. How could the Kimber of three months ago have been so stupid? There, that was a more complex thought.

She balanced on her knees and elbows, pulled herself up the last bit of a sharp slope to find a wide flat spot. It would have to do.

Get high! Get exposed! It was the last thing any Thray would think of, and Eric had to be able to see her . . . if he wasn't still days away, or days dead.

She pulled a signal flare from the backpack, and lay down holding the flare over her stomach. She had a few more, and locators too, but she wouldn't use it until she *saw* him. There was no point in signaling the Thray.

She dozed. It seemed like hours passed. Her watch said it had been thirty minutes. Next time she might not wake at all.

"Kimber?"

She jerked upright. "Eric! What did you find?"

"Later. I think we're in a hurry. Can you see me? Straight above you?"

She fumbled for binoc specs, but already they weren't needed. *Star Surveyor II* was straight up, tiny and bright. Wouldn't his orbit take him around, out of sight? A tinier speck diverged.

His voice continued. "Kimber, it's amazing what you can do when you just don't have to think about running out of fuel. I've left the ship on autopilot, hovering at less than half a G, about three thousand miles up. The Thray are still thinking in terms of orbits, so they just went behind the planet. Gives us at least half an hour. *Eagle* can do two G. See me now?"

"Yes." Forget the flare. "Did you find anything?"

"I said I'd be back when I did. I'm here. For a moment I thought that might be *you* at the Skidder. What happened?"

"It died."

"Sabotage?"

"Who knows?"

The silver speck grew fast. Slowed, hovered. Kimber tried to get up. No go.

Eagle set down. Eric came out at a run.

"Thank god I found you," he said. "I thought you'd be dead." He dropped to the snow. "We need to get your message off. I would have done it myself, but I can't. I wrote everything up for the Verification Link, though. It's ready to go."

"I've got more pictures."

He stood briskly. "We've got to go before the Thray know we're here." Eric took her wrists and pulled her up, and supported her weight while she gained a semblance of balance. He half dragged her to the *Eagle* and left her propped up while he returned for her backpack.

Kimber called, "I think you were right. The Thray want me dead for what I know. Can't be my personality, right? But they're not doing anything direct, Eric, and I think it's because they can't."

Eric guffawed. "Wouldn't that be nice!"

He dropped his pack. "I found this." He pulled out something flat, and skimmed it at her like a big Frisbee.

She threw up an arm to block, and caught it. It was square,

and weightless, amazingly light. She looked at herself . . .
filthy, not fit for human company, but wearing a grin much
nastier than she was used to . . . and then at what she held.

A flat square mirror half a meter on a side, amazingly
brilliant, with edges four or five centimeters wide that tried
to shift under her hand. She wiggled the mirror, letting it
find its own direction. The flaps relaxed when the mirror
faced flat into the sun.

"I aimed the ship to drift through the L1 point. When I got
close I saw a black speck on the sun. I was wrong all along,"
Eric said. "You *couldn't* put this thing in the L1 point and
expect it to stay there. Pressure from the sunlight would
push it right out to the stars. But by the time I worked that
out, I was on my way. That's why I'm still alive, maybe. If
the Thray thought I was going to the right place, they'd have
swatted me."

"So . . . ?"

"They needed *hundreds of trillions* of these death mirrors. Little mirrors for flaps to steer with, and tiny brains
with instructions to stay between the sun and Trine, and turn
edgewise and fall back if the sun gets too far away. The
Thray engineers would have put them deep inward, just a
few million miles from the star, where the star's gravity bal-
ances the light pressure. The Thray chilled the planet, then
sent a signal to the death mirrors to disperse . . . one way or
another. There must be a lot of signals that would do what
they want done. But if you raise the death mirror's maximum
distance, it would ride the light right out into the halo of
comets and wait. Later they can bring them back and use
them for the warming.

"Out of hundreds of trillions of the things, a few are
bound to go wrong. Programming fails. Say a few hundred
still stay between Trine and the sun, but they sail outward.
They'll end up in that wastebasket of gravity, the L1 point,
and that's where I found this. Isn't it beautiful?"

"Oh, yeah."

He took it from her, tossed it in the back seat. "What've
you got?

"Videotape of a cave ceiling. It's in the pack. It *nails* them."

There was gravity: *Star Surveyor II* was still hovering. Kimber began plugging widgets into the Verification Link. Plugs were labeled, a big help. Eric climbed straight to the flight deck.

She felt the deck tilt hard over, and kept working. Eric was getting them out of here. And now it was all there. She need only send the verdict.

Gravity disappeared.

Kimber shrieked and convulsed. It was as if she'd fallen off a cliff. She snatched for a handhold and clung like a monkey, hearing Eric's yell like an echo of her own.

"Wait," said a voice she knew.

Althared was on her screen, his alien head turned in profile. Pale blue veins pulsed around a circular mouth lined with lots of tiny teeth. Frankenstein be damned, just because he's ugly doesn't mean he's a victim! *He* doesn't think he's ugly.

"Chief Surveyor, you appear to have misinterpreted. You owe us the ability to respond before you reach a verdict." he stated.

Kimber said, "I see no point." She heard an echo overhead. Eric was in this conversation too.

"You're falling," the alien pointed out.

"Not fast." When she was practicing with the Verification Link, Kimber had seen a bar displayed—universal symbols for **DON'T TOUCH** and **AFFIRM** and **SEND**. Now she was trying to get it back.

"I see you found one of our mirror modules," the alien said. "We brought them here early, before your verdict allows us to act. We must test them, yes? But it will be thought premature."

"It might at that," she said. *Here* it was. She tapped **DON'T TOUCH**.

The screen printed, **You have chosen to deny the mission which you were sent to investigate. VERIFY?**

Eric bellowed, "Make a decision! The big ship is coming down our throats with two heavy lifters!"

"Your arrogance," Althared said, "your presumption, your *hubris*. How dare you presume to judge us? If you send that message, you must die."

"I was selected," she said. She hit **VERIFY**, then **SEND**.

Althared must have seen. He screamed something fluid, then, "Betrayer! Why would you harm us?"

The message was delivered, the flyers would have justice. Kimber spared a few seconds to send Althared her video of the frieze on the cave ceiling. Flyers and a Thray spacecraft. *I did it for them.*

Eric called, "Kimber?

There was nothing more to do here, and suddenly she really wanted to be with Eric. She pulled herself up into the flight deck, and froze.

There in the Shuttle windows, *Thembrlish* loomed huge; but Trine was the whole sky. The Thray ship was pacing them as they fell.

Kimber got her breath back. She moved forward, touched Eric's shoulder. Althared was on-screen here too, left profile and a breathing problem. She ignored him. She asked Eric, "How long?"

Eric said, "Oh, twenty minutes, thirty . . . I don't know. Long enough. This ship can't do a reentry, Kimber. *No* ship reenters straight down."

The Thray ship veered sideways and was gone. Kimber saw thrust distort Althared's features. She said, "Althared, give us back our drive." Worth a try, she thought.

The alien was wheezing . . . sobbing? "I cannot. I do not captain *Thembrlish*. Your death is ordained. You will fall."

Thump.

Eric said, "What—?"

"It came from below. I'll go look." She kicked herself aft.

Thump.

She got her head and shoulders into position in time to see the well in the Verification Link spit out a silver medicine ball. The ball *thumped* against the hull, unfolded into a Pillbug, kicked and wriggled and bounced back at the Verification Link. Two more were already in place, clinging to the filigree along two edges. The third joined them. Its myriad feet slid into tiny holes in the filigree border. A fourth silver ball emerged, hit the hull (*thump*), unfolded and aligned itself along the fourth edge. Four Pillbugs were joined nose to tail.

The VL spoke in the same translator's voice that had been Althared's. "We come to seek explanation for your verdict—"

The voice stopped. Then small machines began popping through the BH (Big Hole). Three Pillbugs peeled loose to lock components together into a blocky toroid.

Kimber crawled down, hoping to see better. One Pillbug came to look her over. She tried to find its eyes.

The floor surged up.

Kimber found her footing as Eric called, "Yow! Kimber, I've got thrust. Ump?" The thrust was still rising. Kimber tried to kneel, but it was too strong. The floor hit her hard.

She saw the Pillbugs crawling up the wall, back into place around the VL. They seemed to be talking to Althared; at least there was a humming warble, and Althared was answering in no human language.

She couldn't reach a window. Two or three times Earth's gravity had her nailed to the floor. She felt the resonance and heard the roar as *Star Surveyor II* plunged into Trine's atmosphere.

She heard and felt the roar die away.

Then four Pillbugs crawled into the BH and were gone.

"Here, take these pills too. Is that any better?"

Kimber drank, swallowed, drank. She said, "Go easy on the neck."

Her left eye hurt. She couldn't open it. Her chin rested on a collar of rubber foam. Eric was wrapping gauze around her head and eye. "Nice shiner, Chief Surveyor. I can't tell if your neck's broken," he said, "so wear the neck brace. Nobody can do anything about a cracked rib, though. We'll be home about as fast as we came, and then someone qualified can look you over."

"Next question. Pillbugs," she said.

"I never even *saw* them, and *you* didn't use the camera."

"I was busy being crushed!"

He shrugged it off. "Do you think those were the Overlords?"

"They don't talk well. Eric, a Pillbug is too small to have anything like a human brain. They'd have to be *components* of an intelligence. I saw them link up head to tail. Communication must be built in, right?"

His face went slack as he thought it through. "Hardwired, nerve to nerve."

"There's nothing in their evolution for just talking, not to each other, certainly not to *us*."

"We can't even ask them if they're servants of something bigger."

"Eric? They've got the VL. Instantaneous communication. With that you could link up the entire species at once! An arbitrarily complex brain. *Sure* they could be the Overlords."

"I think I bent my brain," Eric said.

"Where's *Thembrlish*?"

"The Thray? They left at two gee. They've already done the Shift Trick. There's no way to run far enough, I expect, but they're giving it a try. Damn, you were right. They just can't reach out and *kill*."

"Doesn't cramp their style."

"Oh, hey, I looked in the Institute records. Kimber, our credentials have been upgraded by a *lot*."

She smiled. "Pillbugs to the rescue."

"Only *after* we made our decision."

Kimber smiled weakly at the word "we." Her ribs hurt sharply, but that was fading. She said, "I wish they'd left us some magic bandages."

"You wouldn't want an alien doctor, Kimber. Nobody *wants* to make medical history."

"Vee vill perform an exshperiment upon this . . . creature . . ." She was woozy. "In a minute I'm going to be no fun anymore."

"That's the pills. I'm going to drop back to half a gee so you can sleep."

" 'Night."

" 'Night."

DISCUSSION WITH BRENDA COOPER
RE: "ICE AND MIRRORS"

What follows is email that passed between me and Brenda Cooper while we were working on "Trine's Flyers," the short story that became "Ice and Mirrors." I've included it as instructions on how to write a story using a computer link.

While we worked on this, Brenda was also active as a council-woman and a computer jock. She worked on minimizing the effects of the Y2k bug. We were also working on "Rogue Backup," the short story that became "Finding Myself." You'll find here references to all of these activities, and to novels I was working on at the time.

THE "ICE AND MIRRORS" PAPERS

Subj: Me
Date: 12/3/99

Hi! This is generic; I apologize. I like to think of myself as a good correspondent, but maybe not.

Here's how my life is running:

The winds are back. Howling in the chimney, blowing vegetation around, scaring the fish . . . but not smashing glass tables. We took ours to safety some weeks ago.

I spent ten days up north: three at Orycon, the next seven in Steve Barnes's vicinity. I thought we'd have more work for SATURN'S RACE, but our editor was already happy. I saw some fixes and made them in around four hours; Steve took his pass and smoothed them over.

I stayed because Steve had a working party planned: show up and criticize his concept for an alternate timeline. Most of us had something to say. IMSH'ALLAH is probably Steve's magnum opus. (Became Lion's Blood.)

Steve was busy. I talked writing a lot with one Brenda Cooper . . . her writing. She's unpublished, but she's good. She's my next collaborator, if things work out. Yes, I'm violating a rule I laid out myself in "Collaboration." Thanks for pointing that out, but look at it:

She's the one taking the risks. A collaboration is around 160% as much work as a solo flight, but she's doing her 80% first. Our first flight is a short story she's already drafted. (There are three, I think. What she can fix just from our conversations, won't become a collaboration. Giving up half the money shouldn't be done lightly.) We won't burn up my time this way, if it's a mistake. The biggest story, carved from scratch while we walked, may become a novelet or a novel.

Got home Sunday. A reading copy of THE BURNING CITY (due in March) was waiting, complete with cover. I turned with it in my hand . . . forgot a wastebasket, tripped. The throw rug slid. I dropped. Bad bruising, two ribs out of place . . . but not cracked. Michele Coleman put them back where they belonged (days later, when the bruising had eased off), and made me get an Xray. I'm tired of being injured at LosCon. Every damn Thanksgiving. Last year it was the flu. In '93 I was six weeks out of abdominal surgery.

Today, 12 days after the fall, it's almost healed. It never did incapacitate me. I was able to hike and swim . . .

Swim! My swimming pool is finished! It's deep enough that I don't scratch my toenails! That's five feet at its deepest. I'm not unreasonable; I don't need the fear of drowning to spice up my life, and I didn't need to buy extra depth. But the guy who built this pool (and house) was crazy.

At the beginning of September I logged onto a website dedicated to discussing my works. For awhile I was getting four or five emails a day. I took a lot of notes for a possible fourth Ringworld novel. The flow has eased off now. I'm glad. As for whether they generated a book, time will tell.

And how are you?

Subj: Re: Discussion Notes
Date: 12/1/99

In a message dated 11/30/99 10:54:49 PM Pacific Standard Time, Brenda Cooper writes:

Subj: Re: Discussion Notes
Date: 11/30/99 10:54:49 PM Pacific Standard Time

Our notes, revised as of Thanksgiving or so, are attached.

Larry

Wow! I digested your return on the notes on the plane back. Good insights on communication. The themes make sense. I like the Forward Thrust Systems, the basic situation set-up. And more time talking story will be great. It's usually easy to get me to work.

My understanding of the next step is I take what you sent me, organize it, and outline a story around it. That means characters and events fleshed out, but still in outline format. Could be long. If you keep working on parts, send them as you feel ready and I'll incorporate into working document. Your choice, of course. I may have questions to send you from time to time, and look forward to playing with this. It's like a good yoga stretch. If you want what I have so far at any point, say so. Otherwise I guess I'll send it next time I need feedback.

BC

Good plan,

LN

I did read A Deepness in the Sky—will re-read as he is dealing with time frames like ours and cold sleep. And yeah, I know I'm not honed enough for anything that ambitious yet. I suspect he's been writing longer than I have (*grin*). But I can learn from him.

BC

Vernor's been writing as long as I have (roughly.)

LN

I sent you Dreaming Alioth. We agreed that one wasn't really a collaboration, and that you did help. If it sells, and I get a chance to thank you, I will. I will keep doing my own stuff—it's a way to tell what I'm learning from you and keep developing my own voice. Keeps my eggs in more than one basket. Yes, I'm sure you could improve the story. For now, don't worry with it. I think it works OK. The test is what editors think. If I get more rejections, I get to finish the wallpaper job.

In the meantime, I am working on the story that started out as Magnetic Lies. That's the one where you solved the problem of the frozen world. I'll send it to you when I'm pretty confident it works—my goal will be that you can do one re-write through and have it ready/perfect. This is an intermediate step, a fairly simple first collaboration. Expect something in a week or two.

BC

Okay.

LN

Next, the one that got a LOT longer when we talked about it—the Rogue Backup story set in the virtual world. Same idea. Will take longer. I have to finish saving Longview from Y2K.

BC

As regards "Rogue Backup," what I saw most of were problems. If you solve them on your own, then that's a solo flight . . . and if I see something good enough, I won't claim a collaboration.

LN

In either case, put your name on 'em if and when you're happy. Question—short stories you collaborate on go through your agent?

BC

Yes, through Eleanor Wood, but I'd better ask her, or at least alert her.

LN

Got your letter and notes on collaboration. Good notes. You own the veto. Yes, you could be a fool to work with an amateur. I admit to not being a hundred percent sure why you're doing it, but I'm glad you are. Instinct says this might work. I don't see any way I can lose—the lessons and work can't hurt me. If I work hard enough to make it a win/win, the win for me saves me years. I need those years. And no matter what, we have some good conversations. The only way we can lose is if we lose something from our friendship. Any way I can help you, tell me.

—BC

I saw the problems. I decided it was worth the risk.

—LN

Take care. I'll send you the current story when it's done.

—Brenda

Stet.

—Larry

Subj: L1
Date: 12/1/99

I've just learned (coincidence) that the L1 point is indeed the gravitationally metastable point between Earth and Sun (or between Moon and Earth, for that matter.) Yesterday I was guessing.

In Sol system, the L1 (or first Lagrange) point is 1,500,000 kilometers inward from Earth. Earth's pull counteracts the Sun's by a little bit, so whatever you put there can do a little slower in its orbit than Earth does. Covering a slightly smaller circle, it still orbits in an Earth year. (And it's metastable because if you leave something in there and then nudge it a little, it falls out. Only the L4 and L5 points are *stable*.)

Larry

Subj: Re: Story Attached
Date: 12/4/99

I'm in.

Something has popped up in the literature since I read your first draft of "Trine's Flyers". (That, by the way, is the proper way to write the title of a short story. You probably knew that already, from Steve.)

The Earth has been frozen from pole to pole, right across the equator, twice at least.

What I just said is not certain. That is, its proponents are certain;

they've found what they believe is clear evidence; but the rest of the scientific community will have to decide. But we can use it, and with "Trine's Flyers" half written, we'll be first in print!

There are other matters I can improve.

Keenan may be in a snit, but—being who he is—he can hardly resist lecturing. Walker can use that. I'll use the "Frozen Earth" scenario.

"I went looking in other libraries"—duh? What kind of communications has this guy got? But then I rethought. An instant link would allow him to accuse the Thray before Althared can react. And he's got a defense:

"Show your toy (the mirrors.) We began preparation to warm this world early. It is a minor offense."

I rethought the matter of the L1 point. It's both right and wrong. Putting the black (not mirror) barriers there wouldn't work: they're still absorbing photons, and will be kicked out. Put 'em closer. But when they're discarded . . . a few will end up in the L1 point!

A thing that needs saying:

A woman, an established writer whom I'd met twice at OutsideCons in Kentucky, phoned me at home one evening. She had a proposition. "I'll write a book. We'll put your name on it with mine. You get half the money."

I don't expect to speak to her again.

Because you're going to do most of your work first, and I'll do most of mine after, I have to be careful deciding if I can contribute. I won't ever jump into a story as collaborator if I can tell you how to fix it and stand back.

As for the rest, this looks like a couple of weeks' work. That doesn't mean you'll see it in two weeks . . . but then, you knew that.

Larry

In a message dated 12/3/99 11:04:01 PM Pacific Standard Time,

<<OK—your turn. I've obsessed over this about as much as I can take. It's a lot better. I'm happy with progress, the results not perfect. When I went back I was surprised at how rough some of it was—four months ago it was the best I could do. So anyway, I cleaned up the language, wrote it with only the first flashback, changed Kimber's

personality some so she's not quite as selfish, added the disks from the L1 point, and incorporated everything else we talked about that I had the sense to make notes for. I also made some changes based on comments from the reviewers at Orycon.

Please feel free to do what you want with it, or nothing if it's not to your standards yet. Areas I think it may need help in are: Ships' details—what they fly isn't very important to the story, but I'm over my head when trying to make it realistic, so I just didn't mess with stuff I didn't know. I'm assuming FTL for the story's sake and pretty instant communication between them and the Institute at the end (although that can be changed if they get out of it some other way). The FTL can maybe be ignored, but the communication maybe can't be. Do they need to get all the way away to end the story? Or is it OK to end it where I do?

What would make their relationship clearer/richer/less flat? Or is it defined enough?

Subj: Re: Technique
Date: 12/6/99

I'm having fun.

As I see it, a water world HAS to be easier to make habitable than a frozen world. One takes . . . at least a huge heat input; maybe an altered atmosphere. The other takes an arbitrarily large raft.

New basic assumptions: Humans are junior members. The top of the interstellar hierarchy is unseen. The Thray follow the law . . . maybe (at first) because they're good guys, or maybe (it will appear) they're afraid.

So I made your swimmer a Hawaiian and gave him some trouble with surfer's ear, sounds go fuzzy and his balance isn't good. But he wants the job.

Onward . . .

                                                                    Larry

Subj: Technique
Date: 12/6/99

Do you know how to do a MERGE FILES?

I haven't done it. I've watched Jerry do it. He generally messes up, curses, talks himself through it until he's got it. It looks learnable.

I'm asking because I'm tempted to send you my current text. It's got big block notes in it. But it would be cruel to send this and then make you hold off from working on it.

Anyway . . . I'm near the beginning. I'll take a full pass before I do anything. But, hey, Brenda, what is this nonsense about a human colony on a water world? While the Thray are fighting (and killing!) for an iceball? And how does a reluctant swimmer get to be a world's best diver?

Nah.

Larry

Subj: Re: Technique
Date: 12/8/99

It took me a while to absorb how powerful you've made humans. This is something I change almost automatically.

My assumption for this story is: by interstellar law, we hold only the Solar System. We might terraform Mars or Venus without seeking permission, but our ambitions haven't even reached that far. There's an interstellar community; we are junior members.

If we made it easy to get the right to terraform a world, even for humans, we lose all of the Thrays' motive to commit genocide. Why would they bother?

I hope we haven't been haring off in opposite directions here.

I've named the faster-than-light drive the Shift Trick. Implication: humans name it but don't understand it. A better name might derive from stage magic. Find out if there's a trade name for making a woman (or tiger) disappear out of a "sealed" box.

I've given the Thray ship artificial gravity only on gold-carpeted walkways; no gravity on the survey ship. You want gold carpet, you got it. Have to see if I can make it work. Free fall makes coffee more complicated.

Larry

Subj: Re: Waking Up
Date: 12/8/99

In a message dated 12/8/99 9:27:37 AM Pacific Standard Time,
<<FYI—I have been waking up at 3:30 every morning this week and adding to the outline—is this stuff that addictive for you? What fun.

Have a good day.

>>

I remember. Enjoy! This is part of the fun.

It didn't stop being that addictive. What happened was, I grew aware that if I didn't bother to go write it down, I'd still remember it. So I stayed in bed/shower/finished the hike/whatever.

LN

Subj: Re: Terraforming
Date: 12/9/99

In a message dated 12/8/99 9:48:57 PM Pacific Standard Time,

<<Do you know anything about this book/have it? Found reference at http://www.reston.com/astro/terraforming.html.

Book Reviews
by Jeff Foust and Harold Hamblet
"Generation Gap"
Terraforming: Engineering Planetary Environments
by Martyn J. Fogg
544 pp, illus.
SAE, 1995
ISBN 1-56091-609-5
review by Jeff Foust

>>

I went to the site. The reference is no longer connected. Can you get hold of this? Because I'd better have read it when we start serious work on GENERATION GAP.

Larry

Subj: Re: Terraforming
Date: 12/10/99

I've thought of an ending.

But stand by. I think it'll work, given that I have to get "extreme" with our communications device anyway.

(We have to do that. Otherwise your instinct was dead on: letting these two discover the truth happens just before they get swatted like one-winged files.)

There's another thing that goes with being a novice. It's reeeally obvious in "There's a Wolf in my Time Machine". A novice will tend to avoid the hard scenes, the confrontations. We try to imply them. Watch out for that.

Larry

LN

Subj: Re: Terraforming
Date: 12/11/99

I'm going with mirrors. The Thray can 1.use them to rewarm the planet too; 2. claim that they brought them in early for that purpose, as opposed to using them to freeze the planet first. Make them half a meter by half a

meter, and the numbers become neat. (You need 4(Pi)¥10,000 squared if Althared pulls from 10,000 km. around. That's 1200 trillion . . . I think. I'll look again.)

Larry

Subj: Re: various
Date: 12/13/99

In a message dated 12/13/99 8:45:22 AM Pacific Standard Time, Title BURNING TOWER noted.

Del Rey retains some of its, well, strange characteristics, but the new editor-in-chief of Ballantine, Greg Tobin, is a level-headed, smart guy who seems to be easing the situation at Del Rey a little. Still, it's hard to know how much support Bertelsmann is planning to give to the Del Rey operation, other than maintaining Star Wars line. I suggest you go ahead with RINGWORLD'S CHILD. If Del Rey bites, fine. If not, what's to keep me from taking such a big name as "Ringworld" elsewhere?

Eleanor

What I'll do, subject to your sanity check..is work **both** THE GHOST SHIPS and RINGWORLD'S CHILD into outlines. (Don't expect these until January.) Give 'em their choice, or sell as a package. What do you think?

LN

I do hope those Draco Tavern stories keep coming. It's hard to imagine Rick getting sloshed on ordinary human booze. On the other hand, it's easy to imagine him being tempted to try some exotic offworld brew.

                                                                    Eleanor

I hope so too. Offworld brew: I did that in "The Real Thing", and that inclines me to try something else. Bad homeworld booze altered by alien tech. A glig's attempt to make a cordial . . . with side effects. . . .

Meanwhile, expect a 10,000 word collaboration story shortly "Ice and Mirrors" . . . and expect a Draco Tavern-ish flavor. I *did* not link the two universes. I suspected you would not approve . . . but am I wrong?

(Read it first. If I went this route, it would be set a generation later than the chirps landings. I haven't raised the subject with Brenda; but she's read the stories.)

                                                                         LN

(to BC)

Equally warm regards . . . and I'll think of you at 9 PM on the 31st. By the time we have to face Y2K, New York will be three hours into the New Year. We'll have the news . . . or a dead TV, lights, power. . . .

                                                                    Larry

Subj: Intermediate draft
Date: 12/14/99

I'm sending you a printout of what you sent me as "Trine's Flyers" in early December, which I covered with red pencil marks.

Keep it for reference. Shortly I'll be sending you what I think is a final draft of "Trine's Flyers", possibly renamed. I want you to compare the two. Wherever you don't see why I made a change, *think about it,* then ask me.

I did a lot of work on this story. I did it partly so you could see what the process of elaboration and trimming looks like. Future stories, I'll make you make the changes for as long as I think I can guide you, and then I'll finish the polish.

It's windy as hell here. In this area and in this age, only a crazy person would put a fireplace in a house. Crazy Dr. Kane gave us five. The chimneys howl like all the damned in Inferno.

Be well, have fun, stay busy.

Larry Niven

Subj: Re: intermediate draft
Date: 12/14/99
    In a message dated 12/14/99 2:53:42 PM Pacific Standard Time,
<<Subj: Re: intermediate draft
Date: 12/14/99 2:53:42 PM Pacific Standard Time
From:
    Thanks for the work. I do get it—what your time is worth. Is it more fun, for you to guide and teach or to really write (as in collaboratively or alone—but doing early drafts as well as finishes?). A side thought—do you think we should have someone else who is not one of us read the story when we think it's done?

BC

I dunno. When I was a lot younger, I was never (in my own head) more a teacher than a collaborator. I'm used to that—I guess I like it that way—but teaching myself is what I'm doing when I pontificate.

It's an invitation to catch me in a mistake, or offer me another viewpoint.

Anyway, it always works out as both.

LN

If it's a helpful trade, I have been working on the outline for GENERATION GAP—will get it to you for feedback soon, if just to tell if I am on a reasonable track and thinking in the right order. Maybe a week or just after Christmas.

BC

Yeah! But, hey, I don't need a helpful trade. Any story has to be the best it can be, and I'm having fun.

Warning: the ending has changed greatly. Be ready. I couldn't leave Kimber doing nothing at all, still in denial, and ready to be swatted like a fly. That last leg of the investigation is now a cross-country skiing trip, intended as a distraction to protect Eric.

And—whether it becomes overt; it hasn't yet—the Thray have real trouble killing face-to-face.

LN

I am looking for places I can be useful to you so you win as much as I do—and I think maybe one of them, besides raw bright beginner enthusiasm, is in technology and understanding that pretty well—seeing how it may affect social choices. I spend a lot of my work day there.

BC

Yeah! As a general thing, my collaborator has usually done the research. (Even the first one. David Gerrold did the research on balloons, and weaving.) I'm delighted you can help with the terraforming research . . . but I'd sure better read that book. Not for Trine, but for Generation Gap.

LN

I'm in San Francisco today, at a conference on ecommerce and for the GII awards, then back home tomorrow. Staying at the Westin (on the City) and Christmas shopping at Macy's after each day's events. People in Longview will get a kick out of Macy's stuff even if it is as cheap (I shop sale racks!). Got a great story from the bus driver about Mars. I'll write and send it along if I get time.

Have a wonderful day.

BC

It's been good, even though I have a cold coming on. Leah (yoga instructor) took it easy on me. "Warming Trine" (alternate title) runs well. I made red marks all over my printout while Roland Dobbins was fiddling with my computers, and input them today, and kept going.

LN

Speaking of Christmas, I sent you a card. On the shopping end, I'll love getting you something that says "Larry" loudly—if I find it. But I won't buy something just for the sake of sending a gift. I have to imagine you have enough general "stuff." So please feel like I wish you a great Holiday whether any gift arrives.

BC

Okay. Your card in hand; your message received and understood. I haven't done it yet, but——my gift to you will reflect my missionary urge: It's a terrific sonic toothbrush.

Larry

Subj: Re: intermediate draft
Date: 12/15/99
   In a message dated 12/14/99 11:35:23 PM Pacific Standard Time,
   I guess my thought on another reader is just 'cause the nature of the collaboration between us is new and different——sometimes I like a reality check from outside. Your call——I don't have any risk here.

BC

Okay. I'll email to Steven as well as you, when it's ready, which will be in about two hours. I've got a cold, but it hasn't reached my brain yet . . . I think. So, who besides Steven? Let's get a sanity check from your circle of writers.

LN

   >For Generation Gap, I'm sure we'll need your basic design on terraforming. Partly because you sounded interested in it when we were talking story——which tags something in my barin as at least partly yours. Sort of like you designing the ships——it's something in your heart. But more importantly, I think you have an intuitive sense of space——things like ships and planets and worlds. I don't yet. Trine was my first attempt to write about space, and mostly I learned I am really still pretty badly clueless. I might learn that about computer and communications tech too, but I don't think so——I think I have some intuitive sense of those and we can shine in that area.

BC

   Ask Steven about THE DESCENT OF ANANSI. He needed some practice in free fall (that is, watching characters move in his head and writing about it.)

So do you. That in particular is why you need to compare the manuscripts. I don't think you even wondered if there was gravity in any given scene; no clue unless a character took it into her head to sit down.

LN

Remind me when I or we get an award to shut up fast.

BC

You'll remember. You're in politics.

Marilyn got us an artificial tree yesterday, after a lot of shopping. The forgotten top to the damn thing arrived this morning. We haven't put it up yet. I'm tired of hiring an overpriced hit man to kill a damn tree every year. I have sympathy for the Green cause; I rage against those who espouse the wrong cause through sheer stubborn ignorance.

I'm sucking on a Cold-Eez to kill what's established a colony in my throat. (Reminds me: I've got to get a January Playboy; I hear it's out.) It's midmorning and the wind is raging . . .

LN

Enough prattle. G'night.

BC

G'night.

Larry

Subj: Re: intermediate draft
Date: 12/15/99
    File: C:/My Documents/Brenda/Trine.doc (1673728 bytes)
    DL Time (32000 bps): < 14 minutes
    Fixed (at 10 pm.)
My first draft put Eric and Kimber each in a place where they couldn't see the action! Duh. I had her getting knocked out; that's what had to be fixed.

I think this does the job. If you find a show stopper, let me know. If it's good enough, show it to whomever you like.

And now I can let my cold have its way.

Larry

Subj: Re: intermediate draft
Date: 12/16/99
    In a message dated 12/15/99 11:47:24 PM Pacific Standard Time,
<<Subj: Re: intermediate draft
Date: 12/15/99 11:47:24 PM Pacific Standard Time
From: bjcooper@teleport.com (Brenda Cooper)
To: Fithp@aol.com
    I can tell I'm sleepy—sentences don't want to end.

Brenda

    Yeah, you can judge readability that way. But do it without the red
pencil.

LN

    Mom says I need a wife, and I agree, except every time I've tried a
beta male it's been good for about an hour.

Brenda

    Jeez, no! Wrong choice.

LN

    Something interesting happened—a woman in the group I met
with tonight gave a few thousand dollars to build a concrete walkway
between an elementary school and an old folks home so the kids
could visit even in the rain and the old folks could get to the school
even with walkers and wheelchairs. It built a bridge between
generations. I think I have a place for it in the still very very rough
plotting of the outline. . . . Bueno.

Brenda

    Sleep good. I hope you feel better. I will think good thoughts about
you.

Brenda

    Thank you. I'm still joyful . . . but a cold rarely lets me go until I've
tasted every symptom.
    I'm going to do a writer's trick: let "Warming Trine" sit for as long

as I can stand it, then hit it fresh. That is, I'll wait for your responses and revisions.

Larry

Subj: Re: intermediate draft
Date: 12/17/99
    In a message dated 12/16/99 10:25:10 PM Pacific Standard Time,
    << I do trust you.
    When Eric goes out to do the pole to pole and see if the CO_2 is freezing out what is he supposed to find? That it isn't?

BC

    Infrared will tell him that both poles are warmer than the freezing point of CO_2. Maybe we'd better say so: "The poles are too warm."

LN

    I'm not making any big changes—some word choices, a few little things. It's little enough I can use "Mark Revisions" so you can see them, or I can just do it. Preference?

BC

    << Just make the changes.

LN

Subj: Re: geration gap
Date: 12/19/99
File: C:/My Documents/Brenda/generation gap.doc (158208 bytes)
DL Time (32000 bps): < 1 minute
    I took a pass through GENERATION GAP.
    I like your names. (Might fiddle anyway, somewhere down the line.)
    Change: the original plan was to use a different moon. From the colonists' POV it would still be too close: accidents are likely, and an accident would greatly damage the ecology on Selene.
    Regarding Trine . . . and this may be redundant, but I'm saying it anyway, because you were thinking in terms of a sequel once.
    All the changes made were driven by a basic assumption: An alien species found it worthwhile to destroy a sapient race in order to get a terraformable world, and also worthwhile to hide it. Let's look at some of the fallout:

Something else has to be telling the Thray what to do. Somebody is conspicuously more powerful than a race with that much power!

Hence the need for the Overlords.

Habitable worlds are rare. Even worlds that can be manipulated into shape are scarce.

Hence EITHER Humanity will have no worlds of their own

OR they've become too powerful to be interesting. You'd spend all your word length deciding what they had evolved into, then trying to describe it.

Set humans up as judges, you have to protect them somehow. The Thray have powerful motive to swat them. We need reasons why they don't.

The Thray had better not be instinctive killers! The eyes are a nice touch: they're herbivores.

Help has to arrive fast, and be seen to arrive.

A hive mentality might well be mute: might communicate with aliens only with difficulty. It's still a nice touch, in that the Thray can't expect to argue their way around the evidence.

So, two points:

In any sequel, we're stuck with all of the previous assumptions. (And if you don't like them, pick another universe.)

Test your initial assumptions this way, every time. "Ask the next question." (Theodore Sturgeon.)

Larry

Subj: Re: "Warming Trine"
Date: 12/20/99
File: C:\My Documents\Brenda\trines fliers.doc (165376 bytes)
DL Time (32000 bps): < 1 minute

I read through it again, finding no change but good change; making small cosmetic changes of my own . . . until I was near the end. Then I started compulsive fiddling.

No facts have changed. I trimmed a little, I added some detail. I reworked dialogue. My intent: at the end, they're talking, they're actually conversing, following old habits that had been shelved. And . . . I eased Kimber off to sleep.

So look it over. But I'm going to mail it to Eleanor Wood, my agent, to be sold.

Larry

Subj: Re: Generation Gap Outline
Date: 12/27/99

In a message dated 12/26/99 8:05:12 AM Pacific Standard Time,
<< Subj: Generation Gap Outline
Got it.

LN

Hope you and Marilyn had a great Christmas. We did up here—
very nice day.

BC

We had a very nice two days.

It's tradition around here: Christmas Eve lunch gathering the whole
Doheny clan; evening, fannish-flavored gathering to open gifts at the
Pelz place. Christmas morning at my mother's. Add a dinner at a
friend's.

The Doheny clan has grown enormous. As they say of fandom . . .
we could rule the world if we could all be pointed in the same
direction. We were given badges with our names and lineage, no
kidding, and we needed them too. (At least, I did.)

LN

Ok. Here's what I've done:

Gone through and integrated your comments from the last run
through. Added a lot to the story plot line—the front and back have a
shape if you like it. The middle needs comprehension of the
terraforming project to take its shape further, but the ghosts of it are
there.

Added bits of stuff I've learned from bits of research.

Added a to-do list so you can look at it and let me know if it's a
good set and what's missing (remember I'm a true novice here—this
will be longer than anything I've even thought of before).

What I could use help with:

Take a look at this when you get time. It's not an emergency—I'm
temporarily on to other things and it's time in my process for this to lie
fallow so my hind brain can think about it undisturbed.

When you do look, add, play, enjoy. Please review/comment on
plot ideas—this is an easy time to change any of it. I don't want to get
too attached to anybody you're going to want to delete.

Don't worry about keeping things in their places if that's not
conducive to how you work. I can reorganize any time—and when I'm

on a creative bent with it I ignore the organization and go back for it later.

BC

I'm on it. If you can keep us organized, that would be great!

LN

My next steps:

Ignore this except the broad research stuff. I won't add directly to the outline document until I get it back from you.

Work on stories. Send them to you when I've done my next re-writes. It'll be two weeks probably for Dreaming Alioth to show up—this week I've got to catch up on web client work, do the town Y2K coordinator work, and play with insurance adjusters and car salesmen.

BC

Good plan.

LN

PS—my teeth are clean!

BC

I can grasp that it's an odd Christmas present; but I haven't forgotten how born-again *clean* my teeth felt the first time I used it. Jerry was going to buy *me* one until he saw I'd beat him to it.

Happy New Year!

Love, Larry

Subj: Re: Space Access 2000
Date: 1/17/00
    In a message dated 1/17/00 6:31:42 PM Pacific Standard Time,
    << Subj: Re: Space Access 2000
    Date:1/17/00 6:31:42 PM Pacific Standard Time
    Oh—and I'm not sure terraforming is forbidden—but rather genocide is. The crime was killing the fliers. Terraforming itself is fine—as long as you're not terraforming someone else's home out of existence.

BC

Think again. Another species was randomly chosen to JUDGE the Thray's intent. As humans clearly didn't have the weaponry to enforce a judgment, someone else must be standing by. We see no evidence that the Thray were suspected of genocide; why would their judges' lives have been given into their hands?

And why would they be suspected, why would anyone be, unless terraforming is very, very difficult? If terraformable worlds are scarce enough, the Thray action becomes reasonable. They know they'll get a habitable world because they know (and nobody else does) that they started with one.

Keep this wording. We may need to use it. Kimber may not have under-stood how difficult terraforming a *dead* world is. Any difficulty with Mars, she may attribute to ineptitude from unskilled humanity.

LN

(I learned that Stapledon's "Fifth Men" story already established that as a problem—he had his long lived terraforming men have to regretfully kill off Venusians, but that's a different story . . .)

BC

Different species too: no longer mankind.

LN

In the Terraforming book, I found a word: "Soletta"—A space based mirror designed to enhance a planet's insolation (amount of Solar Radiation . . .). The book even appears to suggest that ice is the best volatile to be affecting with soletta's since it would warm more easily that regolith (non soil planet crust). Fogg talks about arrays of mirrors, but given the way we are going with robotics I think the large numbers of tiny ones is a real plausible answer. We'll be ahead of the crowd!

BC

Dang—you're smart. I knew I liked you for a reason or two . . .

Brenda

Hee hee hee!

Larry

Subj: Re: Magnetic Lies comments—continued
Date: 1/18/00

You *didn't* write of an oil company's impact report. I want to remind you of why:

An oil company can't be defeated. There's no entity powerful enough to cause them to cease. A corporation can't go to jail, though a corporation officer can. Their spin doctors will blur the truth if the truth is damning. The truths are generally mushy anyway. My sources say that there are spotted owls everywhere; they're not even a distinct species.

There's no *story*. Especially, there's no *short* story.

The way to make a short story is to build boundaries around it. We are restricted by the reach of Kimber's knowledge.

If we *really* dealt with humanity as an interstellar civilization with equals and superiors, we'd be planning a novel the size of the Known Space canon. I don't want to. I've done that dance.

Whereas I have not danced the evolution of a terraform-capable civilization under restrictive rules. (I mean GENERATION GAP.)

LN

—grinning and enjoying the conversation. So remember email is a little one dimensional. Conversation hopefully makes us clear TOGETHER rather than each clear on our own with an intersecting set. We'll confuse readers with the part outside the intersections. I can be talked around—your point works as well—this is just where I started.

BC

Yes! We're overdue for a meet. These matters should have been thrashed out face to face. This is what worried me about writing a novel with Steven two states away. And we'd had practice.

Keep up the email dialogue. Things unsaid will otherwise foul us up.

Love, Larry

Subj: Re: Space Access 2000
Date: 1/17/00

I have a response from Eleanor Wood (my agent) on "Ice and Mirrors."

Today is King's Day. I'll mail it tomorrow, and await a response.

My own responses—save these until you have the manuscript—

She's right: I said Thray faces don't signal as human faces do (because that's the way to bet.) So: Take out the adjective ("approvingly").

The way you wrote the original story, someone had to be enforcing the rules. I took that as a given, and made something up. As we wanted a short story, I didn't show them much.

You showed human culture not much changed. I took that as a given. Thus, First Contact must have been recent, and humans don't have vast power. That plus the Thray's crime implies: terraforming is generally forbidden, and humans won't have done that.

Eleanor's last question is reasonable: how have your readers reacted? If they don't find any of this confusing or implausible . . . and if you haven't been inspired to more rewriting . . . we'll run with this.

love, Larry

Subj: Re: Got Eleanor's Comments
Date: 1/22/00

In a message dated 1/22/00 12:57:48 AM Pacific Standard Time,
Thank you for sending along Eleanor's comments. She's good and talks straight—I like that.

BC

Yes. Finding a good agent is very difficult, largely luck.

LN

The 'ordinary use of language' hurt a bit—but it's a good comment. I'll read through the whole thing tomorrow and look for ordinary wordings—but I don't want to get unclear to be clever. Challenge is good. I don't think it has to sound entirely like you—our combined voice shouldn't be your voice exactly or why collaborate? I want it to be as good a voice as yours alone is though.

BC

In every collaboration, we've learned a mutual voice. I don't know any quick way.

LN

The bit on "looked approvingly" was a good catch—and an easy fix. Bravo Eleanor.

My take on the last paragraph "How could the pillbugs enforce rules . . ." is more complex:

I'll read through and look for ways to deal with "nothing much seems changed from present day"—there should be some good answers to that one in minor technology changes. I don't think much is changed in how the humans ARE, but maybe in their tools . . . and a few very small tweaks might fix that.

BC

Changes in technology cause changes in "how the humans are". I've been trying, will keep trying, to teach you how to anticipate that. In OATH OF FEALTY (don't bother to look it up) Jerry put in a coffee dispenser that makes one cup at a time, in the guardroom. I wrote, "It tasted wonderful. Even cliches change."

You gave these students instant access to information, but they gather anyway to learn their grades. Good. A little more of that.

LN

Regarding Eleanor's comments in the last paragraph, my initial thought is that not everything needs to be known—the mysterious is OK as long as the story itself is not mysterious. I'm with you, I don't want a novel from this one, I want a finished success that readers love!

But confusion is not OK—so far the readers I've shared with have not said they are confused, nor have they seemed to be confused. I'm expecting the best feedback from Joe Green, and should have that fairly soon. He does not pull punches. I'll check in with what he has to say, and then see how I feel, but gut feeling says we are OK. Have you had anyone else read it? If so, what did they say?

BC

I haven't had anyone else read it. Yes, I think we're okay: unanswered mysteries, but no confusion. I'll look again on my last pass.

LN

It will probably be mid-week before I get all comments back, but I'll push for them since I have a huge desire to see this done.

BC

[LINE MISSING]
and "nothing seems much changed from present day" and fix the little "approvingly" glitch. Gather feedback and see if I think more needs to be done and if a clue as to what to do shows up in the feedback.

I'll turn it around back to you as soon as I can and you can swing through it once again as well. Next week is grueling—I have a story due for class, a writers meeting, a writers dinner, class, a part day workshop with Molly Gloss that Joe arranged at the college, and a Council meeting so every night is busy—it might be next Friday night before I get a 'final' re-write to you.

Does that sound about right to you?

BC

Yeah, nibble at it. No hurry. Let your brain work.

LN

Maybe I should re-read "Rogue" for ordinary use of language as well (she grins tiredly). Anyway—as always, open to suggestions. Boy, am I learning a lot!

BC

Okay, here's my take on "Rogue"—
DC Comics published a global graphic novel called "Zero Hour".

They bought from me, through Eleanor, an hour of my time on the phone, to be broken up as needed. And they wanted my name.

For their price, I couldn't give them my name. With my name on it, I would have had to do a lot more work and keep a lot more control. Comics people don't have our education. In fact it would have been impossible, but even trying it would have eaten a week or two, not an hour.

My name doesn't go on "Rogue Backup" unless it gets a lot better than I expect it to.

Working on your best story, not the most difficult, is probably the best use of your time. Pay no attention to me if you get inspired. Writing will polish your skills, even with Rogue, and you'll hone your inspirations.

Example: "sat down, finally letting myself shake with the feelings . . ."

Yeah, right. That involuntary shiver has to be written into her program. It would use all of her imaginary muscles: damn near as difficult as a sneeze.

Example: The Board has allowed the two women to merge: summation of their memories. Again, the mechanism isn't automatic, each choice is made consciously. Why choose to leave two bodies and then erase one? What's the point?

James (if permitted to witness) might see a momentary blur of static, then one Christa acting like a spastic while she tries to sort her memories.

LN

Take care and have a great day.

BC

Will try. Did I say my pool is finally in decent shape? It isn't. The outfit that replastered the pool, and the spa too, allowed not-yet-dried cement into one of the spa pipes. It's screwed up the entire piping system. I'm a swimmer, but I can't swim.

That sounds trivial, and it is. Jerry and I had a dynamite hike-and-work session yesterday. Plotted the first third of BURNING TOWER. I'll just call him and requisition *his* pool and spa.

You have a great day too.

Love, Larry

Subj: Re: "Ice and Mirrors"
Date: 2/23/00

In a message dated 2/23/00 7:17:50 AM Pacific Standard Time,
> Hey, I thought the Big Complaint in Southern California was dry wells, lack
> of water.
> Not now, eh?

> BC

"It never rains; it pours."

I looked out at the rainstorm this morning and thought, "This looks bad." Then, "No it doesn't. My mental picture of the freeway looks bad. My memory of the Tarzana house, with no drainage and water creeping up the steps and covering the pool, looks bad. This looks like my new house, only wet."

"Ice and Mirrors" went out yesterday, should reach you at noon.

Love, Larry

SMUT TALK
A DRACO TAVERN STORY

I was delighted to hit *Playboy* magazine again. They're a user-friendly market, and it had been thirty years since they published "Leviathan!"

They did something flattering and frustrating: they made me wait over a year so that they could get "Smut Talk" into the January 2000 issue, beginning the new millennium.

The Draco Tavern isn't just a pub. It's how humanity interacts with at least twenty-eight sapient species throughout the galaxy. Somewhere among these trillions of alien minds are the answers to all of the universal questions.

So it's worth the expense, but costs are high. Keeping supplies in hand grows more difficult every time a new species appears. Siberian weather tears the Draco Tavern down as fast as we can rebuild it.

When a year passed without a chirpsithra ship, we were glad of the respite. The Tavern got some repairs. I got several months of vacation in Wyoming and Tahiti. Then that tremendous chirpsithra soap bubble drifted inward from near the Moon, and landers flowed down along the Earth's magnetic lines to Mount Forel in Siberia.

For four days and nights the Draco Tavern was very busy.

On the fifth morning, way too early, one hundred and twenty-four individuals of ten species boarded the landers and were gone.

The next day Gail and Herman called in sick. I didn't get in until midafternoon, alone on duty and fighting a dull headache.

* * *

We weren't crowded. The security programs had let the few customers in and powered up various life support systems. The few who didn't mind staying another year or two were all gathered around our biggest table. Eight individuals, five . . . make it four species including a woman.

I'd never seen her before. She was dressed in a short-skirted Italian or American business suit. Late twenties. Olive Arabic features. Nose like a blade, eyes like a hawk. I thought she was trying to look professionally severe. She was stunning.

The average citizen never reaches the Draco Tavern. To get here this woman must have been passed by her own government, then by the current UN psychiatric programs, Free Siberia, and several other political entities. She'd be some variety of biologist. It's the most common credential.

Old habit pulled my eyes away. The way I was feeling, I wasn't exactly on the make, and I didn't need to wonder what a human would eat, drink, or breathe. *Tee tee hatch nex ool*, her chirpsithra life support code was the same as mine. My concern was with the aliens.

I recognized the contours of a lone Wahartht from news coverage. They're hexapods with six greatly exaggerated hands, from a world that must be all winds. They'd gone up Kilimanjaro in competition with an Olympic climbing team. Travelers are supposed to be all male. This one had faced a high-backed chair around and was clinging to the back, looking quite comfortable. He was wearing a breather.

The three Folk had been living in the Kalahari, hunting with the natives. They looked lean and hungry. That was good. When they look like Cujo escaped from Belsen with his head on upside down, then they're mean and ravenous and not good bar company.

Gray Mourners were new to Earth. They're spidery creatures, with narrow torsos and ten long limbs that require lots of room, and big heads that are mostly mouth. I'd taken them for two species; the sexual disparity was that great.

Two males and a female, if the little ones were males, if that protrusion was what I thought it was.

The gathering of species all seemed to be getting along. You do have to watch that.

As I stepped into the privacy bubble the woman was saying, "Men mate with anything—" and then she sensed me there and turned, flushing.

"Welcome," I said, letting the translator program handle details of formality. "Whatever you need for comfort, we may conceivably have it. Ask me. Folk, I know your need."

One of the Folk (I'd hunted with these, and *still* never learned to tell their gender) said, "Greeting, Rick. You will join us? We would drink bouillon or glacier water. We know you don't keep live prey."

I grinned and said, "Whatever you see may be a customer." I turned to the woman.

She said, "I'm Jehaneh Miller."

"I'm Rick Schumann. I run this place. Miller?"

"My mother was American." So was her accent. Briskly she continued, "We were talking about sex. I was saying that men make billions of sperm, women make scores of eggs. Men mate with anything, women are choosy." She spoke as if in challenge, but she was definitely blushing.

"I follow. There's more to be said on *that* topic. What are you drinking?"

"Screwdriver, light."

"Like hers," the Wahartht said. Aliens rarely order alcoholic drinks twice, but some just have to try it.

The female Gray Mourner asked, "Did our supplies arrive?" They had. I went back to the bar.

Beef bouillon and glacier water for the Folk. Screwdrivers, light, for the woman and the Wahartht, but first I checked my database to be sure a Wahartht could digest orange juice. I made one for myself, for the raspy throat.

The Gray Mourners were eating stuff that I'd never seen until that afternoon, an orange mash that arrived frozen. Tang sherbet?

I assembled it all quickly. I wanted to hear what they were

saying. A great many aliens had left Earth very suddenly, and I hoped for a hint as to why.

And . . . given the conversational bent, I might learn something of Jehaneh Miller.

As I set down the drinks the Wahartht was saying, "Our child bearers cannot leave their forests, cannot bear change of smells and shading and diet, nor free fall nor biorhythm upset. We can never possess much of our own planet, let alone others. The females send us forth and wait for us to bring back stories."

A Folk said, "You are all male. Do you live without sex?"

The Wahartht jumped; he tapped his translator. " 'Survive without impregnation activity.' Was that accurately your question?"

"Yes."

"Without scent and sonic cues, we never miss it."

Jehaneh nodded and said to me, "Most life-forms, the mating action is wired in." To the Wahartht, "Does that hold for sapient species too?"

The Wahartht said, "Impregnation is reflex to us. Our minds almost do not participate. Away from our females, we take a tranquilizing biochemical to inhibit a sometime suicidal rage."

I said, "I'm not surprised."

"But what should I miss?"

A Gray Mourner male cried out, "To return from orgasmic joy and be still alive!"

The other male chimed in. "Yes, Wajee! It always feels like we're getting away with something." I grinned because I agreed, but he was saying, "We think this began our civilization. Species like ours, female eats male just after take his generative pellet."

I think I flinched. The woman Jehaneh didn't. She cogitated, then asked, "What if you shove a beefsteak in her mouth?"

They're not insects, I wanted to say. *Aliens!* But nobody took offense. All three Gray Mourners chittered in, I assumed, laughter.

Wajee said, "Easy to say! No male can think of such a thing when giving generative pellet. Like design and build a parachute while riding hurricane! But what if two males? One male have sex. The other male, he put turkey in Sfillirrath's mouth."

Jehaneh jumped. "A whole turkey?"

The female smiled widely. Yike! Her jaw hinges disjointed like a snake's. Sfillirrath was twice the mass of either male, and her smile could have engulfed my head and shoulders too.

She said, "On Earth, a turkey or dog will serve. Taste wrong, even if feed spices to the animal, but size is right. Size of Wajee's head, or Shkatht's head. See you the advantage? Can have sex twice with the same male! Get better with practice, yes, Shkatht?"

"Almost got it right," Shkatht said complacently. "Next time for sure."

Wajee said, "Got to get one part right every time."

They chittered laughter. Wajee said, "Accident can happen. Turkey can escape. Resting male can be distracted, or remember old offense and not move quick."

Sfillirrath said, "But see anti-advantage? Males don't die. Too many males. Soon every female must have many mates, or else rogue males tear down cities."

Wajee said, "Mating frequency rises too. Too many mouths. Must invent herding."

"Herd, then tend crop to feed herd. Then cities and factories. Then barrier bag over placer tube," Sfillirrath said, "so don't make a clutch of infants every curse time! Now we mate without mating, but need cities to support factories to make barrier bags, laws and lawmakers to enforce use. Control air and water flow, cycle waste, spacecraft to moons for raw resources, first contact with chirpsithra, beg ride to see the universe and here are we. All for a perversion of nature."

Jehaneh asked the Folk, "How do you keep your numbers in bounds?"

"Breed more dangerous prey," one answered.

The female Gray Mourner asked, "How do humans pervert sex practice?"

I asked the woman, "Shall I take this?" She gestured, *Go*.

I suppose I shaded the truth a bit toward what she might want to hear. "What Jehaneh said isn't all true. Most of us don't mate with anything but adults of the other gender. Most men *know* that most women want one mate. Most women *know* that any man can be seduced. We make bargains and promises and contracts. We compromise. To go against human nature is the most human thing a human being can do."

Both Folk laughed. Jehaneh was watching me. I said, "We're a young species. In an older species the sexual reflexes would be hardwired." I wasn't sure that would translate, but none of the devices paused. Any space traveler uses computers. "But with us, sex involves the mind. We're versatile."

"We have barrier bags too," Jehaneh said. A moment's eye contact—*Condoms, of course, and had I caught the reference?* I flashed a smirk.

Still, I wouldn't be needing a barrier bag tonight. The rasp at the back of my throat told me that I'd be snuffling and coughing and gender free. I was lucky it had held off this long.

A Folk asked, "How are you versatile? Male with male? With sexual immature? Outside species?"

Sfillirrath asked, "Triads?"

"You've been reading the tabloids," I guessed.

Jehaneh said primly, "All of that has been known to happen. We discourage it."

"There are legends," I said. "Old stories that weren't written down until centuries after they were made. Mermaids were half woman, half sea life—"

"And mermen," she said.

"Jehaneh, those are modern," I said. "When sailors were all men, mermaids were all women with fish tails and wonderful voices."

Jehaneh asked, "Are you an anthropologist, Rick?"

"Sure."

"What discipline? What's your education?"

I'd been lecturing on her turf. My head throbbed. It does that sometimes when I'm challenged, but this was the day's low-level headache lurching into high gear. I must have caught what Gail and Herman had.

I reeled off some of my credits. "If you think about it, I need *every* life science to run this place, and e-mail addresses for everyone in the Science Fiction Writers of America. If you're an anthropologist, you might consider working here for a year or so. We rotate fairly frequently, and both my steadies are out at the moment—"

"No, I'm a bacteriologist."

Bacteriologist? How was I going to get closer to a bacteriologist? I was trying to plan for the long range . . . and the aliens weren't following this at all.

I said, "We humans, we do seem wired up to mate with strangers, outside the tribe. At least in fiction, yeah, Jehaneh, we'd mate with anything. Fairies were powerful aliens, nearly human, not very well described. Humans with goat horns or animal heads, goat legs, fish tails, wings. Some were *that* tall"—hands eight inches apart—"others the size of mountains. Spirits in trees and pools of water, angels and devils and gods from various myths and religions, they all mated with human beings in some stories. I'm telling you what's buried in our instincts. We don't always act on our instincts." I realized I was rambling.

"Rick, do you have any visual aids about?"

I gaped. Jehaneh's smile seemed innocent, but the question was impish.

"I don't think so." A raunchy thought crossed my mind. "Do a demonstration?"

"I don't think you'll be up for that," Jehaneh said.

"No, not tonight . . . flu."

She shook her head. "Invader. I came here to keep it confined."

Confined. Invader. Bacteriologist. A murky truth congealed: I didn't have the flu. Some alien disease had come with the chirpsithra ship. I started to say something to Jehaneh, tried to stop myself, and found my thoughts running away like water.

The Wahartht leapt to the table, then the wall. He scuttled toward an upper window, his thirty-six fingers finding purchase where there was none. Jehaneh reached into her purse.

In that moment's distraction I turned to run ... wondered what I was doing ... and every muscle locked in terror. Not even my scream could get out. The God damned flu was thinking with my brain!

Jehaneh aimed her purse. The Wahartht fell, stunned. I saw it all from the corner of my eye. I couldn't turn my head to watch.

Jehaneh reached forward and turned off my translator. She spoke into her own. "Bring them in."

I couldn't lift my arms. Escape was impossible: the host was fighting me. My head was beating like a big drum.

Sfillirrath's long, fragile arms set a cap of metal mesh on my head. She spoke into her own translator. It was a chirp make, crudely rewired. I heard, but not with my ears and not in any language of Earth, ~For your life, you must speak.~

I chose not to answer.

Two armored men took charge of the Wahartht. One took his breather and dropped it in a bag and sealed it, and set another on his face.

Gail and Herman came in. They bent above me, looking worried. Gail said, "Rick? You're very sick. We were too, but they cured us—"

"Don't agree to anything!" Herman said fiercely. "Not unless you want to make medical history!"

Sfillirrath spoke. ~See you these humans. You took them for hosts some days ago, you and your Wahartht pawn. Your colonies bred too fast for their health. In another day they would have killed them, but human defenders acted first. Most of your colonies on the ship are dead too. How did you reward a Wahartht, to make him betray so many?~

I said, not with my voice, ~Simulate mating. The drug he

takes to tranquilize depression does not leave him alert and happy. I do.~

~And what fool would assume that sapient beings cannot fight bacterial invasion? It may be you are not truly sapient.~

Stung, I answered, ~Am a star-traveling species. Hold many worlds.~

~Your number in the host is?~

~Currently ten to the ninth operators, one entity. Operators are not sapient, not *me*.~

~Breed to ten times as many, entity becomes smarter?~

~Only a little.~

~But too many for host. Rick Schumann would die. Kill host, is that intelligent?~

The voice in my mind asked, ~Fool, do you expect intelligence to stop an entity from breeding?~ I thought that was a funny remark, so I added, "Ask any elected official." My voice was an inaudible whisper.

Gail said, "Rick, the chirp liner is still near the moon. The point was to get all the tourists into closed cycle life support and not start a panic on Earth. There's a sapient microscopic life-form loose. This rogue Wahartht has been leaning over our drinks with his breather on, distributing the bacterium as a powder, in encysted form. Normally it spreads as a, um, a social disease. Under proper circumstances it is a civilized entity, not especially trustworthy but it can be held to contracts. But as a disease it could ravage the Earth."

I could barely blink.

"We can make treaties with sapient clusters of the bacterium. That's you. Some species can't tolerate it at all, and some clusters won't negotiate. Some aliens won't volunteer as carriers, either. Herman and me, we would have. Hell, we're grad students! But there wasn't time. They rushed us to the Medical facility and shot us full of sulfa drugs."

Sfillirrath had gone on talking. ~There is a chemical approach to halt your cell division. Antibiotics would kill you entirely, as they have killed your other colonies. Which will you have?~

I felt terror from both sides of my mind. ~If my operators

do not fission, still they die. When the numbers drop enough, I am gone. You would make me mortal!~

~Give you empathy with your host.~

~Monster, pervert! What would you know of empathy? I will accept the contraceptive.~

~You must buy it,~ Sfillirrath said coolly. ~This first dose is our gift.~ "Jehaneh, give him the first shot." ~Two boosters to come, else the sulfa drugs. We will discuss terms.~

Jehaneh pulled down my belt and pushed a hypodermic needle into the gluteal muscle. I barely felt the sting.

I listened to Sfillirrath's terms, and agreed to them. They included measures for the health of my host. My host was to be treated for arthritis, cholesterol buildup, distorted eyesight, a knee injury, flawed teeth. I was not to make colonies without permission of a willing host. Jehaneh offered herself as a host, under rigidly defined conditions, and I agreed to those. Xenologists of many species would interview me periodically.

I was feeling more lucid. When I could stand up, they escorted me off to the Medical facility.

Morning. I lay on a flat plate with a sensor array above me. I'd never seen the Draco Tavern Medical facility from this viewpoint.

I felt wonderful. Rolled out of bed and did a handstand, something I hadn't done in some time.

Jehaneh caught me at it. "I'm glad to see you're up to exercise," she said. "What do you remember?"

"First flu, then an invasion, now it's an embassy. Jehaneh, I can hear it. It's thinking with my brain. I think it's got the hots for you, but that could be just me."

"We agreed that I'll take a colony from you. Remember?"

"No. That sounds risky! Jehaneh, it would be like being an ambassador to, well, Iraq."

"They do build embassies in Iraq," she said, "and this is a star-traveling intelligence. What might I learn?"

"Huh. Your choice. And it'll fix . . ." I was remembering

more of the negotiations. "I thought I was in pretty good health, but it wants to do a lot of fixing. To show how useful it can be. You're the brain it really wants."

"Do you remember that it's a sexually transmitted, um, entity?"

I did. I leered.

We talked much as we had last night, but on a more personal level. Ultimately she asked, "We've both had the usual blood tests, yes? Our guest would fix that anyway. Do you have room for me here? Just until I can get infected." She didn't like that word. "Colonized," she said.

"Positively. Maybe I can talk you into staying longer? My bed has one or two unearthly entertainment features. And if a hundred breeds of alien are going to be interviewing your guest, well, the Draco Tavern has the best communication and life support systems on Earth."

She smiled. "We'll see."

TELEPRESENCE BY MARVIN MINSKY AND LARRY NIVEN 8/8/97 AT THE CACNSP MEETING, TARZANA

1970—People were interested in astronauts as celebrities, but never dreamed of going themselves. It got boring. Each of us came to realize that he or she would never go to space.

1997—Times have changed. Try this:

We can drop 20 kg robots on the Moon for a few million dollars each. Start with three, so we can lose one or two. Stop with a hundred . . . or not.

We develop the robots by testing on a desert and undersea. Take a climbing version up Everest. When we've made all the easiest mistakes, and sold ten thousand hours of operating the test robots to gamers, then: **Moonbug**.

We run a lottery. It's just like a state lottery, with profits to go to a good cause: explore more of space and build more Moonbugs. Winner gets, not big bucks, but 20 minutes operating a Moonbug. He can SELL or AUCTION what he won, or use it.

Winner gets 10 tickets so friends/family/lovers can watch and coach. He practices first with a simulator. There will be simulators in every mall, and cruder simulator programs on the Internet.

Yes, *we will* run the system at night!

That means 27,000 20—minute sessions per year, minus maintenance time and the frequent need for an expert to steer one or another Moonbug back out of a gully or roll it off its back. Call it 15,000 sessions in a year, or 60,000 per presidential term, per rover. Given ten Moonbugs—replaced from time to time, naturally—we can offer the experience of building structures on the Moon to 600,000 citizens.

Add a dedicated channel on every TV set in the world, and the vicarious experience can reach billions. (Of course it's *all* vicarious.)

The lottery pays for space travel, like any state lottery. But meanwhile we're training expert teleoperators by the thousands.

Notice that—although the lottery winners are randomly chosen—the operators aren't. They're the ones who kept their tickets rather than selling them, plus those who bought them from winners less interested. We've got the dedicated ones. Now we train them on the simulators. Twenty minutes with the real thing tests their training, and we keep the names of anyone who doesn't dump his Moonbug in a gully. We'll need those names.

Options:

A Moonbug might benefit from three or four operators running different systems or tools. This permits groups and even families to become proficient.

Low-cost access to space will allow sample return from the moon periodically. Therefore, during your time on the rover, you can collect your personal moon rock for an additional cost. Or collect one for the government for an extra five minutes!

Winner could write whatever he wished on the moon: his name, or Sally Loves Fred, or Think of It As Evolution in Action. Each rover remembers where it has been and leaves the writings intact . . . For perhaps the next billion or so years.

* * *

Corporate sponsorship. Moonbugs displaying company logos, or custom Moonbugs in the *shape* of company logos.

We intend ultimately to develop a lunar colony. We will hard-land a warehouse of modular components. For continuous power and a high probability of water, we may initially land at the pole. Our Moonbugs and trained operators will do the building:

Signal Relay Stations (for transferring signals to rovers away from the poles or on the "back" side).

Exploration. We want water if we can get it. The midcentury will want Helium3.

Observatory.

A habitat (involves mainly digging).

Build and deploy solar collectors. It will be some time before we can fabricate photovoltaics on-site, so some form of heat engine might be preferred.

Serious applications. There are many things to do on the Moon.

Mining.

Fabrication.

Geological exploration.

Principal industries will eventually include: manufacturing and launching orbital fuel. Hydrogen will be in short supply, but aluminum and oxygen are plentiful, and can make a moderately energetic fuel.

What we're building here is a subculture that will outlast anyone now alive. When the cost of transport to the Moon drops, and an audience of millions has announced itself, we'll see competition. Expect a demolition derby in Clavius Crater, run from the Luxor Hotel, with robots to be designed and operated by the competitors and lofted at Luxor expense.

Expect human teleoperators, originally teens who won a lottery, to travel to Mars orbit, where the familiar second-and-a-half delay won't interfere with the exploration of Mars, and the construction of Marsport City.

LEARNING TO LOVE THE SPACE STATION

I've been losing my arrogance, my faith in my own wisdom. That's hard on a science fiction writer.

Last year I wrote six articles for SPACE.COM, then ran out of inspiration. That was before the World Trade Center fell; it was even before the stock market fell from its amazing zenith. We were supposed to have cities on the Moon by now—and labs for our more dangerous biological experiments. My problem was that we were getting nowhere in space.

But that's a wrong perception, isn't it?

There's a lot going on in space! New domains I can write about! We've found free-floating planets, and weird super-jovians that huddle right up against their parent stars. ("Free Floaters," written with Brenda Cooper, soon in *Analog*.) Archeologists find evidence that the Earth has been frozen from pole to pole, four times over, and recovered. ("Ice and Mirrors," with Brenda Cooper again.) We find hints of a universal negative gravity effect. From quantum physics "entanglement" comes possible faster-than-light communications. There's been an endless run of discoveries, from comets and trans-Neptunian objects to the edge of the universe, so many that I have trouble keeping up.

We don't have a Moonbase, no, but there are men in space. The International Space Station is in place, and working, and growing.

In the 1980s, Ronald Reagan's science advisor was one of Dr. Jerry Pournelle's top students. Jerry gathered fifty-odd good men and women at the Niven house in Tarzana, to work out a proposed space program, with costs and schedules, to put before the President. We met four times during the Reagan Administration and twice since. One result was SDI—"Star Wars"—and the collapse of the Soviet Union. Another was the DC-X1, which landed on its tail and could be flown again the next day, and might have led to a single-stage ground-to-orbit spacecraft.

In one of these first meetings, we were persuaded to support Space Station Freedom.

Dr. Pournelle later told me that this was our worst mistake. Freedom became a great bleeding wound in the economy, sucking up most of the funding that might have gone to something real. The space station became a stack of designs and specs and changes that might have reached the Moon itself.

I have a T-shirt from that date. On the front, a design for Freedom, now many years obsolete. On the back,

"9 years

9 billion dollars

and all we got was this lousy shirt."

For all those years humanity had one station in space, and that was Mir. We're told that most activity aboard Mir was to keep Mir habitable. When the USSR went bankrupt, newly freed political entities argued among themselves while their astronaut was marooned in orbit. Mir was the best we had.

You can't build a political space station. We (various of the Citizens Advisory Council) had watched them build the Shuttle. Stories came down of the compromises between politics and design. Devices mounted on the rocket motor itself, subjected to that much stress, rather than fight through another contract. Clumsy designs intended to keep thousands of employees doing a job the DC-X1 did with three. If building a political spacecraft is that close to impossible, if the result is that close to unflyable, what would a political *space station* look like?

And they changed the design with every administration! I listened to a NASA man laying out possible new designs after Clinton took office. He had a beaten look. He showed hardware that would have to be thrown away.

I came to believe that we should have been launching a space station every time some purpose required one. You can't build a political space station; you have to build a dozen.

With all of that as background, it takes effort to realize that my T-shirt is obsolete. It's been many more than nine billion dollars, and more like twenty than nine years, but the damn thing is up there and doing its job!

I may be preaching to the converted here. I never did read minds worth a damn. If you already love the space station, don't let me bring you down. My viewpoint is special.

I'm sixty-three.

During the golden age—when I would have been twelve, but I grew up a little slow—an issue of *Analog* included a Von Braun spacecraft for a cover, and an article called "Rocket to Nowhere." Until then, even most science fiction writers had not perceived the value of "near Earth orbit"— an empty domain, with nothing there but what we might bring with us.

Von Braun's "The Conquest of Space" converted us all. We all fell in love with Werner Von Braun's wheel-shaped space station.

What *would* we sixty-odds think of the array of plumbing work they're putting together in orbit today? It doesn't spin! Even for fans of science and science fiction, it's hard to fight a prejudice. But Von Braun's wheel is obsolete.

The bigger the circumference, the more closely spin resembles gravity. Given too small a circle, sitting or standing requires a velocity change: it feels like you've been kicked in the head. Why not use a tether instead of a ring? You get a much bigger radius. That idea is as old as the Von Braun wheel.

Good design work has been done on tethers, particularly by Robert Forward. There's a gravity gradient in near Earth orbit. Spin isn't even needed if you don't mind low gravity, and you can use a long conducting cable to pick up electrical power too . . . or pump power in or out to change altitude.

Or you live with microgravity and fight it with exercise and diet supplements. We'll see how that works out. I need to keep better track of what they're doing up there.

From Earth you can't see footprints on the Moon, but you can see the ISS in orbit—a dot to the naked eye, more to binoculars—and it gets brighter as they make it bigger. A fool can still disbelieve in mankind in space, but it takes a conscious effort now. The fool dares not look up.

Once you're in orbit you're halfway to anywhere.

In an earlier article I wondered if virtual travel would become the normal mode; if real travelers, tourists, would become a few highly paid professionals wired to record their experiences for mass-market sale. We would see the Taj Mahal on the Geographic channel, the way we expect to see Mars. The events of September 11 may have brought that about.

Let's find out. I'm pretending the world is normal and I'm flying to New York, then on to a science fiction convention in Albany. Afterward I'll report what flying is like for the likes of me and us, after the airlines adjust to the new reality.

AUTOGRAPH ETIQUETTE

Autographing isn't the fun part.
　　In my lust to bring order out of chaos, I have created a set of rules for authors and autograph hunters. Feel free to disagree with any of this. It's only one man's opinion.

FOR WRITERS

You're not a movie star. You have to go to a convention or a bookstore if you want to sign autographs. You won't be accosted in random restaurants because nobody knows your face.°

Your purpose here is to sell books and have fun. All else follows from that.

1) Don't short-sheet the seeker. Give him your name, his name if he wants it, the date if he wants it. "Best wishes." Special inscription if it's not too long. Don't refuse to sign paperbacks or a story in a magazine. You didn't have to come here to tell someone what he can't have.

   The exception is "generic" autographs for dealers. These have no emotional significance. Do it or don't do it, depending on how you feel.

2) If the committee (store manager) wants to put a limit on the number of books a seeker may submit, that's fine. Let him enforce it too. Or not. **Riot control isn't your problem.**

3) Keep telling yourself: if the seeker's carrying two grocery bags full of your books, he must have *bought* two grocery bags full of your books.

4) Get the convention committee to schedule you for a formal autographing, and advertise it. Otherwise, they'll mob you elsewhere: in halls or at parties. You'll find yourself looking for flat spaces or giving your drink and pipe to some-

one to hold; another flat space for the book, or someone's back; fish out a pen or borrow one, and remember which, because you want to give back a borrowed pen and KEEP YOUR OWN. . . . All of this is worth avoiding.

5) At the formal autographing, borrow a pen from the committee/manager, or use your own. *Know* it's yours. *Don't* give it away. Use a cheap pen, because sure as hell you'll hand it to someone anyway . . .

6) Your brain will turn to mush long before your hand gives out. Never make promises while autographing. (The good news is, it's amazing how fast hand and brain recover afterward.)

7) Since some clown dropped his book into Robert Heinlein's mashed potatoes when he was GOH at the Kansas Worldcon, I've *never* signed a book if the seeker got me while I was eating; and I've been willing to lecture him on the subject. Then again, I'm a compulsive teacher. Take your choice.

FOR SEEKERS

You're here because you want to be. Enjoy it. If you admire the writer who's doing all the signing, give him a break. He's not necessarily having fun right now.

1) If the store put a limit on number of books signed, don't violate it. Go through the line four times. It won't kill you.

2) Sure you hate standing in line. You'd rather accost the poor suffering author in the halls or at a party; but it's not as if you were among strangers. Start a conversation.

3) Talking with an author can be an act of mercy, if he's not exactly being mobbed. However, don't interfere with his signing books. His brain may have turned to mush by now, so don't expect him to be sensible. He won't remember dates or promises. If you leave him a note so he can get back to you, he may lose the note.

4) If he spells your name wrong in the autograph, it's your fault. Best move is to show him your card or your convention badge.

5) Never accost anyone while he's eating. Or ordering. Or sitting in a restaurant. The bar is marginal (and you're buying). Don't interrupt a conversation. At a convention, any

writer may be trying to do business, and that takes precedence over an autograph hunter.

6) No author leaves an autographing if there's still a line, unless it's something serious. He may be keeping an appointment, a chance to make some money or get married or laid. Maybe his thumb and/or little finger feel like they've been smashed. Yours would. Maybe it's his back that's killing him.

So **let the poor bastard go.**

7) Two minutes after the autographing is over, the author **doesn't remember your name**. He won't remember it two years later either, and making him feel guilty about it is rude.

TABLETOP FUSION

When cold fusion broke into the news, *Reason* magazine asked me for an article on how it would affect the future.

The news had gone cold by the time I turned it in. They bought it anyway, but chose not to publish it.

The subject is warming up again.

The viewpoint of the physicists here is easy to understand. They spend money like a drunken government, trying to get enough heat and pressure to make solar-style fusion work. The money is committed years in advance. They did not warm to the notion of being beaten by chemists. Now they've admitted that something is going on: they get radiation, tritium, and other indications that it ain't just chemistry. Nuclear fusion is happening at some level.

But even without that, it's a fit subject for science fiction.

When the news hit, I bought stock in platinum mines. I had to explain to my broker that I had no interest in platinum, just the mines. They're the only source of palladium. I held for a bit, then sold it. It isn't that I lost faith. But it seems that the lattice structure of the palladium electrodes somehow absorbs the shock of two deterium nuclei becoming one helium nucleus, so that the nucleus doesn't have to spit out most of the energy as a neutron. Palladium can't be the only substance with the right lattice structure.

Now my stockbroker wants to hire me. The man she actually wants is Jerry Pournelle: these were his suggestions.

I'm a science fiction writer. It always feels as if I actually know all that stuff. In May 1989 I was prepared to tell you:

The wonderful thing is that you'll know, and soon. The experimental setup at the University of Utah is cheap. Pons and Fleischmann used their own money. For a hundred thousand dollars you can try it yourself! A lot of universities and laboratories will. Before I have quite finished typing, you should know whether this is another Dean Drive or a discovery to rank with the electric motor.

Hah! A panel discussion at Baycon in May changed my perspective.

What's the melt? Lithium deuteroxide, but was it doped with something else? Is it the deuterium that undergoes fusion, or the lithium? Or both?

Platinum and palladium electrodes seem to be the key. But "making the electrodes is a black art." You do everything right, meticulously, and you still don't know what you'll get. Panelists spoke of electrodes used for isotope separation: melted in vacuum, and recast, fifteen times! After the tenth remelting, a spectrum change indicates that the melt is still losing trapped gas!

That black art is called alchemy, and it's old. Or else it's the infant science of chaos, like weather prediction, the stock market, disease control, and a score of other undisciplined disciplines. Results are very sensitive to initial conditions. Wobble the sixth or tenth decimal place, and everything changes. A bright calm day becomes a hurricane. A vaccine that had AIDS stopped cold hits a sudden spike in the death rate.

Pons and Fleischmann are saying very little. Their reputations are solid; their papers are not; their methods are secret pending patent applications. The brightest friends I've got are all using the word "intuition."

So here's the future. I'm making optimistic assumptions because that's what *Reason* asked for, and because it makes the most interesting story.

If tabletop fusion is real, then we know something about it.

1) A tabletop fusion plant—call it a *fusor*—would be a billion times cleaner (per output in kilowatts) than a hot plasma fusion plant. That makes it cleaner than every form of power now in use except hydroelectric (which is clean if you're not downstream when the dam goes) and solar.

2) Interestingly, the tabletop fusor has no more weapons potential than a teddy bear. There's not enough power output for a decent weapons laser, and if anything goes wrong, it just stops.

   You can't build it bigger because there's an upper temperature limit. The fusion takes place in the crystal lattice of the palladium, where an electric charge can concentrate deuterium nuclei to an effective 10^{24} atmospheres of pressure. That's close enough to allow fusion. Swell; but if the electrodes melt (and the theory doesn't), the crystal lattice in the palladium is lost and everything stops.

   So don't expect big power plants: there's no economy of scale. There's no way to make it explode either.

3) Are we talking about running a car around the world on a quart of lithium deuteride? Today's gas-driven car *always* bursts into a fireball, whatever you do to it, at least in the movies. Deuterium burns like hydrogen, sure, but a quart of the stuff isn't terribly dangerous.

   I can't see fusor automobiles. The fusor won't get that small, not soon.

   But we might see eighteen-wheel trucks running on fusors. Small businesses and apartment buildings and individual houses could have fusors in their basements, if the price dropped enough. The big power companies would lose customers.

   Eighteen-wheelers use a lot of oil. The United States produces fuel enough to run our cars ourselves, or near enough. I'm surprised that Pons and Fleischmann haven't published everything they've got, damn quick, before Iran sets a price on their heads. They can do more harm to the oil-producing nations than any novelist.

Run the eighteen-wheelers on deuterium and we'll find city air growing cleaner.

With small power plants in our basements, we would attain an independence we've long thought to be lost . . .

Wait a minute. We've seen how difficult it is to get one of these things to work at all. Wouldn't that push the commercial product a long way into the future? and make it hellishly expensive to manufacture? and a pain in the ass to own?

Yes. Sorry. For the foreseeable future, the fusor will be a rich man's toy. And he's a survivalist. And he hasn't stopped paying his electric bill because he doesn't quite *trust* his fusor.

Then again: *everything* starts as a rich man's toy. *Be the first on your block* . . . The wealthy test new products for us. The best designs ultimately surface, dependability goes up and the price drops. Maybe by A.D. 2050.

4) Don't expect high efficiency here. This is a heat engine, but we've got to keep the electrodes below the melting point. Thermodynamics tells us that the *maximum* efficiency of a heat motor depends on the ratio between operating and ambient temperature, counting from absolute zero.

That's not good, but it's not awful.

Contrast the OTEC power plant (Ocean Thermal Energy Conversion). It gets its power from the difference in temperature between the surface and bottom of an ocean. It's expected to run on a temperature difference of ten Centigrade degrees. A sea bottom is always at $4° C = 277° A$; so the ratio would be $10/277$ = theoretical maximum of 3.6 percent efficiency. Lousy. But there's a lot of ocean; and seawater is *very* conductive; and because you're stirring up nutrients in the sea bottom mud, the only pollution is an excess of fish. Low-efficiency, clean-running, infinite fuel supply . . . and OTEC remains useful, if you have a warm-water ocean.

Fusors are fueled by the deuterium in water. Low-efficiency, clean-running, infinite fuel. We could use up all of Earth's deuterium over the next hundred thousand years and not deplete the seas by much, because most seawater isn't deuterium oxide. And when we run out, the moons of the outer planets are water cores inside ice shells!

5) Still, fusors will operate best where it's *coldest,* where the heat sink is most useful.

Hey, that's interesting! Solar power needs sunlight. An OTEC operates best in tropic summer seas. Even *orbiting* solar plants would deliver power most easily to the equator. But a fusor operates best during a six-month winter night at the Antarctic Pole!

If you put a fusor in every basement in Alaska, Siberia, Greenland, and Antarctica, and institute a regular deuterium delivery, what do you get?

Civilization. Where nothing lives, that's where you want to put your fusor industry. What makes civilization work is a good heat sink.

Every nation that borders the Arctic Circle is already exploiting that environment to some extent, except Canada and the United States. But fusors could make the North Pole worth having, and the South Pole worth even more (because there's land under it). The Soviets could laugh at our warm-water ports.

6) I was in a physics class at Cal Tech the day I realized that the proper place for a power plant is Pluto. My teacher was not impressed. Bright guy, but all these decades later, he still hates science fiction.

So let's talk about space.

Launch to orbit has always been the bottleneck, and the fusor won't help us here. The power output will be too low. But "Once you're in orbit you're halfway to anywhere," said Robert Heinlein. The fusor brings everything closer.

A fusor is the obvious power plant for a lunar base, or for anyplace in the solar system that experiences long nights.

Light sails are still the way to explore the inner solar system. But inward from Earth there's not much besides the sun. Outward from Earth, the sunlight gets thin. You want

your own power supply even if you keep the sail. The black
sky makes a terrific heat sink, too.

A fusor ought to work fine with an ion drive.

Your fuel supply weighs almost nothing and lasts almost
forever (though you can still run out of reaction mass. Shall
we stop at various outer moons?). The colder it gets, the
better your fusor motor likes it. This is what we really need
to explore Jupiter and its moon system . . . and the rest of
the solar planets, and the comets of the Oort Cloud . . . and
ultimately the nearer stars. The domain of the fusor-
powered ion drive reaches from lunar orbit, to infinity.

Jeremy Rifkin's response was quick. Cold fusion is evil,
not because of an intrinsic danger, but because any form of
power encourages the destruction of the environment.

Then it all began to look like vaporware.

The fusor assuredly isn't a hoax. At worst it's a blind al-
ley, and not even an expensive one. At best—

Have you ever wished that you'd gotten in on a fad while
it still worked? We could have been on Mars with a refitted
submarine, before the Dean Drive evaporated. We could
have got thin on the beef and bourbon diet; become indecently healthy on brown rice. We could reshape civilization
with fusor power.

Anything that makes Jeremy Rifkin unhappy can't be
all bad.

COLLABORATION

But how can *anyone* collaborate? Dreams are sacred! Somebody else's sticky fingers muddying your ideas, playing ignorant games in your personal mental playground—and what if you find yourselves trying to gallop off in different directions? How can you stand it?

Well, it's nothing to go into lightly.

I've done it, though. As of 12/10/1982 I have written:

A novel and three scripts for *Land of the Lost* with David Gerrold.

Five and a half novels, two novellas, and an alternate ending to a movie, with Jerry Pournelle.

A triple collaboration with Jerry Pournelle and Steven Barnes. (Another triple is at dead stall. Triples may be overcomplex.)

A short story and two-and-a-fraction novels with Steven Barnes.

A short story with Dian Girard.

Several stories set in "franchise universes," in other people's playgrounds.

Two solar systems, *Medea* and *Thraxisp*, with ten and eight collaborators, respectively.

I've been advised to kick the habit. I think it's too late. I suppose I should add that I've *never* followed *all* of the following set of rules. That's how I learned them.

1) You must trust each other absolutely.

It helps if each of you has a track record. You don't write with an amateur . . . and if you've never published, you don't ask a professional to collaborate with you. He might say yes—and you'd be collaborating with a known fool!

2) Keep talking.

Michael Kurland and I once spent a lovely afternoon walking around Berkeley while we plotted out a collaboration novel. We had a wonderful time. When we got back to his office we realized that neither of us wanted to write the damn thing, together or separately.

Never regret such "wasted" time. Talk is recreation. Writing is work. Until you're sure you want to do the work, keep talking.

3) There's an exception, a fail-safe method that can't cost you anything at all.

When Hank Stine and I were both novice writers, there was a short story I found unsalable. I handed it to Hank with the idea that if he could improve it, we'd split the take. It worked to this extent: we sold it five years later, to Ted White, for what Hank says was the dirtiest check he'd ever seen in his life.

Again: "The Locusts" broke my heart. I didn't have the skills; I couldn't get it to come right. Somewhere in there was a powerful story, but I couldn't find the right approach. Ten years later I handed the old manuscript to Steven Barnes. Could he make anything of it? He did. *We* did.

What's the worst that can happen? The time *you've* expended is gone. *He* does no work unless he sees possibilities. How can either of you lose? And you'll learn whether you can trust each other.

So: he fixes it . . . and you find you can't stand the resulting story. Now you know. You should not write together.

4) A writer has his own ideas of how the universe runs. He makes his own worlds to fit. People who interfere with his world-picture can cripple him. Television writing is notorious for this.

Most writers aren't built for collaborations.

If you're in that class, don't let it affect your self-esteem. People who should never collaborate included the likes of Robert Heinlein.

5) You each go into it expecting to do 80 percent of the work.

Total: 160 percent. Collaborations are hard. Don't expect a collaborator to save you work!

6) Every collaboration is different. Each pairing needs different rules; it has to be learned all over again. I can offer some examples:

David Gerrold and I found that we could work in the same room, trading off at the typewriter. We were writing a funny story. Our senses of humor matched nicely. The plot was loose and simple. We knew what the characters were trying to do, we knew how difficult it would be, and we knew they could solve it. We explored likely and unlikely consequences, and did our best to amuse each other. We took turns doing the homework—which was extensive: weaving, balloon flight, magic in anthropology.

(David's got the typewriter going like an air hammer. I'm on the couch, admiring. Suddenly he shoots to his feet screaming, "All right, I've started a riot. You get them out of it.")

(I read what he's written. I ask, "Why do I want to get them out of it?" and I write the riot.)

Jerry Pournelle plots our novels with infinite intricacy before we start. We hold frequent, intensive discussion sessions, then go off and write alone. We didn't start writing *together* until near the end of *Footfall*, maybe twelve years after *A Mote in God's Eye*.

We discovered early that each of us had skills to match the other's blind spots. Therefore, we carve stories to use our combined strong points to the fullest extent—and we trade the novel off, one keeping it for weeks at a time. Jerry handles politics, warfare, and conversations among large groups of people better than I do, while I run aliens and oddballs and small, revealing conversations. A hero working his way through a sea of troubles on sheer guts is Jerry's. When a character gets hysterical, that's me.

Steven Barnes didn't have all of his skills developed yet, so we worked a little differently. The work still had to be outlined until we'd included *everything*. (It's never true, but it should look that way.) Then he did first draft—which he does well, but it's the hard part—and I did final rewrite, which is the easy part once you've been at it for twenty years.

I'm using the past tense because he's learned everything I could teach by now. Today we trade off, and we're writing together for fun.

Dian Girard and I had incompatible computers and lived too far apart. We just mailed *Talisman* back and forth. It produced a good story, but I don't really recommend the method. If you've got compatible computers and a modem, that might work. Jerry and I do; but we live close enough, and like each other enough, that we just carry the disks back and forth by car.

7) Decide two things at the outset.
   a) One of you has a veto. (Usually me.) I used it with David where our senses of humor *didn't* match, or where his TV training had grown too strong. I almost never used it with Jerry. It gets used with Steven sometimes. Without the veto, a single argument could stop your work dead in its tracks.
   b) Someone has to do the final rewrite.

Look: a collaboration won't automatically read smoothly. You'll learn each other's styles to some extent, but the first full draft will still read rough. One of you does an entire final rewrite, not only because he will spot things you have both missed, but because you *must* remove those jarring inconsistencies of style.

If neither of you volunteers for that final rewrite, play showdown or flip a coin. (Steven Barnes is a martial arts enthusiast. I do the final rewrite.) You might even wait until you've got a full first draft, so that the loser won't lose interest while contemplating that final backbreaking job.

8) Outline what you're doing. You never *really* know exactly how it's going to go, but it should *look* that way. David and I didn't do enough of that, and I think it shows. Jerry and I wind up with enough notes to fill a normal book.

When you see a better path than the one you outlined, take it! But discuss it first.

9) Make frequent copies!

 If you're still using a typewriter—or a quill pen, for that matter—you'll find this a hassle. Do it anyway. You'll make marks in the margins of each other's photocopies, and wind up with nonidentical manuscripts. Not to worry. The melding of two copies took *one afternoon* for *one* of us for a 150,000-word intermediate draft. I was startled.

10) It doesn't matter who contributed what idea. Argue or brag about it if you like, but keep this in mind: if your friends can't tell who wrote what by reading the work, you did it right. If they can, one of you should have done that final rewrite you skipped because it was too much work.

11) If you find your novel coming apart, you must decide who gets what ideas for his own use. In general, two writers working from the same ideas produce utterly different works; you might start with that assumption.

But why do it? I tried it the first time just to see if I could. I went into the second collaboration because the first was so much fun. It became easier. I got hooked.

1) I have this quirk. I can only write so far on a novel before I have to turn to something else. With collaborations I never have that problem; there's plenty of time for short stories and nonfact articles while the novel is elsewhere.

2) It's a wonderful thing to know that your novel is writing itself elsewhere while you're goofing off. It's almost eery to see your scenes improve themselves, shape themselves into what you were trying to say but couldn't get quite right.

3) You know the feeling you get while talking to a fan about the intricacies of your universe? I get it when I meet someone who's done the math for *Neutron Star* or computed the exact instability of the Ringworld or *really* worked out Pierson's puppeteer physiology. Well, there's a touch of that here. Each of you seems to be flattering the other. When you're stuck on a scene, your other half can get you off the dime, or even take over the writing until you can see where you're going next.

4) You catch each other's mistakes!

5) The characters will deepen and develop through the inter-actions of two writers. Inevitably, you'll each pick favorite characters and speak through these. The opposing view-points can make a more interesting story.

6) If you're lucky or careful, your different skills will match. You write something neither of you could have written alone—and that's the only *real* excuse for a collaboration. Otherwise, it's too much work.

7) Corollary to above: you learn from each other.

From David I learned not to hesitate before jumping into a scene. You can always burn it afterward.

From Jerry I've learned to write of boardroom power and precedence battles; I get a glimmering of military strategy; I can write of duty-oriented characters (though I'm still more comfortable with tourists like Beowulf Shaeffer or Kevin Renner).

Steven has a different approach to character development. And his characters have such fun! Dian does nice detail work re daily life in an odd environment. Working with them adds to my own skills. I need all the skills I can get. *So do you.*

How do you get into a collaboration? I don't know. David and I started a short story one night. Jerry and I sat down with coffee and brandy and spent a long night working out ideas, exploring possibilities and jotting notes. I handed Steven a failed story, looking for a new approach; he took my own ap-proach and made it work. Then he showed me a map of Dream Park. Jerry showed me a map of Todos Santos and I put a high diving board at the edge of the roof. I told him I wanted to write a sequel to Dante's Inferno, and he told me that Benito Mussolini was a much-misunderstood man. Joel Hagen got eight of us in a room for a three-day convention, and we produced notes and sheets of math and paintings and maps and sculpture and relief globes and music . . .

The opportunities just happen. Be ready to talk. At the be-ginning of a collaboration you both have a good deal to lose. You may have a great deal to gain.

INTERCON TRIP REPORT

INTERCON is a once-per-two-years convention at the University of Oslo, Norway. At the Holland Worldcon they asked me to attend as the Guest of Honor from USA, with Mary Gentle from England, and two locals.

Sunday: I drove Marilyn to Los Angeles International. She's running next year's Old Lacers convention. This year's is in New Jersey. So it's Marilyn in New Jersey and her husband in Oslo.

Monday: I wrote down the exact location of the car in Lot C, phoned and left it on my answering service for Michelle Coleman to transmit to Marilyn in New Jersey.

SAS boosted me to Business Class. The seats are perfectly orthopedic when reclined, and a shelf pops up under your legs too. They'll bust your back when upright if you don't kill the curve with a pillow, but SAS supplies a pillow.

Tuesday afternoon: Landed at Oslo Airport. Nine-hour time difference. My back felt fine. The seats work!

Bjørn Vermo had volunteered to escort me around. He drove me to the Nobel Hotel, then walked me around Oslo for a couple of hours. Walking after a long plane flight seems to be a powerful antidote: I felt wonderful. And I collapsed right quick.

Wednesday: The Nobel serves a wonderful breakfast, brunchlike, terminating at 10 A.M. No problem. My body had shifted by twelve hours, and stayed that way.

Bjørn drove us to Alfred Nobel's historic dynamite works, now a museum, at Engene. Interesting. Then more . . . I was still jet-lagged, dozing in the car.

He had me back by evening. I wandered the territory I'd

seen Tuesday. Street music, lots of parks and fountains, a roofless restaurant.

Thursday: An old industrial site in a deep valley. "They've locked up the waterfall"—in pipes running down the cliff to a power plant, all decades old. "Sometimes they let it out." There's a turbine on display, designed for not much water and a pressure head of half a mile, with a jet that could cut Superman in half.

The old captains of industry followed powerful obligations to their workers. Early this century, one noticed his people were going nuts without sunlight in winter. He set up an early cable car system to get his people up to the crest in winter, where the sunlight was.

We went up and wandered the crest for a while. Wonderful view.

Up the canyon to the power plant, and the site of the Nazi heavy water plant. Allies tried to bomb it, but the canyon's too deep. They couldn't get an angle. Norwegian saboteurs went in, blew it up, went out, a hairy exercise that ran smooth as silk. They later starred in a movie about it. The Nazis fixed the plant, we *did* bomb it, and the Nazis (believing that they needed heavy water to make their bomb) quit.

Upslope still, to a dam made with no concrete, just rock. It's a Norwegian technique. Dinner: an isolated restaurant, wonderful view, an unfamiliar but delicious fish. Then—

Bruce Pelz had warned me not to leave Norway without seeing a stave church. Bjørn took us to a working stave church at dusk (9 P.M.) It's truly wonderful, and indescribable.

Friday: Five in the morning, I woke with an allergy attack. It gets me in the eyes. Cause: fatigue, shortage of sleep. It eased off after four hours or so. I got some shopping in before Bjørn showed up at noon.

Oslo is surrounded by primeval forest. Bjørn was set to take me walking there. But Intercon was due to start at 6 P.M., and my GOH speech would follow. "Get me to the hotel for a couple of hours on my back," I said, "or I'll collapse."

Nordik law allows anyone to pick berries in the forest; it's one reason the forest has to be protected with such ferocity.

We ate blueberries and wild strawberries as we went. Bjørn took us to a tremendous view over Oslo.

Then he got us lost. Three kilometers down a wrong path, in the rain, and back too far, before he realized that he'd been reading his compass with his knife blade directly underneath it. I didn't make it back to the car. I boarded a bus a kilometer short of that target; sat around ten to fifteen minutes waiting for the bus to move; and saw Bjørn in his car at the next stop.

The hotel shower was all that I'd dreamed of during the walk in the rain. Heaven.

I'm afraid I short-changed the speech somewhat. My mind just turned off. But I'd gone for show-and-tell, because of the language gap: I'd tossed stuff in my luggage, Ringworld Game and Comic illustrations, design specs for Dream Park paraphernalia, interesting badges, the Trantor-Con Restaurant Guide, *Fallen Angels* and the T-shirt with the cover, other books: things to pass around. I hope they spoke for me. (I think I'll try it again at my next convention.)

Saturday: Everyone in Olso seems to speak English. It was like a standard little convention in some respects. In others, no. They take it for granted that the GOHs will vanish frequently to do tourist things.

I was lucid again for the morning panel. Then we (Bjørn and Mary Gentle and her husband and some others) went to lunch and the Viking Ship Museum. Viking ships are awesome in the complexity and skill of their creation.

Sirius magazine had published one of my stories. They fed me Danish beer and Linie Aquavit: chive-flavored vodka that has been shipped to the southern hemisphere and back (across the Line) as a guaranteed means of aging. It's wonderful.

Nightfall, 9 P.M.: Heidi Lyshol (the energy source for Oslo fandom) and her husband took me and Mike Jitlov to Emmanuel Vigeland's Sculpture Garden. This is the right time, she says. See it in half darkness, without swarming tourists. We wandered among over a hundred statues of people at every age and in almost every possible human mood, and not a scrap of clothing among them. Nice, somber mood.

Sunday: My back was still fine: good enough that I

admitted I'd sign autographs. Good enough that I went back to Vigeland's sculpture garden to see it by daylight. Heidi's wrong. The statues fit just *fine* among a seething swarm of tourists. (One artist's vision shaped all of these, with apprentice help. They have a generic look, as if Vigeland forbade any detail beyond some level.)

When I reached the U, Mary and her husband were fighting. Swords. Demonstrating a technique they evolved themselves, swordsmanship turned on its side so that nobody gets hurt. Meanwhile, someone had made off with around $900 in convention receipts, a paper bag of Norwegian kroner clearly labled as to value and left sitting at the desk. Oslo is delightfully crime-free, but Intercon may have to invent security real soon now.

A Soviet publisher brought his wife with him to translate, and his one-and-a-half-year-old daughter. He wants rights to some of my books. The baby's just learning Russian. When her mother begins speaking gibberish, she flies into an instant screaming rage.

So Daddy would speak; then Mommy would begin to tell me in English what stories were wanted, conditions, terms; and the girl would begin a shrieking fit. She didn't like me talking either!

They tried various approaches. Mother retreated, nursed her, got her calm . . . returned and spoke English, and BOOM.

The format that ultimately worked must have been fun to watch. Daddy's carrying the girl, swinging her, soothing her, way the hell at the far end of the hall. Back he comes, and he speaks several paragraphs of Russian to *me*. Then he's briskly off with Daughter, out of earshot while Mommy translates. I answer. Daddy swings back for more . . . a long elliptical orbit. . . .

He asked me to attend a Russian convention. Annual. In February. Sounds cold. Nineteen ninety-two looks busy for me, so I begged to be asked for 1993. . . .

(And now Gorbachev's down and back up, the Gang of Eight Stooges is imprisoned, and who knows?)

Two o'clock, Heidi takes us off to a *different* sculptor

Vigelund's mausoleum, "the most secret museum in Europe." Pass through an outer and inner door: the tomb is dimly lit, with rows of chairs down the center. Vigelund shaped statues inappropriate to a public sculpture garden, and painted the walls with human figures, and skulls, and his own portrait twice, living and dead. Every door handle is a snake in a unique configuration. The urn with his ashes sits over the inner door, under the only complete skeletons in the place: they're fucking in missionary position. It's awesome, it's somber, it shouldn't be missed.

As the convention wound down, so did I. After closing, a handful of us retreated to Ellen Andresen's for dinner. I was nearly comatose. Dinner was late but both good and strange, built around hot cereal with a sour cream base. And Heidi took us (me and Mike Jitlov) home.

Monday: I packed the bottle of PAN liqueur Bjørn gave me. But I found and bought Linie Aquavit duty-free. Now my backpack weighs a ton.

The plane takes off at ten-thirty, no sweat, bound south for Copenhagen. I'll change planes and double back over the North Pole.

Yeah . . . but they can't get our plane to start. From twelve-thirty they've postponed to seven. But they've arranged to take us all to lunch at Tivoli Gardens. It could be worse. I didn't phone Marilyn yet; it was 3 A.M. in Los Angeles.

Three busses reached Tivoli. I'd forgotten where we were bound for, so I just stuck with the crowd . . . and lost them, and may have gotten two other passengers lost too. Two twenty-year-old girls, one from California, one from Sweden. We did our best to hunt down the restaurant, and finally I bought them lunch at random.

We wandered around together, then they went off to shop. My energy was dwindling. Music, flowers, games, crowds . . . and my back was starting to hurt, so I sat down a lot. I got rained on. I'd checked my backpack at the airport, sweater and all. No sweat. I drank a cappuccino under a roof, and waited for sunshine.

Back aboard a bus at five. The guy in front of me was a fan; had gone to college with Alex Pournelle; was just starting Brin's *Earth*, which I had finished on the trip. He had some data for me if I ever planned to go to Russia. We talked a little. He says he's very prone to coincidence. . . .

And SAS had postponed to seven-thirty, to use a plane due in from Japan.

I asked for the return of the money I'd spent on three lunches, and an SAS man got it for me. I bought a haircut, and a ton of chocolate. I phoned Marilyn.

It took off on time. They boosted me forward again: reclining seats. The guy next to me was an engineer with an intense interest in the sciences and none in science fiction. A fascinating conversationalist. We all pretended to sleep, as the plane flew through an endless whiteout afternoon. . . .

And when the flight was over, my back had stopped hurting. I LOVE SAS.

Marilyn met me, jet-lagged herself on New Jersey time, and drove us home. I opened the bottle of PAN. It's a Norwegian liqueur made from forest berries, and it's wonderful.

HANDICAP

I

Handicapped people are pro-technology. That's not an opinion; it's an order. You will vote against neo-Luddites. You will not shut down atomic plants. You need the tools. You need the energy that makes the tools. You need the energy that runs the tools. You need the ingenuity of the people who play with technology. Most of all, the civilization around you must be wealthy, or you will not survive.

The Sierra Club wants to shut down any form of energy source that works. The Nader bloc tends to agree. You wouldn't expect a man on a kidney machine to go along with that. It's surprising that Sierra Club members don't notice the tools that make it so much easier to hike: belly bands, lightweight fabrics and aluminum structures in the packs, self-inflating mattresses and geodesic tents.

Stephen Hawking has Lou Gehrig's disease: amyotrophic lateral sclerosis. He belongs to a club with damn few members. Hawking made headlines by killing his own theory: he invented quantum black holes, then looked again at the quantum-mechanical implications, and set a lower limit on their size.

In the couple of decades during which any normal patient would have been dead, Hawking has expanded our understanding of the universe enormously. It takes a wealthy civilization to afford Stephen Hawking; yet no civilization could afford to lose him.

So, what are we calling a *handicap?*

II

What might our descendants consider a handicap?

Glasses. Reading glasses. Orthopedic shoes. These are tools to compensate for handicaps; but they are so nearly perfected, and so prevalent, that moderately bad eyes or feet hardly count as handicaps.

So: tools compensate for handicaps. So what about telescopes, infrared and ultraviolet detectors, radio and TV, radio and X-ray telescopes? Were we handicapped because we could not see by heat waves?

Yes, we were. We still are, until someone markets a pair of IR/UV glasses light enough to wear on our noses or as contact lenses.

A book is an ancient prosthetic device, a compensation not only for ignorance but for stupidity and poor memory. A book has its limits—you have to be bright enough to read—but consider the wonderful things you *don't* have to figure out because someone already did that, and did the research, and took the risks. Isaac Newton got mercury poisoning while doing his research, but you don't have to. You don't have to ruin your eyes on a homemade telescope.

Consider the artificial limb. If it can be made to do what a real arm or leg can do, there's no reason why it can't do other things too.

Consider an arm and hand with feedback to the nerves, and all the flexibility of a natural arm and hand. Why not give it an override control that will multiply the strength of the machinery by ten? It's a machine. Machines are strong. The danger is that it might be stronger than the human joint it's connected to.

The bone struts in an artificial leg might be designed to include a spring. Unlatch and you're riding an extremely sensitive pogo stick. Or include a solid fuel rocket. With properly designed prosthetics you could shock hell out of James Bond.

I used to be a smoker. I'm waiting for a safe way to clean out a lung.

Psychological tools? Social tools? The social sciences get

above themselves when they refer to themselves as sciences, but that may not hold true forever . . .

The true handicap, for each of us, may be that we were born too early.

III

Comparing ourselves to our ancestors isn't really fair here. Certain of the blind have been remembered forever, like Homer and Milton; but remember that a blind man's most important prosthetic device is a friend who can see. We've become better at curing blindness, but where we can't cure it we substitute a trained dog for the friend.

Throughout most of history the handicapped have tended to die. For the civilizations of the past, caring for the handicapped was a luxury. That statement holds true today . . . but it's harder to notice.

I'm not being sarcastic. (I've been accused of that.) A government's basic necessity is to keep the army happy. Even keeping farmers productive is minor compared to that, as Josef Stalin demonstrated. We are a wealthy civilization—perhaps we are the first wealthy civilization—and we like our luxuries. Voting booths are an expensive luxury. A wheelchair industry is a luxury. Building ramps into our concrete sidewalks is a luxury.

What will our descendants regard as their necessities, their rights? Perfect health? Perfect eyesight and hearing, replaceable teeth, replacement organs?

Do you have the right to a dead man's organs? Maybe. What are we calling dead? His heart is still going but his brain waves are flat? Okay . . .

But let's say he's been frozen. No heartbeat, no brain waves. He's in a tank of liquid nitrogen; he expected to be revived when someone finds a cure for whatever was killing him, and also for the damage done by freezing. Let's speculate that we can learn how to revive him as parts. *Now* do you own his organs?

Okay, try this one. Is a patient dead, do the hospitals have a right to his organs, because he has been *condemned to death?*

The law says *no*. Laws can be changed. There are enough healthy organs in Charles Manson to save a dozen lives . . . or at least, there were the day he was convicted. Because of advances in medicine, convicted criminals on Death Row may make restitution for their crimes, voluntarily or not. But the same argument applies to one convicted of income tax fraud!

Should you have the right to choose your own age? Your own shape? In John Varley's "Eight Worlds" universe, a teacher takes a six-year-old body to teach six-year-olds; surgeons transplant hands to a client's ankles instead of feet, for greater dexterity in free fall; insurance finances his revival from stored memory if he's killed.

In Samuel R. Delany's *Nova* there were the "cyborg studs." Plugs at both wrists and your spine link you directly to whatever machine you choose. Your nervous system becomes an automobile, or a shoe factory. Delany's major villain was handicapped: his body could not accommodate the cyborg studs.

Direct brain-to-computer link? Stupidity is a handicap that may someday be cured. Computers are like artificial limbs, in that if you can make a computer that thinks as well as a man, there is no reason to stop there. The human link may end as the minor part of the gestalt . . .

IV

You can't have any of this. It's all science fiction: it may be reality someday, if somebody makes it so. The point is this—

What constitutes a handicap is at least partly a matter of circumstances. What you are, where you are, when you are: these are the tools you work with.

An intelligent being may still make an art form of his life, whatever his handicaps.

DID THE MOON MOVE FOR YOU TOO?

At Swampcon (March 1989) there was a late-night panel on "Sex in Microgravity." We wondered: have there been experiments in free fall fucking?

Probably not. If we haven't tried it, the Russ are even less likely to. They're prudes.

Of course either group might have experimented in secret. The answer is worth knowing. If they are to our taste—if mating is achieved—then NASA can send up a verifiable husband-wife team. We'd choose a long-term marriage, *not* a honeymoon, and give the couple privacy. Nothing of the event would appear on the news, save for afterthoughts.

One attendee remarked, "Nothing else about that mission would ever be noticed!"

Me: "Yeah, you could run a secret mission in plain sight . . ."

COUPLE TO ATTEMPT SEX IN FREE FALL

NASA Third VP Ernest Pabst also said that a trillion-megaton antimatter bomb would be deployed in an attempt to move the Moon . . .

Did the Moon move for you too?

HUGO AWARD ANECDOTES BY LARRY NIVEN
FOR USE AT THE HUGO AWARD CEREMONIES
OF 1996

I

I haven't won a Hugo Award in twenty years; but there was a year in which I was up for *three*.

That's no record. Bob Silverberg has done the same several times. The trouble was, Jerry Pournelle and I were up for the novel award with *Inferno*, and were competing for the novelette with "He Fell into a Dark Hole" and "The Borderland of Sol."

That night they gave me the award for "The Borderland of Sol." Then a gopher led me backstage into a concrete maze of stairs. Escher style. Somewhere out front they were announcing the novella awards, and I wanted to hear that. So I was in a hurry, and I followed the running gopher through that infinite maze. . . .

The worst thing I'd been able to think of was that the only award I'd win would be the one I'd have to take away from Jerry. It had never occurred to me that I would then stumble over concrete steps at a dead run, breaking—not my kneecaps, though that was likely enough—but the Hugo.

Jerry Pournelle heard my yell of pain and anger. He dashed backstage just long enough to be sure I hadn't broken a bone, then back to his seat to watch the other awards disappear.

To this day he still hasn't won a Hugo Award.

The committee gave me an unbroken Hugo, and the base of the broken one with its plaque still attached.

If you want to see the broken base, ask Harlan Ellison. It's in his possession.

II

Jerry used to say, "Money will get you through times of no Hugos better than Hugos will get you through times of no money."

We got tired of hearing it. In 1984 we had plans to fix that.

The beauty of it was that Jerry was master of ceremonies. No way could he escape. The committee decided to present him with a chocolate Hugo Award! And they chose me to present it.

So: the Award ceremonies are in progress, and I am summoned backstage. Miller hands me a rocket ship and base, both chocolate and wrapped in foil. Two separate pieces.

"It cracked in the mold," he told me.

"I know what to do," I said.

So I went out on stage and presented Jerry Pournelle with the only Hugo that will genuinely get you through times of no money. "But," I said, "I dropped the damn thing and broke it."

INTRODUCTION TO PETER HAMILTON STORY "WATCHING TREES GROW"

Now, this is why I'm not a professional critic. I'm holding a mystery, and the surest way to *really* tell you what Peter Hamilton has accomplished is to blow away all his secrets. You may want to read the story first.

Here goes—

He's written a murder story covering several centuries, in which the solution depends upon the sociology of immortal families evolved during the Roman empire, and upon forensic techniques that change massively during the course of the story.

A story that opens in an altered Regency era, ends centuries later, when humanity has attained near-godlike powers. Why wouldn't Edward Raleigh—the detective—drop the case and move on to something else? Hamilton makes it plausible: near-immortal families are tight and clannish.

New forensic techniques develop and are used on old evidence. How and why was that evidence kept? That's plausible too: immortals have seen times change and can anticipate.

Notice: answers don't have to be inevitable or even likely. They only have to be plausible, as long as they are well thought out, internally consistent, and *shown*. The author can't light them up in neon or *that* will blow away the puzzle. What makes the solution work has to be seen: the text has to paint pictures of an alien world.

And we're obliged to make it look easy. Whatever the author is seen to struggle with is bound to be a clue.

Detective stories are as difficult as the author wants them to be.

The only law is that a reader must know everything he

needs to solve the puzzle. We're not looking for an "Aha" as much as an "I should have seen that!" Agatha Christie broke every other presumptive law over and over: victim as killer, everyone's guilty, *author* as killer . . . but not that one.

Aside from that stricture, a puzzle may be arbitrarily difficult or simple. The level of puzzle selects the reader.

"Sure it's a miserable mystery, but the writing and characters are so *neat!*" (*Death Wore a Fabulous New Fragrance*)

It may be set anywhere, anywhen. Ancient Rome or British Dark Ages or ancient China, South America infested with Hitler clones (*The Boys from Brazil*), alternate time tracks (*Fatherland*). (If the critics say that's mainstream, it's okay with me.) But Author is obliged to educate Reader in every important detail of his background universe. Reader must learn to know Ancient Rome or Hitler's England well enough to understand the motives, the tools, and the attitudes behind the killings.

Science fiction detective stories are harder yet . . . as hard as the author desires. If the weapon is something yet to be invented, it has to be fully described. ("The Hole Man": the weapon was a mini black hole. The killer will escape because no lawyer will try to describe the weapon to a jury.) If motivation derives from quirks in a civilization yet to evolve, that civilization must be described. Mickey Spillane sets action in a bar half his readers have seen themselves, and saves himself a hell of a lot of work. But if I work in centuries yet to be born, with suspects evolved on other worlds, then I have to decide whether the murals in a theme restaurant are live-action holograms and whether the tables float . . . or caused too much trouble when they floated, so they had to be grounded . . .

Example: *Footfall*. Earth is invaded by aliens; you see alien viewpoints as well as human. A book too heavy to carry on an airplane is half over before the Herdmaster's Advisor is dead. With what we know of the aliens, war and politics and family life, the mother ship, the human prisoners, you must determine who killed the Herdmaster's Advisor and buried him in the mudpool, and why.

An author's problem doesn't change if it's an Philadelphia detective protecting an Amish woman who witnessed a murder, or if everyone involved is an Australian outback Abo. The author doesn't have to invent Amish or Abos; but the research can be difficult . . . as difficult as the author desires. Motivation for a murder depends powerfully on sociology. The author is always obliged to understand the people he's writing about.

That's why I don't write more Gil "the ARM" Hamilton stories. I love working on a world of eighteen billion people, with a United Nations cop whose main concerns are organleggers and the Fertility Laws. But the puzzles are hard to write!

And yet the games are endlessly entertaining. In *The Patchwork Girl* I used all the classics—dying message, disappearing weapon made of ice, murder done with mirrors— and the motive. Nothing is more fun than trickery done with motives:

"The Defenseless Dead." Why did never-seen Anubis turn from organlegging to kidnapping, and only once? Because he only needed one hiding place. . . .

Why did Teela Brown arrange her own death? Because she was being watched by a vampire protector, and Louis Wu must choose his successor. . . .

And I'm talking about my own work because I dare not expose Peter Hamilton's puzzle.

But pay attention to motivation as you read "Watching Trees Grow."

James Patrick Baen

Dear Jim:
   Here's introductory material for Man-Kzin Wars II.
                                        Best wishes,
                                        Larry Niven

INTRODUCTORY MATERIAL FOR MAN-KZIN WARS II

The franchise universe lives!
   When I first began sneaking into the playgrounds of
other authors, I had my doubts. Still, Phil Farmer seemed to
be having a lovely time reshaping the worlds he'd played in
as a child. So I wrote a Dunsany story and an extrapolation
of Lovecraft and an attempt at a Black Cat detective story
and a study of Superman's sex life.
   Fred Saberhagen invited me to write a Berserker story,
and I found it indecently easy.
   Medea: Harlan's World was a collaboration universe.
Slow to become a book, it ultimately became a classic study
of how creative minds may build and populate a solar system.
   So Jim Baen and I invited selected authors to write stories
set fourteen thousand years ago, when magic still worked.
We filled two books with tales of the Warlock's era. (We also
drove Niven half-nuts. The idea was for Jim to do all the

work and me to take all the credit. But Jim parted company with ACE Books, and I had to learn more than I ever wanted to know about being an editor!)

I entered a universe infested with lizardlike pirate-slavers, because of David Drake's urging, and because of a notion I found irresistible: the murder of Halley's Comet. When Susan Shwartz asked several of us to write new tales of the Thousand and One Nights, I rapidly realized that Scheherazade had overlooked a serious threat. I stayed out of *Thieves' World*—too busy—but I was tempted.

Still, would readers and the publishing industry continue to support this kind of thing? It seemed like too much fun.

And now DC Comics has me reworking the background universe of the Green Lantern! Green Lantern is almost as old as I am! But his mythos will be mine, for the next few years at least.

I'm having a wonderful time. I've got to say, being paid for this stuff feels like cheating.

What began with "The Warriors" has evolved further than my own ambitions would have carried it.

Jim Baen and I decided to open up the Man-Kzin Wars period of known space, because I don't have the background to tell war stories. Still, I had my doubts. I have friends who can write of war; but any writer good enough to be invited to play in my universe will have demonstrated that he can make his own. Would anyone accept my offer? I worried also that intruders might mess up the playground, by violating my background assumptions.

But the kzinti have been well treated, and I'm learning more about them than I ever expected. You too will be charmed and fascinated by kzinti family life as shown in "The Children's Hour," not to mention Pournelle's and Stirling's innovative use of stasis fields. Likewise there is Dean Ing's look at intelligent stone-age kzinti females: Ing finished his story for the first volume, then just kept writing. Now Pournelle and Stirling are talking about doing the same.

I too have found that *known space* stories keep getting longer. It's a fun universe, easier to enter than to leave.

One thing I hoped for when I opened up the Warlock's universe to other writers. I had run out of ideas. I hoped to be reinspired. My wish was granted, and I have written several Warlock's-era stories since.

If the same doesn't hold for the era of the Man-Kzin Wars, it won't be the fault of the authors represented here. I'm having a wonderful time reading *known space* stories that I didn't have to write. If I do find myself reinspired, these stories will have done it.

James Patrick Baen

Dear Jim:

   I enclose:

   Photocopied material from the Ringworld Game.

   Material of my own.

   Two letters from John Hewitt, along with several pages (his work) of selected quotes and suggestions for stories and story material.

   My letter to Hewitt.

   Together, these ought to be enough to make up our "bible" for the Man-Kzin Wars.

   I offered John $500 for permission to photocopy this stuff. I am told that I don't need his permission; I don't care. In any case, he's gone much further than he was asked to. He's given references I missed and made suggestions for the anthology itself, and saved me a lot of work.

   Look it over. I think we have our "bible."

   Who shall be our writers? I haven't exactly been keeping my mouth shut, and one result is that Roland Green wants to write one of our stories. I'm not familiar with his work. We've already asked David Brin and Jerry Pournelle. Maybe we've asked Poul Anderson; if not, we should. Joe Haldeman should be in.

I got Chaosium's permission to photocopy Game material. They like that. They avow that it's exactly what they want: the Ringworld Game material becoming part of the known space canon. Further, they made an interesting suggestion. Shall we ask John Hewitt to submit a story? He's sure as hell researched the subject.

Four to six writers. If we want more, you or Jerry know who wrote the best stories for There Shall Be War. [Jerry Pournelle's anthology series.]

Best wishes,
Larry Niven

CANON FOR THE MAN-KZIN WARS

I've included a couple of pages of my own; but most of this material consists of two letters from John Hewitt, several pages of his suggestions for stories, story backgrounds, soft spots in the known space literature, and so forth; and many photocopied pages from the Ringworld Game by Chaosium.

The Ringworld Game material is for reference only. (If you quote, quote from my work. However, a lot of this *is* quotes from my work.) On any given story you probably won't need most of this material; so don't be daunted by the bulk. Most of the material was written by John Hewitt, from my books and from extensive conversations at conventions.

Hewitt's notes are current for the Ringworld era, centuries after the Fourth Man-Kzin War. Dates are sometimes given. In every case you'll have to scale things backward. Example: asteroids as described in the Belt section are not nearly so civilized, and some haven't even been settled, as of the First Man-Kzin War (or War with Men.)

Believe the dates in the notes if they conflict with dates given in the Niven stories. Believe later Niven stories in preference to earlier. Hewitt and I half busted our minds reconciling inconsistencies.

There were major "incidents" as well as the four wars. ("The Soft Weapon" in *Neutron Star* describes a minor "incident.") "Six times over several centuries, the kzinti attacked the worlds of men . . ." I've forgotten where the quote comes from, but at least two "incidents" must have been major ones.

I've included a bibliography. You may or may not need it.

Over twenty years I've set no stories during any of the Man-Kzin Wars. Get the dates and place names right, get the technology right, and you'll have an otherwise free hand.

TECHNOLOGY

FIRST WAR: the kzinti have been using gravity generators for at least hundreds of years, probably thousands. Human ships often use Bussard ramjets, manufactured by Skyhook Enterprises.

Human society is pacifistic—partly due to Brennan's efforts; see *Protector* and the notes on the Pak—but they find they can use many of their reaction drives as weapons. Examples: fusion drives, the lasers used to launch interstellar light sails, ramrobots used as missiles moving at relativistic velocities . . .

When We Made It buys the hyperdrive, it's the beginning of the end for the kzinti. (Note, however, that the singularity around a Sol-type star extends beyond Pluto. Hyperdrive is most useful for reconnaissance, courier ships, and for attacking the kzinti in deep space, en route to a battle. Strategy might be to find a fleet en route, use hyperdrive to get within a light-minute, fire a big laser, and be gone before the light alerts the fleet to your presence.)

SECOND WAR: the hyperdrive will have proliferated. Skyhook Enterprises will have died in bankruptcy. Hyperdrive motors will have been barred from the Patriarchy, but the Patriarchy will have a few anyway. The gravity generator will be coming into extensive use in human space.

THIRD WAR: given as a bigger push than the second.

FOURTH WAR: given as a desperation move, with kzinti suicide attacks.

SLAVER STASIS BOXES may contain odd bits of technology: anything that can be lost during the story, and anything that I have given as later technology (such as the thrusters used in the Ringworld stories). May be found by kzinti or by men.

EARTH: officially Earth is going through an ice age. The sun's output of neutrinos hasn't varied, and it indicates that the sun is not presently undergoing fusion, or not much. Earth doesn't notice. What heat the sun doesn't supply is easily replaced by fusion plants and beamed power from solar power satellites.

KZIN: there are descriptions of a hunting park and of the House of the Patriarch's Past, the major museum on Kzin, both in RINGWORLD.

PUPPETEERS: are probably active behind the scenes, but humans don't know of them, and the kzinti don't either.

Larry Niven

THE KNOWN SPACE BIBLIOGRAPHY

WORLD OF PTAVVS paperback novel, Ballantine, 1966. Material is probably not important to the Wars. Earth in the early 22nd century.

NEUTRON STAR collected stories, paperback, from Ballantine. Most of these stories follow the Wars. Includes:

"NEUTRON STAR"

"AT THE CORE"

"A RELIC OF EMPIRE"

"THE SOFT WEAPON" was a minor incident between wars. Could have turned major.

"FLATLANDER"

"THE ETHICS OF MADNESS" takes place before the First War with Men.

"THE HANDICAPPED"

"GRENDEL"

A GIFT FROM EARTH paperback novel, Ballantine, 1968. A look at Plateau civilization. By the end of the novel, kzinti may well be entering Sol system.

RINGWORLD novel, Ballantine, paperback. Details of kzinti and puppeteer society; but beware! Kzinti were more pacifistic and reasonable, and had better control of their tempers, after four Wars winnowed out the tough ones.

PROTECTOR novel, paperback, Ballantine. Detailed treatment of Pak and human protectors. Sol system, as found by the kzinti, was rendered pacifistic partly by Brennan's maneuverings; though Brennan was dead before the kzinti reached Sol.

TALES OF KNOWN SPACE collected stories, paper, Ballantine. Includes:

"THE COLDEST PLACE"

"BECALMED IN HELL"

"WAIT IT OUT"

"EYE OF AN OCTOPUS"—Martians

"HOW THE HEROES DIE"—Martians

"THE JIGSAW MAN"

"AT THE BOTTOM OF A HOLE"—Martians

AFTERTHOUGHTS AND BIBLIOGRAPHY
"INTENT TO DECEIVE"
"CLOAK OF ANARCHY"
"THE WARRIORS" IS OUR FIRST GLIMPSE OF THE KZINTI.
"THE BORDERLAND OF SOL"
"THERE IS A TIDE"
"SAFE AT ANY SPEED"

THE LONG ARM OF GIL HAMILTON collected stories, paper, Ballantine. A look at Sol in early twenty-second century. With this or *The Patchwork Girl* you probably don't need *World of Ptavvs*. Includes:

"DEATH BY ECSTASY"
"THE DEFENSELESS DEAD"
"ARM"
"AFTERWORD"

THE RINGWORLD ENGINEERS serial: Galileo, July, September, November 1979, and January 1980 paperback, Ballantine

THE PATCHWORK GIRL trade paperback, illustrated, Ace

The Long Arm of Gil Hamilton and *The Patchwork Girl* were specifically exempted from the Chaosium game. If you want material on that era, you'll have to buy the books themselves; but the Man-Kzin Wars took place hundreds of years later.

—*LARRY NIVEN*
Tarzana, CA 91356
October 15, 1984

John Hewitt
418 Boynton Ave.
Berkeley, CA 94707
.vs 16

Dear John:

I don't think we'll need to reprint any of this material. If we do, we'll discuss it separately. My specific intent is to send photocopies of it to Jim Baen and to anyone whom we invite to write a story for the book(s).

I'm told I don't have to buy such a limited right. I don't care. Your supplementary material is easily worth the price in terms of the time you've saved me.

I deem the $500 flat fee to cover not only your material from the Ringworld Game (of which I photocopied just about every section on your list) but also your letters and the material that came with them. By cashing this check you express yourself to be in enthusiastic agreement.

Chaosium have expressed themselves as delighted with the use I intend to make of their material. They also suggested (as you did) that you should be asked to write one of the stories. God knows you've researched the background. I'll pass the suggestion to my coeditor, Jim Baen.

Be braced for the possibility that we will plan for two books. We may take the stories in order of appearance; or you may be invited to submit for the second book. If you're asked to submit a story, be aware that it may be turned down. That happens even to me.

Best wishes,
Larry

3/3/2003: Nine tales of the Man-Kzin Wars are published with a tenth in the pipeline.
Larry Niven

EPILOGUE: WHAT I TELL LIBRARIANS

It's an August day, hot outside, air-conditioned in. The pool is open. I'll try it in a minute. Swimming is good for the recovering muscles of my leg.

I tore up my left knee April 12, 2001. One Dr. Friedland opened it up April 18, drilled holes in the kneecap, and reattached the quadriceps tendon along a Dacron strip. This was the same thing President Clinton did to himself during his first term. He was recovered six months later, I'm told.

Today is August 14. I'm rid of the leg brace. That means I can wear long pants! The brace runs from hip to ankle, and it always slips down; in shorts I can reach to adjust it.

This whole four months has been a string of rites of passage.

There was the day I could make my own breakfast. I wrote up the experience and sent it out as e-mail afterward, to everyone I'd complained to after the accident. I'm printing it here in full:

BREAKFAST

Though I've lost count of the weeks, it strikes me that I owe all of you a progress report on my life. Trouble is, nothing much changes when you're laid up.

I'm still not allowed to bend my left leg.

For $2^1/_2$ weeks I was in a cast. I've been in a leg brace for 3. The brace is just like a cast except I can open it and wash my leg.

I can't go upstairs, so I'm camping out in the den downstairs in a rented hospital bed. Jerry Pournelle and Eric Pobirs have set up my computer equipment in the library.

I can write. I did 1600 words yesterday on *Burning Tower.* Friday the Pournelles took me on a research mission to the Los Angeles County Museum of Art, claiming that museums are wheelchair-friendly. They were dead right, and the display of Olmec history was invaluable.

My skills as an invalid grow. I hope my knee is growing back together too. So I wait.

What I want to tell you about is making breakfast.

Six weeks after the accident, five weeks after the operation, yesterday Marilyn asked, "Can I sleep late tomorrow morning?" She hasn't done that since the accident. She was even leery about sleeping upstairs.

I said, "Sure."

"Can you make your own breakfast?"

"Sure." I'd done it before, up to a point.

It's morning. Marilyn bought a papaya; I saw it in the fridge. I want half the papaya, toast with peanut butter and jam, and a cappuccino.

Step one: use the walker, hopping on one foot. I can't carry anything with the walker, but I can turn around with something in one hand, the other on the walker. I go to the refrigerator and get the papaya, peanut butter, jam, putting them on the island. (It's an island kitchen.) I get a knife from the knife rack. (From the wheelchair it's too high.) Cut the papaya. Clean out the seeds. I bag half and put it back in the fridge. I put toast in the toaster oven.

Forget any of that and I lose two or three minutes.

Step two: hop back to the den, transfer to the wheelchair. Marilyn found me a box-shaped carry thing with a strap. The strap goes around my waist. I can carry anything solid in my lap now. I can't carry fluids.

I put a plate in the carry thing. The toaster pops and I put that in the plate and move it to the island. I deal with the toast. I roll into the dining room where there's a new translation of the *Odyssey*. Eat and read.

What's left? The cappuccino.

I've got an expresso and cappuccino maker in the bar. The bar is two steps down. For weeks I thought that couldn't be done. Then a trip to visit Tim and Shannon Griffin hit me with a two-step, and I found out I could do it with the walker.

So: get the walker. Lunge to place the walker, hop two steps down. Pour grounds, run the coffee, add milk and sugar, steam it all. Marilyn has to keep milk and ground coffee supplied; I can't carry anything with the walker. But I can turn around and put coffee on the bar proper.

What I can't do is take it anywhere.

I can carry a magazine in the wheelchair. I put a magazine where I'm going to be. I try to use a normal chair there, but my straight leg defeats me. So I hop the walker to the wheelchair and sit in that while I drink my cappuccino.

Somewhere in there the cat nags me into feeding her. All that takes is the carry thing, if the cat will only get out of my way and let me wheel into the pantry . . .

Breakfast.

It's a lifestyle. I can hope it won't last more than six months.

When the cast came off I could wash my leg with a moisturizing wipe. Luxuries beyond your wildest dreams. The day I was allowed to set my left foot on the ground, I went upstairs to my own bed. A day later I fit myself into a dry bathtub, ran water, bathed, let the water drain and dried myself there, Marilyn supervising, and didn't try to move until the leg brace was back on. One day I was allowed to bend the knee, not by bloody much, but still. One day I sat in a barber's chair and got a haircut! Though the leg wasn't quite *that* flexible.

Getting independent was always the goal. I've been on the

other side of this, when Marilyn's back problem had her paralyzed. (An operation healed her. That's rare, it seems.) So I knew I was holding her prisoner. Early on, she had to feed me. She had to drive me everywhere. Manipulating the wheelchair, lifting it in and out of the wagon, folding it, getting the footrests back in place, was a hell of a lot of work for her. We were glad to send it back.

One day I knew I could still write fiction. I was afraid I'd lost that ability, grown too self-involved as a handicapped person.

Today, stretching first, I can pedal a stationary bike, both feet going all the way around. "Go past the comfort zone," my physical therapists have been saying. Right. I can drive (Marilyn is grateful). I can swim. A minute ago the cat lured me into chasing her in a sort of wobbling jog.

Rites of passage.

It's like growing up. Every day it's a little better. The leg stretches a little more, supports a little more weight. It's the opposite of growing old.

Next time you see a fogey grinning on crutches or a wheelchair, that's the answer. He's injured, but he's learning new skills, and he's improving. He can see it happening. If children knew what we knew, they'd grin all the time too.

An hour ago I found myself jittery with the urge to be someone else. Symptoms: restlessness, a dither as to what to do next, mind running around inside its cage.

I assume this is normal for a writer. I've had it all my life.

What bothers me is that I noticed. I didn't go straight into thinking like Twisted Cloud or Louis Wu or whatever character I'm currently working with. I learn to know my characters from the inside, rarely noticing what they look like, but learning how they think and react. Today, with three novels looking at me and several possible short stories, why am I thinking about who *I* am?

Who a writer is, is not of primary importance. A writer

who thinks writing is the only interesting profession, isn't likely to write well about anyone else, is he?

But, being in an introspective mood, I'll work on *Scatterbrain*.

My first short stories were shaped by my presumption—not always a fact—that I know something the Reader doesn't. *Here, let me show you something wonderful! Pluto on fire . . . the inside of a telepath's mind . . . the real Venus . . . Earth after time stops its rotation . . . the laws after organ transplants become easy . . .*

But several things have happened in the past thirty-five years.

First, the science fiction field is crowded with fine writers. They're popping up faster than I can learn their names.

Second . . . well, the computer has changed the writing profession beyond recall. It's a magic typewriter: it erases mistakes faster than they can be made. Writing has become much easier for me, and for all my competition too.

Of this year's contenders for the Hugo, each one would have been a sure thing when I began writing.

Third, computer and Internet access have made knowledge available on every conceivable subject. Isaac Asimov once wrote of "the sound of panting," the difficulty he had keeping up with advances in the sciences. Today he'd complain that everyone else learns it all just as fast as he does.

What can I do? Writers don't retire. What would I retire from, if every passing stimulus starts a daydream? We tell stories to ourselves. If we're lucky, someone else wants to hear them too.

Besides, sometimes I do see something nobody else has seen. Sometimes I can beat the rest of the field into print. I enjoy that.

* * *

Another matter: how do I know when I'm at work?

Everything I see or do *could* spark a story, or story scene, or character.

Anything interesting in my life should be tax deductible, right? Right down to good restaurants, given the way all my main characters seem to be turning into chefs. (It happened after I quit smoking. My taste buds grew back.)

Once upon a time I had myself persuaded that I was getting my best ideas in bars. I'm glad that didn't last. It turns out that ideas come from everywhere. Take . . . ants.

Ants drive Marilyn crazy. I don't have to wait for them to drive me crazy; we do something about them long before that happens. Assuming that creation derives from a god or gods, that it all has some purpose, what is the point of ants?

Thinking like this can be valuable.

For instance: The Ringworld is a huge artificial habitat. Its ecology isn't in balance, isn't Gaea-esque. It never was intended to be. Protector-stage protohumans (a key invention in the "known space" series) seeded the Ringworld with whatever creations they thought would improve the comfort of their breeders. They didn't bring mosquitoes or jackals. If the ecology got out of whack, they'd fiddle where needed.

When the protectors disappeared, the breeders began to evolve, began to move into empty ecological niches. The author has had a lot of fun with that.

I got quite a different answer when writing of the Warlock's era, fourteen thousand years ago, when magic was running out on Earth. The Warlock's world eventually evolves into our own. What are ants doing there?

This is how the shaman Twisted Cloud explained it in *Burning Tower*:

Twisted Cloud looked at her doubtfully, then at the Sage Egmatel, who was holding a perfect poker face. "Well. The god was Logi or Zoosh or Ghuju, depends on who's speaking. His tribe didn't like to clean up after themselves. Men tired of the women's complaints, and leftover bones got too much attention from coyotes and other predators. Logi made a tiny creature to clean up after them, to carry garbage away. But ants are supposed to stay out of sight, and they're not supposed to swarm over food that's ready for the evening meal!"

Roni said, "So you send a message (to the queen). And what if they don't take the hint?"

But that's another story.

A few years ago the Chicago in 2000 Committee printed up some cards to advertise their bid for the World Science Fiction Convention. The cards resemble bubble gum cards honoring science fiction's professional writers, artists, and editors. Yesterday's mail brought me hundreds of copies of my card. The face shows me in dark glasses in a glare of sunshine, with the DC-X1 experimental rocket ship in the background. Jerry Pournelle took this shot before the first public flight. The back displays some biographical material.

What shall I do with these? I like Marilyn's suggestion: take them to signings and give them away there.

A writer's perks are wonderful and strange.

My e-mail for yesterday included this:

Please pardon the intrusion.

I recently borrowed your book "Lucifer's Hammer" from a friend of mine . . . managed to leave it on a plane and it is lost.

Diana . . . immediately began joking with me that it was a hardcover 1st edition, signed by the authors. It was really a somewhat worn paperback, but I would certainly love to surprise her with what she "claimed" it was.

Well, I managed to find a hardcover copy of it in beautiful condition . . . My request is that if I send the book to you with a self-addressed, stamped book carrier, would you be willing to sign it and send it back? I could also use some assistance in contacting Mr. Pournelle.

My point is, doing favors and repaying debts can often be done with just a signature or a dedication. I wasn't born gracious; I grew up socially inept. This makes life a little easier.

It has been twelve years since I hung the title *Playgrounds of the Mind* on a retrospective collection from Tor Books. That book, and its companion volume *N-Space*, were made up of excerpts from novels, every short story I couldn't stand to leave out, and any neat stuff that just didn't fit anywhere else. Political sniping. The script for a Masquerade presentation. Some notes on rishathra—sex outside one's species— illustrated by obscene cartoons from Bill Rotsler. A letter from an ex–Soviet Union publisher.

The books make great calling cards.

The notion of an imaginary playground now seems downright ordinary, given today's rapid improvement of computer games. It was never strange to me. When I was a child, fantasy stories by L. Frank Baum about the land of Oz turned every aperture into imaginary doorways to another world. When I got a little older I loved Andre Norton's science fiction. She doesn't exactly write stories. They don't have endings. She'll set up a situation and environment, drop some people or mutated animals or aliens into it, and then leave the playground wide open.

As we grow up, we learn to demand that stories have an ending and a point to make. But we don't have to stop thinking after we close the book.

I read Dante's *Inferno* for a college course. Then I read it again. Then spent some time daydreaming. How would you get through Hell if you couldn't call on angels? Ultimately I made Jerry Pournelle write a sequel with me, because he had the theological background I needed.

Years have passed since *N-Space* and *Playgrounds of the Mind*. Now Tor Books is publishing a new collection of my stuff. With any luck at all, you're holding it: a book called *Scatterbrain*.

We had hoped to include a CD in the book. Instead, Aldo will be selling that separately. Aldo Spadoni is a rocket scientist who paints on a computer. The first I ever knew of him was a handful of glorious paintings of *Lying Bastard*, the spacecraft from *Ringworld*. He's been painting the spacecraft I've spent thirty-five years writing about, not just slowboats and General Products designs from known space, but ships and habitats from the Empire of Man and the Mote Prime system, the hastily built warship *Michael* from *Footfall*, and the primitive ground-to-orbit ships from *Destiny's Road*. Now Aldo plans to market the CD.

I'm a scatterbrain. It's something I came to terms with long ago. My retrieval system is a mess. I can't remember your name. If I try, my brain follows a nightmare maze.

I've somehow persuaded myself that this is a not a bug, but a feature. That is, I need the scatterbrained state to write. Things link in my head that barely belong in the same universe.

Rainbow Mars shows how far the deterioration has gone: Time travel as fantasy, links up with fantasy Mars. Orbital tethers link with Jack and the Beanstalk and the legend of Phaeton. I loved writing *Rainbow Mars*, but I wish I could remember phone numbers too.

Last October, Kathleen Doherty of Tor Books arranged for three of us—Vernor Vinge, Pat Murphy, and me—to address a convention of 130 Los Angeles County librarians. My mission: to tell them anything librarians might need to know, that even Pat Murphy and Vernor Vinge couldn't tell them.

Kathleen told them that I would speak about my work. I fudged on that one. I only had twenty minutes to talk; let them read the damn books. If my work needs a critic to explain it, it means I should have fixed it in rewrite. The story I tell should speak for itself.

I jumped around a lot in that speech, and I'm doing that here too. My emphasis is on science fiction, of course. Why should librarians give special consideration to science fiction?

I can tell you something specific.

It's very difficult for a black man to get out of South-Central Los Angeles, and get out civilized. Women may find it easier, for all I know. The only men I know who have escaped, all began reading Robert Heinlein at age ten.

Of those men, I've written nine books with Steven Barnes. I see Ken Porter every few weeks. The third guy was installing my copier when the subject came up. It's a tiny sample, and all three men were in their forties.

So even if I'm right, the book that rescues a ten-year-old child from a bad environment may not be Heinlein anymore.

Robert Heinlein's planets have become fantasy due to half a century of exploration by NASA probes. He was always a teacher of moral lessons, but if his worlds have become unrealistic, his lessons will be suspect too—though to me they still hold true.

Forty years ago, Ken Porter was a black kid growing up in South-Central. Ken's peers tried to tell him that no white man could ever understand what he was going through. Ken knew they were wrong because he had read *Citizen of the Galaxy* by Robert Heinlein. Robert Heinlein was white, but he understood Ken Porter perfectly, and Ken knew it.

The solar system keeps changing—and so does the wider universe—but *Citizen of the Galaxy* is still readable. Its basic truth remains.

I still recommend much of Heinlein's earlier work—try *Double Star*—but it's not vital. Several generations of science fiction writers have all borrowed from Robert Heinlein. He's the most copied man in the field. Writers of hard science fiction, in particular, are all compulsive teachers, and maybe we learned that from Heinlein too.

So almost any name will do.

It's important to let kids into the adult section of the library. A librarian may give appropriate warning if he knows the book, but any child who demands to read in the adult section is probably ready.

Twenty years ago a fifth grade teacher told me that half her class was reading *Ringworld*. That surprised me, and I've heard it again since, but I figured it out. The parts that children don't understand, they just take the author's word for it *if* it moves the story along, *if* it's a good story.

And that is why you let children into the adult section, but you steer them to science fiction instead of fantasy. Because they believe!

So how does a librarian tell the difference?

There were librarians in Kathleen's crowd who refused to admit that *1984* is science fiction. One guy was grinning and baiting me like I was silly and hadn't realized it. Some causes really are hopeless.

The brightest minds in our field have been trying to find a definition of science fiction for these past seventy years. The short answer is, science fiction stories are given as possible, not necessarily here and now, but somewhere, sometime.

Where have all the poets gone?

We've had immortal poets in every century but the twentieth. Did something peculiar happen during the twentieth century?

Yes, something did.

The immortal poets always understood the sexiest science of their day, the science in which advances were being made, and they all wrote science fiction and fantasy! Edgar

Allan Poe's "The Gold Bug" is a classic demonstration of logical thinking, scientific process-of-elimination techniques. Alexander Pope understood and used his version of atomic theory. Rudyard Kipling understood engineering and war, the queen sciences of *his* age, and used them in poetry *and* fiction. Homer understood sailing and winemaking. Dante Alighieri used Greek science, theology, astronomy, and astrology. In fact he designed an astrologically perfect Easter weekend for his *Divine Comedy*—the first science fiction trilogy. And he set it in a structure that is large compared to a Dyson shell.

It's not Dante's fault if his science has become fantasy. That's happened to Heinlein too, and (in some cases) me.

But in the twentieth century the critics decided that science fiction is not worthy of consideration.

The best poets have always been drawn to write fantasy and science fiction. Unless you have a precise, global, detailed picture of how the universe works, you can't be a real poet. Without that your prose becomes mushy and ambiguous. Your work comes out diffuse and unreadable. So you *will* write science fiction, if you are a potential poet, like all of your spiritual ancestors have for thousands of years. When you get around to writing actual poetry, you will find that Harvard and *The New Yorker* magazine and the librarians' conspiracy have locked you out.

So the question becomes: Why would critics avoid science fiction?

I must refer you to a book by C. P. Snow, *The Two Cultures*. I don't know who still reads this thing, *I* sure never did, but the core idea has become a part of Western civilization. Snow said that science majors and liberal arts majors have trouble talking to each other. Their brains don't work alike. Their interests are different, their line of thinking is different.

Now, if you're a science fiction fan, *you* know he was wrong. You and most of the people you know understand

and love science, literature, music, art, puzzles, the whole vast domain in which human beings find ways to kill time and play with their minds.

C. P. Snow was mistaken, and he may have known it. In practice, and in my experience, working scientists are just as intrigued as any liberal arts major by good writing, good music, and good art. They don't have as much time to pursue these things because what they're doing is more important, or maybe more fun.

Greg Benford, plasma physicist and science fiction writer, writes like he swallowed an English teacher. Not even a librarian can think he's not literate, but he's writing on the frontiers of all we know and all we're learning.

What the liberal arts graduates forget—and what they will never say to each other—is this. They didn't go into science because it was too hard. They didn't know how to do the math. And these are the mainstream critics who have swallowed C. P. Snow's *Two Cultures* book, line, and sinker.

It's hard to say they're making a mistake.

A mainstream critic who forms an opinion of a work of science fiction can make himself look like a fool. He might rave over a brilliant new idea in a not-really-science-fiction novel, something way beyond science fiction, and it turns out to be only Robert Heinlein's "Universe" ship . . . which *is* a brilliant notion, but *everybody's* stolen that one. And filed off the serial number, just like Robert said to, and called it something else . . . like . . . *slowboat*.

It's worth remembering that for most of humanity, science is hard work. But the *scientists* know that they're playing a vast game, and being paid to do it. It feels ridiculous. One day they know they'll be caught.

Last August I came home from NASFIC with an e-mail address, *larrynivenl@bucknell.edu*, a group that exists for the purpose of discussing my work. (That address will have changed by now.) I do sometimes go ego-surfing. I logged on and found myself eavesdropping on discussions of whether you can clone a protector, and whether Teela Brown is likely to have left a child. Within a month of lurking, I had enough material for a fourth Ringworld novel.

I just want to point out that these people do huge levels of research for the simple pleasure of it. They make up their own homework! Mundanes pay full price for a book and then they only read it.

So I'm still facing 130 librarians while I use up my twenty minutes, but now I want to establish my credibility so they'll listen to the rest of what I have to say. So I tell them Conan Doyle didn't write like Mickey Spillane. I said that a quill pen allows you to write with only your right hand and the left side of your brain, but a typewriter or computer keyboard makes you use both sides of your brain simultaneously. Writing from any previous century reads intellectual rather than visceral, straight lines rather than patterns. It's all left-brain. The keyboard forces us to use our whole brains.

I should add that Connie Willis thinks I'm dead wrong here.

I told them why people talk to themselves. One of the librarians tried to tell me that was the mark of a poet. That's ridiculous. Plumbers do it too. It's because our corpus callosum is so narrow. The corpus callosum is that arc of tissue between the left and right sides of your forebrain. There are a lot of nerves in the corpus callosum, but it's too narrow to carry all the messages you want sent between two lobes. If you're trying to do something complicated with your hands, you may well want to talk your way through it, to get the information from one side to the other. If you're in a hurry, if there's a fire in the kitchen and you can't find a pail, you may find yourself yelling orders at yourself.

Librarians still use the term *escape reading*.

I told them that science fiction fans are all compulsive

teachers, and the authors are even worse, and if we can get readers' attention by showing them escape reading, we'll teach them before they can escape.

In July 2000, during a panel at the Hawaii Westercon, I solved a puzzle. Where have all the short story markets gone?

It's movies and television, of course.

What I see is that movies do not replace novels. A novel is too long to make a good movie. *Dr. Zhivago* showed just the love story. *Dune* should have been a movie trilogy. Movies replace short stories, novelettes, and *abridged* novels. When was the last time you saw anyone selling Reader's Digest Condensed Novels? We see the markets for short stories constantly dwindling. Every writer knows that novels are where the money is, but the real money used to be in cracking *Black Mask* or *Argosy* or the *Saturday Evening Post*.

Robert Forward tells me I beat him into print with a line of cement dust.

This was during the eighties, and Bob was still working at Hughes Research. He was sure that a quantum black hole—they were still calling it that, back before Stephen Hawking changed his mind—a mini black hole falling through the Earth must interact with the Earth somehow, but Bob hadn't seen how yet. In a short story called "The Hole Man" I showed a line of dust running through a concrete floor, no wider than a pencil lead, the track of a mini black hole. This is tides operating on a minute scale: the tides around a black hole tearing molecule from molecule as it passes through concrete, or bone, or flesh.

I love it when I can beat the scientists into print.

I thought I had another one once. I thought it up independently and put it in "Neutron Star." It turns out Albert Einstein's name was already on it. "Einstein rings." They call it "gravitational lensing" now. This is what gives you several images of a galaxy if there's a mass in front of it. Looking for gravitational lensing lets you place galaxies and measure their mass.

But I'm not finished yet.

Abisko is a biological research station in Sweden, two hundred kilometers north of the Arctic Circle. I had never heard of it. It's the site of an annual seminar backed by Umea University. Greg Benford got me into the annual Abisko seminar. About twenty-five people, all the place will hold, gather to lecture each other on a chosen topic. Most of these were British or Swedes. We spoke English; they got tired of Brits trying to speak Swedish.

I was trying to tell them something of my work as a skilled professional daydreamer. So I offered an explanation of the "missing mass" as presently understood in astrophysics. It's an idea that relates the fate of the universe to the energy of the vacuum and the problem of how galaxies form. Another attendee, Dr. Phil Barringer of the University of Kansas, tried to tell me why it won't work. I got e-mail from him later saying that he may have been wrong.

So my Nobel prize isn't hopelessly lost, and I've beaten the rest of the field into print. I turned these related concepts into a short story, a Draco Tavern story which appeared in Analog in 2001 as "The Missing Mass." It's won a Locus Award, my first award in this millennium.

All of the Abisko speeches were to be followed by questions and comments. During these periods I seem to have developed a reputation for "bullets," that is, for the epigrams and slogans that speakers might project onto a screen so that an audience will remember *something* five minutes after he stops talking.

* * *

I saved you this one:

NOT RESPONSIBLE FOR ADVICE NOT TAKEN. Say the truth as best you can, and hope someone is listening. Liars are not your fault. Gullible fools are not your fault.

And:

THINK OF IT AS EVOLUTION IN ACTION. (From *Oath of Fealty*, where it became a theme.)

I left the librarians with this too. Let me leave it with you:

If there were only one thing you could teach a child, it ought to be this: to play with his mind. To make up his own homework.

It seems that I've spent most of my life designing toys for imaginary playgrounds.

END

Look for

RINGWORLD'S CHILDREN

by Larry Niven

Now available
From Tom Doherty Associates

Turn the page for a preview

CHAPTER ONE: Louis Wu

Louis Wu woke aflame with new life, under a coffin lid.

Displays glowed above his eyes. Bone composition, blood parameters, deep reflexes, urea and potassium and zinc balance: he could identify most of these. The damage listed wasn't great. Punctures and gouges; fatigue; torn ligaments and extensive bruises; two ribs cracked; all relics of the battle with the Vampire protector, Bram. All healed now. The 'doc would have rebuilt him cell by cell. He'd felt dead and cooling when he climbed into the Intensive Care Cavity.

Eighty-four days ago, the display said.

Sixty-seven Ringworld days. Almost a falan; a falan was ten Ringworld rotations, seventy-five thirty-hour days. Twenty or thirty days should have healed him! But he'd known he was injured. What with all the general bruising from the battle with Bram, he hadn't even noticed puncture wounds in his back.

He'd been under repair for twice that long the first time he lay in this box. Then, his internal plumbing systems had been leaking into each other, and he'd been eleven years without the longevity complex called *boosterspice*. He'd been dying, and *old*.

Testosterone was high, adrenalin high and rising.

Louis pushed steadily up against the lid of the 'doc. The lid wouldn't move faster, but his body craved action. He slid out and dropped to a *stone* floor, cold beneath his bare feet. Stone?

He was naked. He stood in a vast cavern. Where was *Needle*?

The interstellar spacecraft *Hot Needle of Inquiry* had been embedded in cooled magma when last he looked, and Carlos Wu's experimental nanotech repair system had been in the crew quarters. Now its components sat within a nest of instruments and cables on a floor of cooled lava. The 'doc had been partly pulled apart. Everything was still running.

Hubristic, massive, awesome: this was a protector's work. Tunesmith, the Ghoul protector, must have been studying the 'doc while it healed Louis.

Nearby, *Hot Needle of Inquiry* had been fileted like a finless fish. A slice of hull running almost nose to tail had been cut away, exposing housing, cargo space, docking for a Lander now destroyed, thruster plates, and the hyperdrive motor housing. More than half of the ship's volume was tanks, and of course they'd been drained. The rim of the cut had been lined with copper or bronze, and cables in the metal led to instruments and a generator.

The cut section had been pulled aside by massive machinery. The cut surface was rimmed in bronze laced with cables.

The hyperdrive motor had run the length of the ship. Now it was laid out on the lava, in a nest of instruments. Tunesmith again?

Louis wandered over to look.

It had been repaired.

Louis had stranded the Hindmost in Ringworld space by chopping the hyperdrive in half, twelve or thirteen years ago. Dismounted, it looked otherwise ready to take *Needle* between the stars at Quantum I speeds, three days to the light year.

I could go home, Louis thought, tasting the notion.

Where is everybody? Louis looked around him, feeling the adrenalin surge. He was starting to shiver with cold.

He'd be almost two hundred and forty years old by now, wouldn't he? Easy to lose track here. But the nano machines in Carlos Wu's experimental 'doc had read his DNA and repaired everything down through the cell nuclei. Louis had done this dance before. His body thought it was just past puberty.

Keep it cool, boy. Nobody's challenged you yet.

*   *   *

The spacecraft, the hull section, the 'doc, machines to move and repair these masses, and crude-looking instruments arrayed to study them, all formed a tight cluster within vaster spaces. The cavern was tremendous and nearly empty. Louis saw float plates like stacks of poker chips, and beyond those a tilted tower of tremendous toroids that ran through a gap in the floor right up to the roof. Cylinders lay near the gap, caged within more of Tunesmith's machinery. They were bigger than *Needle*, each a little different from the others.

He'd passed through this place once before. Louis looked up, knowing what to expect.

Five or six miles up, he thought. The Map of Mars stood forty miles high. This level would be near the roof. Louis could make out its contours. Think of it as the back of a mask . . . the mask of a shield volcano the size of Ceres.

Needle had smashed down through the crater in Mons Olympus, into the repair center that underlay the one-to-one scale Map of Mars. Teela Brown had trapped them there after she turned protector. She had moved the ship eight hundred miles through these corridors, then poured molten rock around them. They'd used stepping disks—the puppeteers' instant transport system—to reach Teela. For all these years since, the ship had been trapped.

Now Tunesmith had brought it back to the workstation under Mons Olympus.

Louis knew Tunesmith, but not well. Louis had set a trap for Tunesmith, the Night Person, the breeder, and Tunesmith had become a protector. He'd watched Tunesmith fight Bram; and that was about all he knew of Tunesmith the protector. Now Tunesmith held Louis's life in his hands, and it was Louis's own doing.

He'd be smarter than Louis. Trying to outguess a protector was . . . futz . . . was both silly and inevitable. No human culture has ever stopped trying to outguess God.

So. *Needle* was an interstellar spacecraft, if someone could remount the hyperdrive. That tremendous tilted tower—forty miles of it if it reached all the way to the Repair Center floor—was a linear accelerator, a launching system. One day Tunesmith might need a spacecraft. Meanwhile he'd leave *Needle* gutted, because Louis Wu and the Hindmost might otherwise use it to run, and the protector couldn't have that.

Louis walked until *Needle* loomed: a hundred-and-ten-foot diameter cylinder with a flattened belly. Not much of the ship was missing. The hyperdrive, the 'doc, what else? The crew housing was a cross section, its floor eighty feet up. Under the floor, all of the kitchen and recycling systems were exposed.

If he could climb that high, he'd have his breakfast, and clothing too. He didn't see any obvious route. Maybe there was a stepping disk link? But he couldn't guess where Tunesmith might place a stepping disk, or where it would lead.

The Hindmost's command deck was exposed too. It was three stories tall, with lower ceilings than a Kzin would need. Louis saw how he could climb up to the lowest floor. A protector would have no trouble at all.

Louis shook his head. What must the Hindmost be *thinking*?

Pierson's puppeteers held to a million-year-old philosophy based on cowardice. When the Hindmost built *Needle*, he had isolated his command deck from any intruders, even from his own alien crew. There were no doors at all, just stepping disks booby-trapped a thousand ways. Now . . . the puppeteer must feel as naked as Louis.

Louis crouched beneath the edge of some flat-topped mass, maybe the breathing-air system. Leapt, pulled up, and kept climbing. The 'doc's repairs had left him thin, almost gaunt; he wasn't lifting much weight. Fifty feet up, he hung by his fingers for a moment.

This was the lowest floor of the Hindmost's cabin, his most private area. There would be defenses. Tunesmith might have turned them off . . . or not.

He pulled up and was in forbidden space.

* * *

He saw the Hindmost. Then he saw his own droud sitting on a table.

The droud was the connector between any wall socket and Louis Wu's brain. Louis had destroyed that . . . had given it to Chmeee and watched the Kzin batter it to bits.

So, a replacement. Bait for Louis Wu, the current addict, the wirehead. Louis's hand crept into the hair at the back of his head, under the queue. Plug in the droud, let it trickle electric current down into the pleasure center . . . where was the socket?

Louis laughed wildly. It wasn't there! The autodoc's nano machines had rebuilt his skull without a socket for the droud!

Louis thought it over. Then he took the droud. When confused, send a confusing message.

The Hindmost lay like a jeweled footstool, his three legs and both heads tucked protectively beneath his torso. Louis's lips curled. He stepped forward to sink his hand into the jeweled mane and shake the puppeteer out of his funk.

"Touch nothing!"

Louis flinched violently. The voice was a blast of contralto music, the Hindmost's voice with the sound turned up, and it spoke Interworld. "Whatever you desire," it said, "instruct me. Touch nothing."

The Hindmost's voice—*Needle's* autopilot—knew him, knew his language at least, and hadn't killed him. Louis found his own voice. "Were you expecting me?"

"Yes. I give you limited freedom in this place. Find a current source next to—"

"No. Breakfast," Louis said as his belly suddenly screamed that it was empty, dying. "I need food."

"There is no kitchen for your kind here."

A shallow ramp wound round the walls to the upper floors. "I'll be back," Louis said.

He walked, then ran up the ramp. He eased around the

wall above a drop of eighty feet—not difficult, just scary—
and was in crew quarters.

A pit showed where the 'doc had been removed. Crew
quarters were not otherwise changed. The plants were still
alive. Louis went to the kitchen wall and dialed cappuccino
and a fruit plate. He ate. He dressed, pants and blouse and a
vest that was all pockets, the droud bulging one of the pockets. He finished the fruit, then dialed up an omelet, potatoes,
another cappuccino, and a waffle.

He thought while he ate. What *was* his desire?

Wake the Hindmost? He needed the Hindmost to tell him
what was going on . . . but puppeteers were manipulative
and secretive, and the balance of power in the Repair Center
kept changing. Best learn more first. Get a little leverage before he reached for the truth.

He dumped the breakfast dishes in the recycler toilet. He
climbed around the wall, carefully. "Hindmost's Voice," he
said.

"At your command. You need not risk a fall. Here is a
stepping-disk link," and a cursor arrowhead showed him a
spot on the floor of crew quarters.

"Show me the Meteor Defense Room."

"That term is unknown." A hologram window popped up
in the portside wall. "Is this the place you mean?"

Meteor Defense beneath the Map of Mars was a vast, dark
space. All the stars in the universe ran round an ellipsoidal
wall thirty feet high, and the floor and ceiling. Three long
swinging booms ended in chairs equipped with lap keyboards, and those stood black-on-black before the wall display.

Past the edge of the pop-up window, under a glare of light,
knobby bones had been laid out for study. This was the oldest protector Louis knew of, and Louis had named him
Cronus. In the far shadows stood pillars with large plates on
top, mechanical mushrooms. Louis pointed into the window.
"What are those?"

"Service stacks," the Hindmost's Voice said, "each made from several float plates topped by a stepping disk."

Louis nodded. The Ringworld engineers had left float plates all through the Repair Center. If you stacked them, they'd lift more. Adding a stepping disk seemed an obvious refinement . . . if you had them to spare.

Louis saw a boom swing across the starscape. It ended in a knobby, angular shadow.

All protectors look something like medieval armor.

The protector was watching a spray of stars. His cameras would be mounted on the Ringworld itself, maybe on the outside of the rim wall, looking away from the sun. He didn't seem aware that he was being spied on.

Louis knew better than to expect asteroids or worlds. Unknown engineers had cleared all that out of the Ringworld system. This drift of moving lights would be spacecraft held by several species. Now the view focused on a gauzy, fragile Outsider ship; now on a glass needle, a General Products' #2 hull, tenant unknown; now a crowbar-shaped ARM warship.

Tunesmith's concentration seemed total. He zoomed on starscape occluded by a foggy lump, a proto-comet. Tiny angular machines drifted around it, marked by blinking cursor circles. A lance of light glared much brighter: some warship's fusion drive. Here came another, zipping across the screen. No weapon fired.

The Fringe War is still cold, Louis thought. He'd wondered how long that could last. A formal truce could not hold among so many different minds.

The protector's arms jittered above the keyboard.

In the corner of Louis's eye, sunlight glared down. Louis spun around.

Above *Needle* the crater in Mons Olympus was sliding open, flooding the cavern with unfiltered light.

The linear accelerator roared; an arc of lightning ran bottom to top.

The crater began to close.

Louis turned back to the display. Looking over Tunesmith's shoulder, he watched fusion light flare from off-screen and dwindle to a bright point. Whatever Tunesmith had launched was already too far to see.

Tunesmith had joined the Fringe War!

A protector could not be expected to do nothing, even if the alternative was to bring war down on their heads. Louis scowled. Bram the protector had been crazy, even if supremely intelligent. Louis must eventually decide if Tunesmith was crazy too, and what to do about it.

Meanwhile this latest maneuver should keep the protector busy. Now, how much freedom had Louis been allotted? Louis said, "Hindmost's Voice, show me the locations of all stepping disks."

The Hindmost's Voice popped up three hundred and sixty degrees of Map Room. The Ringworld surrounded Louis, a ring six hundred million miles around and a million miles wide, banded in blue for day and black for night and broad fuzzy edges for dusk and dawn. Winking orange cursor lights were displayed across its face. Some were shaped like arrowheads.

This pattern had changed greatly since Louis had last seen it. "How many?"

"Ninety-five stepping disks are now in use. Two failed. Three were dropped into deep space and probes launched through them. The fleets shot them down. Ten are held in reserve."

The Hindmost had stocked stepping disks aboard Hot *Needle of Inquiry*, but not a hundred and ten! "Is the Hindmost building more stepping disks?"

"With his help Tunesmith has built a stepping-disk factory. Work proceeds slowly."

The blinking orange lights that marked stepping disks were thick along the near side of the Ringworld, the Great Ocean arc. The far side looked sparse. Two blinking orange arrowheads had nearly reached the edge of the Other Ocean. Others were moving in that direction.

The Other Ocean was a diamond shape sprawling across most of the width of the Ringworld, one hundred eighty degrees around from the Great Ocean. Two such masses of water must counterbalance each other. The Hindmost's crew had not explored the Other Ocean. *High time*, Louis thought.

Most of the stepping disks were clustered around the Great Ocean, and of those, most were in a tight cluster that must be the Map of Mars. Louis pointed at one offshore from Mars. "What is that?"

"That is *Hot Needle of Inquiry*'s lander."

Teela the protector had blasted the lander during their last duel. "It's functional?"

"The stepping-disk link is functional."

"What about the lander?"

"Life support is marginal. Drive systems and weaponry have failed."

"Can some of these service stacks be locked out of the system?"

"That has been done." Lines spread across the map to link the blinking lights. Some had crossed-circle *verboten* marks on them: *closed*. The maze was complicated, and Louis didn't try to understand it. "My Master has override codes," the Voice said.

"May I have those?"

"No."

"Number these stepping-disk sites for me. Then print out a map."

As the Ringworld was vast, the scale was extreme. His naked eye would never get any detail out of it. When the map extruded, he folded it and stuffed it in a pocket anyway.

He broke for lunch and came back.

He set two service stacks moving and changed a number of links. The Hindmost's Voice printed another map with his changes added. He pocketed that too. Better keep both. Now, with luck, he'd have avenues of travel unknown to Tunesmith.

Or it might be wasted effort. The Hindmost, when he woke, could change it all back in a moment.

The Voice refused to make weapons. Of course the kitchen in *Needle*'s crew quarters hadn't done that either.

Tunesmith was still at the end of a boom, still tracking whatever he'd launched.

"Where are the rest of us?" Louis asked the Voice.

"Who do you seek?"

"Acolyte."

"I do not have that name—"

"The Kzin we shared this ship with. Chmeee's child."

"I list that LE as—" blood-curdling howl. Louis had to pry his fingers loose from a table edge. "Rename him Acolyte?"

"Please."

The map was back, and a blinking point next to Fist-of-God . . . a hundred thousand miles port-and-antispin from Fist-of-God—four times the circumference of the Earth—and twice that far to spinward of the Map of Mars. The hugeness of the Ringworld had to be learned over and over. The Voice said, "Here we set Acolyte, with a service stack, thirty-one days ago. He has since moved by eleven hundred miles." The point jumped minutely. "Tunesmith has altered the setting for the stepping disk. It sends to an observation point on the Map of Earth."

Home to Acolyte's father. "Has he used it?"

"No."

"Where are the City Builders?"

"Do you mean the librarians? Kawaresksenjajok and Fortaralisplyar and three children were returned to their origin—"

"Good!" He'd meant to do that himself.

"To the library in the floating city. I note your approval. Who else shall I track?"

Who else had been his companions? Two protectors. Bram the Vampire protector was dead. Tunesmith was . . . still busy, it seemed. In the Meteor Defense Room the protector's telescope screen was following a receding point, the vehicle he'd launched earlier. Its drive was off . . . flared brilliantly and blinked off again.

That was a warship. Reaction motors were still needed for war; modern thrusters couldn't switch on and off as fast.

Louis asked, "Have you kept track of Valavirgillin?"

The map jumped. "Here, near the floating city and a local center of Machine People culture."

Good, and she was well away from vampires. They had not met in twelve years. "*Why* did you track her, Hindmost's Voice?"

"Orders."

Carefully, "Who do you take orders from?"

"From you and Tunesmith and—" a blast of orchestral chaos, piercingly sweet. Louis recognized the Hindmost's true name. "But all such may be countermanded by—" the Hindmost's name again.

"Is Tunesmith restricted from any interesting levels of this ship?"

"Not currently."

The Hindmost was still in wrapped-around-himself catatonia. "How long since he's eaten?" Louis asked.

"Two local days. He wakes to eat."

"Wake him up."

"How shall I wake him without trauma?"

"I saw him in a dance once. Turn that on. Prepare food for him."